Crown And Sceptre
A West Country Story

By

George Manville Fenn

Double 9
BOOKS

Crown And Sceptre
A West Country Story
by George Manville Fenn

Copyright © 2023

All Rights reserved.

ISBN: 978-93-60461-21-8
Published by

DOUBLE 9 BOOKS

2/13-B, Ansari Road
Daryaganj, New Delhi – 110002
info@double9books.com
www.double9books.com
Tel. 011-40042856

ABOUT THE AUTHOR

George Manville Fenn was a very productive author of novels, a writer, an editor, and an educator from England. He was born on January 3, 1831, in Pimlico, London. He mostly learned on his own; he taught himself Italian, French, and German. During the years 1851–1854, he went to Battersea Training College for Teachers and then became the head of a state school in Alford, Lincolnshire. In the early 1850s, Fenn started to write short stories and pieces for newspapers and magazines. The Old Forest Ranger, his first book, came out in 1856. Afterward, he wrote more than 100 books, many of them for teenagers and young adults. He was one of the most famous writers of his time, and his books were well-liked and read by many people. He also worked as a reporter and writer for Fenn. Among the newspapers and magazines, he worked for was The Boy's Own Paper, which he ran from 1866 to 1874. He worked hard to make children's books better and was a strong supporter of education and reading. The Englishman Fenn passed away on August 26, 1909, in Isleworth.

CONTENTS

Chapter One
In the West Countree

"Derry down, derry down, derry down!"

A cheery voice rolling out the chorus of an old west-country ditty.

Then there was a run of a few yards, a sudden stoppage, and a round, red missile was thrown with considerable force after a blackcock, which rose on whirring wings from among the heather, his violet-black plumage glistening in the autumn sun, as he skimmed over the moor, and disappeared down the side of a hollow coombe.

"Missed him," said the thrower, thrusting his hand into his pocket, and bringing out a similar object to that which he had used as a missile, but putting it to a far different purpose; for he raised it to his mouth, drew back his red lips, and with one sharp crunch drove two rows of white teeth through the ruddy skin, cut out a great circular piece of apple, spat it out, and threw the rest away.

"What a sour one!" he cried, as he dived after another, which proved to be more satisfactory, for he went on munching, as he made his short cut over the moor towards where, in a sheltered hollow, a stone building peeped from a grove of huge oaks.

The sun shone brightly as, with elastic tread, the singer, a lad of about sixteen, walked swiftly over the elevated moorland, now descending into a hollow, now climbing a stiff slope, at whose top he could look over the sea, which spread away to north and west, one dazzling plain of damasked silver, dotted with red-sailed boats. Then down another slope facing the south, where for a moment the boy paused to deliver a sharp kick at something on the short fine grass.

"Ah, would you!" he exclaimed, following up the kick by a jump which landed him upon a little writhing object, which repeated its first attack, striking with lightning rapidity at the lad's boot, before lying crushed and helpless, never to bask in the bright sun again.

"Serve you right, you nasty poisonous little beast!" cried the boy, crushing his assailant's head beneath his heel. "You got the worst of it. Think the moor belonged to you? Lucky I had on my boots."

He dropped upon the ground, drew off a deer-skin boot, and, with his good-looking, fair boyish face all in wrinkles, proceeded to examine the toe, removing therefrom a couple of tiny points with his knife.

"What sharp teeth adders have!" he muttered. "Not long enough to go through."

The next minute he had drawn on his boot, and set off at a trot, which took him down to the bottom of the slope, and half up the other side of the coombe, at whose bottom he had had to leap a tiny stream. Then, walking slowly, he climbed the steeper slope; and there was a double astonishment for a moment, the boy staring hard at a noble-looking stag, the avant-guard of a little herd of red deer, which was grazing in the hollow below.

The boy came so suddenly upon the stag, that the great fellow stood at gaze, his branching antlers spreading wide. Then there was a rush, and the little herd was off at full speed, bucks, does, and fawns, seeming almost to fly, till they disappeared over a ridge.

"That's the way!" said the lad. "Now, if Scar and I had been out with our bows, we might have walked all day and never seen a horn."

As the lad trudged on, munching apples and breaking out from time to time into scraps of song, the surroundings of his walk changed, for he passed over a rough stone wall, provided with projections to act as a stile, and left the moorland behind, to enter upon a lovely park-like expanse, dotted with grand oaks and firs, among which he had not journeyed long before, surrounded on three sides by trees, he came in full sight of the fine-looking, ruddy stone hall, glimpses of which he had before seen, while its windows and a wide-spreading lake in front flashed in the bright sunshine.

"Whoa hoo! whoa hoo! Drop it! Hoi!" shouted the boy; but the object addressed, a great grey heron, paid no heed, but went flapping slowly away on its widespread wings, its long legs stretched straight out behind to act as balance, and a small eel writhing and twisting itself into knots as it strove in vain to escape from the scissor-like bill.

"That's where the eels go," muttered the boy, as he hurried on, descending till he reached the shores of the lake, and then skirting it, with eyes searching its sunlit depths, to see here some golden-bronze pike half-hidden among lily leaves, shoals of roach flashing their silver sides in the shallows, and among the denser growth of weeds broad-backed carp basking in the hot sunshine, and at times lazily rolling over to display their golden sides.

"Oh yes, you're big and old enough, but you don't half bite. I'd rather have a day at our moat any time than here, proud as old Scar is of his big pond."

As the lad reached the head of the lake, where the brown, clear waters of a rocky stream drained into it from the moor above, he caught sight of a few small trout, and, after crossing a little rough stone bridge, startled a couple of moor-hens, who in turn roused up some bald coots, the whole party fluttering away with drooping legs towards the other end of the lake. Here they swam about, twitching their tails, and dividing their time between watching the now distant intruder and keeping a sharp look-out for the great pike, which at times sought a change of diet from constant fish, and swallowed moor-hen or duckling, or even, preferring four-footed meat to fowl, seized upon some unfortunate rat.

"Hi, Nat!" shouted the boy, as he neared the grassy terrace in front of the hall, and caught sight of a sturdy-looking young man busy in the garden.

"Hullo, Master Fred!"

"Where's Master Scarlett?"

"Where's Master Scarlett, sir?" said the man, slowly and deliberately straightening his back, and resting upon the tool he handled.

"Yes. Don't you say he has gone with them, or I'll never give you a mug of cider again."

"Well, I wasn't going to say as Master Scar's gone with 'em," said the man, with a look of wonder in his eyes. "He was here a bit ago, though I didn't see him."

"Then, how do you know he was here?"

"Because nobody else wouldn't—"

"Wouldn't what?"

"Well, you see, Master Fred, it was like this here. I was a-stooping over the bed, tidying up the edge o' the grass, when—whop!"

"What, did he hit you, Nat!" said the boy, grinning.

"Well, sir, he did and he didn't, if you can understand that."

"No, I can't. What do you mean?"

"This here fox-whelp come and hit me side o' the head, and it must ha' been him as throwed it; and that made me know as he was at home."

As the man spoke, he took a cider apple from his pocket, a hard, green, three-parts-grown specimen of the fruit, and involuntarily began to rub the place where he had been struck.

"Yes; that looks as if he was at home, Nat," said the boy, showing his white teeth.

"Yes, Master Fred, that looks as if he was at home; but you wouldn't have laughed if you'd had it."

"He did it to wake you up, Nat."

"Oh, I was waken enough, Master Fred; but how's Brother Samson?"

"Like you, Nat, half asleep," cried the boy, looking back as he hurried on toward the house, leaving the man staring after him thoughtfully.

"Yes," he muttered, "Samson is a deal like me. Wonder whether Master Fred ever chucks apples at he?"

Meanwhile the lad addressed as Master Fred made his way along the house front, peering in at first one and then another window, till he reached the great door opening on to the end of the shingled terrace.

Without the slightest hesitation, and behaving like one who was quite at home, he entered the great oak-floored hall, and looked round—not at the groups of weapons and suits of armour that were arranged as trophies about the place, nor yet at the pictures and various interesting objects hung between the stained-glass windows, on the oaken panels surrounded by carving and surmounted by the heads and antlers of deer killed on the adjacent moor.

Fred Forrester had eyes for none of these objects, as he looked here and there, now in the low-ceilinged and carved-oak dining-room, then in the drawing-room, and, lastly, in Sir Godfrey Markham's library—a gloomy, tree-shaded room, where he thought it possible that his friend and companion might be hiding. But all was still, and there was no one behind the heavy curtains, nor inside the huge black oak cabinet beside the great mullioned window.

"Wonder whether he's in the stables?" said Fred, half aloud, as he came slowly out of the gloomy room and stood beneath the broad gallery which crossed the end of the hall. "I know. He's with the dogs," said the lad, taking a step from out of the shelter of the gallery, and then staggering forward and nearly going down on hands and knees; for at that moment a wool mattress, which had been poised ready on the gallery balustrade, was dropped upon his head, and a peal of laughter echoed from the panelled ceiling as Fred recovered himself, and rushed up the broad staircase to attack his aggressor.

There was a good-tempered wrestling bout on the landing, and then the two lads, Fred Forrester and Sir Godfrey Markham's son Scarlett, stood panting and recovering their breath.

"And you are quite alone?" said Fred at last.

"Yes, all but the women; but I knew you'd come over, and I lay wait for you, as soon as I saw you crossing the park."

"Well, what shall we do?"

"Let's fish."

"Come along, then. Got any bait?"

"No; but we'll make Nat dig us some worms. Let's go and get that mattress first. It belongs to the spare-room."

No sooner said than done. The two boys ran down the broad oaken stairs, leaping the last six, and, each seizing one corner of the mattress, they trailed it up the stairs, along the gallery, and into a sombre-looking room, after which Fred rushed to the top of the staircase, seated himself astride the broad balustrade, and began to glide down, but only to be overtaken by Scarlett, with the effect that the latter portion of the descent was achieved with additional velocity.

The ride was so satisfactory, that it was tried again and again, sometimes one first, sometimes the other.

"Wonder whether I could travel all along the gallery and down to the bottom, hanging on to the balusters," said Fred, looking up at the turned supports, which grew thin in one place, and offered a tempting grip for the hands.

"Try," said his companion.

"You'd play some trick!"

"No, I wouldn't."

"Honour bright!"

"Honour bright."

"Here goes, then."

Fred bounded up the stairs, ran along the gallery, climbed over the balustrade, and lowered himself down till he hung by his hands, holding on to the thin part of the balusters, while Scarlett looked up and his grim-looking ancestors looked down.

For as Fred Forrester, son of Colonel Forrester, of the Manor, performed his feat, with no little display of agility, old Sir Gabriel Markham, who had built the hall in the days of Henry the Seventh, frowned from his canvas in one of the panels, and looked as cold and angry as an old knight clad in steel could look.

There, too, was Sir Henry, seeming equally stern in his court suit and hat, and Dame Markham, in stomacher and farthingale and ruff, with quite a look of alarm on their countenances, which was reflected from that of another of the old Markhams—all appearing either angry or startled at such a freak being played in their august presence.

There was one exception though, in the face of a sweet-looking lady of about twenty, whose eyes seemed to follow the boys, while a pleasant, mirthful smile was upon her lip.

But the boys did not even give a thought to the portraits, whose eyes seemed to watch them till the feat, which required the exercise of no little muscular effort, was dexterously performed, and Fred stood on the oaken floor.

"Well, I suppose you think I couldn't do that, do you?" cried Scarlett.

"Not I. Any one could do it if he tried."

"Yes, I should think he could, and in half the time you took. Look here; I'll show you."

"Try if you can do it with your face turned this way, Scar," cried Fred.

For answer, the boy, who had reached the gallery, ran along to the end, climbed over, and then lowered himself down till he hung at full length by both hands clasping the balusters. Then he hung by one, and cleverly swinging round, grasped another baluster, and hung facing his companion, who stood looking up and eagerly watching every movement.

"Go on, Scar."

"Oh yes, it's very easy to say go on; but see how awkward it is this way."

"Well, try the other."

"Going to," said Scarlett, laconically, as he swung himself back, and then hand over hand passed along the front of the gallery, reached the turn, grasped the second of the descending balusters, loosed his hold of the last one on the level of the landing, made a dash to catch the first baluster side by side with that he already held, missed it, and swung round, hanging by one hand only, when suddenly there was a loud *crick-crack*, and, under the impression that the slight wooden pillar had broken, Fred sprang up the stairs to his companion's assistance, but only to trip as he nearly reached the top and fall sprawling upon the landing upon a great deer-skin rug.

Chapter Two
Behind the Stair

Fred was up again in a moment, ready to pass his arms through and help his friend; but the latter had already recovered himself, and was holding on with both hands, now staring between the balusters like a wild beast through the bars of his cage.

"What's the matter?" he said.

"I thought you were falling. Which one broke?"

"I don't know; neither of them."

"But what was that clacking noise?"

"I don't know. The baluster seemed to turn half round, and then fly back as if it had a spring at the bottom."

"I know! Look here. It wrenched this stair loose. I trod on it, and that's what made me fall."

"Wait till I've gone down to the bottom," said Scarlett, "and we'll soon put that right."

As he spoke, the lad went on down, hand by hand, as Fred had made the descent before him, and then came running up the polished oaken stairs to where his companion stood by the top stair but one, upon which lay a broad stain of red and gold, cast by a ray of light passing through one of the painted windows.

"It must have come unnailed," said Scarlett, as he knelt down.

"I don't think it has," replied Fred, as he knelt beside him. "Look here, it's quite loose; and see here, you can push it right in."

He thrust at the oaken board as he spoke, and it glided horizontally from them under the top step which formed the landing, and left a long opening like a narrow box the length and width of the stair.

"Don't push too far," cried Scarlett, "or we shan't get it back. Pull."

The boys pulled together, and the oaken tread glided back toward them with the greatest ease, like a well-made drawer.

"Mind!" shouted Fred. And they snatched away their fingers just in time to save a nasty pinch, for the board came swiftly back into its position. There was a sharp *crick-crack*, and the stair was as solid as before, and the broad stain from the painted window lay in its old place on the dark brown wood.

Scarlett Markham turned and stared at Fred Forrester, and Fred Forrester turned and stared at him.

"I say, what do you think of that?" said Scarlett.

"I don't know. What do you?"

"I don't know either," said Scarlett, trying to move the board again. But it was firm as the rest of the stairs.

"Did you see that baluster?" said Fred.

"See it? No. What do you mean?"

"It seemed to me to move and make that noise."

"Nonsense! How could it?"

"I don't know, but it was just the same noise as it made when you missed your hold and swung round."

"So it was; and I had hold of it," said Scarlett, thoughtfully, as he laid his hand on the piece of turned and carved wood. "But it's quite firm." He gave it a shake, but with no effect. "You come and try," he said.

Fred took his place, and shook the baluster, then the other — its fellow — but there was no result.

"I don't know what to make of this," said Scarlett. "I wonder whether all the stairs are made the same. There, never mind; let's go and fish."

"Stop a moment!" cried Fred, excitedly. "Look here; you can turn this thing half round. See!"

"Well, that's only because it's loose. They're getting old and —"

Crick-crack!

Scarlett Markham started back, so quick and sudden was the sound, but only to resume his position on his knees before the oaken stair-tread, which again yielded to a thrust, and glided under the landing once more, leaving the opening the length and breadth of the great stair.

"Why, it's like the lid of a sliding box, Scar," cried Fred. "Now then, let's pull it over once more. But look here, it won't go any further."

This was the case, for about an inch of the carved front was left for them to take hold of and draw it back, which they did, the board gliding easily toward them, and closing with a loud snap.

"There! I did see it then," cried Scarlett.

"What?"

"That baluster. It half twisted round. Why, Fred, it's a hiding-place. Here, let's open it again. Perhaps it's full of gold."

Fred was quite willing, for his curiosity was excited; so, seizing the baluster with both hands, he gave it a twist. There was the sharp sound as of a catch being set at liberty; the board moved, and was once more thrust back.

"Now let me try," cried Scarlett, "so as to make sure."

The opening was closed again, the baluster twisted, and it was again opened, the lads pausing before the dark cavity, across which the coloured rays played over a bar of dancing motes.

"Seems to me," said Fred, "that we've discovered a secret. Does your father know of it, do you think?"

"I feel sure he doesn't. I say, let's see if there's anything inside."

"Do you think we ought to?"

"I wouldn't, if I thought my father knew about it; but I don't believe he does, so I shall try. Of course I shall tell him."

"Yes, of course," said Fred, whose curiosity pricked him on to action, and who felt relieved by his companion's words. "But do you think it's a secret drawer?"

"Yes, I'm sure it is, or it wouldn't be made like that."

"But perhaps they are all made this way."

This was a damper; for if the stairs were all made in this fashion, there could be no secret.

"Let's try," said Scarlett; and together they turned and twisted with all their might at every baluster from top to bottom, but without result.

"Then it is a secret drawer," said Fred, in a low, husky voice.

"More like a coffin," said Scarlett.

"Ugh!"

"I hope no one's buried here."

"Oh, I say, don't talk like that," cried Fred. "It's too horrible."

"Well, it might be so. Some one been killed years ago, and put there."

"'Tisn't likely," said Fred. "But, if it is a secret place, we oughtn't to let any of the servants know."

"I didn't think of that," replied Scarlett; and, drawing the oaken board back, the spring was closed, and the boys went and looked out to see that Nat Dee was busy over the garden beds; and further investigation proved that the indoor servants were all in the other part of the house.

"They would go up the back-stairs if they wanted anything," said Scarlett, as they returned to the place where the coloured light shone; but it had already somewhat altered its position as Fred seized the baluster, turned it, and the board lay loose.

"Now, then, what are we going to find?" cried Scarlett, as he thrust back the board, and then recoiled a little and looked at his companion.

Fred looked at him, and both lads felt that their hearts were beating fast.

"Not scared, are you, Fred!"

"No, I don't think so."

"Then you may have first try if you like. What do you say?"

"Nothing," replied Fred. "I feel as if I should like to, but all the same I don't like. Let's try with a stick. There may be something nasty there; perhaps rats."

"They wouldn't have stopped; but you're right. Go down and fetch a stick."

"You will not try till I come back?" said Fred, doubtingly.

"No, I shall not try. Make haste."

Fred was not long running down to one corner of the hall, and obtaining a stout ashen cudgel, which he handed to his companion, who, after a moment's hesitation, thrust in the staff, and found that the opening was about half as deep again as the height of the step; but though he tapped the bottom, which seemed to be firm, and tried from side to side, there was nothing solid within, nothing but a fine, impalpable dust, which made its presence known, for both lads began to sneeze.

"I'm glad there are no bones in it," said Scarlett. "It was only meant to put something in; made on purpose, I suppose. Just a long box: nothing more, and— Halloa!"

"What have you found?"

"Nothing, only that it's all open at the back, and I can—yes, so I can!—reach right back; yes, as far as the stick will go."

"That place wouldn't be made for nothing, Scar," cried Fred. "I know. That's the way to somewhere."

"Nonsense!"

"I don't care; I know it is, and you see if—"

"Some one coming," whispered Scarlett, stooping down and dragging the board toward him, when there was a sharp crack, and the stair was once more firm, just as steps were heard coming along the corridor, and one of the servant-maids passed along the gallery and entered a room at the end.

"Wait a bit," whispered Scarlett, as soon as the maid had passed out of hearing. "We'll get a bit of candle and lock the end door, and then we'll see what this means; for, as you say, it must have been made for something. But it can't be a way anywhere, or they would have made it upright like a door."

"If they could," said Fred, thoughtfully. "Perhaps it was meant for people to go through lying down."

"Well, wait a bit," said Scarlett, "and we'll see."

Unkind people say that girls have the bump of curiosity greatly developed, far more so than boys. This is a vulgar error, for the latter are quite as eager to know as their sisters, and from the moment that the heavy oak board was replaced, Fred Forrester and Scar Markham suffered from a fit of excitement which they could not allay. For, as is usually the case, the person they wanted to go seemed determined to stay. That person was the maid, who appeared to have found something very important to do in the room at the end of the corridor; and it was impossible to continue the examination till she had returned to the servants' quarters.

Scar fetched a candlestick with a short piece of candle burning therein, and shut it up in one of the great cupboards in the hall, so as to lose no time.

Then they fidgeted up and down, listening intently the while; examined some of the well-oiled, warlike weapons on the walls; crept upstairs and along the corridor to listen at the bedroom door; ran down again, and waited until the suspense seemed unbearable.

"I believe she has gone to bed and fallen asleep," whispered Fred.

"Nonsense! She dare not in that best room."

"Let's go out in the garden, then, and leave it till another day."

"And when will that be? Why, everybody will be about then. No; we must examine the place to-day."

"What's that?" cried Fred, suddenly. "What's what?"

"I can smell fire."

"Well, they're cooking in the kitchen, I suppose."

"No, no; it's wood burning. Oh, Scar, look there!"

As Fred pointed toward the great closet in one corner of the hall, the lads could see a thin blue film of vapour stealing out through the crack at the top; and their first inclination was to run away and shout "Fire!" But second thoughts are best.

"Come on," cried Scar; and he ran to the closet door, swung it open, and the reason for the smoke was plain enough to see. The candle which they had hidden there till the maid came down had been badly fastened in the socket; had fallen over sidewise, probably when the door was closed, and was now leaning up against the oak wainscot, guttering down rapidly, and burning a long, channel-like hole in the woodwork, which was pouring forth smoke, and would in a few minutes have become serious.

As it was, a little presence of mind was sufficient to avert the danger. The candle was removed, and a handkerchief pressed against the smouldering wainscot stifled the tiny fire, while the windows being open, the pale blue smoke soon evaporated, and the candle was left securely now as the lads re-entered the hall and carefully closed the door once more.

"We should have looked nice if the old hall had been burned down," said Fred.

"Oh, nonsense!" was the reply. "The place is too strong and full of oak and stone. The hall couldn't be burned. Here, it's of no use waiting any longer; she will not come down. Let's go out in the garden."

Fred glanced at the stairs, and followed his companion unwillingly; but no sooner were they outside than Scar called his companion's attention to the bedroom window, where the maid in question was leaning out, watching Nat Lee, as he slowly did his work.

The girl caught sight of the two lads, drew back, and as they waited in the great porch they had the satisfaction of hearing her go back, along the corridor, closing the door at the end.

"Now, Fred," said Scarlett, excitedly, "we're safe at last." He dashed up the stairs and slipped the bolt of the door through which the maid had just passed, and returned to the top of the stairs. "Come along," he whispered. "Don't stand there. Bring the light."

Fred ran to the great closet and obtained the burning candle. The baluster was twisted; there was the familiar *crick-crack*; the loose step was thrust back, and the boys stood looking into the long box-like opening.

"Wouldn't it be safer to fasten the front door too?" said Fred in a whisper.

"Yes, and be quick," replied his companion in the same low, excited manner.

Fred ran down, closed the great oaken door, ran a ponderous bolt into its receptacle, and again joined his companion.

"Now then," whispered Scarlett, "what shall we do?"

As he spoke he knelt down and thrust the candle in as far as he could reach, disclosing the fact that this was no rough back to the staircase, but a smooth, carefully finished piece of work.

"Shall we try if we can creep in?" suggested Fred.

"I hardly like to; but if you will, I will."

"I will," replied Fred, laconically.

"But how are we to get in? It isn't deep enough to crawl."

"Tell you what," cried Fred, "I think the way is to lie down in it and then roll along. There's plenty of room that way."

"Will you try?"

"If you'll come after me."

"Go on, then."

Fred hesitated a few moments, and then holding the candle as far forward as he could he lay down, but instead of rolling, shuffled himself along under the landing, finding plenty of room for his journey, and pushing the light onward as he crept sidewise.

"Coming, Scar?" he whispered rather hoarsely.

"Yes, I'm coming. Mind the candle doesn't set fire to anything. What's that?"

"Only a cobweb burning. The place is full of them; and— Oh, Scar!"

"What is it?"

"I can get my legs down here, and—yes, it's a narrow passage, and I can stand upright."

Wondering more and more, Scarlett shuffled along to his companion, and directly after they were standing together in a passage so strait that they could barely pass along it as they stood square, their shoulders nearly touching the sides.

"Yes, it's a passage, sure enough," said Scarlett, in an awe-stricken whisper, as by the light Fred held he could see that the sides and ceiling were of rough oak panelling, the floor being flagged with stone.

"Shall we go on?" whispered Fred.

"Yes. Why not? You're not afraid, are you?"

"Yes, a little. It's all so strange. Don't you feel a little—"

"Yes, just a little; but there can't be any thing to be afraid of. You must go first."

Fred hesitated a few moments, and then went on for quite forty feet, when the narrow passage turned off at a right angle for about another twenty, when it again bent sharply round in the same direction as at first.

"This cannot be a chimney?" whispered Scarlett, for the darkness and heavy dusty air seemed to oppress them.

"No; they wouldn't make a chimney of wainscotting. Oh!"

"What have you found?"

"Look here; a lot of stone steps."

The boys stood looking at the old stone stairway, which seemed to invite them to a higher region, but still as narrow as the passage.

The stones were dusty, and cobwebs hung in all directions; but everything seemed as if it had been unused ever since the architect put the finishing touches to the place.

The two boys looked at the stairway, Fred holding up the candle, and Scar peering over his shoulder for some moments before the former spoke.

"Think we'd better go back now."

"Yes," said Scarlett; "only doesn't it seem cowardly?"

Fred remained silent for a while, and then said with a sigh—

"I suppose it does. Come on."

"Are you going up?"

"Yes. I don't want to. It's all so dark and creepy; but we should laugh at each other for being frightened when we got out."

Scar nodded his head, and after a little more hesitation, Fred went slowly up the stairs, to find that from the top another narrow passage went off at right angles.

As they stood together on the narrow landing, Scar exclaimed —

"Here, I know. These are only openings through the thick walls to keep them dry."

"Look!" said Fred, pointing before them at a thin pencil of light which made a spot on the wall.

"That's sunshine," cried Scarlett, "and shows what I said. This is one of the walls we are in, and that must be the south."

"Why?" said Fred, trying to touch the slit through which the light came.

"Because the sun shines in. Let's go on to the end."

This was soon reached, for at the end of a dozen steps they came upon a narrow door studded with great nails, and after a little hesitation, Fred pushed this, and the boys started back at the hideous groan which greeted them.

Chapter Three
How the Light was Extinguished

There was something very strange and weird about that sound—one which sent a chill of horror through both the hearers, but they laughed the next moment at their fears, for the noise was only such as could be given out by a pair of rusty hinges from which an unused door had hung for a hundred years, the sound being rendered more startling from the hollow space beyond.

Fred felt more startled than ever, in spite of his forced laugh; but he held the candle before him, and gazed through the narrow opening into a little low-ceiled room, panelled throughout with oak, and festooned with cobwebs, while on one side there was quite a cluster of long, thin, white-looking strands and leaves hanging over and resting upon a heap of crumbling, fungus-covered sticks.

"Why, it's quite a little chamber," Scarlett exclaimed; "and look at the ivy. It has come in through that loop-hole."

"And look at that old jackdaw's nest. I say, Scar, can your father know of this place?"

"No, nor any one else. But it is queer. A regular secret chamber."

"Yes, but what's it for?"

"I don't know. Must have been made when the house was built to keep the plate in for fear of robbers."

"Look at the spiders! There's a big one!"

"Yes, but I'm trying to puzzle out where it is. I know. It must be somewhere at the west corner, because that's where there is most ivy."

"But is it upstairs or downstairs?"

"Up, of course; and look here."

Scarlett pointed to what had at first escaped their sight—to wit, a second door, ingeniously contrived in one angle of the little chamber, and in the dim light shed by the candle hardly distinguishable from the panelling.

"Where can that go?"

"Oh, it's only a cupboard. Stop a moment."

Scarlett went to the other side, crushing down the heap of rotten twigs brought in by the birds, and thrust his hand amongst the mass of sickly ivy strands, to find that the opening through which they came was completely choked up, but after a little feeling about he was able to announce that there was a narrow slit-like window, with an upright rusty iron bar.

"Why, it will be glorious, Scar," cried Fred. "Let's clear the place out, and cut away the ivy, and then we can keep it all a secret."

"Yes, and bring some furniture—chairs and table, and a carpet. Why, we might have a bed too."

"How are you going to get them here?"

Scarlett gave his dark curls a vicious rub. "I never thought of that."

"Never mind; but we could bring some cushions, and store up fruit, and make this our cave. You will not tell anybody?"

"I should think not."

"Not even Lil."

"No; she'd go and tell every one directly. Why, Fred, this will be splendid. What a discovery!"

"When we've cleaned it up it will be a little palace."

"And we can keep our stores in the closet there, and— Think there'll be any rats?"

"No signs of any. Can't smell 'em."

"They've never found their way here. Dare say there are some bats; but we'll soon clear them out. Wish there were a fireplace. We could cook the birds and fish we caught."

"Let's see what's in the cupboard."

Fred crossed the little chamber to the corner where the second door stood ajar, and it was so similar to the panelling that but for its being partly opened, it would not have been seen.

This, too, gave forth a dismal hollow groan as it was drawn inward upon its concealed rusty hinges, and then, as Fred raised the light to see what was inside, he exclaimed—

"Why, it isn't a cupboard. Here's another flight of steps!"

Scarlett pressed forward and stood beside him, peering beneath the candle, and looking down the dusty stone stairs into utter darkness beyond the faint light shed by the candle.

Then he turned to Fred as he grasped his arm and looked inquiringly into his face.

"I will if you will," said Fred, as if his companion had asked him a question.

"Come along, then," cried Scarlett, excitedly. "Only let's keep together."

"Of course. Shall I go first?"

"No, I'll go," said Scarlett, after a momentary hesitation.

He snatched the candle from his friend's hand, and took a step forward on to the little square landing.

"Mind the door doesn't blow to. Push it wide open."

Fred did as he was told, the rusty hinges giving forth another dismal groan, which seemed to echo hollowly and then to die away.

"Come along," said Scarlett, in a low voice; and, holding the candle well before him, he began to descend the narrow steps, the distance from side to side being precisely the same as before.

"Smells cold and damp," whispered Fred, when they had descended about twenty steps; "just like a wine cellar."

"Perhaps it is one when we get to the bottom, and full of old wine."

"Are there many more steps?"

"Can't see. Shall we go any farther?"

"Oh yes; we'll go to the bottom, as we are here."

"Stop a moment. What was that?"

"I didn't hear anything."

"Yes; there it is again."

"Sounded like a drip of water in a pool."

"Perhaps it's a well."

"They wouldn't make a well here. Let's go to the bottom, and then be satisfied for one day."

"Take hold of hands then, in case."

"In case of what?"

"There may be foul air at the bottom, same as there was in the Manor well."

"You are saying that to frighten me."

"No."

"Well, it sounded like it. Let's go on."

The two explorers of this hidden way went on down and down, with the sounds made by their feet echoing strangely; but still there were fresh steps, and the distance seemed in their excited state to be tremendous. Scarlett, however, persevered, though his movements were slower and slower; and more than once he turned back to hold the light as high as possible, so as to gaze up at the way they had come, looking over his shoulder, and still holding tightly by Fred's hand.

"We must be right down ever so much below the house," he said at last. "Shall we go any farther?"

"Oh yes, I'd go on," replied Fred, quietly; and once more the two lads gazed in each other's eyes as if looking for signs of fear.

"Come along then," cried Scarlett, manfully; and he went down and down more steps to stand at last on level stones, a narrow passage stretching out before him, while the stone walls and ceiling gleamed as if slightly damp.

"Hold the light up a little higher, Scar," whispered Fred.

Scarlett raised his left hand to the full length of his arm; there was a soft *dab*, and Fred uttered a subdued "Oh!" as his companion's right hand grasped his with spasmodic violence.

For Scarlett had pressed the candle up against the stone ceding, and the arched surface thoroughly performed the duty of extinguisher, leaving them in total darkness.

Half a minute must have passed, during which they were stunned by the horror of their position, before Scarlett exclaimed —

"Oh, Fred, what shall we do?"

There was no answer, Fred holding the other's hand tightly, and it was not until the question was repeated that he uttered a low gasping sigh.

"We can find our way back," he whispered, in an awe-stricken voice. "There's nothing to mind, for we can't go wrong."

"But we might take a wrong turning, and never find our way out."

"There are no turnings," replied Fred, stolidly. "Come along."

"Listen! Wasn't that something?"

"I don't hear anything, only the echo. Hoi!"

Fred half shouted the last word, and as they listened it seemed to run right away in an echoing, hollow way, to die at last in quite a whisper.

"What a horrible place!" faltered Scarlett. "Let's make haste back. I say, don't you feel scared?"

"I don't know," whispered back Fred. "I feel as if I do. I'd give anything to be out in the sunshine again, and I wish we had not come. Let's make haste."

Scarlett needed no further urging, but pressed on so closely behind his companion that they seemed to move as one, Fred passing his hand along the cold stone wall as they went on, up and up the apparently endless flight of steps, till the landing was reached, and the leader grasped the door.

"There!" he cried, as they passed into the little room, Scarlett closing the door behind them, the hinges creaking dismally. "Now for the other door. I don't seem to mind so much now."

"I don't think I do; but it seems very queer. What's that?"

"Only me. I touched you with my hand."

"It felt so cold on my cheek, it sent a shiver through me. Let's make haste."

"You go first this time, then. You remember where the door is?"

"Yes, I remember," replied Scarlett. "It was just a few steps over here and — I say, Fred, it's gone!"

"Nonsense! It can't have gone. Feel about with your hands."

Scarlett felt here and there, and then uttered a low sigh.

"I can't find it. Come over here."

Fred crept to him, and as he felt about in the utter darkness, he touched his companion, who uttered a cry and rushed away from him.

"Don't be a coward, Scar. It was only I."

"I'm not a coward," cried Scarlett, angrily; "only I fancied something was going to touch me, and you came so quietly. Where are you?"

"Here. And, I say, you made me turn about, and I don't know which nay the door is now. But we'll soon find it."

Nothing seems more simple to talk of, but nothing is more confusing than to be standing in profound darkness, not knowing which way to go, the slightest deviation beginning the confusion, which seems to augment.

Fred's attempt to regain touch of their position was simple enough. He went forward, and after a step or two touched the wall.

"Here we are, Scar," he said. "Come along. The door is just here. Yes; here it is."

He seized the edge, and it gave forth its dismal creak again.

"That's the wrong door," cried Scarlett, excitedly. "The one we just came through."

"Is it?" said Fred, confusedly. "Yes, I suppose it is. Then we must try again. How stupid!"

The second trial was more successful; and slowly and cautiously passing through, they began directly after to make their way along the first passages they had traversed, feeling their course round the angles at the sharp turns, and with their spirits rising fast as they felt that they were approaching the entrance; and as they at last reached it, with the daylight shining through, feeling ready to laugh at their fears.

"Here we are, Scar," cried Fred, as he lay down and rolled himself over and over till he was in the hollow stair, and directly after climbed out, bent down and took the candlestick from his companion's hand, leaving him free to follow, but Scarlett uttered a cry.

"What's the matter?"

"Something has got hold of my jerkin."

Fred burst out laughing.

"Why, it's only that knob. Meant to open the stair from inside, I suppose."

Crick-crack! The board was drawn back into its place, and the boys went slowly down into the hall.

"Why, Scar, you look quite white."

"Do I? So do you," was the reply. "Look, we're covered with dust. Come along, and let's go to my room and have a wash."

"And then we can sit down and talk about it."

Scarlett nodded; and once more ascending the stairs, they passed over the secret entry, unlocked the door in the corridor, and entered Scarlett's bedchamber, where it took some time to get rid of the marks of their journey. After which they sat down in the sunshine by the open window, to discuss their find, and settle two or three points in connection therewith.

Chapter Four
"God Save the King!"

"Seems queer now," said Fred, as they gazed down into the garden, "that we could have felt so scared."

Scarlett was silent.

"What are you thinking about!"

"Whether I oughtn't to tell father about that place."

"I suppose you ought," said Fred, after a pause; "but if you do, we shall have no more fun."

"I didn't see any fun in it," said Scarlett, slowly.

"Not then; but see what we could do with a secret place of our own to retreat to whenever we liked, and no one knowing where we had gone. I say, don't tell anybody."

"But I feel as if I ought to tell my father, as it's his place."

"Yes, I suppose you ought; but let's wait a bit first."

"Well, we might wait a little while. I say, Fred, what cowards we were!"

"But it was so dark, and I couldn't help thinking that we might never find our way out."

"Yes; that's just how I felt, and as if something was coming after us out of the darkness."

"And, of course, there couldn't be anything. You could see by the dust on the steps that nobody had been there for years and years."

There was a long silence here, during which the two lads looked out at the garden flooded with sunshine, where Nat was working very deliberately close by the sun-dial. And beyond him, at the lake, from which the sunbeams flashed whenever a fish or water-fowl disturbed the surface.

"I say," said Fred at last, "don't let's sit here any longer. You're as dull as if you had no tongue. What are you thinking about now?"

"I was wondering whether I shall be such a coward when I grow up to be a man."

"I say, Scar, don't keep on talking like that; it's just as if you kept on calling me a coward too."

"So you were."

"No, I was not; but it was enough to frighten anybody. It was all so dark and strange."

"Should you be afraid to go again?"

"No," said Fred, stoutly.

"Will you go, then?"

"What, alone?"

"No; both together."

"I'll go, if you will. When shall we go?"

"Now," said Scarlett, firmly.

"Now?"

"Yes. I want to know where that place leads to; and I don't like to feel that we were frightened because it was dark. Come along."

"What now—directly?"

"Yes; you're not afraid, are you?"

"No," cried Fred, starting up. "Get two candles this time, and we'll take one apiece."

The lights were obtained, the door at the end of the passage bolted, and once more the two boys stood at the top of the staircase.

"Think we had better go now?" said Fred.

"Yes; we may not have such a chance again for ever so long. Do you feel afraid?"

"Not exactly afraid; only as if I didn't want to go. I'm not so brave as you are, Scar."

This last was said with a bit of a sneer, which made the boy wince, and then draw himself up proudly.

"I'm not brave," he said, "for I feel as if I'd give anything not to go; but it seems to me as if it would be very cowardly to give up, and I mean to go."

He seized the balustrade as he spoke, gave it a wrench, the stair shot from its fastening, was pushed back, and without another word Scarlett thrust in his lighted candle, followed it, and Fred stood looking in as his companion gradually disappeared.

"Come along, Fred," came in muffled tones from beneath the landing; and, uttering a sigh, Fred thrust in his candlestick and followed, to rise, after a slow horizontal progress, to a perpendicular position, behind his leader.

The way seemed far easier now, and in a very few minutes they were standing again in the chamber, where they paused for a few moments before Scarlett drew open the panelled door in the corner, and once more held the light above his head as he gazed down the mysterious stairs.

"Shall I go first?" asked Fred, in a voice which invited a refusal of his services.

"No; it's our place, and I'll lead," was the reply.

"Don't put the candle out again," said Fred, with a sigh of relief, and speaking in warning tones. "I say, Scar, perhaps there's a place like this at the Manor."

"We'll see, when we've found out all about this," replied Scarlett, as he began to descend, while Fred followed closely, the two lights making their task easier, while their confidence began now to increase as they encountered no danger.

The foot of the steps was reached in safety, the candle being held low down, so as to guard against any pitfall or fresh flight of stairs in the way.

But all was perfectly level as the boys went on along the narrow, arched-over passage, their light footfalls sending on before them a curious series of reverberations, while their progress for quite a hundred yards was singularly monotonous and uneventful.

"Why, how far does it go?" said Fred at last, becoming bolder now, but feeling startled as he heard his words go whispering away.

"Very little farther. Look!"

The lights were held up, and they stopped short, for a few yards before them was a narrow, nail-studded door, very similar to the one leading into the chamber, but heavier looking, and with a great rusty bolt at top and bottom.

"That's the end of it, then," said Fred. "I say, I know what it is. That's the vault where they used to bury the old Markhams."

"That it can't be, for they were all buried at the church."

"Well, it looks like it," said Fred. "Shall we go any farther?"

"Yes, of course. I want to see what's behind the door."

Nerving himself to the effort, Scarlett stepped over the intervening space, and took hold of the top bolt, which, like its fellow, was shot into a socket in the stone wall.

But the bolt was rusted to the staples, and he could not move it with one hand.

"Hold the light, Fred," he exclaimed; and his companion stood behind him, bearing both candles, as Scarlett tugged and strained and wrenched vainly at the corroded iron.

"Wants a hammer to start it," said Fred, as the interest in these proceedings drove away the sensations of nervousness. "Shall we go back and fetch one?"

"I'm—afraid—we shall have to," panted Scarlett, as he toiled and strained at the stubborn bolt. "It's of no use to try and—"

There was a sharp creak, the bolt gave way a little, and the rest was only a work of time, for by wriggling it up and down the rust was ground out, and at last it yielded and was drawn back.

"Let me have a try at the other," cried Fred; and Scarlett squeezed by him and took the candles, to stand, hot and panting, watching intently while his companion attacked the lower bolt.

This was even more compactly fixed than the other; but the thumb-piece was projecting, and Fred began on this with his foot, kicking it upward with his toe, and stamping it down again, till it gradually loosened, and, after a little more working, shot back with ease.

Fred drew away from the door then, and looked at his companion.

"Shall we open it now?" he said, with his old hesitation returning.

Scarlett did not answer for a few moments.

"Think it is a tomb?" he said.

"You said it was not," replied Fred.

"It would be very horrible if it is; I shouldn't like to look in."

The door opened from them, and, as they stood there, they could see that it had given a little, so that the edge was nearly half an inch from the stonework, and a faint, damp odour reached their nostrils.

"Don't let's be cowards," cried Fred; and, raising one foot, he placed it against the door, gave a hard thrust, and started back so suddenly that he nearly overset Scarlett with the lights.

But the door did not fly open. It only yielded a few inches, the hinges giving forth a dismal, grating sound, and for a few moments the boys stood hesitating.

"I don't care," cried Fred, excitedly. "I mean to have it open now;" and he rushed at the door, and thrust and drove, each effort moving it a little more and a little more, the ironwork yielding with groan after groan, as if it were remonstrating for being roused from a long, long sleep, till the door struck against the wall with an echoing bang; and once more the boys hesitated.

But there was nothing to alarm them. The heavy, dank odour came more plainly, and, after a few minutes, Fred took one of the candles and advanced into a stone vault about a dozen feet square, with a very low, arched doorway opposite to them, and another flight of steps descending into darkness, while on one side lay a little heap of rusty iron in the last stages of decay.

"Why, the place is nothing but passages and cellars," cried Fred.

"This must be the end, though," replied Scarlett, eagerly. "We have come a good way, and there should be a door at the bottom of these stairs leading into the park."

"Let's come and see, then," cried Fred, advancing boldly enough now. "What fun if we've found another way into the— Here, Scar, look, look!"

The boy had stopped half a dozen steps down, and he was stooping and holding the candle as far as he could stretch as Scarlett reached his side.

"Water?"

"Yes; water."

"What is it—a well?"

"I don't know. We could soon tell, if we had a stick. Here! what are those at the side?"

They went back to the heap of old iron, and to their surprise found that it was a collection of old arms and armour, rusted almost beyond recognition.

From this heap they dragged a long sword, one which must have been heavy, but which was now little better than a thin collection of scales.

"This will do," said Fred, returning to the farther doorway, and descending till he was on the lowest step, where, reaching out, he tried to sound the depth.

This proved an easy task, for, as near as they could make out, the water was about a yard deep, and the steps went to the bottom, where all was level ground.

They stretched out the lights, and gazed before them to where the retreating passage grew lower and lower, till the top of the arch seemed to have dipped down and touched the black water; and having satisfied themselves that no farther progress could be made, Fred turned and said, as he rubbed one ear—

"Now, if we were fishes or water-rats, we might find out some more. But, I say, Scar, we've taken a deal of trouble to find out very little."

"I think we've found out a great deal," replied Scarlett. "This is no well. It's the edge of the lake, and this—"

"Nonsense!"

"I feel sure it is, and this must be a secret way into the house, hidden under water. Fred, we must have a search outside, and see if we can't find the place."

"Then you will not stay here any longer?" said Fred, throwing down the sword upon the rusty heap.

"No; let's go back now. We have found out a very curious thing; and if we can discover the way in from outside, it will be splendid."

"Come along, then," replied Fred, crossing to the heap of old armour, and stooping over it, candle in hand. "But I wonder how old these things are. Do you think we could clean the armour, and make it look bright again?"

Scarlett shook his head as he picked up the remains of an old helmet.

"It must have been a time of war when this house was built," he said thoughtfully; "and the secret passage was forgotten when it became a time of peace."

"But it is not a time of peace now, is it? I heard that there would very likely be war."

"Who told you that?"

"I heard your father and my father talking about it; and they both grew cross, and your father soon got up and went home."

"Then your father must have said something he did not like against the king."

"My father does not like the king," said Fred, sharply.

"And my father does," cried Scarlett, with a flash of the eye.

"Oh, never mind about that now," said Fred, looking at his old companion in a troubled manner. "What has it got to do with us? What shall we do now?"

"Go back," replied Scarlett; "for we cannot get any farther along here. I say, Fred, it does not seem such a terrible place now you are used to it, does it?"

"Terrible!" cried Fred, stoutly. "Why, I like it. Don't, pray don't, tell anybody about it, and we can have fine games here. It's ever so much better than a cave, and we can smuggle all sorts of things up here. I mean up there in that room."

"Yes, if I don't tell my father about it."

"Oh, don't tell him yet! not till we're tired of it. Then I don't mind."

Scarlett made no reply, but holding his candle above his head, went out of the vault, stopping afterwards while Fred drew to the door. Then, with the ease begotten of use, they went along the tunnel, up the steps to the chamber, and then along the passages to the great staircase, lying down and rolling themselves over, and emerging to listen intently before closing the opening, and hurrying to Scarlett's room for another wash and clearance of the cobwebs and dust.

This done, they hurried out, full of eagerness to run down to the side of the great lake, where they fully expected to find the opening at once.

Failing in this, they stopped by a sandy bank, and, taking a piece of stick, Fred set to work to sketch on the sand a plan of their wanderings.

"You see, we started from here, Scar; then we went off so far to the left, then to the right, then to the left again, and then up into the chamber. Then we went out of the right-hand corner, and down that long flight of stairs to the passage, which led straight away to the vault, and down into the water."

"Well?" said Scarlett, coolly.

"Yes, of course, I see it now. Then, according to my plan, the way into the lake must be just under where we are sitting."

"Where is it, then?"

Fred looked up at his companion, rubbed his ear again, and then looked down at the water's edge.

"It must be here somewhere," he said. "Let's have another look round."

Scarlett rose to his feet from where he had been lying, and they once more searched the side of the lake, which toward the house was deep and dark below its high bank.

There were places where it might be possible for a tunnel to run down into the water, shady spots where willows and alders overhung the lake; places where birch and hazels grew close up to the patches of rushes and reed-mace, with its tall broken pokers standing high above the waving leaves.

In one indentation—a spot where the flat-bottomed boat lay moored—Scarlett felt certain that they had found the entrance; but when they lay flat on the overhanging bank and peered down below, there was nothing to be seen but black leaves and dead branches far below, while in mid-water, bar-sided perch in golden green armour, floated slowly to and fro, seeming to watch the movements of sundry carp close to the surface, gliding in and out among the stems of the lilies and nestling beneath the leaves.

"It's of no use, Fred. I'm afraid we have made a mistake. That must be a kind of well made to supply the house with water, and it is all fancy about the passage coming down here."

At that moment there was a loud burst of barking, and the lads started up to run towards the house, for two mounted men were on their way along the winding road which crossed the park, evidently making for the great entrance-door of the Hall.

"They've come back together," cried Fred as he ran; but before they could reach the door, one of the horsemen had swung himself down, thrown the reins to Nat, who was waiting, and walked up to the top of the steps. Here he turned, and stood frowning for a few moments, while his companion sat beating his boot with his whip so vigorously that the horse kept starting and fidgeting about, making a plunge sufficient to unseat a bad rider.

"Will you come in, Forrester?" said the dismounted man.

"What for?" was the stern reply. "To renew the argument, and have harsh words said to me?"

"Nonsense, my dear Forrester," said the other. "I only spoke out as a loyal man should, and I am sorry you took it so ill."

"And I only spoke out as a loyal man should."

"Loyal?"

"Yes, to his country, sir."

"Why, my dear Forrester—" began the dismounted man, angrily. "There, I beg your pardon. I was a little heated. Come in, Forrester. Stay and dine with me, and we can chat matters over coolly."

"Better not," said the mounted man, coldly. "Fred!"

"Yes, father."

"You were coming home with me?"

"No, father; I was going to stop with Scar for a bit."

"Humph! Better come home now, my boy. I think Sir Godfrey wishes to talk to his son."

"I was not going to do anything of the kind, Forrester; but if you are bent upon a division between us, I am not the man to baulk you."

"Very good, sir, very good. Then be it so."

"But it seems to me a great pity that two old friends should be divided, and our boys, who have been like brothers, should be separated upon a question about which you must feel, upon calm consideration, that you are wrong."

"If I felt that I was wrong, Sir Godfrey Markham, I should at once apologise; but I am not wrong."

"And our boys?"

"It is impossible for our boys to be friends, Sir Godfrey, until you have apologised for what you have said."

"Apologised, Colonel Forrester! Why, sir, I commend myself for my restraint. If it had been any other man than my oldest friend who had dared to utter such disloyal thoughts against the king, I should have struck him from his horse. Good day, sir, and I pray Heaven to place better thoughts in your mind! Scarlett, my boy."

"Yes, father."

"Come here."

"Mayn't I shake hands with Fred Forrester first?"

"No. Yes. You boys have no quarrel. But it will be better that you should keep at home for the present."

"Oh, Fred, what's the matter?" whispered Scarlett.

"Don't you know?"

"Ye–es, I'm afraid I do."

"That's it. I didn't know we were going to have trouble about it down here in Coombeland. But, I say, Scar, we're good friends, aren't we?"

"Yes, of course."

"That's right. They're both cross to-day; they'll make it up to-morrow."

"Fred!" said Colonel Forrester over his shoulder as he rode off.

"Coming, father. Good-bye, Scar; and, I say, don't tell anybody about the secret place just yet."

"Very well."

"It will be all right again directly. Father soon gets good-tempered again after he has been cross; but it always makes him angry if anybody praises up the king."

"Fred!"

"Coming, father."

The boy darted off after the departing horseman, and Scarlett sat watching them till they disappeared among the trees, when he went slowly into the house, catching sight of his father striding up and down in the dining-room, and with a more serious look in his face than he remembered to have seen before.

"I hope there is not going to be trouble and fighting, the same as there has been elsewhere," thought the boy; and he involuntarily glanced through the open hall-door at the beautiful landscape, across which seemed to float visions of soldiers and burning homesteads, and destruction such as had been brought to them in the shape of news from far distant parts.

The coming of his father roused him from his reverie.

"Why, Scar, lad, don't look so serious," cried Sir Godfrey, clapping the boy on the shoulder. "I spoke angrily, didn't I, my boy? Well, I was obliged in these rebellious times. Remember this, Scar, no matter what comes, 'God save the king!'"

"Yes, father," cried the boy, flushing as he took off his cap and tossed it in the air, "'God save the king!'"

Chapter Five
Another Discovery

Fred was right; the two elders did soon make it up, and the political ebullition seemed to be forgotten. The boys were soon together again, enjoying their simple country ways as of yore, while the clouds gathering around only looked golden in their sunshiny life.

The search for the outlet to the secret passage was renewed without success, and then given up for a time. There was so much to see and do that glorious autumn time when the apples were ripening fast, and hanging in great ropes from the heavily laden trees, beneath whose tangled boughs all was grey and green leaves and gloom, every orchard being an improvised wilderness, which was allowed to bear or be barren according to its will.

There was always so much to do. Trout to hunt up the little moorland streams; loaches to impale among the stones of the swift torrents; rides over the long undulating stretches of the moor, from far inland to where it ended abruptly in steep cliffs by the sea.

And so life glided on at Manor and Hall. The king and country were not mentioned; Colonel and Mistress Forrester supped at the Hall, and little Lil listened to the sweet old-fashioned ballads the visitor sang. Then the Scarletts spent pleasant evenings at the Manor, and the two fathers discussed the future of their sons, while Dame Markham and Mistress Forrester seemed to be like sisters.

But all the while the storm-clouds were gathering, and a distant muttering of thunder told that the tempest threatened to break over the pleasant west-country land.

"There's going to be a big change o' some kind, Master Scarlett," said Nat, the gardener; "and if there is, it won't be any too soon, for it will put my brother Samson in his proper place, and keep him there."

"Yes, Master Fred, I went and had a mug o' cider down in the village last night, poor winegar wee sort o' stuff—three apples to a bucket o' water— such as my brother Nat makes up at the Hall; and there they all were talking about it. People all taking sides all over England. Some's Cavaliers and some's Roundheads, so they say, and one party's for the king, and the other isn't. Precious awful, aren't it?"

"Perhaps it's only talk, Samson?"

"No, Master Fred, sir, I don't think it's all talk; but there is a deal o' talk."

"Ah, well, it's nothing to do with us, Samson. Let them quarrel. We're too busy out here to bother about their quarrels."

"Well, I dunno, sir. I'm not a quarrelsome chap, but I heard things as my brother Nat has said quite bad enough to make me want to go again him, for we two never did agree; and when it comes to your own brother telling downright out-and-out lies about the Manor vegetables and fruit, I think it's time to speak, don't you?"

"Oh, I wish you and Nat would meet some day, and shake hands, or else fight it out and have done with it; brothers oughtn't to quarrel."

"I dunno, Master Fred, I dunno."

"Ah, well, I think all quarrels are a bother, whether they're big ones or whether they're little ones. They say the king and Parliament have fallen out; well, if I had my way, I'd make the king and Parliament shake hands, just as Scar Markham and I will make you and Nat shake yours."

"Nay, Master Fred, never!"

"I'm going to meet him this afternoon, and we'll talk it over."

Samson shook his head.

Home studies were over for the day, and by a natural attraction, Fred started by a short cut to the high point of the moor, just at the same time as Scar Markham left the Hall for the same spot.

"He'll be in some mischief or another before he gets back," said Samson Dee, as he ceased digging, and rested one foot upon the top of his spade, watching his young master contemplatively as he went along the road for a short distance before leaping up the bank, and beginning to tramp among heath, brake, and furze, over the springy turf.

Samson shook his head sadly, and sighed as he watched Fred's progress, the figure growing smaller and smaller, sometimes disappearing altogether in a hollow, and then bounding into sight again like one of the moorland sheep.

"Yes; some mischief!" sighed Samson again, and he watched the lad with the sorrowful expression on the increase, till the object of his consideration was out of sight, when he once more sighed, and recommenced digging. "You don't catch me, though, making it up."

Oddly enough—perhaps it would be more correct to say naturally enough—Nat Dee ceased digging up in the Hall garden to watch Scarlett Markham, who, after sending his sister Lil back into the house in tears, because he refused to take her with him, started off at a rapid pace.

"Wonder what mischief he's going to be at," said Nat, half aloud; and he, too, rested a foot on the top of his spade, and contemplated the retiring form.

Perhaps, after all, digging is exceedingly hard work, and a break is very welcome; but whether it be so or no, the fact is always evident that a gardener is ready to cease lifting the fat mellow earth of a garden, and stand and think upon the slightest excuse.

Nat Dee waited till Scar had disappeared, and then he slowly and sorrowfully resumed his task, and sighed with a feeling of regret for the time when he too was a boy, and indulged in unlimited idleness and endless quarrels with his brother Samson.

Fred Forrester whistled as he slowly climbed the hill, which was shaped like a level surfaced mound, and stood right up above the ordinary undulations of the moor, and Scarlett Markham whistled as he slowly climbed the other side, while high overhead, to turn the duet into a trio, there was another whistler in the shape of a speckled lark, soaring round and round as if he were describing the figure of a gigantic corkscrew, whose point was intended to pierce the clouds.

There had been a shower earlier in the day, and the earth sent forth a sweet fragrance, which mingled with the soft salt breeze, and sent a thrill of pleasure through the frames of the two lads hastening to their trysting-place. They did not know that their feet crushed the wild thyme, or caused fresh odours to float upon the air, or whether the breeze came from north, south, or west; all that they knew was that they felt very happy, and that they were out on the moor, ready to enjoy themselves by doing something, they knew not what. They did not even know that they were each performing a part in a trio, the little lark being so common an object as to be unnoticed, while the top of the hill divided the two terrestrial whistlers from each other.

Fred was at the highest point first, and throwing himself down on the turf, he lay watching the coming figure toiling up, while the grasshoppers *chizzed* and leaped from strand of grass to harebell, and thence to heather, and even on to the figure lying there.

The view was grand. Away to right were the undulations of the moor; to the left the high hills which seemed as if cut off short, and descended almost perpendicularly to the sea, and in front of them the sea itself, glistening in the sunshine beyond the cliff, which from the point where Fred lay looked like a lion *couchant*, end on to him, and passing out to sea. Here and there some boat's sail seemed like a speck upon the sea, while going in different directions—seaward and toward Bristol were a couple of what Fred mentally dubbed "king's ships." Away as far as eye could reach to right and left lay the softly blue Welsh coast; but Fred's attention was divided between the lion's head-like outline of the Rill, and the slowly advancing figure of Scarlett Markham, who finished his ascent by breaking into a trot, and zigzagging up the last steep piece to throw himself down beside his friend.

They lay for some few minutes enjoying themselves, their ideas of enjoyment consisting in lying face downward resting upon their crossed arms, which formed a pillow for their chins, and kicking the turf with their toes. Then, as if moved by the same spirit, they leaped to their feet with all a boy's energy and vital force.

"Let's do something," exclaimed Scar. "Shall we go to the lake?"

"That's just what I was going to say," cried Fred; but they did not go far in an aimless way—they began to descend the hill slowly at first, then at a trot, then at headlong speed, till they stopped a part of the way up the next slope, after crossing the bottom of the little coombe between the hills.

This second hill looked wearisome after their rapid descent, so they contented themselves with walking along its side parallel with the bottom of the little valley, talking of indifferent matters till they came upon a little flock of grey and white gulls feeding amongst the short herbage, where the rain had brought out various soft-bodied creatures good in a gull's eyes for food.

The beautiful white-breasted creatures rose on their long narrow wings, and flapped and floated away.

From force of habit, Fred took up a stone and threw it after the birds, not with any prospect of hitting them, for they were a couple of hundred yards away.

"Wish I could fly like that," said Scarlett. "Look at them; they're going right over the Rill Head."

The two boys stopped and watched until the birds glided out of sight, beyond the lion-like headland, an object, however, which grew less lion-like the nearer they drew.

"What would be the good?" replied Fred. "It would soon be very stupid to go gliding here and there."

"But see how easy it would be to float like that."

"How do you know?" said practical Fred. "I dare say a bird's wings ache sometimes as much as our legs do with running. I say, Scar."

"Yes."

"Let's go and have a look at the caves."

"What caves?"

"Down below the Rill. Now, only think of it; we were born here, and never went and had a look at them. Samson says that one of them is quite big and runs in ever so far, with a place like a chimney at one end, so that you can get down from the land side."

"And Nat said one day that it was all nonsense; that they were just like so many rabbit-holes—and that's what he thought they were."

"But our Samson said he had been in them; and if they were no bigger than rabbit-holes, he couldn't have done that. Let's go and see."

"Bother! I had enough of poking about in that damp old passage, and all for nothing. I thought we were going to find the way in there."

"Well, so we did."

"But I mean the other end."

"Bother, bother! what's the good!"

"How do I know? It's very curious. There's something seems to draw you on when you are underground," said Scarlett, dreamily.

"Hark at the old worm! Why, Scar, I believe you'd like to live underground."

Scarlett shook his head.

"I mean to find that way in to our place some day, whether you help me or whether you do not. Never mind what your Samson said about the Rill caves. He don't know. Let's go and see."

"What's the good?"

"I don't know that it will be any good, but let's see. There may be all kinds of strange things in a cave. I've read about wonderful places that went into the earth for a long way."

"Yes; but our Rill cave would not. My father told me one day about two caves he went into in Derbyshire. One had a little river running out of it, and he went in and walked by the side of the water for a long way till he came to a black arch, and there the gentlemen who were with him lit candles and they waded into the water and crept under the dark arch, and then went on and on for a long way through cave after cave, all wet and dripping from the top. Sometimes they were obliged to wade in the stream, and sometimes they walked along the edge."

"And what did they find?"

"Mud," said Fred, laconically.

"Nothing else?"

"No; only mud, sticky mud, no matter how far they went; and at last they got tired of it, and turned back to find that the water had risen, and was close up to the top of the arch under which they had crept, so that they had to wait half a day before it went down."

"What made the water rise?" asked Scarlett; "the tide?"

"No; there were no tides there right in among the hills."

"Then how was it?"

"There had been a storm, and the water had run down and filled the little river."

As they chatted, the lads walked steadily on, and began to ascend the long, low eminence, which formed, as it were, the large body of the couchant lion, but which from where they were, seemed like the most ordinary of hills.

"There was another cave, too, that my father went into, but that was very different. It was high up in among the hills, and you went down quite a hole to get to it, and then it was just as if the inside of the hill had come full of cracks and splits along which he kept climbing and walking with the two sides just alike, just as if the stone had been broken in two."

"Then this was stone, not mud," said Scarlett, who was deeply interested.

"Yes, solid stone—rock; and every here and there you could see curious shapes, just as if water had been running down, and it had all been turned into stone."

"I should like to go and see a place like that," said Scarlett.

"Yes; I shouldn't mind seeing a cave like that. Father says it went in for miles, and nobody had ever got to the end of it, for it branched off into narrow slits, and sometimes you were walking on shelves, and you could hold the candle over and look down horrible holes that were nobody knows how deep, and there you could hear the water gurgling at the bottom, and hissing and splashing, and— Oh!"

"Scar!" yelled Fred, making a dash at his companion just in time to catch him by the arm as he suddenly dropped down through a narrow opening in the midst of the short green turf over which they were walking.

So narrow was the opening, and so nearly hidden by grass and heath, that Scarlett had no difficulty in supporting himself by spreading out his arms, as soon as he had recovered from the first startling effect of his slip.

But he did not stop many minutes in this position. Fred hung on to his arm. He threw himself sidewise, grasped tightly hold of a stout branch of heath, and scrambled out.

"Who'd have thought of there being a hole like that?" said Scarlett, as soon as he was safe. "But I don't suppose it's very deep, after all. Got a stone?"

"No. Listen."

Fred had thrown himself upon his breast, and craned his neck over the place, trying to peer down, but only into darkness, the hole evidently not going down straight; it being, in fact, a narrow crack, such as he had described in telling of the Derbyshire cavern.

Scarlett, who looked rather white from the shock he had received, joined his companion, and bent down to listen.

"Hear that?" said Fred in a whisper.

"Yes; water."

"Water! Yes, of course; but listen again."

They kept silence, and there ascended from below, through the almost hidden crevice, a low whisper of an echoing roar, which died away in a peculiar hissing sound that was thrilling in its strange suggestiveness.

"There must be a waterfall somewhere below there," said Scarlett at last.

"Why, don't you know what it is?"

"No."

"The sea. Didn't think it was the end of your passage, did you?"

"What there? Nonsense!"

"Yes, it's the cave; and the sea runs right up here."

"It couldn't; it's too far away."

"I don't care; that's the sea. Now listen again, how regularly it comes. Every wave must be rushing in, and you can hear it go whishing out."

Scarlett and his companion listened for a few minutes.

"Yes; it's the sea, sure enough," said Scarlett. "Why, Fred, I didn't think we had such a place here."

"No," said Fred. "But, then, nobody ever comes up here. Why, it's quite a discovery, Scar. Let's get down to the shore, and go in."

"Yes, I'm ready;" and together the two lads made their way to the edge of the slaty cliffs, and then a long way by the edge, before they could find a rift of a sufficient slope to warrant their attempting a descent.

Even this selected path looked far more easy than it proved; but by the exercise of a little care they got about half-way down, and then stopped; for it was plain enough to see, from the point of vantage they had gained, that even if they climbed to the narrow line of black slaty shingle between them and the perpendicular rock, they could not reach the face of the Rill Head, which projected, promontory-like, into the sea, and low down in which for certain the cave must be.

"What a bother!" exclaimed Fred. "I thought we were going to have a fine bit of adventure, and discover seals, and lobsters, and crabs, and all kinds of things. What shall we do?"

"Wait till low water."

"But it's nearly low water now. Can't you see?"

The marks of the last tide were plainly visible high up on the rugged rock-face, the last tide having left every ledge covered with washed-up fucus and bladder-wrack, speckled with white shells and sandy patches.

"Then it must always be deep in water?" said Scarlett.

"Well, I tell you what, then, let's borrow somebody's boat and try and get right in that way."

"I don't know who somebody is," said Scarlett, drily; "and if I did, I don't suppose he has got a boat."

"Don't talk like that," cried Fred. "I say, couldn't we get a boat?"

"There isn't one for miles. Old Porlett bought one—don't you recollect?—and the sea knocked it all to pieces in the first storm."

"Yes, I recollect," said Fred, thoughtfully, "though it was twenty feet up on a broad shelf of rock. Shall we swim to the cave?"

Scarlett shook his head. "No," he said. "It would be too risky."

"What shall we do, then?"

"Give it up."

"And I just won't," cried Fred, emphatically. "I say, Scar, look here."

"Well?"

"If we can't get in one way, let's get in the other."

Scarlett stared at him wonderingly, "Let's go down the same way that you were going, only not in such a hurry," he added with a gun.

"What, climb down the hole?" said Scarlett, thoughtfully, and ignoring the smile. "Yes. Why not?"

"Oh yes, we could, with a rope. Drive an iron bar down into the earth, and tie one end of the rope to it, and then go down."

"You would not dare to go down that way."

"Yes, I would," said Fred, stoutly; "and so would you," he added.

"I don't know," said Scarlett, dreamily. "But I do. Shall we do it? I'm ready if you are. Come along, then, back to our place, and let's make old Samson lend as couple of good ropes."

Scarlett nodded acquiescence, and the two lads, little thinking how their act would be importance in the future, re-climbed the cliff and started toward the Manor at a run.

It proved very easy to propose getting a rope, but much harder to get one, for everything in the shape of hempen cord was under the care of Samson Dee, who had to be found, not at all a difficult task, for he was digging—at least, handling a spade—down the garden.

Samson greeted the coming of the lads with a smile, for it was another excuse for taking a foot from the ground, and resting it upon the spade. But as soon as he heard the want, the smile faded from his face. "You want a what?" he said. "You know what I said, Samson, so no nonsense. Let us have one directly."

"You want a rope, Master Fred?"

"There, I told you that you did hear me. Yes; I want the longest rope about the place directly."

"What yer want it for?"

"Never you mind. I tell you I want the rope."

"To make a swing with, of course. Well, then, you can't have it."

"Can't I?" said Fred, sharply. "We'll soon see about that. Come along, Scar. Any one would think the ropes were his."

"Look here, Master Fred, if you—"

Samson ceased speaking, for he was wise enough to see that he was wasting words in shouting after the two lads. But he began muttering directly about a "passell o' boys" coming and bothering him when he hadn't a moment to spare.

"And look here," he shouted, as he saw his visitors trotting off with a coil of strong new rope belonging to the waggon, "mind you bring that rope back again. Now, I wonder what them two are going to do?" he ended by muttering, and then set to work digging once more, but in so slow and methodical a fashion that the worms had plenty of time to get away from the sharp edge of the spade before it was driven home and cut them in half.

"Poor old Samson!" said Fred; "he seems to think that everything belongs to him."

"So does our Nat," replied Scarlett. "I often fancy he thinks I belong to him as well, from the way he shouts and orders me about."

"But you never do what he tells you."

"Of course not; and— Oh, Fred!"

"What's the matter?"

"We've got the rope; but what are we going to fasten the end to when we go down?" Fred stopped short, and rubbed one ear.

"You hold it while I go down, and I'll hold it while you go down."

"I shouldn't like to try that," said Scarlett. "We're not strong enough."

"Nonsense! Not if we let the rope bite on the edge of the hole?"

"That would not do," said Scarlett, decisively.

"I know, then," cried Fred. "Come along."

"No. Let's go back and get an iron bar to drive down in the earth."

"I've got a better way than that," said Fred. "There's a pole across the opening in that stone wall half-way up the hill. We'll lay that across, and tie the rope to it."

Scarlett nodded acquiescence, and they trotted on to the rough stone wall, built up of loose fragments piled one on the other, the gateway left for the passage of cattle being closed by a couple of poles laid across like bars, their ends being slipped in holes left for the purpose.

The straighter of these two was slipped out by Scarlett and shouldered, and they hastened on, attracted by the discovery they had made, but recalling, as they went on, that they had been told before about the existence of this opening by more than one person, though it had slipped from their memory for the time.

"Who's going down first?" said Fred, as they slowly climbed the last hundred yards of the slope.

"I will."

"No; I think I ought to go first."

"Long bent, short bent," said Scarlett, picking a couple of strands of grass, breaking them off so that one was nearly double the length of the other, and then, after placing two ends level and hiding the others, offering them to his companion to draw one out.

Fred drew the shorter, and Scarlett had the right to go down first—a right which but for the look of the thing he would willingly have surrendered. For as they reached the long, narrow, grass-grown crack, the strange whispering and plashing sounds which came from below suggested unknown dangers, which were more repellent than the attractions of the mysterious hole.

Fred looked curiously at Scarlett, who noted the look, and tightened himself up, assuming a carelessness he did not feel.

"Doesn't go down quite straight, seemingly," he said.

"All the better. I say, shall I go down first?"

"What for? I won the choice, and I'm going," said Scarlett, sharply, as he took one end of the rope and tied it to the middle of the pole, which proved to be of ample length to go well across the opening.

"Tie it tightly, Scar," cried Fred.

"Never fear. Mind the rope is so that it will uncoil easily. There, run it down, and let's see if it is long enough to get to the bottom."

Fred raised the rings of stiff twisted hemp, and dropped them down out of sight; but it was evident that the rope did not descend very far, the main portion lodging only a little way down; but Fred raised it a yard or two and shook it, with the effect that more fell down and lodged, but only to be shaken loose again and again, showing plainly enough that the hole went down in a sharp slope for a long way, and then that the rope had dropped over a perpendicular part, for as it was drawn up and down it fell heavily now.

"There," said Fred, "that's it. I dare say that reaches the bottom. If it doesn't, you must come up again. Ready?"

"Yes."

And with all the recklessness of boys who never see the reality of danger until it is there, Scarlett stripped off his jerkin and lowered himself down into the crack, hanging with one arm over the pole for a few moments before seizing the rope, twisting his legs round it, and letting himself slide down.

"Keep on calling out what it's like; and as soon as you get down, sing 'Bottom!' and then I'll come too."

Scarlett nodded, and let himself slide slowly, to find, and call up to his companion, that the hole went down at a slope into the darkness, so that he was not swinging by the rope, but supporting himself thereby, as he glided down over the shaley earth of which the hill was composed, but only to come to a sudden stop as he found that the hole zigzagged back in the opposite direction at a similar angle to that by which he had descended.

"Are you right?" cried Fred from above.

"Yes."

"Is it easy?"

"Yes, quite."

"Then I shall come down now."

"No, no," cried Scarlett; "the rope is not strong enough for two."

"Make haste, then. I want to see what there is. Found anything good?"

"No," said Scarlett, as he glided slowly down into the darkness, with his companion's words buzzing in his ears, just as if they were spoken close by, and listening as he descended to the peculiar, trickling, rushing noise of the scraps of disintegrating slate which he dislodged in passing, and which fell rapidly before him.

"Keep talking," said Fred from above.

"There's nothing to talk about," cried Scarlett. "I'm only sliding down a slope, and—yes, now I'm hanging clear, and turning round. Hold the rope: it's twisting so."

"I am holding it tight," came back; "but I can't help its turning round. What's it like now?"

"Just like day beginning to break, and I can see something shining down below."

"Is it the water?"

"Yes, I suppose so. Shall I go down any lower?"

"Yes, of course."

"It isn't water that's shining," said Scarlett, after turning slowly round two or three times, as he descended another twenty feet.

"What is it, then?—gold or silver?"

"It's only a reflection, I suppose; but I can't quite see."

"Aren't you at the bottom yet?" cried Fred, impatiently.

"No."

"Make haste, then."

"Yes, I am at the bottom," cried Scarlett, directly after, as his feet touched firm rock.

"Look out, then," cried Fred. "Down I come."

"No, no; wait a moment," was the reply. "I want to try and find out what it's like."

Whirr, whizz!

"What's the matter?" cried Fred, as he heard his companion utter a loud, "Oh!"

"Something rushed by me."

"What was it?"

"I couldn't see. Ah! there it is again."

"Hold tight; I'm coming," cried Fred. "I dare say it was an owl or a bat. Oh my! doesn't it scrape you?"

Scarlett's response was a sharp ejaculation and a jerk at the rope.

"Here, what are you doing?" cried Fred.

There was no answer, only a panting noise.

"Don't swing the rope about like that, Scar! Do you hear? I won't come down, if you don't leave off."

"Hah! that's it," came from below.

"What's the matter? What are you doing?" cried Fred, who had paused at the bottom of the first slope, holding tightly by the rope, which Scarlett seemed to be trying to jerk out of his hand.

"It's all right now," panted Scarlett. "You sent down a lot of slate and earth, and it came on my head."

"Well, I couldn't help it. Why didn't you stand on one side?"

"I did," cried Scarlett, "and stepped back off the edge. Fortunately, I had tight hold of the rope, but slipped down ever so far, and had to climb up again. Come along down, now."

There was a serious sound and a spice of danger in this little recital, which, added to the darkness into which Fred had plunged, made him descend for the rest of the way slowly and very cautiously down the second slope, and then, as he hung perpendicularly, and felt himself slowly turning round, he kept on asking how much farther it was, till his feet touched his companion's hands, and he stood directly by his side in the faint grey light, which seemed to strike up from below, both clutching the rope tightly in the excitement of the novel position, and trying to pierce the gloom.

"Ugh! What's that?" cried Fred, suddenly, as he kicked against something which made a rattling noise.

"I don't know. Sounds like pieces of wood."

"Ugh!" ejaculated Fred again, "bones! Come away, Scar; it's a skeleton."

The two boys shrank away in horror, and for some moments neither ventured to speak, while, as they clung together, each could feel his fellow suffering from no little nervous tremor.

"Some one must have slipped down the hole and died here of starvation," whispered Scarlett at last. "You know how dangerous it is."

"Yes," said Fred, thoughtfully, and with his shrinking feeling on the increase. "No," he exclaimed directly after, "I don't think it's that. I know — at least, I should know if I touched it."

"What do you mean?"

"It's some sheep slipped down when feeding, and never been missed."

"Do you think it's that?" said Scarlett, eagerly.

"I feel sure of it. If it had been a man, he would have found some way of getting out. I say, Scar, will you stoop down and touch it?"

"No," said Scarlett, with a shudder.

"Well, I will, then. Yes; I'm right. It is a sheep's bones."

"How do you know?"

"You can feel some wool down here. If it had been a man, it would have been clothes. Well, I am glad."

Scarlett showed his satisfaction by drawing a long breath full of relief, and the spirits of both seemed relieved by the knowledge that the grisly relics told no tale of a human being's terrible fate.

"I dare say there are more bones about, if we were to search," said Fred. "But what a great gloomy place it is! Who'd have thought that there was such a cave on our shore?"

"I can't see any good, now we have got down in it," said Scarlett, rather discontentedly. "I don't suppose we shall find anything."

"Why, we have found something."

"Yes; bones. I wish we had a light."

"Where was it you stepped over?" said Fred, speaking in a whisper now, for the silence and darkness were not without their effect upon him.

"There."

"Where's there? I can't see which way you mean."

"Exactly behind you," said Scarlett.

Fred made an involuntary movement in the opposite direction, one imitated by Scarlett, with the result that they edged along about a dozen feet before they were stopped by the wall of rock, which sloped away above their heads.

"I wish it wasn't dark," said Fred. "Now let's try how far we can get this way."

Still holding on tightly by the rope, they moved in a fresh direction, finding the rock upon which they stood made irregular by the heaps of slate and earth which had crumbled down from above; but over this they cautiously made their way for seven or eight yards, when they were again stopped by the sloping wall of rock.

The next investigation suggested itself as being the edge over which Scarlett had stepped, and for the moment they shrank from that, and made their way cautiously back, keeping close to the wall.

"Let's see how far it goes in that direction," whispered Scarlett. "I fancy that's where the light comes from."

Fred acquiesced, and the little mounds of slate were crossed, and the way followed till they had nearly reached the limit of the line, when, low down before them, they made out a dark, rough-looking edge, black upon the very pale light which struck into the cave.

"Why, that's the edge of the rough shelf we are standing on," said Scarlett. "Now, let's get close to the line there, and look over."

"Shall we?"

"Yes; why not? I don't feel half so frightened now I've got over that fall."

"I never felt frightened at all," said Fred.

"Oh?"

"Well, not much. Come along."

They approached cautiously, finding that the shelf grew narrower, and evidently ended in a point.

"Mind!"

"Mind what?"

"I've got to the end of the rope."

"Well, let's leave go, and creep to the edge without it."

"No," said Fred, who felt that the rope was like a hand connecting them with the upper surface. "Perhaps it has caught somewhere, and we haven't got it all loose. Wait till I give it a jerk. Here, leave go for a moment."

Scarlett loosened his hold, and Fred stepped back a foot or two before sending a wave along the cord, which was followed by a rattling noise, as if a quantity of the shale and earth had been set at liberty, and was falling in a shower upon the rocky floor.

"There, I told you so," cried Fred. "I can draw yards and yards in, and yards and—"

He was suiting the action to the word, hauling more and more of the rope towards him, when there was an end to the rattling sound, and one dull flap.

"What is it, Fred?"

"I—I'm not sure."

"I am," cried Scarlett, in agony. "Why, you've dragged at the rope till it has come untied."

"I'm afraid so," faltered Fred, in a husky voice.

"And nobody saw us come here," cried Scarlett. "Oh, Fred, Fred, we shall be buried alive!"

Chapter Six
Unexpected Aid

For a few minutes the two lads were so overcome by the horror of their position that they stood there in silence, afraid to move. Then Scarlett recovered himself a little, and said huskily—

"Pull the rope again, and make sure."

"I'm sure enough," said Fred, sulkily. "It's all down here. How could you have tied it so badly?"

"I don't know. I thought it was tight. Ah! there it is again."

There was a whizzing, whirring sound heard above the plash and whisper of the water down below, and for a few moments the boys remained perfectly still.

"Why, I know what that is," cried Fred. "Pigeons. I've often seen them fly into the holes of the rocks. They build in these places, and roost here of a night."

"Wish I was a pigeon," said Scarlett, sadly. "We shall never be able to climb up that hole."

"We shall have to try," said Fred, "unless we can find a way down. Here, let's creep to the edge and look."

Scarlett hesitated for the moment, but it was a work, of stern necessity; and together, using the greatest caution the while, they crept on hands and knees to the edge of the great shelf, and looked over to see that the light came in from some opening away to the right, to be reflected from the wall of rock opposite, and shed sufficiently strong a dawn to let them see fifty feet below them the creamy foaming water which flowed in and then ran back.

"Don't see any way down," said Fred, rather despondently. "This place sticks right out over everything."

"But we can get down by fixing the rope up here, and sliding down."

"I'd forgotten the rope," said Fred, with a deep sigh. "But suppose we do get down. What then?"

"Why, we can find our way to the mouth of the cave, and look out and shout at the first boat that comes by."

Fred brightened up.

"I say, Scar," he said cheerfully, "what a clever fellow you are! Let's try at once."

"Hadn't we better try first whether we can climb up the hole?"

The suggestion was so good that it was at once tried, but without effect; for a very few minutes' search proved that there was a perpendicular face of rock to scale, and, unless they cut steps with their knives, ascent in that way was impossible.

"It's of no use, Scar," said Fred, "unless we can get away by the mouth. I say, is it as dark as it was when we first came down?"

"Our eyes are getting used to it," said Scarlett, as they both stood gazing across the opening at the black-looking rock-face before them, and, gaining courage from familiarity, they once more approached the edge of the shelf, and felt their way about, seeking vainly for the means of descent.

"I'm afraid it's of no use, Fred. The only way is for one of us to let the other down with the rope, and the one who goes down to call for help."

"But why not both go down?"

"Because there is nowhere to fasten the rope; and, after it slipped as it did just now, I should not like to venture."

"That was with your tying. You wait till I've found a place."

There did not seem much risk of a fall after Fred's securing of the rope, for the simple reason that he was not likely to tie it. Everywhere, as they searched, they found smooth rock without a projection, or shivering shaley slate, which crumbled down at a touch, and, at last, Fred gave up with a sigh of despair.

"It's of no use," he said. "One of us must go down and try the mouth of the cave. I don't want to, but I will go if you'll hold the rope."

"I feel so much afraid of not being strong enough, that I ought to go, and let you."

"Let's have a look, and see if we can make out what it's like first," said Fred; and, creeping cautiously to the edge, he lay down, and peered over, Scarlett following his example, and looking into the gloom beneath from close by his side.

"Looks very horrible," said Fred; "but I suppose it's because it's so dark. I don't believe it would be anything to mind, if it was so light we could see clearly."

"Perhaps not," replied Scarlett, gloomily; "but then, it is dark; and how dreadful the water sounds as it rushes into the mouth of the cave!"

"Oh, it always does; but there's nothing to mind."

"But suppose one of us did get down and found the mouth?"

"Well, we must find the mouth, because that's where the light and water come in."

"But if we did, the water's deep outside, and we should have to swim round to somewhere and land."

"Seems to me very stupid that we know so little about the shore under the rocks," said Fred, as he tried to pierce the pale grey light below. "Seems a stupid sort of shore, all steep cliff, and nowhere hardly to get down. Well, what shall we do? Will you go down, or shall I?"

"I'd rather trust to your holding the rope than mine."

"That's just how I feel," cried Fred. "But you went down first, and now it's my turn, so here goes. Now then, let's gather the rope into a coil, and throw one end down. Then you sit flat here on the ledge, with your legs stretched out, hold tight by the rope with both hands, and then let it hang between your legs and over the edge. It won't be hard to hold."

"I'll try," said Scarlett, nervously; "but I hardly like doing it."

"And I don't like going down, but it has got to be done, and the more fuss we make over it, the worse it will be. When you've got to take physic, down with it at once."

"Yes," said Scarlett, drily, "that's the best way, but the best way is often the hardest."

Fred had gathered the rope into rings, and was taking a final glance down at what seemed to be an uglier descent the more it was inspected, and but for very shame he would have given up. He set his teeth, though, and handed one end of the rope to his companion.

"Catch hold—tight," he said in a low voice. "If you let that go we're done. Now then—one, two—"

He did not say three, for at that moment a gruff, husky voice came rumbling and echoing down toward them with the cheery hail of—

"Anybody at home?"

"Now, I wonder what them boys are going to do," said Samson, over and over again, and each time that he said so he sighed and rubbed his back, and ended by resting upon the handle of his spade.

"No good, I'm sure," he muttered. "Yes," he added, after a thoughtful pause, "that's it—going to let one another down over the cliffs so as to break their necks; and if they do, a nice mess I shall be in, for the colonel 'll say it was all my fault for letting them have the rope."

Samson turned over a couple of spadefuls of earth, and then drove the tool in with a fierce stab, leaving it sticking up in the ground.

"Here, I can't go on digging and knowing all the time as them lads is breaking their necks over the cliff side. Never was in such a muddle as this before. Why didn't they say what they were going to do?"

"Here, this must be stopped—this must be stopped!" he cried, with a display of energy such as he had not before shown that day; and, snatching up his jacket, he started off in the direction taken by the lads, he having had no difficulty in seeing that their aim was the mass of slaty rock, rounded and covered with short green turf, known as the Rill Head, up which he climbed just in time to shout down the grassy crevice the words which sent joy into the boys' hearts.

"Hurrah! There's help!" cried Scarlett, starting up.

"Mind! you nearly knocked me over."

"I could not help it, Fred. Here, hi!"

"Anybody at home? Where are you?"

"Why, it's old Samson," cried Fred, groping his way to where he believed the bottom of the crack by which they had descended to be. "Hi! Samson!"

"Hullo!" came back. "Where are you? What are you doing?"

Fred hastily explained their plight.

"Serve you both right," cried Samson; and his voice, as it rumbled down the hole into the cavern, sounded, as Scarlett thought, like the voice of a giant. "Well, what are you going to do? Live there?"

"No; you must help us out."

"Help you out?"

"Yes. How did you know we were here?"

"How did I know you were there, indeed!" growled Samson, with aggravating repetition of the other's words. "Why, I knowed you'd be in some mischief as soon as I saw you both go by with that rope."

"But you didn't see us come down here."

"No; but I see your clothes lying aside the hole. What did you want here? Somebody's sheep tumbled down again?"

"Hear that?" whispered Fred. "No, Samson; but don't stand there talking. Did you bring a rope?"

"How could I bring the rope, when you'd got it?"

"Go and fetch another."

"There isn't one that'll bear you. Can't you throw up the end of that one?"

"Impossible! You must fetch another."

"And who's to do my gardening while I'm hunting all over Coombeland for ropes as nobody won't lend?"

"Look here, Samson," cried Scarlett. "Go up to the Hall, and ask Nat to lend you one of ours."

"Go up and ask my brother Nat to lend me a rope?"

"Yes."

"I'd sooner go and jump off the cliff. There!"

"Well, you must do something, and pray make haste."

"What am I to do?"

"I know," cried Fred. "Go and get your garden line."

"Why, that wouldn't bear a cat, let alone a boy like you."

"You do as I tell you, and bring a big round stone, too, one that you can tie to one end of the line. Be quick."

"Oh, I'll go," said Samson; "but mind you, I warn you it won't bear."

"You do as I tell you," cried Fred, again; "and don't tell my mother where we are."

"I may tell the colonel, I suppose?" said Samson, with a laugh to himself.

"No, no, no!" cried Fred; but the words were not heard, for Samson had set off down the hill at a trot.

"I say, what a pair of stupids we are," said Fred, after trying two or three times over to find out whether Samson was still there.

"Don't talk," replied Scarlett. "Let's listen for his coming back."

"But he must be half an hour, at least; and we know we are all right now. I say, Scar, I've a good mind to go down lower, and see if there's a way to the sea."

"No, you will not," said Scarlett, rather gruffly. "Let's sit down and think."

"It's too dark to think," cried Fred, petulantly. "I wonder how this place came. Think it was made by the hill cracking, or by the sea washing it out?"

"I don't know. But shall we come again, and bring a lanthorn?"

"Yes, and regularly examine the place. We will some day. I wonder whether we're the first people who ever came down into it? I mean," said Fred, "the first people who were not sheep. Here, hi! Scar! what are you thinking about?"

"I was thinking what a hiding-place it would make for anybody who did not want to be found."

"Do for smugglers. Wonder whether any smugglers ever knew of it?"

"No; if they had there would have been some way down to the mouth."

"And perhaps there is, only it's too dark for us to see where it is."

Then the conversation languished, and they sat on the rough shaley earth, trying to pierce the gloom, and listening with quite a start from time to time to the sharp whirr of the pigeons' wings as they darted in and out.

At last, just when they were beginning to think it a terribly long time, Samson's voice was heard.

"Here you are! I've brought my line."

"And a big stone?"

"Yes, Master Fred; eight or nine pounder. But I warn you once more that line won't bear you boys."

"You do as I tell you. Now tie the stone to the line."

There was a few moments' pause, during which they seemed to see the red-faced gardener as he busied himself over his task, and then down came the words—

"All right."

"Lower it down."

"What?—the stone?"

"Yes. Quick."

Directly after, there was a rattling and falling of tiny bits of shale, which went on as Samson shouted —

"She won't come no farther."

"Draw the line and start it again."

Samson started the stone after hauling it up a bit, and this time it glided out of the angle in which it had rested, increased its speed, bringing down quite a shower of shale, and then there was a dull thud.

"That's it, Samson. I've got it."

"Good job, for there ain't much more."

"There's quite enough," cried Fred, as he rapidly set the stone loose, and tied the line to the rope's end. "Now, then, haul away."

"No, no, my lad; I tell you it won't bear you. You'd only have a nasty tumble."

"Haul!"

"And I shall be blamed."

"Will you haul? Oh, only wait till I come up!"

Samson gave quite a snatch at the line, and drew it up rapidly, while the boys waited to hear what he would say when he found their meaning.

"Why couldn't you have said as you meanted that!" he grumbled. "I see now. Want me to make this here fast to the pole."

"Yes, of course; then we can climb up."

"To be sure you can. I see now."

"Make it quite fast, Samson."

"I will, sir. And try it, too," he added under his breath, as he knotted the rope fast, seized and drew it tight, and then lowering himself into the crevice, he began to glide down rapidly, sending a tremendous shower of shale on to Fred's head, and making him start away just as he had drawn the rope tight ready to ascend.

"Why, what are you doing?" he shouted.

"Coming down, sir," panted Samson; and the next minute he was on the broad shelf in company with nearly enough disintegrated rock to bury the skeleton of the sheep.

"Well, 'pon my word, young gentlemen," cried the gardener, "you've got rum sort of ideas. Wouldn't no other place please you for a game but this?"

"We wanted to explore it," exclaimed Fred; "to see if there's a way down to the shore."

"Well, you can hear there is, lads. But why didn't you bring a lanthorn?"

"I wish we had."

"Wish again," said Samson, with a chuckle.

"What for?"

"Because then you'll get one," said the gardener, laughing.

"Why, Samson, what do you mean?" cried Scarlett.

"This here!"

There was a rattling sound, a clicking noise of flint upon steel, and soon after a glowing spark appeared, then a blue flame, a splint burst into a blaze, and directly after Samson's red and shining features could be seen by the light of the candle he had lit inside a lanthorn.

"There, lads," he said, closing the door with a snap; "you didn't think to tell me to bring that, but I thought of it, and there we are. Now we can see what we're about," he continued, as he swung the lanthorn above his head; "and not much to see nayther. Only an 'ole. Yes, of course. There you are. Sheep's bones. Dessay many a one's tumbled down here. Hole don't go up very high," he added, once more raising the lanthorn above his head; "but it goes down to the sea for sartain."

"Oh, Samson, and you've left the line up above. If we had it here, we might have swung the lanthorn down and seen how deep it was."

"That's just like you, Master Fred," said Samson. "You always think other folk will do what you'd do. You'd ha' left the line up at the top, same as you did your clothes, but being only a gardener, and a very bad one, as my brother Nat says, I put that there line in my pocket, and here it is."

Fred's answer was a slap on Samson's hard broad back, as he tied one end of the line to the lanthorn-ring, swung it over the edge of the shelf, and they watched it go down sixty or seventy feet, feebly illumining the sides of the cave, and as it grew lower an additional radiance was displayed by the light striking on the bottom, which proved to be full of water kept slightly in motion by the influx of the waves outside.

"Not much to see, my lads," said Samson. "No gold, nor silver, nor nothing. Shouldn't wonder if there's pigeons' nesties, though, only you couldn't get at 'em without a ladder. There! seen enough?"

"No; I want to see whether there is any way down," said Fred.

"Any way down?" said Samson, swinging the lanthorn to and fro. "No, my lad—yes, there is. Easily get down at that corner. Slide down or slip down. See!"

"Yes," said the lads in a breath; and long afterwards they recalled their eagerness to know about a means of descent from that shelf.

"Yes," said Samson; "you might make a short cut down to the sea this way if you wanted to. But you don't want to, and it wouldn't be any good if you did, because you'd be obliged to have a boat outside; and if the boat wasn't well-minded, it would soon be banged to matchwood among the rocks. There, my bit o' ground's waiting to be dug, and I've got you two out of your hobble, so here goes back."

As he spoke, he rapidly hauled up the lanthorn, forming the line into rings, untying the end from the ring, and, after giving it a twist, thrusting it back into his pocket, while he undid the strap he wore about his waist, thrust an end through the lanthorn-ring, and buckled it on once more.

"Will you go first, Samson?" said Fred.

"No; I mean to go last. I don't leave here till I see you both safe. What should I have said to your mothers if you'd been lost and not found for a hundred years? Nice state of affairs that would ha' been."

"Go on first, Scar," said Fred; "we'll hold the rope tight, so that it will be easy."

Scarlett reached up, seized the rope, and began to climb, getting the thick cord well round his legs, as he struggled up for nearly twenty feet, and then he slipped down again.

"Can't we go down the other way, and climb the cliff?"

"No, you can't," said Samson, gruffly. "You've got to go up as you come down. Here, Master Fred, show him the way."

Fred seized the rope, and began to climb, but with no better success; and he, too, glided down again after a severe struggle.

"The rope's so slippery," he said angrily.

"And you call yourselves young gentlemen!" grunted Samson. "Why, you'd ha' been just as badly off if your rope hadn't slipped. Here, give us hold."

Samson seized the rope, and they heard him grunt and pant and cease his struggle, and then begin to grunt and pant again for quite ten minutes, when, just as they rather maliciously hoped that he would prove as awkward as themselves, they heard the lanthorn bang against the rock, a shower of shale fell as it was kicked off, and Samson's voice came down—

"Line is a bit slithery," he said; "but I'm all right now."

They could not see, but they in imagination felt that he had reached the first slope, up which he was climbing, and then felt when he passed up the second, showers of shale and earth following every moment, till, all at once, there was a cessation of noise, and of the shower, and Samson's bluff voice exclaimed—

"Up a top! Now, then, lay hold, and I'll have you up to where you can climb."

"Go on, Scar."

"Go on, Fred."

The boys spoke together, and, after a little argument, Scarlett seized the rope, felt himself hoisted up, and, once up at the slope, he soon reached daylight, Fred following in the same way, to stand in the sunshine, gazing at his companions, who, like himself, were covered with perspiration and dust.

"You look nice ones, you do," said Samson, grinning; "and all that there trouble for nothing."

But Samson was a very ignorant man, who knew a great deal about gardening, but knew nothing whatever about the future, though in that instance his want of knowledge was shared by Fred and Scarlett, who, after resuming their jerkins, took, one the pole, the other the coil of neatly ringed rope, and trudged back to the Manor with Samson, who delivered quite a discourse upon waste of time; but he did not return to his digging, contenting himself with extracting his spade from the ground, wiping it carefully, and hanging it up in his tool-house, close to the lanthorn.

"Going home, Master Scarlett?" said Samson.

"Yes, directly."

"Won't have a mug o' cider, I suppose?"

"No, thank ye, Samson."

"Because I thought Master Fred was going to fetch some out, and you could have a drop too."

"Hark at him, Scar! There never was such a fellow for cider."

"Oh yes, there was; but I've yearned it anyhow to-day."

"So you have, and I'll fetch you a mug," said Fred, darting off.

"Ah, that's better," grunted Samson. "Never such a fellow for cider! Why, my brother's a deal worse than I am, and you wouldn't ketch him leaving his work to take all the trouble I did to-day, Master Scarlett. Hah! here he comes back. Thank ye, Master Fred, lad. Hah! what good cider. Puzzle your Nat to make such stuff as that."

"He says ours is better," said Scarlett.

"Let him, sir; but that don't make it better."

"Bother the old cider! Who cares?" cried Fred. "Look here, Samson, don't say a word to anybody about our having found that hole."

"No, sir; not I."

"Why did you tell him that!" said Scarlett, as they walked away.

"I don't know," said Fred, starting.

"Perhaps I thought we ought not to tell, in case we wanted to hide some day."

"Hide! What from whom from!"

"I don't know," said Fred again, as he looked in a puzzled way at his companion; and then they parted. Fred felt that he should have liked to have told his friend why he wished the discovery to be kept a secret, but the puzzled feeling grew more intense, and when at last he dismissed it, he was obliged to own that he did not know himself any more than when he spoke.

Chapter Seven
Fred Takes a Jump

The adventure in the Rill cave was talked about for a few days, and several plans were made for its further exploration; but, in spite of the talking, no further visit was made in that direction.

"You see, we ought to get a boat," Fred said, "and row right to the mouth, and go in that way next time, and we haven't got a boat."

"And no likelihood of getting one," said Scarlett, thoughtfully. "Shall we go down again, and take your Samson with us this time?"

"I don't see that there's any good in it; and see what a mess we should be in again. I was full of little tiny bits of slate all in my hair, and down my back, and, after all, it wasn't worth the trouble."

"Made me feel a bit queer. I say, Scar, only fancy being shut up there, and starving to death."

Scarlett gave an involuntary shiver.

"Don't talk about it."

"I say, starving to death makes you think about eating. When are your people coming over again to supper?"

"I don't know," said Scarlett, with an uneasy sensation.

"What's the matter, Scar?"

"I don't know. I'm not sure. I think your father and mine have fallen out again."

"What makes you think that?"

"Something I heard my mother saying to him."

"Well, they'll soon be friends again, I dare say."

"I hope so. But, Fred, how everybody seems to be talking now about the troubles in the east."

"Well, let them," laughed Fred. "We don't want any of their troubles in the west. What do you say to an afternoon's nutting?"

"The nuts are not half ripe."

"Well, let's get your Nat's ferret, and try for a rabbit."

"He would not lend it to us."

"Let's go down on the shore, and collect shells for your Lil."

"She has more than she wants now."

"Well, let's do something. I vote we go down and hunt out the way into that passage. We can do that without getting our heads full of slate."

Scarlett acceded readily, the more so that ever since their adventure in the passage, the place had had a peculiar fascination for both lads. They often stopped in the middle of some pursuit to talk about the curious idea of making a door to be entered by lying down, and contriving it out of a stair. Then there were the ingenious peculiarities of the old passage, and the strange gloom of the oak chamber, and the dark vault, with its heap of old arms, which they regretted not to have brought out to try and restore to something like their former condition.

For, in spite of previous failure, the idea of discovering the second entrance to that passage was often suggesting itself to the lads; and, in consequence, they began to haunt the edge of the lake, feeling sure that some day or another accident would direct them to the very spot they had searched for so long.

Scarlett insisted that they would find the opening right down in the water, while, on the other hand, Fred maintained the opposite.

"Nobody would be such a noodle as to build his back-door right down in the water," he said, "unless he meant the place for a bath. No; we shall find that doorway out in the wood somewhere, you mark my words, Scar. I dare say, if we were to take billhooks and cut and hack away the branches, we should find it soon enough."

Scarlett shook his head, but joined in the search, one which, in spite of their peering about, proved to be in vain, and, after being well scratched by brambles and briars, Scarlett had his own way again, and they began to hunt the shore.

The broad sheet of water ran up in quite a bay toward the fine old English mansion, and round this bay were dense clumps of hazels, patches of alder, and old oak-trees grew right on the edge of the perpendicular bank, their roots deep down beneath the black leaf-mould, which here formed the bottom of the clear water.

"It must be here somewhere," said Scarlett, one sunny afternoon, as they sat on the mossy roots of one of the great oaks, and idly picked off sheets of delicate green vegetable velvet and flakes of creamy and grey lichen to throw into the water.

"Yes, it must be here somewhere, of course; but I don't see any use in getting scratched by briars for nothing. We never seem to get any nearer to it. Perhaps we were wrong, and it's only a kind of well, after all."

"No," said Scarlett; "they would not make a well there."

"Then we got muddled over the way we went, and, perhaps, while we are looking for the entrance this side, it's over the other."

"No," said Scarlett again, "I don't think that."

"But if there had been a way in here from the lake, some one must have seen it before now. We should have noticed it when we were fishing or nesting. Or, if we had not seen it, your Nat or one of the other gardeners must have found it."

"No, they must not. I don't see any must about it. Perhaps it's too cleverly hidden away, or I shouldn't wonder if, since it was made, a tree had grown all over the entrance, and shut it right up."

"And we shall never find it."

"Not unless we cut the tree down."

"And, of course, we don't know which tree to cut."

"And if we did, my father would not have a tree touched on any account. Remember how angry he was with the wind?"

"What, when it blew down the big elm?"

"Yes."

There was a pause.

"I say," said Fred, yawning, "let's give it up. What do we care about where the passage comes out! We know where it goes in."

"Foxes always have two holes," said Scarlett, dreamily.

"So do rabbits. Lots of holes sometimes. But we're not foxes, and we're not rabbits."

"No; but you'll be like a water-rat directly, if you sit on that moss. It's as slippery as can be close to the edge. Come and get some nuts."

"Not ripe enough," said Fred, idly.

"Never mind; let's get some, whether or no."

"Where shall we go? We've got all there are about the edge of the lake."

"Let's go down there by the big oaks. There's a great clump of nuts just beyond, where we have not been yet."

"Oh yes, we have," said Fred, laughing; "leastwise, I have—one day when I came over and you weren't at home."

"That's always your way, Fred. I never come over to your place and take your things."

"Halloa!" laughed Fred, rising slowly from where he had lounged upon the mossy, buttress-like roots. "Who came and helped himself to my gilliflower apples?"

Scarlett laughed. "Well, they looked so tempting, and we were to have picked them that day. Come along."

They went crushing and rustling through the woody wilderness for about a hundred yards from the side of the lake. It was a part sacred to the birds and rabbits, a dense dark thicket where oaks and beeches shut out the light of day, and for generations past the woodman's axe had never struck a blow. Here and there the forest monarchs had fallen from old age, and where they had left a vacancy hazel stubs flourished, springing up gaily, and revelling on the rotten wood and dead leaves which covered the ground, and among which grew patches of nuts and briar, with the dark dewberry and swarthy dwale.

Here, as they walked, the lads' feet crushed in the moss-covered, rotten wood, and at every step a faint damp odour of mould, mingled with the strong scent of crushed ferns and fungi, rose to their nostrils.

"Never mind the nuts," said Fred; "let's get out in the sunshine again. Pst! there he goes."

He stopped short as he spoke, watching the scuttling away of a rabbit, whose white cottony tail was seen for a moment before it disappeared in a tunnel beneath a hazel clump.

"No; we'll have a few while we are here," said Scarlett, making a bound on to the trunk of a huge oak which had been blown down and lay horizontally; but while one portion of its roots stood up shaggy and weird-looking, the rest remained in the ground, and supported the life of the old tree, which along its mighty bole was covered with sturdy young shoots for about thirty feet from the roots. There it forked into two branches, each of which was far bigger than the trunk of an ordinary tree; but while one was fairly green, the other was perfectly dead, and such verdure as it displayed was that of moss and abundant patches of polypody, which flourished upon the decaying wood.

Opposite the spot where Scarlett leaped upon the tree-trunk — that is to say, on the other side — the thicket was too dense to invite descent, and the lad began to walk along toward the fork, pressing the young branches aside as he went, followed by Fred, who had leapt up and joined him.

"Here, I'm getting so hot," cried the latter. "What's the good of slaving along here! Let's go back."

"I don't like going back in anything," replied Scarlett, as he walked on till he reached the fork, and continued his way along the living branch of the old tree, with Fred still following, till they stood in the midst of a maze of jagged and gnarled branches rising high above their heads, and shutting them in.

These dead boughs were from the fellow limb to that on which they stood, the two huge trunks being about six feet apart.

"There, now we must go back," said Fred.

"No. It looks more open there," cried Scarlett. "If we could jump on to the other trunk, we could go on beyond."

"Well, anybody could jump that," said Fred.

"Except Fred Forrester," replied Scarlett, mockingly.

"What! not jump that? I'll soon show you."

"No, no; you can't do it, Fred, and you may hurt yourself."

"Well, that will not hurt you. Here goes."

"Mind that branch there."

"Oh yes, I'll mind the branches; and you have to do it when I've done. Way he!"

Fred stooped down, with his feet close together and his arms pressed to his sides, bent forward and jumped cleverly quite over the intervening space, and came down upon the great dead moss-covered trunk.

There was a crash, and it seemed to Scarlett for the moment that his companion's heels had slipped, and that he had gone down on the other side among the bushy growth that sprung up; but a second glance showed him that the apparently solid trunk was merely a shell, through which Fred had passed completely out of sight.

"Hoi! Fred! Hurt yourself!" cried Scarlett, laughing heartily.

There was no reply.

"Fred! Hoi! Where are you?"

Still no reply. And now, beginning to feel alarmed, Scarlett lowered himself down, and forced his way through the tangle of little shrubby boughs growing round him, to the dead trunk, and found himself within a breastwork of rotten bark as high as he could reach, and which crumbled away as he tried to get up, one great green mossy patch breaking down and covering him with damp, fungus-smelling touchwood.

"Fred! Where are you? Don't be stupid, and play with a fellow. Do you hear?"

Still there was no reply, and Scarlett gave an angry stamp on the soft ground.

"He's hiding away. I won't trouble about him," muttered the boy. Then aloud—"Very well, lad. I shan't come after you. I'm going back to the lake side."

Scarlett began to struggle back, making a great deal of rustling and crackling of dead wood; but he had not the slightest intention of leaving his companion behind, in case anything might have happened to him. So he clambered back through the brush of oak shoots on to the sound limb, and walked slowly back to the folk to try and walk along the dead portion of the tree; but before he had progressed six feet, he began to find that it was giving way, so he descended, and then slowly creeping in and out among the dead branches, sometimes crawling under and sometimes over, he began to make his way to the spot where Fred had disappeared.

It proved, however, a far more difficult task than he had imagined, for pieces of the jagged oak boughs caught in his jerkin; then he found that in stretching over one leg he had stepped into a perfect tangle of bramble, whose hooked thorns laid tight hold of his breeches, and scratched him outrageously as he tried to draw his limb back. Finding that to go forward was the easier, he pushed on, and took three more steps, vowing vengeance against his companion the while.

"It's horribly stupid of me," he muttered. "I don't see why I should take all this trouble to help a fellow who is only playing tricks, and will laugh when I find him. Oh, how sharp!"

Still there was the latent thought that Fred might have hurt himself, and Scarlett pressed on; but, all the same, seeing in imagination Fred's laughing face and mocking eyes. In fact, so sure, after all, did he feel that his companion was watching him from somewhere close by, that he kept thrusting the rough growth aside, and looking in all directions.

"I'll give him such a topper for this," he muttered; and then as he struggled on another foot, he suddenly stopped short, looked straight ahead, and exclaimed loudly, "There, I can see you. Don't be stupid, you old ostrich, hiding there. Now then, come out."

Scarlett's ruse was a failure. "He knows it isn't true," muttered the lad. "Serve me right for telling lies. It was only my fun, Fred," he cried hastily, to make honest confession of his fib. "But don't go on like that. Come out now, and let's get back. It makes me so hot."

He listened, and in the stillness of the wilderness he could have heard any one breathing, if he had been close at hand; but all was perfectly still, until, high up in a neighbouring tree, a greenfinch uttered its mournful little harsh note, which sounded like the utterance of the word *wheeze*.

"Surely he hasn't hurt himself," muttered Scarlett; and then aloud, as an uncomfortable sensation came over him—"Here, Fred! Fred! lad, where are you? Why don't you speak?"

"As if I don't know where he is," muttered Scarlett again, now growing thoroughly alarmed. "He must have slipped and hurt his back.—All right; I'm coming," he cried. "With you directly, as soon as I can get through this horrible tangle.—That's better. Now then, what's the matter? Fred, where are you? I say, do call out, or something. I don't like it. Fred, lad, are you hurt?"

And all this time he was forcing his way onward, the brambles tearing and the old oak wood crackling. The greenfinch uttered its mournful *wheeze* once more, and fled in alarm as Scarlett broke down a good-sized branch which barred his way, the rotten dry wood snapping with a sharp report; and then, panting and hot after his heavy labour to get through so short a space, he forced himself to the place where Fred had landed, and, to his utter astonishment, found that on his side the whole of the trunk was gone, merely leaving the shell-like portion which had impeded him before, while below the crumbled tree-trunk was a great gap.

For a few moments he stood there aghast. Then, recovering his presence of mind, he pushed aside more of the growth which impeded him, and looked down into a narrow pit which was choked with broken wood and ferns.

"Fred!" he shouted; but there was no reply. There, however, beneath him, he could see his companion's head and shoulders, with eyes closed, or seeming to be in the dim light, and only about five feet below where he stood.

Without a moment's hesitation, but trembling the while for fear that this might be some terribly deep pit into which his companion might fall if once the broken boughs which supported him gave way, Scarlett tried bough after bough of the old oak to find one upon which he could depend; but they all crackled in a way that threatened snapping if he trusted one; so, reaching back, he got hold of a stout hazel which seemed to be a dozen or fourteen feet high, dragged it down, and holding it by twisting his hand among the twigs at the top, he began to descend.

At every movement the earth crumbled, and the bed of rotten wood supporting Fred, as he lay back with his face to the light, shook so that at any moment Scarlett expected to see it descend into the profound abyss below. But in spite of this, as he climbed down the short distance, he realised the state of affairs—that in its fall the oak had crushed in the masonry arch over some old well-like place, leaving this terrible hole securely covered till the wood had rotted away; and that now it had been Fred's misfortune to leap upon the spot, go through, and be held up by the broken wood, which formed a kind of rough scaffold a short distance below.

Should he run back for help?

No; he could not leave Fred like that. And yet when he reached him he was afraid that the slightest touch would send him down; and now he realised how fortunate it was that Fred had been hurt, and had remained insensible, for if he had struggled, the possibility was that he must have gone through at once.

Short as the distance was, Scarlett had to take the greatest precautions, for, as he tried to get foothold, something gave way beneath him, and he hung by the hazel, feeling as if all the blood in his body had rushed to his heart, for there was a loud hollow splash, which went echoing horribly away, and he found himself with his eyes on a level with the old crumbling masonry forming an arch.

He recovered himself though directly, for he could stretch out a hand and touch Fred.

The touch had instant effect, for the lad opened his eyes, stared at him wildly, and then said quickly—

"What's the matter?"

"Nothing much, if you are careful. You have fallen, and are hanging here. Now—"

"Fallen? Oh yes, I remember; the tree," cried Fred. "Oh, my head, my head!"

"Never mind your head," whispered Scarlett. "Now listen."

"I say, what hole's this? Is it a well?" said Fred, eagerly.

"Don't, pray don't talk. Now, can you reach up and get hold of the hazel above my hands?"

"Dare say I can," said Fred, coolly. "Yes. There!"

"Then be careful. You are held up by that broken wood. Now try and draw yourself out."

"Can't," said Fred, after one effort. "I'm held tight; wedged in by this wood."

"Try again; but be careful, whatever you do."

"Wait a moment. Oh, my head, my head! I hit the back of it on something."

"Ah, mind!" cried Scarlett, in agony. "Don't think about what is beneath you, but try to climb up."

"Of course: only my head hurts so. I gave it such a knock."

"Yes, yes," cried Scarlett, impatiently; "but do mind."

"Well, I am minding; only don't be in such a fuss. I must get this piece of broken bough away."

"No," cried Scarlett, in agony; "don't leave go your hold."

"But can't you see," cried Fred, impatiently, "that this is just like a wire trap? I've gone through it, and the points are all round me, holding me from coming back."

"Yes, I see something of the sort; but if you leave go, you may fall."

"How?"

"By passing through. Now, I'll pull you if I can. Make a struggle at once before you grow weaker."

"Wait a bit. I'm not going to grow weaker. I mean to get stronger. Don't you fidget. I'll be up there in no time."

Scarlett groaned in his nervous agony, and the great drops stood upon his brow. He had found hold for one foot by thrusting it in above a snake-like root which formed quite a loop in the broken-away soil, and now, reaching down, he thrust his hand within the collar of Fred's jerkin, and held with all his force.

In those moments of excitement, he could not help thinking how often it was that the looker-on suffered far more than the one in peril, and he found himself marvelling at his companion's coolness, suspended there as he was with the dreadful echoing abyss below him, that which had given forth so terrible a splash when the stones of the old arch gave way.

"Now then," cried Fred, as he gazed in his companion's ghastly face, "when I say 'Now,' you give a good tug, and I'll shake myself clear in no time."

"No, no; I dare not," faltered Scarlett.

"What a coward! Well, then, let go, and let me do it myself."

"No, no, Fred; pray take my advice. Don't attempt to stir like that. Only try making one steady draw upward. As soon as you get free of those broken branches, which hold you so tightly, they'll all fall with a splash below."

"Of course they will," said Fred, coolly.

"I don't seem to be able to make you understand your danger."

"Isn't any," said Fred.

"No danger?"

"No; and, look here, it's getting precious cold to my legs, so here goes."

"Fred, listen! If you shake and move those branches which hold you down, you will go to the bottom."

"Can't," cried Fred.

"How can you be so foolish, when I am advising you for your good?"

"I'm not foolish. I want to get out, and you want me to stay."

"But you'll fall to the bottom of this horrible hole."

"Can't," cried Fred.

"Can't?"

"No; I'm standing on the bottom now."

"Fred!"

"Well, so I am, with the water just over my knees."

"Oh!"

"Well, if you don't believe it, come down here and try."

Chapter Eight
The Subterranean Way

Scarlett hung there from the hazel bough staring, and for a few moments utterly unable to realise that which his companion had said, till Fred gave himself a shake, like a great dog coming out of the water, and by degrees got one leg free, then the other, trampling down the broken wood, and standing at last on a level with his companion.

"Did you think it was deep?" said the lad.

"Deep? Yes; I did not know how deep. Then it is not a well?"

"Why, of course not. Don't you see it's the passage we were looking for, and it does go down to the lake."

"The passage?"

"Of course. Look, you can see a little both ways. Of course the top's broken in here. Isn't it droll that we should find it like this. But oh! my head. I gave it such a crack when I fell. It served me just as if I was a rabbit. I don't know how long I've been like that."

Scarlett could not answer him, so excited had he become at the strange turn things had taken.

"There, my head's better now," said Fred, as he sat at the edge of the hole after climbing lightly out: and as he spoke he amused himself by kicking down fragments of the side to listen to the echoing splash. "What do you say to going up to the house for a light? No; let's get Nat's stable lanthorn, and then go down here and see where the way out goes."

"I know," cried Scarlett, eagerly.

"Where?"

"Why, down there, right away by the old tree clump—right out yonder."

"There can't be a way out there, because we should have seen it."

"Perhaps it's covered up so as to keep it hidden till it was wanted."

"Let's go and see. But, stop a moment. We don't want another way in, now we've got this."

"No," said Scarlett. "I don't know, though. Let's go and see."

"All right; it will dry my legs," replied Fred. And, getting up, the two lads made their way down to the head of the little bay nearest to the house, and then worked along among the alders which hung over the lake till they ca.ne to the part of the old forest Scarlett had named—an evergreen patch of about an acre, on which stood a dozen or two of the finest trees in the park.

"Why," cried Scarlett, "I remember old Dee—"

"Nat's father?"

"Yes—saying that there once used to be a boathouse down here."

"Then, why didn't we look there first?"

"Because it was not a likely place, all that distance away."

Neither did it seem a likely place now, as they climbed over a rough, moss grown fence, and entered the unfrequented spot, to find old masses of rock peering out of the soil, ancient trees coated with ivy, and an abundance of thick undergrowth such as they had been fighting with a short time before.

The task was less difficult, and they spent the next half-hour hunting along the edge of the lake, whose shore here was for the most part high and rocky, but broken here and there by shrubby patches of gorse and heather, in company with fine old birches, whose silvery trunks were reflected in the lake.

"I knew you were wrong," said Fred at last, as he sat down in a sunny spot to let his legs dry, "it couldn't be here."

"Why not?"

"Because, if it were here, we should have found it."

Scarlett said nothing, but stood at the edge of the rocky bank, now looking down into the water, now toward the bushes which were overhanging the lake. There were plenty of rather likely places, but none quite likely enough, and reluctantly agreeing at last that he might have been mistaken, he turned slowly away from the ivy covered perpendicular bank, and sauntered slowly back with his companion in silence.

"My legs are getting drier now," said Fred, suddenly. "What do you say—shall we fetch a lanthorn, and go down into the passage?"

"I don't see what you want with dry legs, if you are going to wade," replied Scarlett, thoughtfully.

"You don't want to go."

"Yes, I do."

"You're afraid."

"Perhaps so," replied Scarlett; "but you are not, so let's go and get the lanthorn."

A quarter of an hour later, the lanthorn was secretly obtained, lighted, and a supply of pieces of candle included, and then the question arose, How were they to get it down to the little wilderness unseen?

"Somebody would be sure to come and look what we were doing."

"I know," cried Scarlett. "Let's get a big bucket, and a couple of rods, and they'll think we are going to fish."

The idea was accepted at once, and the lads marched off, rods over shoulder, and the bucket swinging between them, its light unseen in the broad sunshine. The place was soon reached, and, taught by experience, they found a better way to the prostrate oak, and after a little struggling and scratching, stood gazing down.

"Look hear, Scar," cried Fred, "if we find a better way in, we can easily cover this place over with some old branches and fern roots, because it must be a secret way, or it's of no use."

Scarlett quite agreed to this, and there they stood gazing up at the arrowy beams of sunshine which shot down through the leaves. Then they had a look down into the hole which, with its watery floor and darkness, was anything but tempting.

"Don't look very nice, Scar, does it?"

"Not at all. Shall we give it up?"

"If we do, as soon as we get home, we shall say what cowards we were."

"Yes, I shall," replied Scarlett, "but, all the same, I don't want to go down. Do you?"

"No."

"And you don't want me to go alone?"

"No, I don't think so. Here, Scar, don't let's give ourselves a chance to call ourselves cowards. I'll go, if you will."

"I don't want to go, but I will, if you will. Come along."

The hesitation was gone.

"I'll go first," said Scar, "because you have been down, but I suppose we must be careful so as not to loosen any stones."

"Very well," said Fred, rather unwillingly. "Give me the lanthorn to hold."

The light was drawn out of the bucket, and Scarlett prepared to descend; but this proved it longer task than was expected, for it was first necessary to drag out several pieces of broken branch.

This being done, Scarlett looked up at his companion, who let himself down without hesitation, and they stood together with the daylight above them, and the narrow lugged stone passage stretching away to right and left.

"Which way shall we go first?" asked Scarlett.

"This way," cried Fred, and his voice sounded so strange and hollow, that as he stood there up to his knees in water, which glimmered and shimmered on the black surface, he hesitated and wished that he had not agreed to go.

For there before them lay a narrow path of light, ending in quite a sharp point, and seeming to point to the end of their journey.

They both told themselves that they were not likely to meet anything that would do them harm, but, all the same, neither of them could help wondering whether there would be any unpleasant kind of fish in the depths as they neared the lake. That word depth, too, troubled them. It was easy enough to wade now, but suppose it should grow deeper suddenly, and they should step into some horrible hole. Suppose—

"Look here," cried Fred, suddenly, as they waded slowly on, listening to the whisper and splash of the water, "I wish you'd be quiet with your suppose this, and suppose that. You don't want to frighten me, do you?"

"Why, I never spoke," cried Scar.

"Then you must have been thinking aloud, for it seemed to me as if you were saying things on purpose to scare me."

"Well, it is enough to scare anybody, Fred; and I don't mind saying to you that I don't like it."

"But we will not go back?"

"No."

"Only you might hold the light a little higher."

Scarlett obeyed, and they cautiously went on, with the water still about the same depth, and for prospect above, before, and on either side, there was the arch of rugged stones, the dripping wall, and the gleaming water.

That was all, and after going about fifty yards, Fred exclaimed—

"I say, this can never be of any use to us. Who's going to wade through water for the sake of having a secret place?"

"Nobody," replied Scarlett; "but let's go on, as we've gone so far."

"Ugh!"

"What's the matter?" cried Scarlett, stopping short suddenly.

"I thought something laid hold of my leg. Mind!"

Scarlett nearly dropped the lanthorn. "Oh, I say, Scar, that would be too horrible. Do be careful. I don't want to be in the dark again."

"It was your fault, you pretending to be frightened."

"I didn't pretend. I was frightened. It did seem as if something touched my leg. I say, how much farther do you think it is?"

"What! to the end? I don't know. Come along."

"Well, if anyone had told me that I should do such a thing as this, I wouldn't have believed him," grumbled Fred. "How cold the water feels!"

"You wouldn't mind if it was one of the streams, and we were after trout."

"No; because it would be all light and warm there, and we could see what we were doing. Don't you think we might go back?"

"No. Let's go to the end now. I'm sure this is the way down to the lake, and we shall find the entrance. Perhaps we shall find the end blocked up, and then when we open it all the water will rush out, and we shall have a dry passage after all."

"Then you will not give it up?"

"No," said Scarlett, doggedly. "It's our place, and I want to be able to tell father all about it."

"No, no; don't do that," cried Fred, in dismay.

"I don't mean yet. I mean when we've done with it."

"I've done with it now," muttered Fred. "I don't see any fun in going sop, sop, squeeze, squatter, through all this cold, dark water. Eh! what's that—the end of it?"

"I think so," said Scarlett, holding the lanthorn up as high as he could. "Here are some steps and a door."

"Of course; then that must be the door that opens on the lake."

"No, it can't be, for the steps are dry, and—I say, Fred!"

"What is it?"

"Look here," cried Scarlett. "This is strange. Here's a chamber or cellar."

"Just like the other we found."

"Like it," cried Scarlett; "why, it is it!"

"What nonsense! That one was toward the house. This one is toward the lake."

"Nonsense or no, there's the old armour in the corner."

The two lads stood with the lanthorn held up, staring at the heap, and then at the rusty hinged door, and lastly at one another.

"Do you believe in enchantment, Fred?" said Scarlett, at last.

"No, not a bit. Enchantment, and witches, and goblins, and all those sort of things, are nothing but stuff, father says."

"But isn't it curious that we should have found ourselves here? It is the same, isn't it?"

"I think so. Yes, that's the way into the house," said Fred, staring along the dark passage. "But I don't care whether it is or whether it isn't. My legs are so wet that I mean to get out as soon as I can."

Scarlett held the lanthorn up again, and had one more good look round. Then, without a word, he turned, descended the steps into the water, and began to wade back.

"Oh, I say, it is wet!" grumbled Fred, as he followed the lanthorn, watching their grotesque shadows on the wall, the flashing of the light on the water, and the glimmering on the damp walls.

Neither of the lads spoke now as they waded on, for each was trying to puzzle out the problem of how it was that they should have journeyed backward; but no light came.

"I shall make it out," said Fred, "as soon as we get in the sunshine again. Go on a bit faster, Scar."

But there was no temptation to go faster, and the slow wading was continued, till a glimmering of light cheered them; and then quicker progress was made, for the opening seemed to send down more and more light as they approached, till they could see quite a fringe of roots, which had forced their way through the arch of rugged stones, and at last make out how the roof of the passage had been driven in by the fall of the tree.

"Oh! there is something now," cried Scarlett, starting.

"What is it?"

"Something did touch my leg."

"Kick it!" cried Fred, huskily. "Look out, Scar! it's swimming towards you. Mind, mind!"

The boy had raised up his foot to kick, but placed it down again, for the terror proved to be a piece of rotten wood floating on the surface.

"How easy it is to be frightened!" said Scarlett, drawing a long breath, as they stood once more at the opening.

"Yes, far too easy," grumbled Fred. "I wish it wasn't. Shall I go up first, or will you?"

"Isn't it a pity to go up without finding the way?" said Scarlett, hesitatingly.

"It does seem to be; but I've had enough of it. Let's go up now."

"Shall we? I know we shall want to come down again."

"Yes," said Fred, hesitating; "I suppose we shall. Do you feel to mind it so much now?"

"I don't think so."

"Let's go on, then."

"Shall we, Fred?"

"Yes; didn't I say so?" cried Fred, crossly. "Go on; you've got the light."

Without another word, Scarlett held the light above his head.

"It seems very rum though, Scar. That must be the way to the house."

"Well, let's see."

Scarlett started once more with the lanthorn along the tunnel in the other direction, apparently toward the house, while, with a maliciously merry laugh on his face, Fred hung back, and half hid himself among the fallen wood and stones.

Scarlett went on quite a couple of dozen yards, talking the while, every word he said coming back as in a loud whisper distinctly to the mouth of the hole.

"Don't seem to get any deeper, Fred. I'm glad we came, because we shall find it out this time."

Fred chuckled and watched, and, to his surprise, he saw his companion and the light gradually disappear, leaving the tunnel in obscurity.

"Why, I shall have to go in the dark," cried Fred to himself. "Oh!" And, startled more than he had startled his companion, he hurried after him, so eager to overtake the light that he nearly went headlong in the water, for his body went quicker than his legs.

"Hi! stop a minute, Scar!" he cried; and he noted, as he hurried on, that the passage made a great curve, though it was so gradual that he could not tell its extent.

"Why, I thought you were close behind me," said Scarlett, as he overtook him. "Lean a little forward, and you'll find it easier to go along through the water. It's getting just a little deeper now."

"Then this must be the way to the lake, after all."

They persevered, going steadily on for some time, and, with the water gradually creeping up and up till it was mid-thigh, and then higher and higher till it was almost to their hips, and then they stopped.

"I shan't go any farther, Scar," cried Fred. "I don't want to have to swim."

"Yes, it is getting deep," said Scarlett, thoughtfully.

"Couldn't get a boat down here, could we!"

"No; but we might get one of the big tubs," replied Scarlett. "It would hold us both. Shall we go back now?"

"Yes; we're so horribly wet; but hold the lanthorn up higher, and— Oh, I say!"

Scarlett had obeyed, and raised it so high that the lanthorn struck slightly against the rough roof, and, as the candle happened to be already burning away in the socket, this was sufficient to extinguish it, and for the moment they were in total darkness, or so it seemed to them in the sudden change.

Then Fred cried exultantly, "Look! look!" and pointed to a bright, rough-looking star of light.

"Sunshine," cried Scarlett. "Then that is the entrance. Shall we go on?"

Fred had already squeezed by him, and was wading on toward the light, which proved to be not more than fifty feet away.

"Come along!" he cried; "it isn't very much deeper, only up to my middle now. Here, I'm touching it. This is the end, and—it's—it's—no, I can't quite make out where it is," he continued, as he darkened the hole by placing his face to it; "but I can see the lake, and I could see where, only there's a whole lot of ivy hanging down."

"Can you get your head through?"

"No; too small. Come and look."

Fred made way for his companion, and, while he was peering through, the other amused himself by feeling the flat surface which stopped farther progress, and soon made out that there was a wall of rugged stone, built up evidently to stop the entrance; and this was matted together with ivy strands and roots which had forced their way in.

"Yes," said Scarlett, at last, as he drew away; "this is the entrance, and now we've got to find it from outside."

"Yes; but how?"

"Oh, we shall soon find it. Get the boat, and hunt all along till we find a place that has been built like a wall, and then search for this hole."

"And how about the ivy all over it?"

Scarlett was silent for a while.

"I had forgotten all about the ivy," he said.

"If we could tell about where it was, I dare say we could soon find it."

"Yes, but we can't tell yet."

"And we shan't find out by stopping here, Scar; and oh, I say—"

"What's the matter?"

"The water's right up in my pockets. Come along back."

"But we've got to go in the dark."

"Can't help it. I don't mind so much now, for we can't go wrong. Come along."

Fred took the lead now, and they went steadily back, feeling their way along by the damp wall, and casting back from time to time regretful looks at the bright star of light, which grew less and less, and then disappeared; but as it passed from sight, they saw to their great delight that there was a faint dawn, as it were, on ahead, and this grew brighter and brighter, till they seemed to turn a corner, and saw the bright rays shooting down through the hole, which they reached with a rather confused but correct notion that about here the passage took a double curve, somewhat in the shape of the letter S; but they were too eager to get out into the wood again to give much attention to the configuration of the place.

"Hah!" exclaimed Fred, taking a long breath, and then beginning to squeeze the water out of his nether garment, "that's better. I say, hadn't we better hide this hole?"

"I don't think we need; nobody ever comes here. Let's go and have a look down by the lake."

Chapter Nine
Something the Matter

The two lads were so accustomed to rough country life and to making wading expeditions for trout in the little rivers, or rushing in after the waves down by the seashore, that, after giving their garments a thorough good wring, they soon forgot all about the dampness in the interest of searching for the entrance to the secret passage down by the lake.

"I know how it must all have been," said Scarlett. "When our house was built, there must have been wars. I dare say it was in the War of the Roses, and that place was contrived, so that in case of need any one could escape."

"Yes; and if the place was taken, the rightful owners could get in again."

"And now it's all peace," said Scarlett, thoughtfully, "and we can make it our cave, and do what we like there."

"But it isn't all peace," said Fred. "I heard father say that if the king went on much longer as he's going on now, there might be war."

"Who with—France?"

"No; a civil war."

"What Englishmen against Englishmen! They couldn't."

"But they did in the Wars of the Roses."

"Ah, that was when people knew no better, and there were different kings wanted to reign! Such things never could occur again."

"I hope not."

"There! this is where the entrance must be."

The two lads had reached the edge of the lake now, and began once more to search along the most likely spots where the rocky banks were perpendicular and high, and covered with ivy and overhanging trees.

But it was labour in vain, and at last, as the afternoon grew late, they sat down on a piece of slaty rock in the hot sunshine, swinging their legs over the side, gazing out at the bright waters of the lake.

"I don't care," cried Fred, pettishly; "I'm tired of it. I don't mind now whether there's a way in or a way out. It's of no use, and I'm hungry. I shall go home now."

"No; stop and have supper with us."

"Very well. I don't mind; only let's go."

The two boys went straight up to the Hall, passing Nat on the way, ready to exchange a salute and a grin.

"What are you laughing at, Nat?" cried Fred.

"Only at you two, sir. You've been up to some mischief, I know."

The boys exchanged hasty glances, which, being interpreted, meant, "Has he been watching us?"

"I always knows," said Nat, with a chuckle.

"No, you don't," cried Fred. "You're just like our Samson."

"So would you be, Master Fred, if you was a twin."

"I did not mean that. I meant being so precious cunning and sure about everything when you don't know anything at all."

"Ah, don't I, sir! Ha, ha, ha! I could tell Sir Godfrey a deal more than you think for."

"Yes, you'd better," cried Fred. "You do, that's all, and I'll go home and lead Samson such a life."

"Wish you would, sir, for he deserves it. A nasty, stuck-up, obstint fellow as never was. I never meet him without he wants to quarrel with me and fight. Thinks he's the strongest man there is, and that he can do anything. And talk about a temper!"

"Shan't," cried Fred. "What do we want to talk about tempers for? Our Samson has got as good a temper as you have."

"Nay, nay, Master Fred; now that aren't a bit true. And I beg your pardon, sir: our Sampson's father was my father."

"Oh yes! and his mother was your mother. That's what you always say."

"Which it's a truth, Master Fred," said the gardener, reprovingly; "and Master Penrose say as a truth can't be told too often."

"Then I don't think the same as Master Penrose. Do you, Scar?"

"No, of course not. Well, Nat, what were you going to say?"

"Only, sir, that Sampson's my brother; but I'm mortal sorry as he's the gardener for any friends of yours, for a worse man there never was in a garden, and I never see it without feeling reg'lar ashamed of the Manor."

"Ha, ha, ha!" laughed Fred. "Why, that's just what our Samson says about your garden."

"What, sir? Our Samson said that about the Hall garden?"

"Yes, lots of times."

Nat had a hoe in his hand, and he let the shaft fall into the hollow of his arm as he moistened his hands, took a fresh hold of the ash pole as if it was a quarter-staff, and made half a dozen sharp blows at nothing before letting the tool resume its place on the earth.

"That's what's going to happen to Samson Dee next time we meets, Master Fred; so p'raps you'll be good enough to tell him what he has got to expeck."

"Tell him yourself, Nat," said Scarlett, shortly. "Come along, Fred."

The gardener stood looking after them till they disappeared through the great door of the Hall, and then went on hoeing up weeds very gently, as if he did not like to injure their tender fibres.

"Master Samson won't be happy till I've given him stick enough to make his bones sore. Hah! we shall have to get it over somehow. Samson won't be content till we've had it out."

The supper of those days was ready when the boys entered the great dining-room, Fred having declared himself ravenous while upstairs in Scarlett's bedroom, where, the lads being much of a size, he had been accommodated with a complete change, even to dry shoes.

Sir Godfrey and Lady Markham were waiting, the former looking very serious, and his countenance becoming more grave as he saw Fred enter.

"You bad boys," whispered Scarlett's sister, as she ran up to them, with her dark hair tossed about her shoulders. "Father was beginning to scold."

"How do, Lady Markham?" said Fred, and her ladyship looked troubled as she took the boy's hand. "How do, sir? It was so late, and I am so hungry, that I thought you would not mind my stopping to supper with Scar."

"Ahem! No, my boy," said Sir Godfrey, trying to be cordial, but speaking coldly. "Sit down. Been out with Scarlett?"

"Yes, sir. All the afternoon in the woods," replied Fred, looking at the baronet wonderingly, for he had never heard him speak in such a tone before.

Ever since he could remember he had been in and out of the Hall at meal-times, even sleeping there often, and Scarlett's visits to the Manor had been of the same character. To all intents and purposes the life of the boys had been that of brothers, while that of their fathers had been much the same.

It was a genuine old-fashioned Coombeshire repast to which the hungry boys sat down, eating away as boys of fifteen or sixteen can eat, and bread and butter, ham, cake, junket and cream, disappeared at a marvellous rate.

"Is your father poorly?" whispered Fred, after satisfying his hunger to some extent. "I don't know. Don't speak so loud."

"Wasn't speaking so loud," said Fred, kicking Scarlett under the table. "What's the matter with him?"

"I don't know. Heard some bad news, perhaps."

"Shall we tell him about the secret way? He'd like to hear, I dare say."

"No, no; let's keep it to ourselves for the present."

That something was troubling Sir Godfrey was evident, for his supper was hardly tasted, and twice over, when Lady Markham spoke to him, and pressed him to eat, he declined in an irritable way.

"I shall have to join them, if these things go on, Margaret."

"Godfrey!"

"Yes; I feel it is a duty to one's self and country. If we country gentlemen are not staunch now, and do not rally round his majesty, what are we to come to?"

Lady Markham shook her head, and softly applied her handkerchief to her eyes, ending by rising and going to where Sir Godfrey sat and, laying her hand upon his shoulder, she bent down and whispered a few words to him, which seemed to have a calming effect, for he took her hand from where it lay, raised it to his lips, and looked up in his wife's eyes for a few moments before she returned to her place.

All this seemed very strange to the lads, who, feeling uncomfortable, began chatting to Lil, but a complete damp was thrown over what was generally a pleasant, sociable meal, and it was with quite a sense of relief that Fred rose at a hint from Scarlett, and they went out into the hall to walk up and down,—talking for a few minutes before Scarlett ran up the stairs and down once or twice to make sure that all was right by the topmost balusters.

"Glad I did not make up my mind to tell father," he said, as he stood once more by the open door.

"What's the matter?"

"I don't know. Father has had letters, I suppose, that have upset him."

"But he said something about the king—and rallying round him."

"Yes."

"Well, never mind that. Shall we get the boat out to-morrow morning, and have a hunt along the side of the lake? We must find that archway."

"Yes, of course."

"What time shall I come—directly after breakfast?"

"Yes, and I'll have the boat baled out. She's half full of water. Job for Nat."

"Then I'll run home now. Good night.—Good night."

The second good night came from half-way to the west end of the lake, as Fred ran on down to the narrow track which skirted the water-side.

"He will not go and hunt for it by himself," said Scarlett, thoughtfully, as he turned to go in, little thinking what a shadow was falling over his home. "No," he added laconically, "too dark;" and, after a glance toward the woodlands at the east end of the gate, he entered the house whistling merrily.

Chapter Ten
Captain Miles

Fred's way across the fields to the Manor was among sweet autumn scents, and with moth and bird taking his attention at almost every step.

The white owl was out, with its peculiar grating cry; so was the tawny owl, breaking forth into its loud hail—*hoi-hoi-hoi*! Skimming about the oak-trees he saw the nightjars again, every swoop meaning death to some unfortunate moth or beetle.

But all these objects were too familiar to call for more than a passing glance as the boy hurried on. Down in the hollows the mists were gathering and floating a little way above the ground, as if there were a fire near, while far away in the east a bright planet burned like silver opposite to the warm glow left in the west.

"Hurrah! there we are," cried Fred, as he topped the last hill, and looked down at the lights which showed where home lay; and he was not long in getting over the ground, almost quicker than he was satisfied with, for he was making his plans for the next morning respecting the discovery of the entrance to the passage.

For the whole of the incidents in connection with the secret chamber had thoroughly excited him, and he felt as if he could not rest till he had found out everything about the place.

To his great surprise, as he entered the house, he found that supper was not begun.

"Been waiting for me, mother?" he cried to the calm, sweet-faced lady seated working by the light of rather a dim candle.

"No, Fred," she said, smiling gravely, as she drew him down and kissed his brow.

"Because I had mine with Scar. Where's father?"

"In the library. He has a gentleman with him."

"Gentleman?"

"Yes; he has come from Bristol to see your father on business."

"Oh!" said Fred, carelessly; and he sat down and rested his head upon his hand.

"Does your head ache, my boy?" asked his mother.

"Head? No, mother. I was only thinking," said the boy, as his mother's words brought him back from wandering in the water-floored passage.

"Thinking of your studies?"

Fred started a little, for his studies had been rather neglected of late.

"No, mother, only of a hunt Scar and I had in the Hall woods to-day."

It was in the boy's heart to tell his mother all that had passed, and their discovery from beginning to end, but he argued, "If I do, it will not be a secret any longer."

There was a pause.

"Father said that a well-intentioned boy would have no secrets from his father and mother, and that they should be always looked upon as his best friends. But it isn't mine altogether," argued Fred, after another very long pause; "and I've no business to tell Scar's secret to any one till he has told it to his own father and mother; and, besides, as it's a private place, they would not like any one to know about it, and—"

"Yes, Forrester, we may throw away all compunction now," said a loud, firm voice; and Fred rose from his seat as his father entered in company with a tall, broad-shouldered man, whose grizzled, slightly curly hair was cut very close to his head, and whose eyes seemed to pierce the boy, as he gave him a sternly searching look. He had a stiff, military bearing, and he did not walk down the long low room, but seemed to march rather awkwardly, as if he had been riding a great deal.

He nodded familiarly to Mistress Forrester, who looked at him in rather a troubled way, as he marched straight to Fred, slapped him sharply on the shoulder, and gripped it so hard as to give him acute pain. But the boy did not flinch, only set his teeth hard, knit his brow, and gazed resentfully in the visitor's dark eyes, which seemed full of malice and enjoyment in the pain he was giving.

"So this is Fred, is it?" he said in a harsh voice, which sounded as if he was ordering Colonel Forrester to answer.

"Yes, sir," said Mistress Forrester, with dignity, "this is our son;" and she looked wonderfully like her boy in the resentful glance she darted at her guest, for she could read Fred's suffering.

"Hah! made of the right stuff, like his father, Mistress Forrester. Did that hurt you, my boy?"

"Of course it did," said Fred, sharply.

"Then why didn't you cry out or flinch, eh?"

This was accompanied by a tighter grip, which seemed as if the stranger's fingers were made of iron.

The grip was but momentary, and the boy stood like a rock.

"Well," said the stranger again, "why didn't you cry out?"

"Because I would not," replied the boy, frowning.

"Shake hands."

Fred tried to hold back, but the command was so imperious, and the firm, sinewy hand before his face seemed to draw him, and he laid his own within it, to feel the fingers close in a warm but gentle grasp, the pressure being firm and kindly; and in place of the fierce look a pleasant, winning expression came into the visitor's countenance, while the left hand was now clapped upon the boy's shoulder, and closed in a pressure as agreeable as the other was harsh.

"Glad to know you, my lad. That's frank and manly of you. The right stuff in him, Mistress Forrester. He'll make a good man, colonel. Well?"

"I didn't speak, sir," said Fred, in answer to the question and look.

"That's right, too. Don't be in too great a hurry to speak," said the visitor; and somehow, to his own astonishment, Fred felt himself drawn toward this imperious personage, who seemed to take command of every one in the place. "Well, Forrester, you'll make a soldier of him."

"I—"

The hesitatingly spoken pronoun came from Mistress Forrester, who seemed checked by the guest's quick look of reproof.

"I had not decided yet," said Colonel Forrester, gravely; and Fred noticed that his father seemed to have suddenly grown rigid and stern in manner and tone of voice. "What do you say, Fred? should you like to be a soldier?"

"Yes, father; like you have been."

"No, no, Fred, my boy!" cried his mother.

"Madam," said their guest, "ladies do not always understand Latin, but a certain Roman poet called Horace once said, '*Dulce et decorum est pro patriâ mori'*. Let me modify it by saying, 'to offer in time of need to die for your country.' It does not follow that a man who fights for his home and liberty dies. Good lad. Be a soldier."

"I will, sir," said Fred, firmly. "Father didn't die, mother."

"No, nor you shall not, my boy. There, now, we know one another, and I hope we shall become well-tried friends."

"But I don't know you yet, sir. You have not told me your name."

The visitor clapped Fred on the shoulder again, and there was a merry, kindly light in his eyes as he cried—

"Come, I like this, Forrester. Your Coombeland boys are the genuine, frank English stuff. Fred, my lad, I like your out-spoken ways. From some lads it would have been insolence, but from you it seems sturdy, honest independence. You may know me for the present, my boy, as Captain Miles."

"Miles, a soldier," said Fred to himself but the visitor heard him.

"Right," he cried. "Miles, a soldier. Mistress Forrester, I congratulate you on your home and surroundings. And now, pardon my frankness, I have travelled far to-day and I journey far to-morrow, I am a-hungered and a-thirst, madam; and afterwards, as your good husband and tried soldier and I have done our business, I shall be glad to press a pleasant west-country bed."

With winning courtesy, but at the same time with a half-shrinking, troubled look in her eyes, Mistress Forrester led the way to the table, and as soon as he was seated the guest seemed to cast off his imperious military manner, and become the courtly scholarly gentleman who had read much, travelled far, and thought deeply. So pleasant and interesting was his conversation that Fred grew more and more attracted by him, and listened with wide-open eyes to all he said.

Only once did the business-like, firm and decisive officer appear after supper, when he suddenly apologised and rose.

"I have an old-fashioned way of looking after my best friends, Mistress Forrester," he said. "At the present moment, on this journey, my horse is one of my best friends. You will excuse my visiting him?"

"If you will trust me, Captain Miles," said Colonel Forrester, placing some emphasis on the name, "I can promise you that your good horse has everything that will help him to make a long journey to-morrow."

"I do trust you, Forrester," said the visitor, smiling. "I would I had ten men like you, and as worthy of trust."

As he spoke, he subsided into his chair, but Fred was already on his legs.

"I'll go and see after the horse," he said.

The visitor gave him a kindly approving nod, and the boy left the room.

"How old is he, Mistress Forrester?" he said.

"Sixteen," replied the hostess, sadly.

"Just on the dawn of manhood, madam. Hah, Forrester, old friend, it is a grand thing to be sixteen, and with life before you. God bless all boys! How little they know how grand a thing it is to be young!"

There was silence after this speech—a silence which lasted till Fred entered eagerly.

"The horse is quite right, sir," he cried.

"How do you know, boy?"

"How do I know, sir? Because he is eating his corn so well, and feels so comfortable and cool. I say—"

"Well?"

"He's a fine horse."

"Yes. So he is. A splendid fellow. There, my kind hosts, I'll say good night. I would I had come on another mission, but it is only duty, and you must forgive me. I shall be off at dawn. Good night, madam. Good night, Forrester. I knew I could depend on you. Good night, my boy. You'll forgive me for pinching your shoulder so hard. It was to try your mettle."

"Oh, I didn't mind," cried Fred. "Good night, sir; and when I do become a soldier, will you have me in your regiment?"

"I will," thundered out the guest. "Forrester, that's a bargain. Good night."

There was silence in the room as the two men went out together; and as soon as the door was closed, Mistress Forrester dropped into the nearest chair, and covered her face with her hands.

"Mother, dear mother," cried Fred, going on his knees before her, and throwing his arms about her neck, "you are crying because I said I would be a soldier!"

"No, my boy," she said, looking up, "I was weeping for the evil days in store for us all. Heaven be with us, and guide us all aright. Good night, my boy, good night."

Fred kissed her tenderly, and suffered her to lead him to the door on his way to his room.

He passed his father on the stairs, and there was a troubled look in the colonel's eyes, as he bade his son good night.

A quarter of an hour after, Fred was in bed dreaming of secret passages, and the captain helping him to fight men in rusty armour after they had won their way to the inner chamber where the old arms lay; and then it seemed to him that he heard the trampling of horses, and he woke to find it was morning, and the sun shining into his room.

Chapter Eleven
Nat is very much in the Way

Fred lay for some few moments thinking over his vivid dream and unable for a time to realise that he had been fast asleep. That was the morning sunshine sure enough, and this was his room; but his head felt in a whirl, and as if it was mixed up with some puzzle.

But that was not the coinage of his brain that distant *pit-pat* of a horse's hoofs upon the hard road; and springing out of bed, he ran to the window, threw it open, and looked out, straining his neck to get a glimpse of the distant way.

For a few moments he could see nothing. Then there came into sight, rising out of a hollow, the head and broad shoulders of a horseman. As he progressed, more and more of his figure appealed as he ascended a slope, till at last the horse was in full view, but directly afterwards they seemed to top the ascent and begin to go down on the other side, with the sun flashing from stirrup and buckle, and from the hilt of the rider's sword. There were other bright flashes too all around, but they were from the dewdrops which spangled grass and leaf, as the rider seemed to grow shorter, his horse disappearing, till only his head and shoulders appeared above the ridge, and then they passed away, and the *pit-pat* of the horse's hoofs died out.

"Gone!" said Fred, thoughtfully. "No! there he is again;" and he strained his eyes to gaze at the tiny distant form of the military-looking man who had made so strong an impression upon him, but he did not become visible; it was only the sound of his horse's hoofs which were heard for the space of a minute, faint but clear, on the morning air. Then all was silent.

"I half like that Captain Miles," said Fred to himself. "Wish I was going with him. Wonder where he has gone? To Plymouth, perhaps."

Fred began to dress, after hesitating whether he should go to bed again. But the bright morning was so attractive, and after the first application of cold water, he felt a positive eagerness to get out in the fresh air.

All the time he was dressing his head was full of his confused dream and the fight in the narrow passage, while the events of the preceding day had so impressed him that he hurried downstairs, glanced at the hall clock, which pointed to a quarter to five, and, taking his hat, ran out, and down the garden.

"Morning, Master Fred," came from behind the hedge; and it was so sudden that the lad jumped.

"You, Samson?" he cried. "Yes; I've been starting that gen'leman who come yesterday. Had to get up at four and have his horse ready. Going fishing?"

"No; only for a walk."

"Over to the Hall?"

"Yes, Samson," replied the lad, impatiently. "Then, if you see that bad brother o' mine, Master Fred, don't you speak to him. I'm getting ashamed of him."

"No: he's getting ashamed of you, Sam," cried Fred, tauntingly. "What?"

"Well, he said so last night."

"Ashamed of me, sir. I should like to see him be 'shamed of me. I'd give him something to be 'shamed about."

"Oh yes, of course," cried Fred; and he ran on, forgetting all about the gardener in his eagerness to get to the lake.

The birds were twittering and singing in the woods and coppices, the soft, silvery mists were rising from the hollow, and each broad fern frond glistened as if set with tiny jewels of every prismatic hue. Away too in the distance, as he topped a hill, one corner of the Hall lake could be seen glistening like burnished silver set in a frame of vivid green.

But these were too common objects to take the boy's attention as he walked up the hill slope and trotted down the other side, for he was intent upon one thing only, a faint indication of which was given by his exclaiming once—

"How surprised old Scar will be!"

It was not to go under his window and rouse Scar by throwing pebbles up at the lattice-pane, for instead of taking the dewy path round, by the high trees, which would have taken him at once to the house, Fred ran down the sharp slope into the little coombe, through which ran off the surplus waters of the lake. Here there was a clump of alders growing amongst the sandstone rocks, and three of the larger trees had been cut down to act as posts, to one of which the old flat-bottomed boat was fastened by a chain.

The boy had about fifty yards to go through this clump of alders, a little winding path trampled by the cattle forming his way; and along this he turned, so as to get to the opening where the trees had been cut down, and the boat lay.

But before he was three-parts of the way through, he heard a peculiar scraping sound, followed by a splash, and then a repetition, and another repetition, in regular rhythm and measure.

Fred stopped short, listening. "How tiresome!" he muttered. "Scar must have told old Nat to bale her out before he went to bed. Wonder how long he'll be?" Evidently intending to wait until the man whom he heard was gone, Fred crept softly along, listening to the rhythmic splash of water, till he could peer through the thin growth at the person bailing out the boat.

No sooner did he catch sight of him than he dashed forward to where Scarlett sat on the edge of the old punt wielding a shallow iron pot.

"Fred!"

"Scar!"

"Why, what brought you over so soon?"

"What are you doing there?"

"Baling."

"Yes; and you were going over yonder without me?"

Scarlett sat tapping the gunwale of the boat with the pot, having ceased to bale.

"Yes, I knew you were," continued Fred, in an altered tone, as the other remained silent.

"Come, now, confess."

"I don't know that I need call it confessing," said Scarlett, throwing back his head and speaking haughtily. "It's our boat, and our lake, and that place is all ours."

"Yes; but we were schoolfellows, and we found it together."

Scarlett winced a little at this. "And you were going to steal a march and find it all out by yourself. I do call it mean," cried Fred, angrily. "I didn't think you'd do such a thing, Scar, and—"

"You thought just the same," said Scarlett, quickly, "and meant to take the boat before I was up, and that's why you are here."

He looked sharply at Fred, who thrust his hands in his pockets, and suddenly became interested in the movements of a bald coot, which was paddling in and out among the reeds which grew right into the lake.

"There now, you're found out too, and you're as bad as I am," cried Scarlett.

"Well, I only meant it as a surprise. Is she very leaky?"

Scarlett seemed disposed to hold off, but the interest of the project in hand swept all that away, and he replied sociably enough.

"No; she has been so deep in the water and got so soaked, that I don't think much comes in."

"Bale away, then," cried Fred.

"Suppose you have a turn. I'm getting hot."

Fred required no further hint, but stripping off his jerkin and rolling up his sleeves, he was soon at work scooping up the water and sending it flying and sparkling in the morning sunshine, while Scarlett sat and chatted.

"I didn't care to ask Nat to clean out the boat," he said, "for he's such an inquisitive fellow. He'd have wanted to know what I was going to do, and if I hadn't told him—"

"I know," said Fred, making a momentary iris as he sent the water flying, "he'd have hidden away and watched you."

"Yes; sure to."

"And Samson's just the same. I have to cheat him sometimes. But it didn't matter cheating old Nat. What I think was so shabby was trying to cheat me."

Scarlett was silent for a minute.

"I should have told you afterwards," he said. "Here, let me have a turn now."

"No; I shall finish," replied Fred, wielding the old pot with increased energy, "just to show you how forgiving I am."

"Ah! but you're found out too," cried Scarlett.

"Well, I didn't mean any harm," cried Fred, with a droll look, "and should have told you afterwards."

"Yes; but—"

"Look here," cried Fred, "you say another word about it, and I'll throw all the water over you."

"Let's make haste, then, and go and find the way in before breakfast."

For answer Fred scooped away at such a rate that he had soon cleared the boat down to the little well-like hollow arranged to catch the drainings.

"Now then," he cried, "I'm tired. You row."

Scarlett unhooked the chain, gave the boat a good thrust, seized the oars, and in ten minutes more they were coasting along as near to the bank as the overhanging trees and projecting bushes would allow.

For quite half an hour they searched to and fro, but without result. There were plenty of likely looking places overgrown with ivy, and sheltered by the willows, alders, and birches, but not one showed a sign of having been built up with rough blocks of stone, or presented a hole such as they had seen from the inside.

"We shall never find it like this," said Fred, at last.

"How are we to find it, then? And we must go soon, as some one will see us, and wonder what we are doing."

"Oh no; they'll only think we are fishing," said Fred. "I'll tell you how to find it."

"How?"

"We must cut a long willow, and strip it all but the leaves on the end."

"What for?"

"Then one of us must go down the opening yonder, wade along the passage, poke the stick out through the hole, and shout."

"Yes; that would do it nicely," said Scarlett. "But who's to do it?"

"Let's both go."

"Then we should be no wiser, because there would be no one out here to listen."

"No," said Fred; and then, "Let's have another try."

They had another try—a long and careful search, but the entrance had been too cunningly masked.

"It's of no use," said Scarlett, drawing in the oars. "One of us must go."

Silence. And Fred seemed to be deeply interested in the proceedings of a great flap-winged heron which had alighted on the further shore.

"Will you go, Fred?" said Scarlett, at last.

"No. It's your place, and you ought to go."

"Yes," said Scarlett, slowly; "I suppose I ought."

"No, no, I'll go," cried Fred, eagerly. "I will not be so shabby. Let's cut a stick, and then set me ashore."

Scarlett nodded, and resuming the rowing, ran the boat's head ashore, close to a clump of willows. Then, taking out his knife, he hacked off a rod about ten feet long, trimmed off the twigs and leaves, all but a patch on the end, and, before his companion could realise what he intended, he had leaped ashore, given the boat a thrust, and run up the bank.

"No, no," cried Fred. "I'll go."

"It's my place, and I shall go myself," replied his companion. "Take the oars and row gently along. I don't think I shall mind. If I do, I'll come back and you shall go."

"But you have no light."

"No," said Scarlett, gravely; "but I know the way now, and that there's no danger, so I shall not care." Before Fred could offer further remonstrance, Scarlett had run into the nearest patch of woodland and disappeared.

"I don't like letting him go," muttered Fred, as he gazed at the spot where his companion had disappeared. "It seems as if I were a coward. Perhaps I am, for it does seem shivery work to do. Never mind, I'll go next time," he added quickly; and, taking the oars, he sat down where his companion had vacated the seat, and began to row slowly back to where he fancied the entrance must be.

Then followed so long a period of waiting that the boy grew anxious, and after rowing to and fro for some time outside the thick growth which edged that portion of the lake, he made up his mind that something must be wrong, and determined to land and go in search of Scarlett.

"How horrible if he has waded into a deep place, and gone down!" he muttered, as he bent over the oars, to pull with all his might, when he fancied he heard a distant hail.

He ceased rowing, and the water rippled about beneath the front as he listened.

"Where are you?" he cried.

"Here," came from apparently a great distance.

"Where's here?"

"Here, here, here. Can't you see?"

The voice seemed to come from far away, and he drew in the oars, and stood up in the boat to look from side to side, searching eagerly, and trying to pierce the bushes and overhanging ivy, which screened the rocky shore.

"Here! Hoy!"

Fred faced round now, and looked across the lake, to see Nat standing on the farther shore.

"What are you doing? Got any?" shouted Nat.

Fred put his hands to the sides of his mouth, and shouted back.

"No! not yet."

"Where's Master Scarlett?"

"Ashore."

"Oh!"

"He thinks we've been setting eel-lines," muttered Fred, as, to his great annoyance, he saw the gardener seat himself on the distant bank and watch him.

"Oh, what a bother!" he cried, with an impatient stamp on the bottom of the boat. "Well, he must think so, then."

To induce the spy upon his proceedings to go on in this belief, Fred stooped down in the boat, and picked up and threw in an imaginary line. After which, he took up one oar, and, standing upright, began to paddle the boat in toward the bank, where a large birch drooped over and dipped its delicate sprays of leaves almost into the surface of the lake.

"I'll moor her fast here," thought Fred, "and go ashore and warn Scar. We can't do any more, with that fellow watching."

To this end, he paddled the boat close to the silver trunk of the birch, whose roots ran down into the clear water, forming quite a delicate fringe, amongst which the tiny perch loved to play.

He was in the act of fastening the chain as he stood up, and had passed it round one of the lower boughs, being fairly well screened now from Nat's observation by the delicate spray, when a fly seemed to tickle his ear.

Fred struck at it viciously without looking round, and went on fastening the chain, when the fly again seemed to tickle him, this time low down in the nape of his neck.

"Get out! Will you?" he cried: and he turned, sharply struck at the fly, and caught—

The end of the willow rod with its tuft of leaves.

"Oh!" he ejaculated, as the tug he gave at the wand was replied to by another at the end; and as he looked, he saw that it came from out of a dense mass of twiggy alder above his head, where a quantity of ivy grew.

"Scar," he cried, giving the wand a shake, "are you there?"

"Yes," came in a faint whisper that sounded very hollow and strange. "Didn't you hear me shout!"

"No."

"I was afraid to cry too loud, because it goes backward so, rumbling all along the passage. Whereabouts is it?"

"By the big birch-tree; just where we thought it couldn't be."

"Eh? Speak up."

"By the big birch-tree; just where we thought it couldn't be; and I can't speak louder, because Nat's over the other side, watching."

"Can he see you now?"

"No. But are you all right!"

"Yes."

"You're higher up than I thought. Stop till I push the boat closer, and I'll see if I can find any loose stones."

"Stop a minute," said Scarlett, in the same smothered voice, which sounded faint as a whisper. "Let me see if I can move any of them."

Fred waited, and, peering through the twigs, he could see that Nat was patiently waiting for him to come in sight again.

"Some of them seem loose," came from within; "but I can't get them out."

"Don't stop to try now," said Fred. "Let's come another time; we can't make any mistake, now. Oh!"

The cry was involuntary, for all at once a patch of ivy just above the level of the water seemed to be driven outward, and several stones about the size of his head fell with a splash down among the alder roots, followed by a heavy gush of water, which poured forth fiercely into the woody edge of the lake, and continued to pour as if a fresh lake was discharging its waters into the old one.

So near was the edge of the boat, that the water nearly rushed in; but though it was afterwards slightly drawn toward it, a snatch at a bough drew it back, and Fred stood gazing wonderingly at the rush which foamed in.

Then he looked across the lake, wondering whether Nat could hear and see. But he was too far distant to see more than a little ebullition which might have been caused by the movement of the oars and boat, for the water that poured in was discharged in quite a dense thicket of moisture-loving growth.

"I say, Scar," cried Fred, at last, alarmed by the silence, and after listening to the surging noise of the water for a few minutes.

"Yes."

"Are you all safe?"

"Yes, of course."

"What does all this water mean?"

"I was pushing against the wall high up, and slipped, and my knees struck against the bottom, driving out some of the stones."

"Then— Stop a minute; Nat's going away."

The lad held some of the twigs aside, and could see that the gardener was moving off, apparently tired of waiting, and, once he was out of sight, there was no occasion to be so particular about shouting, and a conversation was painfully carried on above the rushing noise of the water.

"I can't understand it, Scar," cried Fred. "There must be a stream running through that passage."

There was no reply; but the willow wand was withdrawn, and the next minute it appeared through the hole where the water was rushing.

"I say, Scar."

"Yes."

"Haven't you done some harm, and oughtn't we to let them know up at the house?"

"I don't know. I couldn't help it."

"I thought the passage was partly under the water," said Fred to himself, "and so it ran in; but it couldn't have been meant to be wet like that. I say, Scar," he cried aloud, "whereabouts is the bottom where your feet are?"

"Eh?"

"I say, where are your feet?"

"Where this stick is," came back more clearly now.

And it suddenly struck Fred that the water was not pouring out in quite so great a volume. But for the moment he could not see the stick for the foam. Directly after, though, he made out where it was being moved to and fro, exactly on a level with the surface of the lake.

"I'm coming back now," cried Scarlett; and his voice was plainly heard, after which Fred sat watching the water, rapidly draining away with less and less violence, till he heard a shout, answered it, and soon after Scarlett came along, forcing his way through the hazels till he reached the edge of the lake, and, by the help of one of the boughs of the birch, swung himself lightly into the boat, and began looking curiously at the opening, nearly hidden by the growth, through which the water still poured.

"No wonder we could not find the place," he said, as he at once placed the right construction on the presence of the water; "and, do you know, all that could not have come from the lake."

"Where could it have come from, then?"

"It must have drained in by degrees from the sides in wet weather, and the stones at the end dammed it up, so that it couldn't get away."

"Nonsense! The water would have pushed the stones down."

"It did, as soon as I pushed too. The wall was only just strong enough before."

"I tell you it must have run in from the lake."

"It couldn't, Fred. The bottom of the passage is higher; and when I came out the water was only just over my shoes. By to-morrow you see if it isn't drained right out. There, you see, it has pretty well stopped now."

Scarlett was quite right, for the water was now flowing out silently, and in very small volume.

"Well, we will not argue about it," said Fred. "Perhaps you're right, but I don't think you are. Anyhow, we've found the way in, and you couldn't have done it without me."

"No; nor you without me, Fred."

"No; and I say— Oh!"

"What's the matter?"

"Don't I want my breakfast."

"Yes; it must be nearly time. Come up and have some with me."

Fred shook his head.

"No," he said. "Your father did not seem to want me there last night."

"Nonsense!"

"Oh no, it was not. You come home with me. What's that?"

Scarlett listened, for there was a rustling and crashing noise, as of some animal forcing its way down through the hazel stubs to get to the edge of the lake to drink.

They waited breathlessly as the sounds grew nearer, and then stopped. The silence only lasted a minute, and then plainly enough came a familiar voice.

"I thought it was just here. Now, where have they got themselves to?"

Then the rustling was continued, and Nat came into sight.

The boys glanced sharply at the place where the water flowed, but there was nothing now but a feeble trickle, not likely to excite attention.

"Oh, there you are, Master Scarlett! Well, how many have you caught?"

"Not one, Nat," cried Fred, sharply.

"You don't put your lines in the right places, lads. Where are they now?"

"Not going to tell you," replied Fred, sharply. "There, hear that? Didn't some one call?"

"No," cried Nat; "I didn't hear nobody. Show me where your lines are laid. Aren't put any down here, have you?"

"No; it wouldn't be any use."

"I should think not. Why, if you hooked an eel, he'd run in and out among the dead wood and roots till your lines would be all tangled together, and you'd lose them."

"Will you come and show us a good place, then, Nat?" said Fred, for Scarlett was a little puzzled as to what was going on.

"Yes; I'll show you," said the gardener, who, like most of his class, was as much interested in the chance of a little fishing as the boys themselves. So, swinging himself into the boat, he took the oars, and, to the great relief of the two lads, rowed right away towards where a little rivulet entered the lake.

"Glad I saw what you were both going to do," continued Nat. "Only waste of time muddling in there among the wood. You might catch a few perch or an old carp, but that would be about all."

Ten minutes later he ceased rowing in front of the mouth of the rivulet.

"There," he said; "set your lines about here, and you'll catch as many as you want, and—breakfast-time. Let's get ashore."

Chapter Twelve
The Colonel's Message

No farther visit was paid to the passage that day; but the next, in the afternoon, the boys made their way down toward the lake, and met Nat, who approached them with rather a mysterious look on his face.

"What's the matter?" asked Scarlett.

"Ah, that's what I want to know, sir. You didn't hear it, of course, because you were out in the boat."

"Hear what?"

"Oh, I don't know, sir," said the gardener, mysteriously. "I've just come from the kitchen, where the servants was talking about it."

"About what?"

"It, sir, it; I don't know what it is. I told 'em it was howls, but I don't think it was. Still, if you tell maid-servants as there's something wrong in the house, they'll either go out of the house or out of their skins."

"Do you know what you are talking about, Nat?"

"Yes, sir. Course I do."

"Well, then, just be a little plain, and don't go smothering your words up as if they were seeds that you'd put in to come up in a month. Now, then, what is it?"

"You needn't be quite so chuff with a man, Master Scarlett—a man as is trying to do his duty."

"Well, go on, then."

"I will, sir. I went into the kitchen, and the women was all talking about it. Her ladyship's maid was the one who heard it, yes'day morning, before breakfast."

"Heard what?"

"Groans, sir, and cries."

"Where?"

"That's what they can't make out. All she could say was that it sounded close to the best bedroom, and it was as if somebody was crying for help in a weak voice, and then shouting, 'Red—red!' which they think means blood."

"Stuff and rubbish, Nat!" cried Fred, hastily.

"That's what I said to them, sir."

"Then go and tell them so again," cried Fred. "Come along, Scar; I want a run."

He hurried his companion away, and they went off down to the lake, leaving Nat staring after them before going slowly away toward the garden, muttering to himself—

"It's all very well," he said; "but it couldn't be howls."

"What made you hurry away so?" cried Scarlett, as they walked on, and he came to a stop. "Let's go back and speak to my father. Something may be wrong. How do we know? Nat—"

Fred burst out laughing.

"Why, don't you see?"

"No: what do you mean?"

"Didn't you tell me you were afraid to shout yesterday because your voice went echoing along the passage?"

"Yes."

"Well, what did you call?"

"Fred—Fred!"

"Well, wouldn't that sound to any one who heard it like, 'Red—red'?"

"Of course," cried Scarlett, laughing. "I never thought of that."

"Now, then, which way shall we go? Straight to the mouth where the water ran, or to the hole in the wood?"

"To the hole;" and, after taking the trouble to make quite a circuit, so as to be sure of avoiding observation, they entered the little wood, made their way to the prostrate oak, and found that the bottom of the hole was dry.

"There!" cried Scarlett, "I was right."

They dropped down, and found that by the time they had reached the end of the portion illumined by the light which came down the hole, faint rays were there to meet them from the other end, the light striking in strongly from the bottom of the walled-up entrance, and showing that the floor which they had to follow was damp, but every drop of water had drained away.

On reaching the end, it was quite light; and a little examination proved that other stones at the bottom were sufficiently loose to be easily pushed out, Fred sending out a couple, which went down into deep water at once.

"I wouldn't have done that," said Scarlett. "It's like opening a way for any one right into our house."

"But any one will not know the way," replied Fred, as he went down on hands and knees, and thrust out his head and shoulders. "Easy enough to get out now," he said, as he thrust the bushes aside, "only we should want the boat. Water's quite deep here. Stop a moment!" he cried excitedly, as he twisted himself round and looked up before drawing his head back. "Why, Scar, we could climb up or down there as easily as could be."

"Could we?"

Scarlett crept partly out in turn, and looked up for a minute or two.

"Yes," he said, as he returned, "that would be easy enough."

"Then, do you know what we have to do next?"

"No."

"Go and stop up the big hole in the wood."

Scarlett thought for a moment, and then agreed, following his companion to the opening, and climbing out in turn.

"How shall we do it?" he said.

"The rougher the better," cried Fred, who was by far the more practical of the two. "Let's get great dead branches, and lay them over anyhow, leaving a hole like a chimney, so as to give light. Come along; I'll show you. The more natural the better, in case any one should come here."

"Which is not likely," replied Scarlett.

"I don't know; Nat might. Work away."

They did work away, and with good effect. They had no difficulty in getting plenty of rough pieces, which they laid across, first like the rafters over a shed, and then piled others upon them in the most careless-looking fashion, after which some long strands of ivy and bramble were dragged across, to act the double purpose of binding all together and looking natural.

"But they seem as if they had been just placed there," said Scarlett, looking rather dissatisfied with their work.

"Of course they do to-day; but before a week has gone by, they'll have all their leaves turned up to the light, and go on growing fast. Now, then, who could tell that there was a way down there?"

Scarlett was fain to confess that the concealment would be perfect as soon as the leaves were right, and a shower of rain had removed their tracks.

"And we shall not want to come here at all now, only get in by the proper way. I wish that hole was not broken through."

"We should not have found it without."

"Oh yes, we should," said Fred; "because some day we should have bought candles, and waded down to the mouth."

"Well," said Scarlett, as they strolled away at last, "what's the good of it all, now we have found it out?"

"It doesn't seem quite so much now we have found everything; but still it is interesting, and it will do to hide in when we want to get away from everybody."

"But we never do."

"No," said Fred. "But never mind; there's no knowing of what use it may be, and it's our secret, isn't it?"

"Oh yes, it's our secret, Fred."

"And how we could scare the servants now, by hiding and groaning."

"Till my father examined and found it all out. I shouldn't like to look him in the face when he did."

"No," said Fred; "it wouldn't be nice. I say, what stupids we should look!"

"Did you get up so early on purpose to come over here yesterday?" said Scarlett, suddenly.

"No. I was woke up by hearing Captain Miles go."

"Captain Miles? Who is he?"

"I don't know; an old fellow-officer of my father, I think. I say, Scarlett, I'm to be a soldier."

Scarlett laughed, and his companion felt nettled.

"Well," he said, "I shall grow older and stronger some day."

"Why, you couldn't pull a sword right out of its sheath," said Scarlett.

"Couldn't I? Let's go into the house and try."

"Come along, then," cried Scarlett; and the two lads ran right into the Hall, where Fred seized an old weapon from one of the suits of armour, and proved his ability by drawing it from the sheath, Scarlett following his example.

"Now, then!" cried Fred; "*en garde!*"

Nothing loth, Scarlett crossed swords with him, just as his father came thoughtfully out of the library, and stopped to watch them.

"I say, this old sword is heavy though," said Fred, as the point of the long blade seemed attracted toward the ground.

"It's because you haven't muscle enough," replied Scarlett, as the blades grated together. "Wonder whether this one ever cut off a man's head?"

"Is this an omen?" said Sir Godfrey to himself. "Friend against friend, perhaps brother against brother, all through our unhappy land. Well, Heaven's will be done! My duty is to my king."

Meanwhile, the two boys were laughingly making a few cuts and guards with the clumsy old weapons; but directly after they started apart in confusion, as Sir Godfrey said aloud—

"Boys, do you remember the words of Scripture!"

Neither answered; but, with the points of the swords resting on the old oak floor, they stared at him abashed.

"'They that take the sword shall perish with the sword.'"

There was silence in the grand old hall for a brief space, as the two boys stood there in the centre, with the bright lights from the stained-glass windows showering down upon them, and the portraits of Scarlett's warlike ancestors seeming to be watching intently all that was taking place.

Then Sir Godfrey moved slowly across the hall, paused and looked back, and then said gently—

"Put the weapons away, my lads. Warfare is too terrible to be even mimicked in sport."

He sighed and passed through the farther door, leaving the boys gazing at each other in silence.

"How serious he is!" said Scarlett, at last. "Let's put them away. I thought he was going to scold us for taking them down."

"Yes, I thought that," said Fred. "But I should like to be a soldier, all the same, only without any war. Ugh! only fancy giving a man a chop with a thing like that," he added, as he replaced the weapon. "Here, I'm off home," he cried, as he ran to the door.

"Good-bye, old soldier without any war. I say, Fred."

"Well?"

"That will be a capital place for you to hide in when you are a soldier, and the war comes."

"That's right," said Fred, good-humouredly; "laugh away. I dare say I am a coward, but I don't believe everybody is brave. Coming over to-night?"

"Perhaps," was the reply; and Fred went off homeward at a trot, thinking of how delightful it would be to grow into a man, and carry a sword and ride about on a horse like Captain Miles.

He thought a good deal about Captain Miles as he went home, and wondered whether he had gone to Plymouth.

"Because he might have been going to Tavistock or Barnstaple."

The recollection of the sturdy, keen-eyed soldier seemed to oust every other thought from the boy's brain, and he saw in imagination the distant figure as it mounted the rising ground, and, passing over, disappeared.

"I wonder what he came for?" thought Fred. "It didn't seem like the visit of a friend, and it could not be about business, because father never does any business now; but they were so serious, and my mother looked so troubled."

Fred gave his ear a rub, as if he were vexed.

"I suppose it was thinking so much about that rabbit-hole of a place up at the Hall," he muttered. "I never thought any more about mother looking so serious, and having tears in her eyes. I'll ask her what's the matter."

He walked slowly on till he came in sight of the western road, which looked like a narrow path crossing the distant hill.

"Why, there's somebody coming," he cried, as he sheltered his eyes to make out what was evidently a mounted man moving slowly along the road. "He's coming this way," said Fred, musingly. "I wonder who it is?"

Not much of a matter for consideration, in modern days; but to the dwellers in that retired part of Coombeland, far away from a town, the coming of a strange horseman was an event, and, regardless of where he put his feet, Fred went on trying to keep the mounted man in view, as he disappeared at times in the hollows, and then came into sight again, evidently moving at a foot's pace.

"It must be Captain Miles coming back," cried Fred, as the figure disappeared from view in consequence of the lad having to descend into a hollow before rising the opposite hill.

"That old place will be no end of a game when we have cleared it out," mused the boy, as he went slowly down the hill. "It will be a lot of trouble though, and we shall have to sweep and clear away the dust and cobwebs too. I wish we could set Samson and Nat to work, only we can't do that, because, if we did, it wouldn't be a secret place; and, besides, they would do nothing but quarrel, and get no work done. Wonder whether brothers always do quarrel. Why, they're worse than Scar and I are, though we do have a pretty good row sometimes."

Ten minutes later he was mounting the hill, and, as he reached the top, he hastened his pace, so as to get within view of the coming horseman, who was for the moment shut out from view by a patch of woodland; but the regular beat of the horse's hoofs came plainly enough.

"Sounds in the distance just like my pony's trot," said Fred, thoughtfully; and directly after he burst out with a loud, "Oh!" full of vexation in its tone. "Why, it's only old Samson, after all," he cried. "Think of me taking him for Captain Miles!"

He set off at a sharp run across the moorland, so as to cut off a great piece of the road, and reach a point by which the Manor gardener must pass.

Samson was not long in recognising him, and, checking the speed of the stout cob he rode, the mutual effort brought the two together at the sought-for spot.

"Here you, Samson, who told you to exercise my pony?"

"Exercise, Master Fred? You look at him."

"Look at him? I am looking at him. Poor old fellow! he's all in a lather."

"Yes; he hasn't had such a gallop for months."

"How dare you, then! Jump off directly, and walk him home."

"Shan't!" was the laconic refusal, accompanied by a grin.

"What!" cried Fred, doubling his fists threateningly.

"Shan't come off, sir. There!"

"Oh, won't you!" cried Fred, seizing Samson by the leg, and proceeding as if to tilt him over.

"You leave your father's special messenger alone, Master Fred, or you'll get into trouble."

"Did my father tell you to take the pony?"

"Course he did, and to take what he called a despatch."

"Despatch?"

"Yes. To Barnstaple."

"What for?"

"How should I know? It was a big letter, all tied round with ribbon and sealed up, and I've got another like it in here."

As he spoke in a voice full of importance, he tapped a leathern wallet slung over his right shoulder.

"Why, Samson, who did you take it to?"

"To that gen'leman who was here the other night."

"Captain Miles?"

"Yes. At Barnstaple, and some more gen'lemen was with him when I got there, and he read the letter, and they read the letter, and then they said they'd write another, and I was to go down and have some bread and cheese and cider, and I did—a lot."

"I wonder what it means?" said Fred, as he walked on beside the pony, holding by its thick mane, for it was uphill.

"I think I know, Master Fred."

"You do? What is it?"

"Well, sir, it's something to do with the king and the Parliament. They were talking about it at the Red Hind."

"King and the Parliament?"

"Yes, Master Fred; and there were some there as said we should most likely have to fight for our rights."

"But we haven't got any rights to fight for."

"Oh yes, we have, Master Fred," said Samson, importantly. "A man there told me all about it."

"What did he say?"

"Well, sir, I don't quite understand, but they're trying to take our rights away."

"Who are?"

"Well, that's what I didn't get quite clear, you see, sir. But it's some'at like this. Every man has—I don't quite remember what it was he said there, but I do recollect he said that if things were not altered, we should have to fight."

Fred looked at him wonderingly.

"I should have got it all quite pat, you see, only just as I was getting into the marrow of it and understanding it all, that captain sent for me, and give me the big letter I've got in here. And now I must hurry on." For the top of the hill was reached, and the pony broke into a sharp trot without urging.

But Fred kept hold of the mane, and ran easily by his side, coming soon after in sight of Colonel Forrester, standing at the garden gate, evidently waiting for his messenger's return.

As soon as he saw them descending the slope, he walked quickly forward to meet them, holding out his hand for the despatch, and looking so anxious and severe that his son forbore to speak.

"Take the cob round to the stables, and treat him well," said the colonel, sharply, as he tore open the missive and began to read.

Fred felt eagerness itself to know its contents, and he was about to stop, examining the missive the while with eager eyes; but, recollecting himself, he went off at a trot after Samson, who had dismounted, and was leading the pony.

"Hope it's good news, Master Fred."

"I dare say it is. I don't know."

"The captain said I was a gardener, wasn't I; and I told him the truth, and said I was."

"Why, of course, stupid."

"Ah, you don't understand, Master Fred. It isn't every day that a gardener has to carry despatches. And then he said, as he give me the answer, 'Well, you say you are a gardener, don't let the grass grow under your feet.' I didn't, Master Fred. Ask Dodder."

"No need to ask him, poor old fellow," said Fred, patting his favourite's neck.

"Fred!" came from the road.

"Yes, father," cried the boy, and he ran back.

"I thought you were by me, my boy," said the colonel, gravely, as he laid one hand upon his son's shoulder, and held the despatch in the other, gazing thoughtfully before him toward the old house they were approaching.

"I hope you have not had bad news, father," hazarded Fred.

"No, on the whole, good. It must come—it must come."

Fred looked at him inquiringly.

"What are you, Fred—sixteen, isn't it?"

"Yes, father."

"Ah, if you had been six and twenty, how useful to me you could have been!"

Fred flushed.

"I could be useful to you now, father, if you would let me be," he said in an injured tone. "I could have ridden over to Barnstaple with your letter quicker than Samson did, and I shouldn't have tired Dodder so much."

"Yes, I thought of that, Fred, but you are only a boy, and you were at play."

There was a silence for a few moments, and then Fred spoke.

"Is it wrong for a boy to play, father?"

"Heaven forbid. No; of course not. Play goes with youth, and it gives boys energy, strength, and decision. Yes, Fred, play while you can. Manfully and well. But play."

Fred looked up at his father in a puzzled way, as he stopped short, and began beating his side with the despatch he had received. There was a dreamy look in his eyes, which were fixed on vacancy, as he muttered—

"Yes; I must be right. I have hesitated long, but it is a duty. But what does it mean—friendships broken; the land in chaos; brother against brother; perhaps father against son. No, no," he added, with a shudder, as he turned sharply on his boy. "Fred, my lad," he tried, "if trouble comes upon our land, and I have to take side with those who fight—"

He stopped short.

"Who fight, father? You are not going to fight."

"I don't know yet, my boy; but if I do, it will be for those I believe to be in the right. What I believe to be right, you, too, must believe in, and follow."

"Of course, father," said the boy, quietly.

"No matter what is said against me, or how you may be influenced. I know about these matters better than you do, and I shall ask you to trust to me."

Fred smiled, as if his father's words amused him, for it seemed absurd that he should have any opinion against his own father.

"Why, of course, I shall do as you tell me," he said, taking hold of his father's arm, and they walked together into the house, where Mistress Forrester, looking pale and large-eyed, was awaiting her husband's return.

She did not speak, but looked up in his eyes with so eager and inquiring an air that he bent down and kissed her forehead.

"Yes," he said.

"Oh, husband!"

"It cannot be avoided. My duty is with the people. That duty I must do."

"But home—me—Fred?"

"You will be safe here," he said. "It is not likely that the tide of trouble will flow this way."

"But Fred," she whispered.

"Fred. Ah, yes, Fred," said the colonel, thoughtfully.

"Oh no, no, no," cried Mistress Forrester, in agony, as she saw her husband's hesitating way, and suspected the truth. "No, no, husband, he is too young."

"He will grow older," said the colonel, with quiet firmness. "Wife, when the country calls for the help of her son, he must give it freely. If your boy is needed in his country's service, he will have to go."

Fred heard these words, and went slowly and thoughtfully away—thoughtfully, for his head was in a whirl—the coming of his father's military friend—his father's old life as a soldier—and these hints about civil war.

"I don't think I should mind," he said to himself, "not if Scar went too. He and I could get on so well together. Of course we should be too young for regular soldiers, but we should soon grow older."

Then he began to recall different things of which he had heard and read, about youths going off to the war in olden times to be esquires, and after deeds of valour to become belted knights who had won their spurs.

Fred's was not a romantic nature, for that night, quite late, after he had gone up to bed, he sat at his window looking out at the starlit sky. And as he gazed all the thoughts of the evening came back to make him burst into a derisive laugh.

"It's all nonsense," he said; "knights and squires never did half the things they say. And if we had a war, and I had to go, I'm afraid it would be all rough and different to life here at home. But if Scar went too, I should not mind. They want all the men at such a time as this. Samson would have to go, and Nat, and no end of the farm lads about."

Fred rose from his seat, and closed the window softly, for fear that he should be heard, and at last lay down, but not to sleep, for his young brain was excited, and a feeling of awe came over him as he began thinking of her who was sleeping only a few yards away.

"If father goes and takes me with him, and there is a terrible war, what will my mother say?"

Chapter Thirteen
The Beginning of Trouble

"Godfrey!"

"Hush, my darling; think of the children. Be firm. Be firm."

"But it is too horrible."

"Is this my dear wife speaking?" said Sir Godfrey, gravely, as he took his dame's hand.

"Yes," said Lady Markham, excitedly. "Would you have me sit silent when such a demand is made?"

Sir Godfrey's brow was knit, and his nether lip quivered as he heard his wife's words, while Lil, who seemed alarmed, crept to her brother's side and held his hand.

"The demand is just, wife," said Sir Godfrey, at last. "I am a soldier, sworn to help my king."

"You were a soldier once, love," interposed Lady Markham.

"I am a soldier, wife. Still a soldier, though during these peaceful years I have been allowed to live peacefully here at home. The time has now come when my master needs the help of all his loyal servants. He calls me to his help, and do you think I am going to play the coward and knave, and hide here in idleness while every rogue is striking at the crown? Come: be a woman. Do your duty."

"My duty is to those children, Godfrey," said Lady Markham, piteously.

"And to your husband. You, as a brave, true woman, now that the perilous time has come when ruin and destruction threatens the kingdom, you, I say, should be the first to buckle on your husband's sword."

"Father!" cried Scarlett, "are you going away?"

"Yes, boy; I am summoned to Exeter. From there, perhaps to Bristol."

"And when do you come back?"

Sir Godfrey was silent for a few moments, and then said calmly—

"Heaven knows!"

"Godfrey!" cried Lady Markham, and she threw herself sobbing on her knees.

"Oh, father, father!" cried Lil, running to him and catching his hand, but only to be snatched up to his breast and kissed passionately; "don't, pray don't go away. You'll break poor mother's heart."

"Hush, child!" said Sir Godfrey, sternly. "Do you think I wish to leave all who are dear to me for the risks of war? Remember there is such a thing as duty."

"Yes, father," sobbed Lil, nestling to his breast.

"Scar, my boy, what have you to say? You have heard the king's throne is in danger, and he calls upon his loyal west-country gentlemen to come to his help. Are we loyal or are we not?"

"Loyal, father, of course."

"And you say, then?"

"That you must go, father. Yes, you must go."

"Right! my brave boy, right!" cried Sir Godfrey, seizing the lad's hand. "I must go—at once. And you, while I am gone, will be your mother's help and support—your sister's protector."

Scarlett did not speak, but looked his father firmly in the face.

"I shall leave everything in your hands, and from this day forward you must cease to be a boy, and act as a calm and thoughtful man. I make you my steward and representative, Scarlett. Do your best, and by your quiet, consistent conduct, make yourself obeyed. You understand?"

"I hear what you say, father."

"Well, sir, why do you speak in that hesitating way?"

"Because, father, I shall not be here."

"Scarlett!" cried Sir Godfrey, in a tone full of displeasure.

"Don't be angry with me, father," cried the lad. "You are going away— because the king wants the help of every loyal heart. Well, father, you will take me too."

"Take—you? Scar! No, no; you are too young."

"I expected to hear you say that, but I shall soon be older; and, though I am only a boy, I could be useful to you in a hundred ways. I suppose I am too young to fight."

"Yes, yes; of course."

"Well, others could do the fighting. Couldn't you make me something—your esquire?"

"Knights do not have esquires now, my boy," said Sir Godfrey, with a smile; "but—"

He stopped short, while his son gazed at him eagerly, waiting for the end of his speech.

"Yes, father—but—?" said Scarlett, after waiting some time.

"I was only thinking, my son, as to which was my duty—to bid you watch over your mother and sister here, or to devote you to the service of your king."

"Devote me to the service of my king, father," cried Scarlett, proudly.

"No, no, my boy," cried Lady Markham. "Don't try to stop me, mother," said Scarlett. "You know I should have to stay here in peace to take care of you who are not in danger; but ought you not rather wish to have me trying to watch over him who will be in the war?"

Lady Markham bowed her head. She could not trust herself to speak, for her son's words had set his going in a new light. But she still hesitated, clinging first to father, then to son, and ending by exclaiming—

"Heaven's will be done! I can say no more."

"No, mother. Let me go, and I will do all I can to protect my father."

She gazed piteously at him through her tears, and then cast herself sobbing upon his breast, while Sir Godfrey gravely set his daughter by her mother's side, and laid his hand upon her head.

"Scarlett is right, dearest. He can do more good by embracing his father's profession at once. He will learn to be a soldier, and—perhaps—he may be able to protect me. Who can tell!"

Lady Markham took and kissed her husband's hand, and then once more embraced her son, ending by taking her daughter to her heart, and weeping over her silently, while Sir Godfrey paced the room.

"Yes, my boy?" he said suddenly, as he caught his son's eye.

"When shall you start, father?"

"To-morrow at the latest. Quite early in the morning, if we can get away."

"So soon?"

"Yes. Have you begun to repent already?"

"Oh no, father; but I thought that I should like to go over to the Manor to say good-bye."

Sir Godfrey held up his hand.

"Impossible, my boy. By the same despatch I learned that Colonel Forrester—unhappy man!—has cast in his lot with the Roundheads. I am told, too, that he has been harbouring one of the enemy's generals, who has been about the country organising revolt against his majesty, under the name of Captain Miles. Scarlett, my boy, the Forresters are the enemies of the king, and therefore ours."

"Poor Fred!" said Scarlett, half aloud.

"Ay, poor Fred!" said Sir Godfrey. "Do you think it possible that you could save him from this fate by bringing him over to us? He is your friend, Scarlett?"

"Yes, father, but—"

"Yes, my boy, you are right. It would be a cowardly deed to try and separate father and son. Would it were otherwise, for I like the boy."

"Like him, father? It seems horrible; just as if one was losing a brother, and could not stretch out a hand. And you would not like me to say good-bye to Fred, father?"

"You cannot now, my boy; neither while he is against us can I take Colonel Forrester's hand again."

There was a painful pause here, broken by Lady Markham's sobs; and then, with a sudden display of soldierly firmness, Sir Godfrey bent down and kissed his wife.

"Come, my darling," he said, "remember your duty as the wife and mother of two soldiers suddenly called away."

"I'll try," said Lady Markham, rising sadly.

"And succeed," replied Sir Godfrey, gently. "Come, Scarlett, my boy. Time flies. You will choose which horse you like, and prepare the very few necessaries that you can carry. We shall get our equipment at Exeter, so work hard, as if you momentarily expected to hear the trumpet call, 'To horse.' Why, it stirs my blood again, after all these years of idleness. That's better, my darling. Women should not weep when those they love are about to leave on duty, but give them smiles."

"Smiles, Godfrey!" said Lady Markham, sadly.

"Yes, smiles. Every soldier who goes to fight does not get hard blows or wounds. Many escape everything, and come back covered with glory and full of the sense of duty done. There, Scarlett, my boy, away with you and pack your valise. Recollect you are a soldier now."

Scarlett dashed at his mother, kissed her, and then, bewildered by excitement, he hurried out to go to the stable and select the horse he might need to carry him in many a perilous time; but before he reached the long range of buildings where Sir Godfrey's horses led their peaceful life, he was attacked by Nat.

"Here, Master Scar," he cried excitedly, catching the lad by the sleeve, "is it true?"

"Is what true?"

"That the war's coming nigher our way, and they've sent for the master to fight?"

"Yes, Nat; true enough," said the lad, proudly drawing himself up. "Sir Godfrey and I are going off to the wars to-morrow morning."

"You, Master Scar? You?"

"Yes, Nat; to-morrow."

"Why, dear heart alive, Master Scar, lad," cried Nat, laying his hand affectionately on the boy's shoulder, "it seems only t'other day as you used to come and coax me to leave my mowing and go on hands and knees to make a horse for you to ride, and now you're talking about going to the war."

"Yes, Nat. Time goes."

"But, dear lad," cried the gardener, letting his hand slide down to Scarlett's biceps, "why, you haven't got the muscle in your arm to handle a scythe, let alone a sword to mow down men."

"I can't help that, Nat," cried Scarlett, angrily. "Let go. There'll be muscle enough to thrash you some day."

"I hope so, dear lad. But try and thrash brother Samson first. I should like to see you do that."

"Don't talk nonsense. And come along. I want to look at the horses."

"But are you really going, Master Scar?"

"I—am—really—going, Nat, and I want to settle which horse I shall ride. So please say no more about it."

Nat took off his hat and scratched his head, his face wrinkling up all over as he followed his young master to the stables, just like one of his own pippins which had been lying in the apple loft all through the winter.

Then, as they reached the door, and Scarlett entered, Nat put on his cap, gave his knee a slap, and with one set of wrinkles disappearing from his countenance to make room for another, like a human dissolving view, he burst out into a low chuckle.

"That'll knock the wind out of old Samson's sails! A miserable, cowardly, fat-headed old puddick. He wouldn't have the courage to do that."

"Nat!"

"Coming, Master Scar;" and Nat hurried into the stables to find his young master standing beside the light cob his father often rode. "Hullo, Master Scar, sir, thinking about having Moorcock?"

"Yes, Nat. My father is sure not to take him for his charger, and he would suit me exactly."

"Well, yes, sir, I dare say he would. But why not have Black Adder?"

"Because I thought my father would like him."

"Nay, sir; master'll choose Thunder, as sure as can be, and— Hush! Here he is."

"Well, my boy, have you made your selection?" said Sir Godfrey, as he entered the stables, where eight horses raised their heads to look round and utter a low whinny.

"Yes, father; I have been hesitating between Moorcock and Black Adder, but I thought you would like the black."

"No, my boy, I have made up my mind to have Thunder."

"I think I'll take Moorcock all the same," said Scarlett, thoughtfully.

"He will suit you better now. Two years hence, I should have said take Black Adder."

"Why not take 'em both, Master Scarlett?" said Nat, respectfully. "Black Adder knows me by heart, and I could ride him and take care of him when you didn't want him, or he'd do for master if Thunder was out o' sorts."

"Why, Nat, my good fellow," said Sir Godfrey, smiling, "you will be here at the Hall, helping to protect her ladyship and cutting cabbages."

"No, I shan't, Sir Godfrey," replied the gardener, with a stubborn look in his bluff English face. "I shan't be here, but along o' you and Master Scarlett, and 'stead of cutting cabbages, I shall be cutting off heads."

"Nonsense, man!" said Sir Godfrey, but with far less conviction in his tone.

"Beg your pardon, sir, but I don't see no nonsense in it. I've sharpened scythes till they cut like razors, and if you don't believe it, look at our lawn. Think, then, if I take my best rubber with me, I can't sharpen a sword?"

"Oh, nobody doubts that, my man; but—"

"Why, look here, Sir Godfrey, I'll keep yours and Master Scar's swords with such an edge on 'em as shall frighten your enemies into fits. You'll let me go, won't you, dear master? I can't stay behind." Sir Godfrey shook his head. "Master Scarlett, sir, put in a word for me. Don't go and leave me behind. I'll be that faithful and true as never was."

"Nobody doubts that, my man."

"Then let me go, Sir Godfrey. Why, see how useful I can be. I can wash for you, and cook for you—anything, and cut a few armfuls of heath of a night to make your beds. And, look here, gen'lemen, soldiers on the march never gets a bit o' vegetable; but if there's any within a dozen miles of where you are, you shall always have it. So there!"

"You do not know the hardships of a soldier's life, my good fellow," said Sir Godfrey, as he patted the neck of the noble-looking, dark-dappled grey in one of the stalls. Nat laughed.

"Well, master," he said, "if you gen'lemen as never gets yourselves wet can bear 'em, I should think I can. Let me go, sir, please." Sir Godfrey hesitated.

"Well, my lad," he said, "I must warn you of the risks of what you ask. We both go with our lives and liberties in our hands."

"All right, sir; and I'll take my life and liberty in my hand, though I don't zackly know what you mean."

"I mean that any day you may be cut down or shot."

"Oh, that, Sir Godfrey! Well, so's our flowers and fruits every day. That's their chance, I suppose, and I'll take mine same as you take yours. Maybe I might help to keep off a bit o' danger from both on you, and I don't suppose Master Scarlett would let any man give me a chop, if he could stop it."

Sir Godfrey gave his horse a final pat on his fine arching neck, and walked back out of the stall, to stand gazing full at his man, who slipped off his hat, and drew himself up awkwardly in soldierly fashion. Then, without a word, and to Nat's dismay, he turned to his son.

"Yes," he said; "take Moorcock, my boy, and the stoutest saddle and bridle you can find."

Then he walked straight out of the stables, leaving Nat gazing after him in dismay.

"And me with such arms, Master Scar!" he cried, in a protesting tone. "Look here, sir."

He stripped off his jerkin and rolled his shirt up over his knotted limbs, right to the shoulder, displaying thew and sinew of which a gladiator might have been proud.

"Well, Master Scar, sir, as I'm not to go, I wish I could chop off them two arms, and give 'em to you, for you'd find 'em very useful when you came to fight."

Just then the stable door was darkened by the figure of Sir Godfrey, who looked in, and said sharply —

"Scarlett, my boy, I have been thinking that over. It would be wise to take Black Adder too, in case one of our steeds breaks down."

Nat's ears gave a visible twitch, and seemed to cock towards the speaker, as he continued —

"I'll leave it in your hands to settle about Nat. You can take him if you wish."

He walked away, and in an instant Nat was squatting down, and going through what is known to boys as the cobbler's hornpipe for a few moments, a triumphal terpsichorean performance, which he ended directly, and ran to the wall, ducked down head and hands, till he planted them on the stone floor, and, throwing up his heels, stood upon his head, and tapped the wall with the backs of his boots.

"Nat, come down," cried Scarlett, laughing. "Why, what does that mean?"

"Mean, sir? Why, I feel as if I could jump out o' my skin."

"Why?"

"Because I'm a-going along o' you, and to show my brother Samson as we've got some stuff in our family."

"But I didn't say that you were to go."

"No, Master Scar; but you're going to, aren't you?"

Scarlett was silent.

"Oh, Master Scar, sir, don't you run back. Do, do pray take me. Ah, I see a twinkle at the corner of your mouth. You're only teasing a fellow. I may go, sir?"

"Yes, Nat; and I'm very, very glad."

Nat startled the horses by throwing his cap to the roof of the stable, and made them tug at their halters, but it did not seem to matter to him, for he caught up a pitchfork, shouldered it, and began to march up and down, shouting rather than singing a snatch of a song he had heard somewhere in the neighbourhood, where the war fever had been catching more men than they knew—

"'So it's up with the sword that will fight for the crown,
And down with the—down with the—down with the—'

"I say, Master Scar, what comes next?"

"I don't know at all. But I'll tell you what must come next."

"Yes sir."

"Pack up and be ready for the march to-morrow, and we've got to say good-bye."

"Yes, Master Scar, and glad I'll be when it's over, for there'll be some wet eyes in the Hall, both parlour and kitchen, before we set away."

Nat was right. There were tears, many and bitter, for master and man that night; and next morning when, after tying a scarf round her son's shoulder, Lady Markham clung to him passionately, till, with a last hasty kiss to his sister, a final embrace to his mother, Scarlett set spurs to his sturdy horse, and galloped off across the park to where Nat was waiting, and there he drew rein to allow his father to come up.

Sir Godfrey rode fast till he was within about twenty yards, when he signed to them to ride on, and the trio went forward slowly till they were at the top of the slope, where they instinctively turned to take a farewell look at the old Hall and the handkerchiefs waving adieu.

"So peaceful and happy," said Scarlett to himself; and then, with a curious sensation as of a film being drawn over his eyes, he turned away, pressed his horse's sides, and when he strained round in the saddle again to look back, it was to see the tops of trees growing about his home, and the moorland spreading away to the sea. Nothing more.

"Hah! I'm glad that's over, Master Scar," said Nat, with a sigh of relief as they went gently along the lane which opened upon the high-road lying to west and east, and there crossed it and led on towards the Manor.

They were within twenty yards of the cross-roads, when Nat looked cautiously back, to see if his master was within hearing, and seeing that he was not, he chuckled and said softly—

"Master Scar, sir."

"Yes," said Scarlett, starting from a reverie full of recollections about the times he and Fred had traversed that road on very different missions to the present.

"I was just thinking, sir, that I'd give every penny I've saved up again I get married, which may happen some day, to see our Samson come shuffling up yonder lane. How he would stare, and how mad he would be, and—"

"Hush, Nat. Look!"

The ex-gardener sat up, round-eyed and as if turned into stone, while the clatter of horse's hoofs behind told that Sir Godfrey had set spurs to his horse, and was riding on to join them, which he did, drawing rein as they reached the cross-roads, an act duly imitated by the group of three horsemen coming up the lane from the opposite direction, and there at the intersection of the great main western road, the two little parties sat gazing at each other, accident having arranged that master, son, and servant from Hall and Manor should be exactly opposite to each other, gazing in each other's eyes.

For full a minute no one spoke, and then Thunder, Sir Godfrey's charger, threw up his noble head and whinnied loudly what might have been taken as a defiance.

"Now, Master Scar," whispered Nat, "isn't the master going to give the word. It's war now, and we can soon do them."

"Silence!" cried Sir Godfrey, sternly; and then, turning to Colonel Forrester, he raised his plumed Cavalier hat, the colonel responding by lifting the steel morion he wore.

Then it was as if Sir Godfrey's command had had its effect upon all present, for they gazed straight at each other, Nat and Samson with the look of a couple of angry dogs waiting to be let loose and fight; the two lads in a puzzled manner, as if ready to shake hands, and held back by some invisible chain; and their fathers with a haughty look of anger and disdain.

Sir Godfrey was the first to speak in a stern tone of voice, as he looked straight in Colonel Forrester's eyes.

"May I ask, sir," he said, "in which direction you are going?"

"No, sir," was the calm reply. "You have no right to make such a demand."

"Then I will address you in a more friendly spirit, Colonel Forrester. The road here to the east leads towards the king's followers—the gentry of the west who are gathering together beneath his banner to put an end to the disorder and anarchy now running riot through the land. You will, I presume, as a loyal gentleman, join us, and we can ride together."

"Is this banter or earnest, Sir Godfrey?" replied the colonel, as the two boys sat with their ears tingling.

"Earnest, Colonel Forrester. What other course could I expect an officer to take?"

"Then, if it be in earnest, sir—no; I ride not with you to help to bolster up a tyranny which makes every true man in England blush for his country."

"Colonel Forrester!"

"Sir Godfrey Markham!"

There was a pause, during which the two old friends gazed defiantly at each other, and then Colonel Forrester continued—

"No, sir; I ride to the west, to join those whom you call the inciters to riot, anarchy, and confusion; but whom we, as true, honest Englishmen, think of as those who are fighting to free our land and to rescue it from the degradation to which it has been brought. Let me entreat you, sir, as a gentleman, to think twice before you take the road to the east, for the way is open still to the west. Ride with us, Sir Godfrey. So old and gallant a soldier would be most welcome to our ranks."

"And a traitor to the king, whose commission I hold, and whose uniform I shall once again wear."

"Traitor!" said Colonel Forrester, starting, and his hand darted to the hilt of his sword; but he drew it back with a hasty "Pish!"

"Yes, sir, traitor, as you seem disposed to prove; but I warn you in time. The king will prove the master over the wretched band of anarchists who have risen against him."

"Enough!" said Colonel Forrester. "That has to be proved."

"Proved or no, sir, I command you to ride with me or to return to your home. You are in arms against the king, the government, and the law of this land. Surrender!"

"Sir Godfrey, too much commanding of slaves to your wishes has rendered you absurd of speech."

"Do you hear me, sir?" cried Sir Godfrey. "I order you to follow me."

Colonel Forrester's hand went again to his sword, but he snatched it back.

"I cannot answer your intemperate words, Sir Godfrey," he said; "and I will not presume to utter so vain a command to you. This is free England, sir, where every man who dares to think, thinks according to his belief. We have been old friends; our boys have grown up together as brothers, but the exigencies of our political faith sunder us widely apart. Ride you your way, sir, and I pray you let me go mine; and may our ways be farther and farther separated, so that we may never meet again till it is in peace."

As he spoke, he turned his horse, and rode slowly away down the western road, leaving Sir Godfrey chafing angrily, and fidgeting with the hilt of his sword, as he sat gazing after his old friend calmly ignoring his presence, and followed by his son and his serving-man.

"I ought to arrest him—a man openly in arms against the law; an enemy to his majesty, who may work him terrible ill. But I cannot do it; I cannot do it. Old friends—brothers; our wives who have been as sisters."

He paused for a few moments, gazing after the retiring figures, and then jerked his horse round so sharply that the poor beast reared.

"Left! Forward!" cried Sir Godfrey then, and he rode on to the east, followed at a short distance by Nat and his son.

Before they had gone a dozen yards, Nat, who was fidgeting about in his saddle, evidently in a state of considerable mental perturbation, wrenched himself round and looked after the Manor people, to see that Samson was waiting for him to do so; and as soon as he did look, it was to see a derisive threatening gesture, Samson, by pantomime, suggesting that if he only had his brother's head under his arm, he would punch his nose till he made it bleed.

"Ur–r–r–r!" snarled Nat, with a growl like that of an irritated dog.

"What's the matter, Nat?"

"Matter, sir? See that Samson—ah, he's a rank bad 'un—shaking his fist at me, and pretending to punch me? Here, I must go and give it him now."

"No, no," cried Scar, catching at Black Adder's rein. "Your orders are to follow your colonel."

"But are we to let that brother of mine insult his majesty's troops?"

"We can afford to treat it with contempt," said Scarlett, solemnly, though Nat's words and allusions made him feel disposed to laugh.

"But I want to treat it to a big leathering, Master Scar. Here, sir, mayn't I ride after him and fetch him off his horse?"

"No; certainly not."

"But, Master Scar, what could your father be thinking of? Here had we got three of the ugliest Philistines in Coombeland in our hand, and we've let 'em go to blight and freeze and blast everything. What could Sir Godfrey be thinking about?"

"Nat."

"Yes, sir."

"Do you know what is a soldier's first duty?"

"To fight, sir."

"No: to obey orders."

"But we aren't soldiers yet."

"I think we are; so be silent."

"Yes, sir; but if I only had leave, I'd draw my sword, gallop after that bad brother of mine, and fetch him off his horse, or jackass, or whatever the miserable beast is that he has his legs across."

"And kill him? Your own brother?"

"Kill him? Not I, sir. He arn't worth it. No; I'd take him prisoner, nearly knock his head off, and then I'd tie his hands to the tail of my horse, and drag him to the king's camp in triumph."

Scarlett made no answer, for he had no faith in his servant's threats; and together they rode on and on after Sir Godfrey, over the pleasant moor, and on to the cultivated lands, and then on and on still into the darkness, which seemed, as it thickened, like the gross darkness of war and destruction, sweeping down upon the fair and sunny west.

So thought Scarlett Markham, as he still rode on through the darkness, and then his thoughts returned to home, and his mother's attitude as she flung herself upon her knees, her clasped hands toward heaven, as she uttered a prayer for the protection of those she loved.

Sir Godfrey made no sign. He merely turned from time to time to see if those he led were close behind, and then rode slowly on to join those whose hands were raised against their brothers—father and sons to plunge into the terrible warfare, which, once begun, seemed to know no end.

Chapter Fourteen
Warlike Experiences

A year rapidly passed away, during which, young and slight as they were, Scarlett Markham and Fred Forrester seemed to have changed into boyish young men. The excitement of a soldier's life had forced them on, and with great rapidity they had mastered the various matters of discipline then known to the army. Sir Godfrey and Colonel Forrester were received by the opposing factions with delight, their old military knowledge making them invaluable, and they were at once placed in command of regiments of horse, newly raised, and whose training caused them immense effort.

But the men were of splendid material, and before long Forrester's and Markham's Horse were looked upon with respect; soon after with envy.

In these two regiments the boys from Coombeland served six months as ordinary soldiers, till, partly for their ability, partly from the dash they had shown, they were nominally raised to the rank of officers, the men of their troops willingly following the lead of the brave boys who rode with them into dangers many enough.

For, in those stern times, no father could spare his son. Those who elected to serve had to run all risks, and the consequence was that on either side the making of a good fighting army took but little time.

"It do me good to see you, Master Scar," Nat used to say, as he rode always at his young master's heels. "Think of a boy like you being an orficer!"

"A very poor one, Nat."

"Nay, Master Scar, I don't know another in the regiment the men would sooner follow."

Equality of situation brings similarity of remark, and it was in like words that Samson, after a tirade about his unnatural brother for fighting against him, would address his young master from the Manor.

And so another six months passed away, with the war-tide setting here and there on the borders of Coombeland, but never spreading its devastating influence there. The two lads grew more and more imbued with the war-faith of their parties, and as they became sturdier and more manly, hardened as they were by the rough, open air life they led, a feeling of bitterness foreign to their natures rapidly increased, till they were ready to speak with hate and contempt of the enemy they blamed for destroying the peace of the land.

And all this time, to Fred and Scar, home was becoming rapidly a memory. By the merest chances, they heard that all was well, and, compelled to be content with this scanty news, they plunged into their work again, till the roar of cannon and clash of steel became familiar as were the terrors of the scene of some desperate fight, such as modern soldiers would speak of as a desultory skirmish.

Eighteen months with the army, and, in spite of exposure, neither of the Coombeland lads had met, or, as far as they knew, been near each other, and neither of the two little parties from Hall and Manor had met with a wound.

But sterner times were near at hand. After much desultory fighting, the Parliamentary forces were mustering strongly in the far west, and those of the king had made Bristol a stronghold, and were moving on.

There were two leaders of opposing ideas, who prayed that the war might not sweep their way, but, as they prayed, they felt that the prayer was vain, and their brows grew rugged as they read how surely what they dreaded must follow, and felt how likely a battle-ground the moor would prove in the neighbourhood of their peaceful homes.

The little petty encounters kept on day after day, week after week, as if each side was practising its men and trying their strength for some great fight to come, and all the while, round and about Barnstaple and away toward Exeter, the forces were gathering, till all at once, when least expected, scouts came in from east and west with news that told of a probable encounter, perhaps before another sun had set.

Those who knew best, however, were not so sanguine till after that sun had set, and among those was General Hedley, who gradually and cautiously advanced, feeling his way step by step, each step being a natural stronghold, which would help him against the dashing onslaughts of Charles's cavaliers.

But forty-eight hours had not elapsed before the rival forces were face to face, when a little skirmishing took place, and then darkness put an end to the varied encounters, the combatants waiting for daylight, when a battle was bound to ensue. This fight must inevitably prove serious to one or the other side, and either the Parliamentarian forces would be driven back into the far west, where their scattered strength could be quenched as the remains of a fire are beaten out, or else the king's men would be driven towards Exeter, after what must prove a deadly blow.

That night the occupants of Hall and Manor lay down to sleep within hearing of the sentinels of each army, and the two lads, worn out with fatigue, slept heavily, to dream of the homes they were so near—dreams full of trouble and anxiety, as they seemed to see the sweet faces of those they loved anxiously listening to the roar of gun and clash of sword, and wondering what was to be their fate and where they could flee if matters came to the worst.

A trumpet roused Scarlett Markham from his dream of home. The deep roll of drums awakened Fred, and as daylight came, and the larks sprang from the dewy moor to carol high in the soft, grey, gold flecked sky, there was the trampling of men and the snorting of horses, and then the first gun belched forth its destroying message against the advancing forces of the king.

Needless to tell of that fight of brother against brother with the horrors of the field. Hour after hour went by, hours of manoeuvring and change of front, and always with the king's men gaining ground, and driving back the Parliamentarians, whose position seemed to be growing desperate. And as the Royalist leaders saw their advantage, they grew more reckless, and urged their men on, till it seemed as if a dozen lesser fights were in progress, the grim men of the Commonwealth fighting hard to hold their own.

This went on till the afternoon, when, in their exhaustion, the king's men paused almost with wonder at the stubborn front still presented to their steel.

"It is their last despairing stand," said the Royalist general to himself, and he gathered his men for a final advance upon the low hill crowned by the enemy.

The advance was made by men wearied out, against those who had not done half the marching and counter-marching, and as they swept on, they saw the change in the front for which they had looked so long—at first with triumph, then with despair. For now General Hedley sent forward his grim squadrons, held so long in reserve, and, raging with their long inaction, they dashed down the slope like a thunderbolt which met the Cavaliers half-way, broke through them, rode them down, and before the two parts into which they were divided could recover in the slightest degree, from the right and left flanks fresh squadrons broke down upon them, and in five minutes the imaginary triumph had become a rout.

The king's banner that day lay low, the royal standard trailing in the dust, as a wild shout of victory was raised by the soldiers of the Parliament, and the gaily caparisoned Cavaliers in bitter despair fled broken and in disorder for their lives.

"Oh, evil fortune!" groaned Sir Godfrey, as he reluctantly galloped away beside his son, their jaded horses going heavily, with heaving flanks. "Quick, my boy, quick!"

"Oh, father," cried Scarlett, "and we are galloping away from home."

Chapter Fifteen
Fred Forrester's Prisoner

Wild nearly with excitement, Fred Forrester kept his place in the ranks of his father's regiment all through that busy day of advance, retreat, and skirmish; but the Forresters were held in reserve during the final charge which resulted in the scattering of the king's forces before the warriors of the Parliament.

The day was won, and pursuit was going on in all directions; but the main body of the Parliamentarians were camping for the night, and tents were being set up, the wounded brought in, and strong parties engaged in burying the dead, while, as troop after troop returned with batches of prisoners, these were placed under guard, after being carefully disarmed.

The Forresters had dismounted at the edge of a beautiful, grove-like patch of timber at the foot of a hill. A stream of pure water babbled among the rocks, and, as the soft summer evening came slowly on, the grim, warlike aspect of the scene seemed to die out, and the smoke of the camp-fires, the pennons fluttering in the evening breeze, and the glinting of breastplate and morion formed a picture against the background of green, which might from a distance have been taken for one of peace.

Fred had dismounted, and, after taking off his heavy morion, which he would never own was too big and uncomfortable to a degree, hung it from the pommel of his saddle, while he patted and made much of his horse, unbuckling the bit, and leading the handsome beast to where it could make a meal from the soft, green grass.

"Poor old lad!" he said; "you must be nearly tired out."

The horse whinnied, and began feeding at once, while, after watching the men making their preparations for the bivouac, Fred was about to throw himself down, being too weary after his many hours in the saddle to care for food, when his father rode up, followed by a couple of the officers.

"Ah, Fred, my boy," he cried; "that's right: take care of your horse. There will be some supper ready in about half an hour. A glorious day, my boy, a glorious day; and I'm proud of the way you behaved!"

"Are you, father," said Fred, sadly. "I don't think I have done much."

"You have done all I could wish to see you do. But, there, I must go and see after our men. Come up to my quarters soon, and eat, and then lie down and sleep. I may want you before long."

"To go on guard, sir?"

"No; for any little duty—to take charge of prisoners, perhaps. Where is Samson?"

"Gone, father."

"What? Not killed?"

"I hope not, father; but after that gallop, when we last changed front, I missed him, and, though we have searched, we can't find him. I'm afraid the enemy carried him off."

"Poor lad! A brave fellow, Fred. There, I must go."

"Shall I come with you now, father?"

"No; lie down and rest till the meal is ready."

Colonel Forrester rode off with his followers, and his son walked wearily to where his horse was feeding, and led it where it could have a hearty drink of the pure water. Then, having turned it loose again, he threw himself down, and lay gazing at the sunlit scene, wishing that the war was over, and that he could go back to the dear old manor house, and enjoy the pleasures of home and peace.

How beautiful it all looked, the golden sunshine glorifying the oak-trees with their tender leaves, and turning the pine trunks bronze-red! The films of wood smoke from the camp-fires spread in a pale blue vapour, and the babbling stream flashed. But, restful as the scene was, and pleasant as the reclining posture was to his aching bones, Fred did not feel happy, for he knew that not far away men were lying in fever and weariness, cut, stabbed, trampled by horse hoof, and shattered by bullet, many of them waiting anxiously for death, the same death that had come upon so many of their fellows, who were lying stark on the field, or being hastily laid in rows in their shallow grave.

"When will it all be over?" he said to himself. "I wonder where Scar is;" and then he thought how horrible it would be if ever he were to meet his old friend in action.

"And him with a sword in his hand and me with a sword in mine," he muttered. "Should we fight? I suppose so," he added, after a few moments' thought. "We are enemies now."

He started up on his elbow, for just then there was a cheer, in salutation of a man who was coming slowly up, leading his horse; and it only needed a second glance to show that it was Samson.

Fred forgot his weariness, sprang up, and ran toward his follower, who caught sight of him directly, and hastened to meet him.

"Oh!" ejaculated Fred, as he drew nearer and caught sight of the man's face. "What a horrible wound! Samson, lad, we thought you a prisoner, or dead."

"I arn't a prisoner, because I'm here," grumbled Samson; "and I arn't dead yet, thank ye, Master Fred."

"But your wound. Come on to the surgeon at once."

"My wound, sir?"

"Yes. Your face looks terrible. How did you manage to get here?"

"Face looks terrible—manage to get here! I'll tell you, sir. A big fellow with a broad grey hat and feathers, and all long hair and ragged lace, spurred at me, and, if I hadn't been tidy sharpish, he'd have rode me down. Hit at me, too, he did, with his sword, and caught me on the shoulder, but it didn't cut through the leather; and, 'fore he could get another cut at me, I give him a wipe on the head as made him rise up in his sterrups and hit at me with his fist."

"His fist, Samson?"

"Yes, sir. There was his sword in it, of course, and the pommel hit me right on the nose; and before I could get over it, he was off along with the rest, full gallop, and I was sitting on the ground, thinking about my mother and what a mess I was in, and my horse looking as if he was ashamed of me, as I was of myself. I wonder he didn't gallop off, too; but I s'pose he thought he wouldn't get a better master."

"But your face, Samson? It looks horrid."

"Well, I can't help that, Master Fred, can I? Didn't make my own face. Good enough to come and fight with."

"Come along with me to the surgeon."

"What, and leave my horse? Not I, sir."

"A man's wounds are of more consequence than a horse."

"Who says so? I think a mortal deal more o' my horse than I do o' my wounds. 'Sides I arn't got no wounds."

"You have, and don't know it. You have quite a mask of blood on your face. It is hideous."

"Yah! that's nothing. It's my nose. It always was a one to bleed. Whenever that brother o' mine, who went to grief and soldiering, used to make me smell his fist, my nose always bled, and his fist was quite as hard as that hard-riding R'y'list chap's. Called me a Roundhead dog, too, he did, as he hit me. If I'd caught him, I'd ha' rounded his head for him."

"Yes, yes, of course, Samson; but come down to the stream, and bathe your face. Your horse is grazing now."

"You're getting too vain and partic'lar, Master Fred," grumbled Samson. "You're thinking of looking nice, like the R'y'lists, when you ought to be proud of a little blood shed in the good cause."

"I am proud and ready too, Samson; but come and wash your face."

"I'll come," grumbled Samson; "and I never kears about washing myself now. Never a drop o' hot water, no towels, no soap, and no well, and no buckets. Once a week seems quite enough, specially as you has to wait till you get dry."

By a little persuasion, Samson was led to the stream, where he knelt down and bathed his face, looking up to his master from time to time to ask if that was better, the final result being that, beyond a little swelling on one side, Samson's nose was none the worse for the encounter.

"There!" he cried at last; "I suppose that will do, sir."

"Yes, my lad, and I'm very, very glad you have escaped so well."

"Oh, I've 'scaped well enough, Master Fred; deal better than I deserved. We're a wicked, bad, good-for-nothing family. Look at our Nat, fighting against his own brother."

"It is very sad, Samson," said Fred; "but, remember, you are fighting against him."

"That I arn't, sir. It's him fighting against me, and I only wish I may run against him some day. I'd make him so sore that he'll lie down and howl for his mother, poor soul, and she breaking her heart about him turning out so badly; and, I say, Master Fred, if I don't have something to eat, I shall be only fit to bury to-morrow."

"Come with me, Samson; I'm going up to my father's quarters. I'll see that you have plenty to eat, if there is anything."

"Who'd be without a good master?" muttered Samson; and then aloud, "Here he comes."

For Colonel Forrester came cantering up.

"Alive and well, Samson? Good lad! We couldn't spare you. Fred, my boy, news has come in that a little party of the enemy has taken shelter in the woodland yonder over the hill. Take a dozen men, surround them, and bring them in. Don't let one of them escape. Turned back by one of the regiments crossing their path as they were in retreat. Now, then, to horse and away!"

Burning with excitement, Fred forgot all his weariness, buckled his horse's bit, mounted, and turned to select his men, when he found Samson already mounted, and at his elbow.

"Here, what do you want, sir?" he cried.

"What do I want, Master Fred? Why, to go with you."

"Nonsense! You are fagged out. Go and rest, and your horse too."

"Now, I do call that likely, Master Fred. Let you go without me. I should just think not."

"But this is nonsense, Samson. I want fresh men."

"Just what I thought, sir. Nonsense for you to go without me, and you don't want no fresh men. You want me, and I'm coming—there!"

Fred had neither time nor inclination to combat his follower's desire; in fact, he was rather glad to have the sturdy, west-country man at his elbow, so he rode up to the main portion of the regiment, selected eleven out of a hundred who wanted to go with the young officer, and rode off at a moderate trot across country, forded the stream, and then, bearing away from the woodland, made as if to leave it on his right, so as not to excite suspicion in case they were seen. But just as he was well opposite, he gave an order, the men divided in two parties, and set off at a gallop to surround the trees, the mounted men halting at about a hundred yards apart, and waiting for the signal to advance.

The manoeuvre was soon executed, and the circle moved steadily toward the centre of the park-like patch of ground, so open that as the ring grew smaller there was not the slightest prospect of any of the enemy breaking through unseen.

Fred, in his anxiety to carry out his father's commands successfully, had remained at the foot of the wooded slope, Samson being on his right and another trustworthy fellow on his left, for he felt sure that those of whom they were in search would break out in his direction. In fact, he sat there waiting for his men to drive the intended prisoners down for him to take.

The task was not long, for the tramping of horses was heard, and the rustling and crackling of the undergrowth; but the enemy did not break cover.

At last, though, there was a rush and the clash of steel, and, with his heart throbbing, the lad signed to his nearest men to close up, and they advanced together, then set spur to their horses, and made a dash for a clump of bushes, where three horsemen were striving to get out through the tangle; and as they reached them Fred uttered an exclamation full of anger.

"Look at that!" cried Samson. "Why, they're our own men."

Fred uttered an impatient cry.

"Couldn't you see them?" he said to the first man who struggled out of the bushes.

"No, sir; nobody there."

"Then you must have missed them, and they are there now."

"We searched the place well," said another man; and one by one, as the party closed up, they told the same tale.

"Father was deceived," thought Fred; and the more readily, that it was not the first example by many of pieces of false news brought in by spies.

"Here!" he cried aloud, "we'll all ride through again. Ah! look yonder. Forward! Gallop!" he shouted; and, setting spurs to his horse, he dashed off, followed by his men, for there, a quarter of a mile to the left, was a little party of six horsemen stealing along a narrow coombe, after evading their pursuers in some way.

They were well in view as Fred emerged from the wooded land, and were evidently spurring hard to escape, and for the next quarter of an hour the chances seemed even, for the distance was maintained, and each party kept well together; but after that the pace began to tell, and horse and man tailed off till both parties seemed to be straggling over the ground, the better-mounted to the front, the worse hanging behind.

It was soon evident that the pursuers' horses were far fresher than those of the Royalists; and after shouting to his men to come on, Fred raced forward, with Samson close behind, and after a headlong gallop of about ten minutes, the young leader had overtaken the hindmost horseman, who was standing in his stirrups, his morion close down over his eyes, his back up, and apparently blind to everything that was before him as well as behind.

"Have him, Samson, lad," cried Fred, as he spurred on past this fugitive to try and overtake the leader, a young-looking man in showy cavalier hat and feathers, who kept on turning in his saddle and encouraging his men to fresh exertions.

The next minute, as they thundered along, Samson rode straight at the man with the morion over his eyes, but before he could reach him the fugitive's horse made a poor attempt to clear a bush in his way, stumbled, fell headlong, and shot his rider half a dozen yards in front.

"Prisoners; and don't hurt them," shouted Fred, waving his sword, and his men gave an answering yell. So did the pursued, for no sooner did the young leader discover that one of his men was down than he checked his horse, held up his sword for the others to rally round him, and turned at once on the party headed by Fred.

It was a gallant attempt, but useless. Their horses were spent, and as they were checked before they could make any effective stand, Fred's party literally sprung at them. There was a sharp shock; the exchange of a few blows, and it was all over, the little party being literally ridden down, their leader going over, horse and all, at Fred's charge.

The young Cavalier struggled free from his fallen horse, and tried to drag a pistol from the holster at his saddle-bow, for his sword had flown a dozen yards away among the bushes; but Fred had him by the neck directly, his hand well inside the steel gorget he wore, and in one breath he shouted, as he held his sword at his breast, "Surrender!" and then, "Scar Markham! You!"

"Yes. Give up, my lads," cried the prisoner. "We've done all we could. Let the crop-ears have a few prisoners for once in a way."

Chapter Sixteen
Teasing a Prisoner

Fred Forrester was too much astonished at the result of his pursuit to make any sharp retort, but sat holding his prisoner by the gorget, staring wildly at his old playmate, who seemed wonderfully changed since their last meeting, and who had looked, in spite of dust and sweat, tall and handsome in his gay frippery, scarf, scarlet feather, and long curling hair.

"Well, rebel," cried the prisoner; and Fred started from his reverie. "Am I the first you ever had the luck to take that you stare in that way? Don't choke me."

Fred's tanned cheeks grew crimson, and his brow was knit as he turned away his face to look after his men, who in the meantime had taken the whole of the little party, dismounted those who needed it, bound their arms behind; their back, and collected the horses.

"Look ye here, sir," cried Samson, dragging forward the man in the morion, who came behind limping, "I've got him at last. This is my wretch of a brother, who has taken up arms against me."

"Against you—you ill-looking dog!" cried Scarlett, fiercely. "How dare you! Crop-eared rebel!"

"That will do, sir," said Fred, sternly; for, after being a little overawed by the gallant aspect of his prisoner, he was recovering himself, and recollecting his position. "Will you give your promise not to escape, or must I have you bound?"

"Promise to a set of knaves like you?" cried the youth, fiercely. "No. Do what you will; only, mind this—our time will come."

"Yes; and when it does," cried Nat, shaking his head to get rid of the iron cap which was over his eyes, for his hands were bound, "we'll show them what it is to be rebels, eh, Master Scarlett—captain, I mean?"

"Silence, sir!" cried Fred, angrily; and, after giving the men orders, the little party returned with their prisoners in their midst, Scarlett behind, gazing haughtily before him, and paying no heed to a few words addressed to him at first by his captor, who reined back at the slight, and followed afterwards at the rear of his little troop, angry and indignant at Scarlett's contemptuous manner, and at the same time sorry and glad, the latter feeling perhaps predominating, for he had successfully carried out his father's commands.

"I wish it had been some one else," he was thinking, as the little party rode on, the prisoners mounted on their horses, but looking in sorry plight with their hands bound behind. "What will my father say when he sees who it is?"

At that moment the sound of angry voices and a hoarse laugh from the troopers made Fred urge his horse forward.

"What is this?" he said. "I will not have the prisoners insulted."

"It's the prisoners insulting us, Master Fred—I mean captain. It's this ne'er-do-well of a brother o' mine bragging and bouncing because his hair's grown a bit longer than mine. He keeps calling me crop-ears, sir, and showing off as if he was a Cavalier."

"So you are a crop-ear and a rebel," said Nat, for his fall had hurt him, and made him disagreeable.

"Silence, sir!" cried Fred, as he made a gesture as if to strike the ex-gardener a blow with the flat of his sword.

"Shan't silence," said Nat. "You're not my master. Rebels can't be masters, and you daren't hit me now I'm tied up, much as you'd like to. Cowards, all of you!"

"Beg pardon, captain," said Samson, "but may I untie his arms, sir, and have him down under the trees with our buffs off? I could give him such a leathering in five minutes."

"Silence! Forward! Samson, rein back;" and they rode slowly on till the outskirts of the camping place were reached, sentries challenging and men cheering the little party as they came in with their captives right to where the regiment lounged about the camp-fires.

Here Colonel Forrester strode out from his tent, followed by half a dozen officers, all ready to cheer the boy who had so successfully carried out the reconnaissance.

"Any one hurt?" asked the colonel, looking very cold and stern, and hardly glancing at his son.

"Only a few scratches and bruises, sir. We took the whole party."

"That's well. Which is the leader? Here, you!"

Scarlett paid no heed to the command, but a couple of the troopers seized his arms, and hurried him before the colonel.

"Which way has the main body of your forces gone, sir?"

"You had better follow and find out for yourself, Colonel Forrester," said the prisoner, coldly. "You will get no information from me."

"Scar Markham!" exclaimed the colonel, in astonishment. "My poor boy, I am sorry that we should meet like this."

"And I am glad, sir," cried Scarlett, excitedly, "for it gives me an opportunity to say that I, too, am sorry to see you like this, a rebel and traitor to your king."

"Silence, sir! How dare you! Take the prisoners away, and see that they are well used."

"Yes, father," replied Fred; and he saw the five men disposed of, and then led Scarlett to his own little tent which he had placed at his disposal, and saw that he had an ample supply of food.

He then took his own, of which he was in sore need, and began to eat in silence, furtively watching the prisoner, who remained silent, and refused the food, though he was famishing.

Fred's anger had subsided now, and remembering the old days before these times of civil war and dissension, he said quietly —

"I am sorry I have nothing better to offer you."

Scarlett turned upon him sharply, with a flash of the eye, as if about to speak; but he turned away again, and sat looking straight before him.

There was a long silence then, during which Fred thought how hard it was for his old friend to be dragged there a prisoner, and he said softly —

"I was only doing my duty, Scar. I was sent out to take the party seen from our outposts."

"Have the goodness to keep your pity for those who need it, crop-ear," said Scarlett, scornfully; "and recollect that I am, though a prisoner, one of his Majesty's officers, one who holds no converse with rebels."

Fred's cheeks flushed again, and his brow wrinkled.

"Very well," he said angrily. "We are fighting on opposite sides, but I did not know that we need insult each other when we met."

As he spoke he left the tent, and Scarlett winced, and his eyes softened.

"Poor old Fred!" he said below his breath; "and I used to think he was like a brother."

It was a glorious evening as Fred Forrester strolled away from the tent, stopping to speak to one of the sentries about the prisoner in the little tent, though he felt that he need hardly take any precaution, for Scarlett was not likely to try to escape and leave his men behind.

"Wonder whether we shall ever be friends again," he thought, "and be back at the old places as before. This terrible fighting cannot always go on. What's that?"

A great deal of shouting and laughter in the centre of a little crowd of soldiers took his attention, and one of the voices sounding familiar, he walked slowly toward the group, hardly caring in which direction he went so that it was away from his tent.

"What are they doing?" he asked of one of the men.

"Don't quite know, sir. Teasing one of the prisoners, I think."

Feeling that his father would be angry if the prisoners were annoyed in any way, he walked sharply to the throng, and, as he reached it, he heard a familiar voice say—

"Now, that's what I call behaving like a brother should, gentlemen. He goes away into bad company and disgraces his name, lets his hair grow ragged and greasy and long, and comes here a prisoner with a nasty dirty face, so what have I done? I give him my supper because he was hungry, and he ate it all, and called me a crop-eared rebel for my pains. So after that I washed his face for him and cut his hair, and made him look decent, but I didn't crop his ears, though the shears went very near them two or three times. But look at him now."

There was a roar of laughter at this, and Fred could hardly keep from joining in, so comical was the aspect of Sir Godfrey Markham's old servant, as he stood there with his hands bound behind him.

For, as Samson said, his brother was now quite clean, and he had cut his hair, which had grown long, in a bad imitation of a Cavalier's. But this was not merely cut off now, but closely cropped, so that Nat's head was round and close as a great ball.

"All right, Sam," he said, as his brother came close to him. "Wait a bit till our side wins, and then perhaps I may take you prisoner, and if so—"

"Well, if you do—what then?"

"Wait, my lad, and see."

Fred Forrester could never after fully explain his feelings. He left the group feeling as if some spirit of mischief had taken possession of him, and kept suggesting that he too had fed his brother, had given up everything to him, and been reviled for his pains. Why should not he show Scarlett Markham that courtesy was due to those who had made him prisoner of war? As it was, his old companion seemed to have grown arrogant and overbearing. He had spoken to him as if he were a dog, and looked at him as if he were one of the most contemptible objects under the sun.

"No," he said, with a half-laugh, "I could not do it."

Then he recalled a long list of injuries he had received from Scarlett, things which had made his blood boil, and he felt tempted again.

But his better self prevailed the next minute, and, shaking his head, he returned to his tent, to find that after all Scarlett had partaken of the food, and had now thrown himself down on Fred's cloak and gone to sleep.

As he lay there in the dim light, Fred gazed at his old companion's handsome young face, flowing curls, and soiled but still handsome uniform, with something like envy. But this passed away; and soon after he lay down outside the tent, to fall into a fit of musing, which was mingled with the pace of sentries, hoarse orders, and the blare of trumpets. Then all was silent, and he fell fast asleep, out there on the bare ground, only to awaken at the morning calls.

Chapter Seventeen
A Lesson in Self-Control

"You will take twelve men as escort, and guard those prisoners to Newton Abbott; there you will give them up, and return as quickly as you can to me."

"Yes, sir. The men need not be bound?"

"Yes; every one."

"Scar Markham, father?"

"Yes; you must run no risks. You might meet a party of the enemy, and if your prisoners fought against you, what then? Let them be bound while on the road. They will have comparative freedom when you have given them up."

The stern school of war in which Fred Forrester was taking his early lessons of discipline and obedience had already taught him to hear and to obey.

This was after a halt of three days in their temporary camp, during which the careful general of the little army had thought it better to rest and recruit his men than to weary them in a vain pursuit at a time when they were pretty well exhausted with previous work.

Fred had seen a great deal of the prisoners during the time, but only for the estrangement between him and his old companion to grow greater. For Scarlett was suffering bitterly from the reverses which had befallen his party, and was in agony about his father's fate. He had tried to obtain some news of the division to which they had been attached, but all he could learn was that in the late engagement it had been cut to pieces, and its components who remained had fled in all directions, while he could not discover whether his father had been among the many slain.

Stung by his sufferings, and irritable to a degree, he was in no mood to meet Fred's advances, looking upon him, as he did, as one of his father's murderers, and when he did not give him a fierce look of resentment, he turned his back upon him, and treated him with the greatest scorn and contempt.

Their relations under these circumstances did not promise well, then, for their journey to Newton Abbott, and matters seemed to culminate for ill when the escort was ready, the prisoners' horses brought out, and Fred announced that the time of departure had come. Scarlett rose from where he had been lying upon his cloak in silence; but the sight of his old companion seemed to rouse him to speak; and in a bitterly contemptuous way he turned to his men, saying to Nat—

"They might have sent a man to take charge of us, my lads."

Fred winced, and felt small in his military uniform. He bit his lip, and told himself that he would not notice the petty remark, but the words leaped out—

"I dare say I shall be man enough to take you safely to your prison, sir;" but Scarlett turned angrily away.

The prisoners took their cue from their leader, and behaved in an exaggerated, swaggering manner, that was galling in the extreme.

"Seem to have starved our horses," said Nat, to one of his fellows; and, less fall of control than his leader, Samson spoke out.

"No, we haven't, for we've given the poor things a good fill out, such as they hadn't had for a month; and my word, Nat, you look quite respectable without those long greasy corkscrews hanging about your ears." Nat turned upon him fiercely. "Do I?" he cried. "Wait till our turn comes, and I'll crop you."

"Don't want it," cried Samson, gleeful at his brother's rage.

"Your hair don't, but your ears do, so look out."

"Silence!" cried Fred, sternly; and then he gave the order for all to mount.

As he was obeyed, and Scarlett swung himself into the saddle, his nostrils dilated, and as he felt the sturdy horse between his knees, he involuntarily glanced round at the surrounding country.

Fred saw it, and smiled. "No, sir, not this time," he said. "I think you will be too well guarded for that."

Scarlett showed that he was well dubbed; for his pale cheeks flushed the colour of his name as he turned away, feeling hot that his action should have been plain enough for his enemy to read his thoughts.

Then he set his teeth fast, and they grated together, as he heard Fred's next orders, and saw a couple of men close up on either side of the prisoners, thrust a stake beneath their arms and across their backs, to which stake their arms were firmly bound, and the ends of the cords which formed their bonds made fast to their horses' necks.

"No fear o' you cantering off, Master Nat," said Samson, as, with keen appreciation of his masterful position, he tied his brother as tightly as he could, while Nat resisted and struggled so that he had to be held by Samson's companion, his steel headpiece falling off in the encounter. "That's got him, I think," said Samson, tightening the last knot which held him to the horse. "Dropped your cap, have you? All right, you shall have it. There!"

A burst of laughter followed Samson's act of politeness, for he had stuck on the steel jockey-like cap with its peak towards the back, and the curve, which was meant to protect the back of the head, well down over his eyes.

"Only wait," grumbled Nat; "I'll save all this up for you."

"Thank ye, Nat. I say, you haven't got a feather in your cap. Anybody got a feather? No. I've a good mind to cut off his horse's tail for a plume; the root of the tail would just stick upon that spike. Hallo, what's the matter there?"

Nat turned sharply from his brother to where Scarlett was hotly protesting.

"It is a mistake," he said, angrily, to the two men who had approached him on either side with stake and cord. "I am an officer and a gentleman, and refuse to be bound."

"It's the captain's orders, sir," said one of the men, surlily.

"Then go and tell him that you have mistaken his orders," cried Scarlett, ignoring the fact that Fred was seated within half a dozen yards.

The men turned to their officer, who pressed his horse's sides and closed up.

"What is the matter?" he said. "Of what do you complain, Master Markham?"

"Tell your officer I am Captain Markham, of Prince Rupert's cavalry," said Scarlett, haughtily.

"I beg your pardon, captain," said Fred, coldly. "Now, then, of what do you complain?"

"Of your scoundrelly rabble, sir," cried Scarlett, turning upon him fiercely. "You see, they are about to treat me as if I were a dog."

"They were going to bind you, sir, as your men are bound. In our army, the officers are not above suffering and sharing with their men."

Scarlett winced at this, and flushed more deeply, but he tried to turn it off by a fierce attack.

"Then this is some cowardly plot of yours to insult one who has fallen into your hands."

"I am obeying the orders of my superior officer, who placed you and the other prisoners in my charge, with instructions that they were to be conveyed bound to their destination."

"The men, not their officer, sir."

"Ah," replied Fred, coldly. And then, laconically, "Bind him."

"You insolent dog!" cried Scarlett, in his rage. "It is your malignant spite. You shall not bind me, if I die for it."

As he spoke, he struck his spurs into his horse's flanks, snatched the stout ash stall one of the men held from his hand, leaned forward, and then, as Fred seized his horse's bridle to stop him from galloping off, struck his captor with all his might.

The blow was intended for Fred's head, but the movement of the horses in the *mêlée* caused the staff to fall heavily across the young officer's thigh.

Unable to restrain a cry of rage and pain, Fred snatched his sword three-parts from its sheath, and then thrust it back, angry with himself for his loss of temper, while Scarlett sat struggling vainly, for the man who held the rope had skilfully used it just as a child would a skipping rope, throwing it over the prisoner's arms, crossing his hands, and passing one end to a soldier on the other side. In an instant, Scarlett's elbows were bound tightly to his ribs, and there held, while a couple more men thrust a fresh staff behind his back and under his arms, another rope was used, and with the rapidity which comes of practice upon hundreds of previous prisoners, the passionate young officer was literally bound and trussed, the ends of rope being made fast to the horse he rode.

The men who were looking on, murmured angrily at the blow which they saw fall on their young officer.

"Hang him to the nearest tree," shouted one of the party.

"Silence!" cried Fred, sternly; and speaking quite calmly now, though he was quivering with pain, he pressed his horse closely to that upon which his prisoner rode.

"That was a cowardly blow, Scar Markham," he said, in a whisper. "I was only doing my duty. You'll ask my pardon yet."

"Pardon?" raged the lad; "never! Oh, if I only were free and had my sword, I'd make you beg mine for this indignity. Miserable wretch! Rebel! I shall live yet to see you and your traitor of a father hung."

Fred started angrily at this, but he checked himself, reined back his horse, and looking very white now from anger and pain, he gave the word of command. Six of his men formed up in front of the prisoners, the other six took their places behind; swords were drawn, and the horses bearing the prisoners needed no guiding, but in accordance with their training as cavalry mounts, set off in rank as the word "March!" was given, the young leader waiting till all had passed, and then taking his place beside the last two men, one of whom was Samson.

Chapter Eighteen
A Cowardly Revenge

No word was spoken as they crossed the fields that separated them from the road, which they reached by the leading men turning their horses into the rapid stream, and letting them wade for a few yards through the flashing water knee-deep, and sending the drops foaming and sparkling in the bright morning sun.

"Left," shouted Fred, as the road was reached, and the next minute the little detachment was trampling up the dust which rose behind them.

"Did it hurt you much, Master Fred?" whispered Samson.

"Hurt me? I felt as if my leg was cut off; and it is just now as if the bone was broken."

"Perhaps you'd better not go, sir."

"Not go? I'd go if it was ten times as bad."

"And what are you going to do to Master Scar?"

"Half kill him some day."

"Why not to-day, sir? Draw up somewhere in a wood, and we'll all see fair. You can whip him, Master Fred; I know you can. We'll set them free for a bit, and I'll stand by you, and Nat shall stand by his young master."

"Don't talk nonsense, Samson."

"'Tisn't nonsense, sir. You nearly always used to whip him when you two fell out, and you're bigger and stronger now."

"But we are in different positions now, Samson," said Fred, thoughtfully; "and it is impossible."

"Don't say that, sir. The men would like to see you whip him for what he did."

"No, Samson. It could not be done."

"You aren't afraid of him, are you, sir?"

"Afraid? How dare you?"

"Oh, I beg pardon, sir. I was only saying so because I thought the men would think you were, for putting up with a crack like that."

Samson's words stung more deeply than he expected, though he had meant then to rankle, for to his mind nothing would have been more fairer or more acceptable than for his young leader to face the Royalist prisoner with nature's weapons, and engage in a regular up and down fight, such as would, he felt sure, result in victory for their side.

They rode on in silence for some time before Samson hazarded another word.

"Beg pardon, sir," he then said, humbly. "I didn't mean to hurt your feelings."

"No, no; I know that, Samson."

"It was only because I thought that the men might think you afraid of Master Scarlett."

Fred turned upon him angrily.

"I beg your pardon again, sir," whispered Samson; "but it's just as I say. I know you aren't scared of him a bit, because I've knowed you ever since you was a little tot as I give pigabacks and rides a-top of the grass when I'd a barrow full. But the men don't know you as I do, sir. Call a halt, sir, and fight him."

"Samson, I am talking to you as my old friend now, not as your officer. It is impossible."

"Not it, sir. The men would like it. So would you; and as for me—let me fight brother Nat same time, and I'll give him such a beating as he won't know whether it's next We'n'sday or last We'n'sday, or the year before last."

"I tell you, man, it's impossible, so say no more."

"Very well, Master Fred. I only tell you the truth; and if you find the lads aren't so willing to follow you, mind, it's that."

"I have my duty to do, sir, so say no more."

"What a nuisance dooty is," said Samson to himself, as his young leader went slowly to the front, and rode for a time beside the leading file. "They'll set him down as a coward. 'Course I know he isn't, but they'll think so. Ha, ha, ha!"

"What are you laughing at?" said the man on his right.

"At him," cried Samson, pointing forward at his brother. "Looks just like a trussed turkey."

"Ah," said the man, quietly, "and who knows when it may be our turn to ride prisoners just the same? Knew him before, didn't you?"

"Eh? knew him? Well, just a little," said Samson, drily. "Come from the same part o' Coombeland. Me and him's had many a fight when we was boys."

"And the young captain and that long-haired popinjay met before, haven't they?"

"Often. I was gardener to our captain's father—the colonel, you know; and that fellow with his headpiece on wrong was gardener to his father as hit our officer."

"Took it pretty quiet, didn't he?" said the man.

"Well, just a little. That's his way."

"Wasn't afraid of him, was he?"

"Afraid? Why, he don't know what it means!"

"Humph! Looked as if he did," grumbled the man; and further conversation was stayed by Fred checking his horse, and letting the detachment pass on till he was in the rear.

They rode on hour after hour, till the horses began to show the need of water, and the men were eager for a halt to be called, so that they might dine and rest for a couple of hours under some shady tree; but for some time no suitable spot was found, and the advance and rear guards rode on, keeping a keen look-out for danger one minute, for a shady grove and water the next.

Once there was an alarm. One of the advance guard came galloping back after seeing a body of horsemen about half a mile away, their arms glittering in the sun; but the party, whatever it was, seemed to be crossing the road at right angles, and for safety's sake, Fred drew back his men and took refuge among some trees in a hollow a hundred yards from the road, where, to the great satisfaction of all, a spring was found rushing out of the rock.

Here in a regular military fashion the horses' girths were loosened, they were watered, and allowed to crop the grass. Outposts were planted, hidden by the trees; sentries were placed over the prisoners, whose bonds were not unloosed, and the men opened their wallets to partake of a hasty meal.

As soon as all the arrangements had been made, Fred saw that his prisoners were supplied with food, a man being deputed to attend to their wants, and this done, the young officer strolled off to the edge of the woodland, where the road could be seen east and west, and stood there watching for the first approach of danger.

His thoughts were divided between his charge and Scar's blow and insulting, contemptuous conduct, which rankled bitterly, for he could not help feeling that the men would judge him according to their lights; and, think of the matter how he would, he felt that he had placed himself at a disadvantage.

"If I had only struck him back I wouldn't have cared."

"Thought that over, sir?"

Fred started, and turned to find that Samson had followed him and approached over the soft moist ground beneath the trees unheard.

"Thought that over?" faltered the young officer.

"Yes, sir. Here's a splendid place for it just below among the big trees. Nice bit of open turf, quite soft for when you tumble down; and it would just please the men to see my young dandy cockerel's comb cut after what he did for you."

"Samson, you are talking nonsense. After serving so long in the army, you ought to know something of what an officer's duties are."

"No, sir; I shall never learn nothing about dooties. I can fight, because it comes nat'ral to a man, and I'm obliged to; but I shall never make a good soldier."

"You don't know, then, what you are saying."

"Oh yes, I do, sir; and I know what the men are saying; and if you won't fight, it must be me, for there's bound to be a rumpus if they go on saying you behaved as if you had a white feather in your cap."

"Who dared to say that?"

"Several of 'em, sir; and I wouldn't hit out, because I thought you would think better of it and fight."

Fred turned away angrily.

"Well, sir, I can't help speaking plainly; and I thought it better to tell you what the lads are saying about it."

"I cannot help what they say, sir; I am doing my duty. Now go back to yours."

"Yes, captain; but don't be angry with your old servant as followed you to the wars. Give me leave to fight Nat, and that will be something."

"Impossible, sir."

"But it would keep the men's tongues quiet, sir. Just about a quarter of an hour would do for me to thrash him, and it would be all right afterwards. The men wouldn't talk so much about you."

Fred marched up and down without a word.

"You see, sir, it's like this. Young Master Scar Markham's bouncing about and ordering and behaving as if he was everybody.—You won't fight him, sir?"

"No!"—emphatically.

"Then why not do something just to show him he isn't everybody, and that you are not afraid of him?"

"You know I am not afraid of him, Samson," cried Fred, hotly.

"Of course I do, sir; but the men don't know. How could they? There isn't one there as took you in hand from a little one, when you was always tumbling down and knocking the skin off your knees."

Fred made an impatient gesture.

"You see, sir, if you'd only do something it wouldn't so much matter. Any one would think, to see the airs he puts on, that he was Prince Rupert himself."

Fred turned away, and stood with his back to his henchman, lest Samson should see from his face how he longed to forget his duty, and to cease being an officer for a few minutes, becoming once more the careless boy who could retaliate sharply for the blow received.

"He's sitting yonder, sir, in his scarlet and gold and feathers, and tossing his head so as to make his ringlets shake all over his shoulders. Proud as a peacock he is, and looking down on us all like my brother Nat did till I sheared off his long hair, and made him a crop-ear too. It's done him no end of good. I only wish some one would serve his lordship the same."

Samson little thought what effect his words would have on his young leader, who again turned away and walked up and down to master the emotion which troubled him. The blow he had received seemed to smart; he pictured the faces of his men looking at him with covert smiles on their lips, and he seemed to see Scarlett sneering at him as some one so cowardly as to be utterly beneath his notice; and he was suffering all this because he believed it to be his duty.

The blood rushed up into Fred's cheeks, and then to his brain, making him feel giddy as he strode away to avoid temptation, for his nerves were all a-tingle, and the desire kept on intensifying to seize some stout staff and thrash his prisoner till he begged his pardon before all the men.

But he could not do such a thing. He told himself he must suffer and be strong. He had certain duties to perform, and he would do them, boy as he was, like a man. And to this end he walked quietly back to the little camp, giving a long look round to see that all was safe.

The mossy ground beneath the trees deadened his footsteps as he approached his prisoners to see that all were right; and there, as Samson had described, sat Scarlett, looking proud and handsome in his uniform, while he fanned his face with his broad-leafed felt hat and feathers, each waft of air sending his curls back from, his face.

Fred had involuntarily stopped short among the bushes to gaze at the prisoner, heedless of the fact that Nat and the other men were just before him, hidden by a screen of hazels.

Then the blood seemed to rush back to his breast, for a familiar voice said —

"Don't tell me. He used to be a decent young fellow when he came over to our place in the old days; but since he turned rebel and associated with my bad brother, he's a regular coward — a cur — good for nothing but to be beaten. See how white he turned when the captain hit him with that staff. White-livered, that's what he is. Do you hear, sentries? White-livered!"

The men on guard uttered a low growl, but they did not say a word in their officer's defence; and a bitter sensation of misery crept through Fred, seeming for the moment to paralyse him, and as he felt himself touched, he turned slowly to look in a despondent way at Samson, who stood close behind him, pointing toward the group as another prisoner said —

"Why, if we had our hands free, and our swords and pistols, we'd soon send these wretched rebels to the right-about. Miserable rabble, with a miserable beggar of a boy to lead them, while we — just look at the young captain! That's the sort of man to be over a troop of soldiers."

It was doubtful whether Scarlett heard them, as he sat there still fanning his face, till at last, in a fit of half-maddening pique, Fred turned again on Samson, and signed to him to follow.

Then, striding forward, he made his way to the sentry nearest to where Scarlett was seated.

"Why are your prisoner's arms at liberty, sir?" he cried.

"Don't know, sir," said the man, surlily. "I didn't undo them."

Fred gazed at him fiercely, for he had never been spoken to before like this, and he grasped the fact that he was losing the confidence of those who ought to have looked up to him as one who had almost the power of life and death over them.

"How came your lianas at liberty, sir?" cried Fred, sternly, as he turned now on Scarlett.

The latter looked in his direction for a moment, raised his eyebrows, glanced away, then back, in the most supercilious manner, and went on fanning himself.

"I asked you, sir, how your hands came to be at liberty?"

"And, pray, how dare you ask me, insolent dog?" flashed out Scarlett.

The altercation brought three more of the guard up to where they stood, and just in time to see Fred's passion master him.

"Dog, yourself, you miserable popinjay!" cried Fred. "Here, Samson! Another of you—a fresh rope and stake. You must be taught, sir, the virtue of humility in a prisoner."

Without a moment's hesitation, he sprang at the young officer, and seized him by the wrists, but only to hold him for a moment before one hand was wrenched away, and a back-handed blow sent Fred staggering back.

He recovered himself directly, and was dashing at his assailant to take prompt revenge for this second blow; but Samson already had Scarlett by the shoulders, holding on tightly while the staff was thrust under his armpits, and he was rapidly bound as firmly as two strong men could fasten the bonds.

Fred woke to the fact that his followers were watching him curiously, as if to see what steps he would take now, after receiving this second blow; but, to their disgust, he was white as ashes, and visibly trembling.

"Be careful," he said. "Don't spoil his plumage. We don't have so fine a bird as this every day. Mind that feathered hat, Samson, my lad. He will want it again directly. Here, follow me."

Scarlett burst into an insulting laugh as Fred strode away—a laugh foreign to the young fellow's nature; but his position had half maddened him, and he was ready to do and say anything, almost, to one who, he felt, was, in a minor way, one of the betrayers of his father; while as Fred went on, gazing straight before him, he could not but note the peculiar looks of his men, who were glancing from one to the other.

Fred felt that he must do something, or his position with his men would be gone for ever. They could not judge him fairly; all they could measure him by was the fact that they had seen him struck twice without resenting the blows.

What should he do?

He could not challenge and meet his prisoner as men too often fought, and he could not fight him after the fashion of schoolboys, and as they had fought after a quarrel of old.

Fred was very pale as he stopped short suddenly and beckoned Samson to his side, the result being that the ex-gardener ran to his horse, was busy for a few moments with his haversack, and then returned to where his master was standing, looking a shy white now, and with the drops of agony standing upon his brow.

The next minute Fred had tossed off the heavy steel morion he wore, throwing it to his follower, who caught it dexterously, and then followed closely at his leader's heels.

"Master or Captain Scarlett Markham," he said, in a husky voice, "you have taken advantage of your position as a prisoner to strike me twice in the presence of my men. It was a cowardly act, for I could not retaliate."

Scarlett uttered a mocking laugh, which was insolently echoed by his men.

Fred winced slightly, but he went on—

"All this comes, sir, from the pride and haughtiness consequent upon your keeping the company of wild, roystering blades, who call themselves Cavaliers—men without the fear of God before their eyes, and certainly without love for their country. You must be taught humility, sir."

Scarlett laughed scornfully, and his men again echoed his forced mirth.

"Pride, sir," continued Fred, quietly, "goes with gay trappings, and silken scarves, and feathered hats. Here, Samson, give this prisoner a decent headpiece while he is with us."

He snatched off the plumed hat, and tossed it carelessly to his follower.

"And while you are with us, sir, you must be taught behaviour. You are too hot-headed, Master Scarlett. You will be better soon."

Scarlett was gazing fiercely and defiantly in his old companion's face, hot, angry, and flushed, as he felt himself seized by the collar. Then he sat there as if paralysed, unable to move, stunned, as it were mentally, in his surprise, and gradually turning as white as Fred as there were a few rapid snips given with a pair of sheep shears, and roughly but effectively his glossy ringlets were shorn away, to fall upon his shoulders.

Then he flung himself back with a cry of rage. But it was too late; the curls were gone, and he was closely cropped as one of the Parliamentarian soldiers, while his enemy-guard burst into a roar.

"There, Master Scarlett Markham," said Fred, quietly, "your head will be cooler now; and you will not be so ready to use your hands against one whose position makes him unarmed. Samson, the headpiece. Yes, that will do. Master Scarlett, shall I put it on, as your hands are bound?"

"You coward!" cried Scarlett, hoarsely, as he gazed full in Fred's eyes; and then again, with his face deadly pale, "You miserable coward! Bah!"

He turned away with a withering look of scorn, and, amid the cheering of his men, Fred tossed the shears to Samson, and strode away sick at heart and eager to walk right off into the wood, where, as soon as he was out of eye-shot, he threw himself down and buried his face in his hands.

"Miserable coward!" he said hoarsely. "Yes, he is right. How could I do such a despicable thing!"

Chapter Nineteen
A Clever Schemer

Fred Forrester felt that he had had his revenge—that he had hit back in a way that humbled and wounded his enemy more deeply than any physical stroke could possibly have done; and, as has been the case with thousands before and since, he had found out that the trite old aphorism, "Revenge is sweet," is a contemptible fallacy. For even if there is a sweet taste in the mouth, it is followed by a twang of such intense bitterness that no sensible being ever feels disposed to taste again.

He had struck back fiercely, and bruised himself, so that he felt sore in a way which made him writhe; and at last, when, urged by the knowledge that he must attend to his duty, he rose, instead of walking back to where his men were waiting the orders to continue the route, proud and elate, he felt as if he were guilty and ashamed to look his prisoners in the face.

No sooner, however, was he seen by his men than there was a loud buzz of voices, and he learned what a change had taken place between them, for instead of being welcomed back with sidelong glances and a half meaning look, the soldiers saluted him with a loud cheer, in which sentries and the two outposts joined.

His action, then, was endorsed by his followers, who began laughing and talking merrily among themselves, looking from time to time at the prisoners, among whom sat Scarlett, with his arms upon his knees and his face lowered into his hands.

Fred's first inclination was to go straight to his captive, offer him his hand, and beg his pardon for what he had done; but two strong powers held him back—shame and dread. What would Scarlett say to him for the degradation? and what would his men say? They would think him ten times the coward they thought him before.

It was impossible; so giving his orders stoutly and sharply, the horses were bitted and the girths tightened. The prisoners were then helped into their saddles, and the ends of the ropes made fast after an examination to see that the bonds were secure, and once more they sought the road, the advance guard well to the front, and the relative positions of the early part of the march resumed.

There does not seem to be much in a few snips with a pair of big scissors; but the young leader's use of those cutting implements had completely changed the state of affairs in the little party. For while the guard were merry, and looked in the best of spirits, the common prisoners seemed as if they felt most bitterly the insult offered to their young captain, sitting heavily in their saddles, with their chins down upon their chests, and neither looking to right nor left, while Scarlett Markham gazed straight before him, his eyes flashing beneath the steel headpiece he now wore. His face was very pale, and his whole form was rigid as he sat there with his arms well secured to the cross staff at his back, and his lips tightened and slightly drawn back from his teeth as he drew his breath with a low hissing sound.

A few hours before, although a prisoner, he had looked the dashing young Cavalier in his scarlet, feathers, and gold, and, in spite of his uniform being stained and frayed with hard service, the lad's mien had hidden all that, and he seemed one to look up to and respect.

Now all was changed: the gay hat and feathers had been replaced by the battered steel morion; the long clustering effeminate curls were shorn away, and the poor fellow looked forlorn, degraded, and essentially an object for pity; his uniform showed every stain, and the places where the gold lace was frayed—and all through the working of a pair of shears among his locks. A short time before the smart young Cavalier, now only Fred Forrester's prisoner—nothing more.

As they rode onward the men commented upon the change aloud; but not half so intently as did Fred Forrester in silence.

The afternoon grew hotter; there was a glorious look of summer everywhere, for nature was in her brightest livery; but to the young leader everything seemed shrouded in gloom, and twice over he found himself wishing that a party of the enemy would come upon them suddenly and rescue those of whom he had charge.

As they rode on slowly with Fred in the rear, he noted that the two men who formed the advance guard were not in their proper places; and, seeking relief from his torturing thoughts in striving to give the strictest attention to his father's military lessons, he turned to Samson.

"Ride forward and tell those men to advance another hundred yards. They are far too near in case of surprise."

Samson spurred his horse, cantered forward, gave the order, and then halted as the advance guard trotted on for a hundred yards or so.

As the party came up, Samson exchanged looks with his brother, whose lips moved as if he were saying—

"Only just you wait, my fine fellow, and I'll serve you out for this."

But Samson laughed and rode to his old place in the rear beside his captain.

As Samson went by Fred, the latter caught sight of something scarlet, and the colour suggesting his prisoner, he turned sharply upon his follower.

"What's that?" he said.

"Only the young captain's hat, sir."

Fred frowned as he saw that Samson had fastened the grey felt hat with its gay feathers to his saddle, and then glanced forward at Scarlett, whose cropped head was sheltered by the heavy, uneasy steel cap.

"Ride forward," he said, "and give the prisoner back his hat."

Samson stared, but of course obeyed. Untying the hat from his saddle, he rode forward to where Scarlett sat, gazing straight before him.

"Captain sent your hat, sir. Shall I put it on?"

There was no reply.

"Your hat, sir. Shall I put it on?"

Scarlett took not the slightest notice, and after a momentary hesitation Samson uttered a grunt, pressed his horse a little closer, took the steel cap from the young prisoner's head, and placed the feathered felt there instead.

Then, backing his horse, he allowed the party to pass on, while he resumed his place, hanging the steel headpiece to his saddle-bow by the strap and chain.

"What's that? Look!" cried Fred, sharply.

He checked his horse as he spoke, and looked back, needing no answer, for there behind them in the dusty road, battered and disfigured, lay Scarlett's dashing head-gear; for so badly had it been replaced that, in his suppressed rage, the prisoner had given his head an angry toss, the felt hat had fallen, and it seemed as if, out of malice, every horse had passed over it, and trampled it down in the dust.

"Shall I pick it up, sir?" said Samson.

"No; let it be there," was the reply. "Take the prisoner the headpiece again."

Samson muttered to himself as he unhooked the steel cap and rode forward, while, in his resentment at having to go through the same duty twice, he took pains to treat the helmet as if it were an extinguisher, literally putting Scarlett out, so far as seeing was concerned.

And all the while, with his arms bound behind him, Scarlett Markham rode on with his head erect.

"Another insult," he said to himself. "The miserable coward! I could kill him as I would a wasp!"

The afternoon glided slowly by, and the detachment kept to a walk, for the heat was great, there was no special haste needed, and Fred wanted to spare his horses as much as possible. But after a short halt for refreshment at a roadside inn, where the landlord dispensed cider and bread-and-cheese liberally to either side, so long as he was well paid, but all the same with a strong leaning toward the Royalists, the little party rode on at a trot, very much to the disgust of the landlord, who stood watching them from his door.

"Poor lad!" he said. "Must be Sir Godfrey Markham's son from over yonder toward the sea. How glad he seemed of that draught of milk the lass gave him! Seems hard to be a prisoner, and to his old schoolfellow, for that's young Forrester, sure enough. I've a good mind to. No; it's interfering, and I might be found out, and have to hang on one of my own apple-trees as a traitor. But I've a good mind to. Yes, I will. Dick!"

"Yes, master," came from the stable, and a stout boy with some oat chaff in his rough hair made his appearance.

"How long would it take you to get to Brownsand?"

"On the pony?"

"Of course."

"Four hours by road. Two hours across the moor."

"Take the pony, then, and go across the moor. There's a regiment of horse there."

"Them as went by day afore yesterday?"

"Yes. Ride straight there and tell the officer. No, I can't do it."

"Oh, do, father, please—please!"

"You here, Polly?"

"Yes, father," said his rosy-cheeked daughter, who had fetched the mug of milk from the dairy. "You were going to send and ask them to save the prisoners."

"Was I, mistress? And pray how do you know?"

"I guessed it, father. That poor boy!"

"Perhaps I was," grumbled the landlord; "but I'm not going to do so now."

"Oh, don't say that, father!"

"But I have said it; and now, both of you go about your work."

"Oh, father, pray, pray send!"

"Do you want to see me hung, madam?"

"No, no, father; but nobody will know."

"I know—you know—he knows; and there's an end of it. Be off!"

The girl and boy both went out, and directly after the former made a sign which the latter interpreted to mean "Come round to the kitchen."

As soon as the landlord was left alone he drew himself a mug of cider, lit his pipe, and chuckled.

"Wonder how my apples are getting on?" he said. "I must have a good cider year this time; ought to be, anyhow." Then aloud at the door, "Keep an eye to the door, Polly," he cried. "I'm going down the orchard."

"Yes, father; I'll mind."

"That'll do it," said the landlord, laughing till his face grew as red as his own apples. "Nobody can't come and accuse me of sending the boy, and they'll never suspect her."

He walked right down the orchard, and then crept quickly to the hedge, stooped down, went nearer to the house, and then watched and listened.

"Ha! ha! ha!" he laughed softly. "I knew she would. Good-hearted girl! There he goes."

The landlord rubbed his hands as, turning to a hole in the hedge, he saw his boy Dick go off at a canter, lying flat down on the back of a little Exmoor pony, his arms on each side of the pony's neck, till he was over the nearest hill and descending into the valley, when he sat up and urged the pony on at as fast a gallop as the little beast could go.

"Nice promise of apples," said the landlord, contentedly smiling up at the green clusters. "Now, if I could have my wish, I should like a splendid crop of fox-whelps and gennet-moyles. Then I should like peace. Lastly, I should like to see all the gentry who are fighting and cutting one another's throats shake hands outside my door, and have a mug of my best cider. And all these wishes I wish I may get. There, now I'll go in."

He went slowly back to the house, puffing away at his pipe, and directly after encountered his red-faced daughter, who looked ruddier than ever as the old man looked at her searchingly, chuckling to himself the while. "I'll give her such a scare," he said.

"Want me, father?"

"Want you? Of course I do. Go and call Dick."

"Dick, father?" she faltered.

"Yes; didn't I speak plainly! Call Dick."

"He's—he's out."

"Who sent him out?"

"I—I did, father."

"Oh, you did, did you—without my leave?"

"Oh, father—father," cried the girl, sobbing, "don't—don't be angry with me!"

"Not I, Polly," he cried, bending down and kissing her. "Only I don't know anything, and I don't want to know anything, mind."

"And you're not cross about it?"

"I'm not cross about anything; but I shall be if I don't have a mug of cider, for I've been thinking, and thinking's thirsty work."

"Then you had been thinking that—"

"Never you mind what I had been thinking, my lass. My thoughts are mine, and your thoughts are yours, so keep 'em to yourself. When I've had my drop o' cider, I think I shall go out for a ride."

"Oh father!" cried the girl.

The old man chuckled.

"Don't you tell me that the pony has gone out, too," he said. "There, it's all right, Polly, only I don't know anything, and I won't be told."

Chapter Twenty
A Sudden Reverse

And all this time Fred Forrester rode on at the rear of his little detachment, longing to get to Newton Abbot and be rid of his painful charge. The evening grew more pleasant and cool, the moths came out, and with them the bats, to dart and flit, and capture the myriad gnats which danced here and there beneath the trees. Then, as they passed beneath some umbrageous oak, which stretched its ponderous and gnarled arms across the road, a night-hawk swooped from where it had been resting upon its parrot toes, its beak toward the bole of the tree, and skimmed round and round for a time to capture a great moth or two in its widespread, bristly-edged gape, before swiftly darting back to its perch, where it commenced its loud, continuous purring noise, which died softly away as the party rode on.

Sweet moist scents rose from the dewy ground, and as they neared a marshy pool, a low, musical whining and croaking told that the frogs which made the stagnant place their home had a full belief that before long it would rain.

Tired though the party were, it was pleasant travelling now, and as some horse, feeling freshened by the cool moist air, snorted and tossed its head, there followed a loud tinkling of accoutrements and an uncalled-for increase of pace.

As they rode on deep down in a hollow between mighty hedges, a loud hail seemed to come from the road on the hillside, "Hoi, hoi!" which was followed by another on the opposite slope, but no one stirred. The call of the hoot-owl was too familiar to the Coombeland men to deceive.

It was so dark at times down there amid the trees that the horses' heads were hardly visible, and when fire was struck by an impatient hoof from a loose stone, the flash given forth seemed by comparison to lighten up the lane.

Half an hour's increasing darkness was followed by a glow in the east, and then, slowly rolling up, came the moon, to silver the patches of firs, to lighten the pensile birches, and make the glossy-leaved beeches glisten as if wet with rain or frosted with silver. The little river which ran at the bottom of the valley, meandering on its way, shone out with flashes of light, as the moon rose higher; and once, in the midst of Fred's gloomiest thoughts, came, like a gleam of the moon on the water to lighten all around, the feeling that the world was, after all, a very beautiful place, and that it was man himself who made it miserable.

"I mean boy," said Fred, in his musings. "No, I do not; I mean man, for he is to blame for all this terrible war in which we are going against the king. But my father says it is just, so I have no right to think differently."

"How far are we from Newton, Samson?" he asked his follower.

"'Bout four miles now, sir. We've got to turn out of the main west road, and go through the wood next. Soon be there now."

The turning was reached at the end of another half mile, and the advance guard soon after came to the edge of the wood, through which a good road had been cut, the only drawback being that the overhanging trees made it dark.

Upon this occasion, though, the moon was rising higher and higher, pouring down a flood of silver light, which lit up the denser part with its soft diaphanous rays.

The solemn beauty of the scene, with its velvety shadows and silvery light, impressed every member of the party, so that they rode on in silence, the horses' hoofs sounding loudly, and the night being so still that the patter of the advance guard and of those in the rear was plainly audible.

"How much more is there of this woodland, Samson?" asked Fred, after a time.

"Not much more, sir, though I can't be sure—it's so many years since I rode through it with your father—when I was quite a boy."

"What's that?"

"Nothing, sir. Fox, perhaps, or a deer. Everything sounds so plainly on a night like this. Hear the advance?"

"Yes. Keep close, my lads," cried Fred. "No straggling in the darkness."

The men closed up, and they were going steadily on, congratulating themselves on the fact that they would soon be out in the open. A keen eye was kept upon the prisoners, though there was very little chance for their escape. The bonds were secure, and their horses' bridles out of their reach, while, had there been a disposition to urge a horse away from the rest, and make a dash for it in the darkness, the chances were that the poor beast would have declined to stir from his companions. The horse is by nature an animal which, for mutual protection, goes with a drove of his fellows; and, allowing for the formality of cavalry movements, there is something in the formation of troops and squadrons so similar to the natural habits of the horse, that they keep together, to such an extent that in warfare the "trooper" that has lost his rider regains the regiment and keeps in his place.

They were so near the edge of the wood now that the advance guard had passed through into the clear moonlight, and were going calmly on in full security, as they believed, when all at once a clear sharp order rang out on the night air; there was a quick trampling of horses, and the road in front was occupied by a strong body of men, whose position was between Fred's little detachment and their advance guard.

To have gone on burdened with their prisoners would have meant failure, to have plunged to right or left into the dense black wood no better than madness. There was only one course open—retreat; and in the emergency, young as he was in military evolutions, Fred proved himself worthy of his charge.

Setting spurs to his horse, he dashed to the front, giving his orders promptly. The men faced round ready for action, and, in defiance of the loudly shouted commands to surrender, the prisoners' bridles were seized and a rapid retreat commenced; but only for the little party to realise that they were in a trap, for in the darkness ahead they heard fresh shouts to surrender, from a second body of horsemen, who had been hidden in the wood till they had passed, and now occupied the road—how strong it was impossible to tell.

However, here lay their route now. If he had known that he had an enemy in his rear, Fred would have made a dash forward to try and reach his advance guard. Under the circumstances, it would have been fresh waste of time to turn, so again rushing to the front, he cheered on his men, and, sword in hand, charged, hoping by a bold manoeuvre to reach his rear guard now, and gallop back with his prisoners.

It was a vain hope. He had time to get his men well in hand, and the compact little body charged along the dark road, captors and captives together, for about a hundred yards, when there was the shock of meeting an advancing troop of the Royalist cavalry. The clashing of swords and the sharp rattle of blows struck at helmet and breast-piece; the plunging of horses, yells, and shouts; the deep groans of wounded men; and then, in the midst of the wild turmoil and hopeless struggle, it seemed to Fred that there was a short sharp crash of thunder, accompanied by a mingling of tiny flashes of lightning, and then the noise and confusion of the skirmish died away—and that was all.

Chapter Twenty One
Companions in Misfortune

It was quite in keeping with his life for Fred Forrester to be awakened by the blast of a trumpet, and, according to his habit, he made one turn and was about to spring from his rough pallet.

But he did nothing of the kind. He let his head fall back and his arm drop, as he uttered a groan of pain and weakness, which seemed to be echoed from close at hand.

Then there was a peculiar dizzy feeling of sickness; mists floated before his eyes, and, in a confused, feverish, dreamy fashion, he lay wondering what it all meant.

After a time he felt clearer, and found himself gazing at a small square window, unglazed, one through which a great beam of sunshine fell, making a widening bar of light which cast a distorted image of the opening upon a rough brick wall. That beam of light was full of tiny motes which rose and fell and danced into the brightest part, and away into the gloom till, as they skurried and floated here and there, it seemed as if he were gazing at a miniature snowstorm, of which all the flakes were gold.

There were sounds outside of trampling feet; of hoofs and the snorting of horses; but all seemed distant and confused, as if his ears were stopped or the sounds were coming from a distance; but directly after a very familiar note arose—the sharp, cheery chirping of a sparrow, followed by a low groan.

But it did not seem to matter, for he was tired and sleepy and in pain, and he seemed to drop off to sleep and wake again wondering what it all meant, and why it was, and how he came to be lying there.

After a time he stretched out one hand in a feeble way, to find that he was touching straw, and that beneath the straw there were boards. But there was straw everywhere; even the ceiling seemed to be straw, coarse straw, till he realised that it was reed thatch, and by degrees that he must be in the upper part of a stable—the loft, for he could smell hay; and as he satisfied himself that he was right so far, he discovered something more—that there were horses somewhere below, for there was a loud snorting and the rattle of a headstall.

But still it did not seem to matter, for everything connected with the war and his duties had passed entirely from his mind, till he heard once more a groan from somewhere close at hand, and then a familiar voice said—

"Don't go on like that, lad. I dare say you're very bad, but so am I; and you'll disturb the captain."

"Captain? what captain?" thought Fred, dreamily, and who was he that he should not be disturbed?

But he felt no inclination to speak, but lay listening to the chirping of the sparrows, and moved his head slightly to find that it was resting upon a piece of sacking laid over the straw.

That movement brought on the dizzy sensation again, and his head throbbed painfully for a time.

But the pain grew easier, and he lay perfectly still, watching the beautiful beam of sunshine which came through the open window, above which the roof went into a point, showing him that this was the gable end of the loft where he lay.

This did not surprise him, for he had been accustomed for months past to sleep in shed, stable, or loft, as well as in houses with decent rooms. At one time for a month a church had been the barracks where he had lain. Rough quarters had become a matter of course, and he lay quite still, for how long he did not know, to be roused once more by a deep groan.

"Do you hear, lad? What's the good of going on like that?" said the familiar voice again.

"My head—my head!" moaned some one.

"Well, and my head, and my ribs, if you come to that; but I don't howl and groan."

"Samson!"

"Master Fred! Captain, I mean. Hey, but it does a man good to hear you speak, again. Don't die this time, dear lad."

"Die? I don't understand you."

"Then the Lord be praised, you are not going to die!"

Fred lay wondering, for there came something like a sob from close at hand, though when he tried to turn towards the sound the horrible dizziness came back.

"Samson!"

"Yes, Master Fred."

"What are you doing there?"

"Blubbering, dear lad, like a great calf as has lost its mother; but it's only because I'm so glad."

"But, Samson, what does it all mean?"

"What, don't you know, my lad?"

"No."

"Not that you are badly wounded—cut down same as I was when we charged?"

"When we charged?"

"Yes, when they took us front and rear in the dark wood."

"Dark—wood?"

"Yes, lad. Some of us killed—I don't mean us—Smithers and Pelldike. The advance escaped, and so did the rear. All of us with the prisoners got hurt more or less."

"Oh!"

The scene in the gloomy wood came back now clearly enough; and in an excited tone Fred exclaimed—

"And the prisoners, Samson?"

"Oh, they were taken again! They're right enough."

"Scarlett Markham?"

"Yes; he came up here yesterday to see how we were."

"Oh!"

"What's the matter, my lad?"

"My father—my charge. Samson, I'm disgraced for ever."

"What, because about sixty men surprised us in that hollow road, and cut us all down? I don't see no disgrace in fighting like a man, and being beaten by five to one, or more than that."

"But how came we to be surprised so suddenly?"

"Dunno, Master Fred. Some one must have known we were going through that wood, and set a trap for us."

"And I allowed my poor fellows to walk right into it. Oh, Samson, I can never look my father in the face again!"

"Hark at him! Nonsense! It's all ups and downs—sometimes one side wins, sometimes t'other side. We had the best of it, and then they have the best of it, and we're prisoners. Wait till we get well, and it will be our side again. Long as we're not killed, what does it matter?"

"Then you are wounded, Samson?"

"Well, yes, lad; I got a tidy chop aside of the head, and a kick in the ribs from a horse in the scrummage. Leastwise, it wasn't a kick, 'cause it was done with a fore leg, when somebody's horse reared up after I'd cut his master down."

"And there is some one else wounded?"

"Yes, sir—Duggen."

"Badly?"

"Tidy, sir; tidy chop. But we shall soon mend again. Bark 'll grow over, same as it does when we've chopped an apple tree. I was afraid, though, as you was badly, sir?"

"Was I wounded, Samson? I feel so weak."

"Wounded, sir! Well, it was a mercy you wasn't killed!"

"It seems all so confused. I cannot recollect much."

"Of course you can't, sir. All the sense was knocked out of your head. But it'll soon come back again."

"Samson!"

"Yes, sir."

There was a pause, and Fred's henchman rose painfully on one arm to try and make out the reason of the silence, but he could only see that the young officer was staring at the window.

"Poor boy!" said Samson to himself. "Seems hard for him to be made into a soldier at his time o' life. Ought to be at school instead of wearing a sword."

"Yes, sir," he said aloud.

"Yes?"

"You called me, sir."

"Did I?" said Fred, vacantly.

"Yes, sir; you said 'Samson.'"

"Oh yes, I remember. Did you see much of the fight, Samson?"

"As much as any one could for the dark."

"We were attacked front and rear, weren't we?"

"That's it, sir. Trapped."

"It was all my fault, I suppose," said Fred, with a sigh.

"Fault, sir; not it. Nobody's fault. People can't do impossibilities. Why, there was sixty-five of 'em in the troop, and of course they regularly rode us down!"

"But you did see something of the fighting?"

"To be sure I did, sir."

"Did—did I disgrace myself, Samson?"

"Did you what yourself, sir? Come, I like that! If digging your spurs into your horse, and shouting to us to come on, and then going to work with your sword as if it was a scythe, and the pleasaunce hadn't been cut for a month in June's disgracing yourself, why, I suppose you did!"

"Then I did fight?"

"Fight! I should think you aid."

"Like a man, Samson—like an officer should?"

"Why, of course you did, sir!"

"As my father would have liked to see me fight, if he had been there?"

"Well, sir, that question's a puzzler. You see, fathers is fathers, and, as far as ever I've been able to find out, they don't like their boys to fight. Why, my father was always giving me and Nat the strap for fighting, because we was always at it—strap as he wore round his waist, when he wasn't banging our heads together. You see, Nat was always at me, and knocking me about. We never did agree; but our old man wouldn't let us fight, and I don't believe your father would have liked to see you trying to cut people's heads off with that sword of yours."

"Well, then," said Fred, smiling faintly, "would my colonel have been satisfied with what I did to save the prisoners and my men?"

"Wouldn't be much of a colonel if he wasn't. There, dear lad, don't you fret yourself about that. I've heered the men here say you did wonders for such a boy, and a big sergeant who fetched you off your horse was up here yesterday—"

"Yesterday?" interrupted Fred. "Why, we were travelling yesterday!"

"That we were not, my lad, for we've been lying here two days."

"Oh!" ejaculated Fred.

"While you've been off your head."

"Oh, Samson!"

"Well, sir, that's better than your head being off you."

"Then you are sure I did my duty?"

"Duty, sir? Yes; that's what I was going to tell you. The big six-foot sergeant who fetched you off your horse with a great cut of his heavy sword was up here yesterday to see you; and I heered him say to himself, 'Poor boy! I feel ashamed of myself for cutting him down. What would his poor mother say to me if she knew?'"

"I can lie patiently now till I get well," said Fred, after a pause. "I was frightened by my thoughts, Samson."

"Yes; them's what frightens most of us, sir."

"I mean by the thought that I had not done my duty by my charge."

"But you did, sir; and it's the fortune o' war. They was prisoners the other day; now we're prisoners this day."

"And Master Scarlett Markham, and your brother, and the other men?"

"All here, sir. There's about a thousand of the enemy about, waiting, I suppose, to drop upon our side, if our side doesn't drop upon them. Fortune o' wars sir—fortune o' war."

Samson waited for Fred to speak again; but as he remained silent, the ex-gardener went on—

"I've been expecting to hear some news of my beautiful brother, but I haven't heered a word, only that he's about somewhere. Oh, I am proud of him, Master Fred! I shouldn't wonder if we was to be sent off somewhere—Exeter or Bristol, maybe, and Master Scarlett and my brother had charge of us. Be rum, wouldn't it?"

Fred sighed as he recalled the past.

"Couldn't cut our hair short, sir, could they?"

Fred remained silent, and his follower went on.

"Nat said first chance he had, he'd crop my ears. That's like him all over. But he dursn't, sir. Not he. I should just like to catch him at it. Pst! some one coming."

Fred had already heard steps below, and then the creaking of a rickety ladder, as if some one were ascending.

Directly after a door on his left was thrown open, a flood of sunshine burst into the cobweb-hung loft, and an officer and a private of cavalry came rustling through the straw till they were within the scope of the wounded lad's gaze, and a chill of misery ran through him like a shudder as he saw Scarlett Markham, followed by Samson's brother Nat.

Chapter Twenty Two
Samson and his Brother

In spite of the cropped appearance of his head, a cropping that was still closer now in consequence of his having had Fred Forrester's clumsy shearing regulated, Scarlett Markham had pretty well regained his old dashing cavalier aspect. He had somehow obtained a fresh hat and feathers, and, as he stood at the foot of Fred's straw bed, with one hand resting upon the hilt of his long sword, the other carelessly beating a pair of leather gauntlet gloves against his leg, he looked, in his smart scarlet and gold uniform, the beau ideal of a young officer.

Following the action of his leader, Nat passed on, and stopped at the spot where his brother lay, to stand gazing down at the wounded man.

Fred was too weak to do more than move his head slightly, so as to gaze back at his enemy; but he met Scarlett's stern look defiantly, and waited for him to speak.

And as he lay there the rough loft and its straw seemed to pass away, for the background of his mental picture to become the park and grounds about the old Hall, on one of the old sunny days when he and Scarlett had had a quarrel about some trivial matter, and were gazing threateningly at each other after uttering dire words, and were declaring that everything between them was quite at an end, and that they were never going to speak to each other again.

Then the present came back, and there stood Scarlett, looking stern and frowning, as he involuntarily passed his great gloves into his left hand, and began to let his finger and thumb play about his lips, where he tried to find—and failed—an imaginary moustache, which, all the same, he twisted up into airy points to add to his fierce aspect. A little bit of conceit which he had picked up during his soldier life.

"What a miserable peacock he has grown!" thought Fred. "And I am in the power now of such a court fop, whose only idea is dress and show. Well, I'm glad I belong to the haul, quiet Parliamentarians. Better than being like that."

But somehow, all the while, Fred could not help thinking of his own plain buff-leather uniform, with its heavy, clumsy, steel breast and back plates, which, like his hard, head-aching helmet, were more often rusty than bright, and, though he would not have owned it, he could not help admiring the figure before him, and looking at it with something like envy.

"Why don't he speak?" thought Fred, with a faint flush coming into his cheeks. "Does he think he is going to stare me down?"

The faint flush deepened a little, as he grew indignant at his enemy coming to triumph over him in his helplessness; and then he thought of how he had triumphed when it was his day, and how he had humbled his old companion to the dust.

"And what a mean, contemptible triumph it was, and how it stung me far more than it did him! But he shan't humble me. I can be as defiant as he is, and I'll die before I'll show him that he has gained the day."

But as Fred defiantly returned Scarlett's calm, stern look, a thick mist seemed to gather slowly between them, making the face of the young Cavalier grow faint and distant, a singing noise came in his ears, and slowly and painfully everything seemed to pass away till all was dark once more.

Meanwhile, Nat Dee had crept close to his brother's head, and, kneeling in the straw, allowed a grin to overspread his rustic countenance.

"You've got it, then, this time?" he whispered.

Samson had "got it this time," indeed, for his bandages wanted changing, and his wounds were hot and painful; but, in spite of his anguish, he echoed, so to speak—visibly echoed his brother's broad grin, and acknowledged the fact, fully resolved that, as Nat had come to triumph over him, he should be disappointed.

"Yes," he said in a cheerful whisper; "I've got it this time, Natty."

"Don't you feel ashamed of yourself?"

"Not a bit."

"Then you ought to. Suppose your poor mother saw you now, what do you think she would say?"

"Say? Say, 'Get your ugly great carcase out of the way, and let poor Samson have room to breathe.'"

"Nay, she would not; she'd say, 'Here's my wicked young black sheep as leaped out of the fold to go among the wolves, properly punished, and I'm very glad of it.'"

"Well, then, I'm very glad she isn't here to listen to her ugly son Nat telling such a pack of lies."

"Nay, it's the truth."

"Not it," said Samson, cheerily. "My poor old mother couldn't say such words as that. She'd more likely say, 'If I didn't know you two boys was my twins, I should say that Nat belonged to some one else, and was picked up by accident.'"

"Nay, she wouldn't; she'd be ashamed of you."

"Never was yet, Nat; and if I wasn't lying here too weak and worn-out to move, I'd get up and punch your ugly head, Nat, till you could see better, and make you feel sorry for saying such wicked things about my poor old mother."

"She's my mother as much as she is yours."

"Yes, poor old soul; and sick and sorry she is to have such a son as you."

"Nay, it's sick and sorry she is to have a son as deserts his king, and goes robbing and murdering all over the country with a pack of ruffians scraped from everywhere."

"No, I didn't; I never desarted no king. I wasn't the king's servant, lad."

"Yes, you was."

"Not I, Natty. I was master's servant, and he says, 'Will you come and fight for me, Samson,' he says, 'against oppression?' ''Course I will, master,' I says. 'And handle a sword instead of a spade,' he says. 'You give me hold of one, master,' I says, 'and I'll show you.' That's how it was, Natty."

"Your master's a bad man, and him and you will be hung or chopped as sure as you're alive."

"You always was a muddlehead, Natty. It's your master as is the bad man; Colonel Forrester's a thorough gentleman, and we always had better fruit and garden stuff at the Manor than you had at the Hall, and that's what makes you so wild against me."

"Yah! Why, you never grew anything but weeds at the Manor. Your garden was just as if pigs had got into it."

"Did you think so, Natty?" said Samson, good-temperedly.

"Yes."

"That shows what I say 's right. You always was such a muddlehead that you couldn't tell good from bad, and you don't know any better now.

Poor old Nat, I don't bear you any malice or hatred in my heart. I'm sorry for you."

Nat ground his teeth gently, for his brother's easy-going way angered him.

"Sorry for me?" he said. "Why, you're a miserable rebel, that's what you are."

"Not I, Natty; not a bit miserable. If you was not here, I should lie back and sing."

"Shall you sing when they take you out and hang you?"

"Not going to hang me, Natty; not ugly enough. Now, if it had been you— I say, Nat, I should like to have you hung up in the Manor garden to keep away the birds."

"What?"

"To scare 'em. You do look such an old Guy Fawkes. I say, who cut your hair?"

Nat's hand went involuntarily to his freshly shorn head, and a dull red glow came into his cheeks.

"You wait till I get better, and I'll crop it for you neatly. Why, you don't look one thing nor the other now. Cavaliers wouldn't own you, and I should be ashamed to set aside you in our ranks."

"Go on," said Nat, grinning viciously. "That's your nastiness; but it don't tease me. I'm sorry for you, Samson. What a pass for a respectable Dee to come to, only you never was respectable. But there's an end to all things. Made your will?"

"Nay, Natty, not yet."

"Thought you might like to leave any clothes you've got to your brother."

"Well, I did think about it, Natty; but, you see, my brother's grown to be such a high and mighty sort of chap as wouldn't care for anything that wasn't scarlet and gold. I say, Natty, I have got something though as you may as well have—hidden away in the roof of my tool-shed."

"Eh? What is it?" said Nat, who was betrayed into eagerness by the idea that perhaps his brother had a pot of money hidden away in the thatch.

"Perhaps I'd better not let you have it. You're proud enough as it is."

"You can do as you like with it, of course," said Nat, with assumed indifference.

"Ah, well, it will be useful to you, if what you say's true about me. It would be a pity for any one else to get it, wouldn't it?"

"Well, I am your brother, after all," said Nat, quietly.

"Yes, so you are, Natty; and you're just the chap to be proud of it, and wear it stuck in your steel pot. Look here, you go into the tool-shed at the Manor, first time you're that way, and as soon as you're inside the door, reach up your hand, and in the dark corner you'll find a bundle of our old peacock's moultings when he dropped his tail. You shall have 'em, Nat, and I hope I shall live to see you with 'em in your iron cap. My! you will look fine!"

"If you wasn't such a miserable scrunched-up garden-worm of a man, I'd baste you with my sword-belt, Samson," whispered Nat, angrily.

"Thank ye, Nat, lad. Thank ye. It's very kind of you to say so. Save it up, lad, till I'm better. It will be pleasanter then for us both."

"Nat," said Scarlett just then.

"Yes, sir."

"Come here."

Chapter Twenty Three
An Exciting Watch

Fred lay insensible for a few minutes, and when he did struggle back into consciousness, it seemed to him that he must be still dreaming, or else that the bewildering excitement of the civil war, with the misery, despair, and wretchedness, was all the result of his fevered imagination.

What did it all mean? he asked himself. Were they back at home, and had he fallen from the pony and struck his head against a rock? or was he over at the Hall, and was this the time when he climbed the great elm to get the magpie's nest, and had that horrible fall?

No; it was all true—this was the war time—he was badly wounded, and his enemy, Scarlett Markham, the young Cavalier, was bending over him in mocking triumph at his downfall, and revenging himself for the insult he had received in the loss of his flowing curls.

It was a cruel revenge—one which, in spite of his efforts, brought the weak tears to his eyes, and, as he closed them tightly to hide his emotion three or four great drops were shut out by the lids, and rolled slowly down on either side, tickling him for the time before they were washed away.

Then, as the time glided on, Fred opened his eyes, and looked up in Scarlett's, as he again asked himself whether it was all a dream, the consequence of his fevered state.

For there, kneeling in the straw, was Scarlett Markham, his buff gauntlet gloves thrust in his sword-belt, his cavalier hat cast aside, and his brow knit and glistening with perspiration, as he kept on dipping a white kerchief in a bowl of cold water held by some one at the back, and carefully bathed Fred's forehead.

How cool and delightful that water felt as the kerchief was opened out, and spread right across the brow from temple to temple! Then how hot it grew, till it was softly removed, to be resoaked and applied once more with all the tender solicitude that would have been shown by a woman.

Fred wanted to speak, but no words would come; he could only lie there, with his breast heaving, as he watched the calmly stern, handsome face bending over him, and thought of the past—their old boyish friendship, the delightful days when they frolicked in the park; and fished, and sought for plovers' eggs on the moor. How short a time ago it seemed, and now they were acting the parts of men fighting on either side in the terrible civil war which was devastating old England; enemies—deadly enemies, and Scarlett Markham was pouring coals of fire upon his head.

"Shall I fetch some more water, sir? This is getting quite warm," said a pleasant voice.

"Yes, I was going to ask you to get some more," said Scarlett. "Be quick, my lass; we shall be called away directly."

Then Fred had a glimpse of a bonny, little, round-faced lass, with red cheeks and hands, as the bowl was borne away. The straw rustled, and steps were heard upon the rough loft ladder, to be followed by the rattle of a chain, and the creaking of a windlass, Fred seeming to see all as plainly as if he were there, and watching the girl's actions at the draw-well in the yard below.

And all this time the two boys gazed at each other in silence—a silence that was broken by the splash of water; then there were footsteps on the ladder again, and the red-faced lass came back, knelt down behind the injured lad's head, the kerchief was soaked, and the cool refreshing water did its work.

"And we are enemies," thought Fred, with his eyes now closed, and a calm restful feeling coming over him like the beginning of sleep, from which he started, for there was the loud trampling of horses, the jingling of accoutrements, and the brazen bray of a trumpet.

Scarlett started up, shook the water from his hands, snatched up his broad-leafed hat, and took his gloves from his belt.

"Bathe his forehead for a few minutes longer, and then let him sleep. We shall be back before many hours, but the surgeon will be here before then."

"Yes, sir."

"And tell your father that General Markham will see that he is paid for all his trouble."

"Oh, sir," said the girl, "you need not think of that. We'll do our best."

By this time Scarlett was at the door, and Fred had turned his eyes toward him, but he did not look back.

"Come, Nat," he cried loudly; and his follower stumped over the rough straw; the steps creaked, and voices were heard below. Loud orders followed. Then the trumpet brayed out again, the trampling of horses followed, and the girl set down the bowl, and went to the end of the loft, where she climbed up and looked through the little window, staying there till the trampling of the horses had died away.

"Gone," she said, as she returned to Fred's side, and prepared to bathe his brow once more.

"No," he said gently; "let me sleep now. But haven't I seen you before?"

"Yes, sir; you came here and brought Captain Markham and the prisoners," said the girl, turning a deeper red, as she recalled her own action upon that occasion, and gazed suspiciously in his face for signs that he knew of all that she had done.

"Yes, I remember now."

"And I suppose you were wounded when they were rescued by a party of the king's horse?"

"Yes," sighed Fred. "I thought I remembered you. The little inn near the moor."

"Yes, sir. Father's inn."

"And you are Royalists, I suppose?"

"I don't know what we are, sir. We only wish the war was over, and we want to do all we can for the poor wounded folk."

"For rebels, too?" said Fred, bitterly.

"For any one who is in trouble, sir; and if you don't want me to bathe your head again, I'll go and attend to your servant. Father says there's nothing like clean cold water for a cut."

"Yes, go and help the two poor fellows; but, one moment—there was quite a regiment there, was there not?"

"Yes, sir; the greater part of one. Came from the town."

"Do you know where they have gone?"

"No, sir, only along the Exeter road. News came, I think, of the enemy being there, and I'm afraid we shall be having more wounded to-night."

The girl went on to where Samson and the other man lay, and soon afterward the landlord's red face appeared at the head of the stairs, to cry hastily—

"Here, Polly! Dick has just come in from the top of the hill, and he could see soldiers riding this way to meet the regiment going along the road. There'll be a fight not far from here, I'll wager, and— Hark at that!"

"I don't hear anything, father."

"But I do. Horses galloping. Now can you hear?"

There was a faint distant sound, gradually increasing—a sound which soon developed into the rapid beat of horses' hoofs, and the girl climbed to the window to look out again.

"Yes, father, I can see them," she cried.

"Well, well, what is it? the king's regiment?"

"Yes, father, coming galloping back along the road, and—yes, I can see them too, a great regiment of the other side galloping after them, and you can see more soldiers off on the moor."

"Coming this way?"

"No; going right off behind the wood."

"To cut them off," cried the landlord. "It's some one who knows the country, and if the king's regiment keeps to the road those last will get before them; they'll be between two parties of the rebels, and they'll be cut to pieces."

"Hooray!" came from the straw where Samson lay, and the landlord turned upon him angrily, but there was too much that was exciting outside to let him find words of reproof.

The clatter of hoofs and jingle of sword against stirrup increased, and Fred lay with his eyes glittering, panting heavily as, full of excitement, he listened to the sounds of hurried flight.

Then came another trumpet blast, sounding distant, and a rushing sound as of a coming storm, ever increasing in power.

Then another blast, and another, both sounding farther away, and as the wounded lad lay there, he pictured to himself the advance of two more regiments of the Parliamentary cavalry rapidly coming on in pursuit, his mental pictures being endorsed by the words of the landlord's daughter, as she forced her head out of the little opening to watch the retreat and pursuit, turning from time to time to speak to her father in answer to some eager question.

"Are they keeping to the road, Polly? Quick, my girl? Why don't you speak?"

"Yes, father; they are keeping to the road."

"Can't you tell 'em to turn off across the moor?"

"No, father; they are too far away."

"Shout to them."

"It's of no use, father. One, two, three rebel regiments are coming along at full gallop."

"All on the road?"

"No; one on the road, the others across the moor."

"The poor fellows will be cut all to pieces. Can nothing be done? Here, Polly, come down, and let me look."

"There is plenty of room beside me, father. How they are galloping now!"

In spite of his weakness, Fred had turned himself a little on one side, so as to watch the backs of the pair who were now blocking out the little light which came from the window; and as the exciting events went on, and he listened to the galloping of the horses, the shouts of the horsemen—his own party—and the trumpet calls, the perspiration due to excitement stood upon his brow, and he at last groaned out—

"Oh, if I could only see!"

"Ay, Master Fred, if we could only see!" came from close at hand. "Hark at 'em! hark at 'em!"

There was no need for Samson's adjuration, for Fred's sense of hearing was strained to the utmost, and he was picturing mentally the effects of the scattered shots which were now being fired.

"All waste, Samson; all waste," he said hoarsely. "No man can take aim when he's galloping full stretch."

"No, Master Fred; but it'll scare t'other side a bit, p'raps make some of 'em surrender."

Fred shook his head slowly, and then listened again as the girl exclaimed excitedly—

"Look, father; there's one down!"

"Ay, how could he expect to leap the wall on a horse blown like that?"

"Those two have galloped up to him. Ah, cowards! two to one. Father, they're killing him. Oh!"

"They're not," cried Fred, hotly. "They're taking him prisoner."

"Right!" cried the landlord, turning sharply; "but how did you know?"

"Because I know our side would not act like butchers with a defenceless man," said Fred, proudly, "They take prisoners, sir, and always give quarter."

The landlord uttered a grunt, and turned sharply to watch the progress of the fight and pursuit.

"Look, Polly!" he cried; "they have got to the top of the hill, and see their danger."

"Yes, father; look, look—they have halted and turned. Yes; they are coming back."

"Can the two regiments trying to cut them off see them?"

"No, I think not; they are down in the hollows. Look, father; they're coming back."

"The enemy?"

"No; the king's men. Can't you see!"

"See? yes," cried the landlord, with increased excitement. "Why, they're mad. They're coming right into danger. Whatever do they mean?"

"I don't know, father. Why, they'll all be taken."

"They must have a fool for leader."

"Ah!" sighed Fred, as he strained his ears to catch every word and sound from outside.

But the landlord was wrong. The king's regiment of horse had no fool for colonel. On the contrary, he had suddenly woke to the fact that a regiment of Ironsides on his left, and another on his right, were trying to get round him by short cuts, so as to head him back to the regiment in pursuit; and, what was more, he saw that there could be no doubt of the success of the manoeuvre.

With a gallantry that almost approached recklessness he faced round his regiment, and in the full intent of attacking his enemies, corps by corps, he gave the order to charge, and dashed right at the pursuing regiment.

This movement resulted in bringing the engagement well within view of the spectators in the loft, or rather, it should be said, of the spectator; for, as soon as the landlord's daughter saw that a deadly shock was inevitable, she covered her face with her hands, stepped down from beside her father, and fell upon her knees in the straw close to where Fred lay.

"God help them, poor men!" she murmured. "How horrible it is!"

Then there was a painful silence within that straw-spread loft, while without there was a rushing sound, as of two great torrents hurrying to meet, and above this came the jingling of sword and spur, the hoarse shouting of words of command; then the brazen blare of trumpets, followed by a distant cheer; then one more near; and then one horrible, crashing, hurtling noise, as man and beast dashed at man and beast, and came into collision. There was the clash of sword upon sword, of sword upon helmet, and again of sword upon breastplate. Yells of pain, wild shrieks, shouts of defiance, and then one confused din, broken by a loud "Hah!" from the landlord.

"Polly," he cried, "it's awful! Ah, here comes another regiment, and—yes, here comes the other!"

Almost as he spoke, came the sound of another shock, and then of another, followed by desperate clashing of steel, which grew less and less and less, and then gradually died out, to be followed by a dull, low murmur, and then silence, which lasted only a few moments, to be succeeded by a series of deafening cheers.

"Is it all over, father?" whispered Polly, with hands over her face.

"Yes, my girl," said the landlord, in a sad voice; "it is all over for the poor fellows."

"Who have won, father?"

"What's the use of asking that? What could you expect, when it was three to one? Plenty of killed and wounded, and not a man escaped. Yes; there they are, two or three hundred of them, and all prisoners."

"Will they bring the wounded here, father?"

"I don't know, Polly. Where are we to put them, if they do?"

"Ah!" sighed the girl, rising and wiping her eyes, "it is very dreadful, and I nearly swooned away when they brought the first wounded men here; but I must be about and ready to help when they come. They'll want all we can do."

She smoothed down her apron in a calm, matter-of-fact way, and then moved over the rustling straw, as if ready for any duty; but she seemed to recollect something, and came back to where Fred lay.

"It's your side that has won, sir," she said. "You will not be a prisoner any longer, and—"

"Yes?" said Fred, for she stopped short.

"You heard what my father said, sir? You know he likes the Royalists, and if he fought would fight for the king?"

"Yes, I could see all that from his manner. I had no need to hear his words."

"But he is so good and kind, sir. He would not hurt a hair of any man's head. You will not betray him to the soldiers, sir, and let him be treated as a spy."

Fred was conscious that the girl was talking to him, but her words seemed to be coming through a thick mist, and she looked far away somewhere down a long vista of light, which stretched right away into space, beginning upon the straw where he was lying, and passing right out through the end of the loft. And there, within this vista of light, surrounded by dancing motes, was the landlord's daughter. Then, as if a thin filmy cloud had passed over the sun, a cloud which grew thicker and thicker, so that the broad beam of light gradually died away, the pleasant young homely face grew less and less distinct, and, lastly, all was confused and mingled with singing noises and murmurs in his head, and then—a complete blank.

Chapter Twenty Four
Discovering the Traitor

When Fred came to himself, he was no longer lying upon straw, but upon a comfortable bed, in a clean, white-washed room. It was evening, for the sun seemed to be low, and sending a ruddy glow through the open window.

For a time he felt puzzled, and wondered why he was there; and as he tried to collect his thoughts, and the memory of the fight which he had heard came back, it seemed as if it was all a dream.

But no; that was no dream. Tramp—tramp! tramp—tramp!—the heavy march of an armed man. It was a sentinel going to and fro beneath the window sure enough; for the footsteps sounded faint, grew gradually louder, as if passing close to the window, became gradually fainter, and then grew louder once more, and this over and over again.

At the same time that he was listening to this, he became aware of a peculiar scratching noise close by, but until in his heavy drowsy state he had settled in his own mind that it was a sentinel, he could not pay any heed to the scratching.

By degrees he recognised the sound as being that of a pen, and knew that some one was writing, and just as he had arrived at this conclusion, there was the faint scrape of a chair, a clinking noise such as might be made by the hilt of a sword against a breastplate, and directly after a sun-browned, anxious face was gazing earnestly into his.

"Father!" whispered Fred, feebly.

"My dear boy! Thank Heaven!"

The first sentence was uttered aloud—the second breathed softly.

"How is it with you, Fred?"

"Bad, father, bad," he murmured. "I seem to have no strength left, and—and—and—oh, father," he gasped, as he clung to the hand which took his, "I did—indeed, I did my best."

"Why, Fred, my boy, Fred. Don't—don't take it so seriously as that. You were overpowered and wounded."

"Yes, father, but you trusted me with the prisoners, and I allowed myself to be out-manoeuvred, and I have disgraced myself."

"What! How?"

"And I did try so hard to do my duty. I wish now I had been killed."

"Fred! My son!"

"Don't be angry with me now I am so weak."

"Yes, too weak, my dear boy," said Colonel Forrester, as he knelt down by the bedside, and passed his arm beneath the lad's neck as he kissed his forehead, "too weak to talk about all this. Be silent and listen to me."

Fred answered by a look.

"You think you have disgraced yourself by letting your enemies out-manoeuvre you, and with the prisoners turn the table on your little escort?"

Fred gave another pitiful look.

"That you have disgraced yourself for ever as a young officer?"

"Yes," whispered the wounded lad.

"And that I, your father and your colonel, am angry for what you look upon as a lapse?"

Fred tried to bow his head, but failed.

"Well, then, my dear boy, let me set your poor weak head at rest. I know everything you did from your start until you were trapped in the wood, the enemy letting you pass one troop, and having another waiting for you at the end of the wood."

"Yes, that is how it was, and I did not take sufficient care."

"Yes, you did, my boy; your precautions were all that an officer on such a duty could take, and all that I should have taken."

"You seem to be giving me fresh life, father," whispered Fred. "But how did you know?"

"Partly from the advance guard, partly from Samson; and both join in saying that my son behaved as a gallant officer should. I am quite satisfied, my boy. I sent you upon a dangerous expedition, and in spite of the perils of your journey, you have escaped with life, and you are no longer a prisoner. In fact, we have turned the tables on the enemy again, and read them a lesson they will not forget."

"Yes; I heard the fighting, father."

"And do you know whose men they were?"

"No."

"Sir Godfrey Markham's."

"Father?"

"Yes; and his son, lately your prisoner, was with them."

"And they are prisoners now?"

"No, my boy; they cut their way out with about a hundred mere, and escaped. This war is one of constant change."

"Then you are not angry with me, father?"

"On the contrary, Fred, I am proud. You acted better than many older officers would have done."

"You say that to comfort me over my disgrace."

"I say it because it is true, and because you are not in disgrace. A far more experienced man would easily have been led into such an ambush, betrayed as you were."

"Betrayed?" said Fred.

"Yes; some one must have carried information to the enemy."

"You think that?"

"Of course."

"But who could have done so? We had no traitors with us."

"Perhaps not, but the enemy may have had friends near."

"Impossible, father!"

"Quite possible, my boy. Where did you stay to refresh your men?"

"Here, father—at this very place. At least," added Fred, as he glanced round, "if this is the little inn where I was a prisoner in the loft."

"The very place, my boy; and now the secret is out. Lie still now, and don't speak."

Fred gazed at his father eagerly as he rose from his knees and crossed to the door, which he opened, passed out on to the landing, called for the host, and returned.

Instead of the florid landlord, there was a heavy step on the stairs, and the shock-headed boy of the place entered the room to look from Fred to Colonel Forrester and back.

"Where does the nearest doctor live?" said the colonel, quietly.

"At Brownsand," replied the lad, with another sympathetic glance at the wounded officer.

"Rather a long ride?"

"Only twelve miles, sir."

"But that's where a body of the king's men lie, is it not?"

"Well, no, sir, I don't think so now. Those is them that you had to fight with. They were at Brownsand t'other day."

"You have a horse here, have you not?"

"No, sir, only a pony; and if I took the short cut it would not be a long journey."

"But could the pony do the journey to-day?"

"Do it to-day, sir? Yes; she's as hard as a stag."

"That will do for the present," said Colonel Forrester.

"Shall I ride over for the doctor, sir?"

"No. Send up your master."

The lad went down quite sulkily, and delivered his message, while Colonel Forrester smiled at his son.

"Well, Fred," he said, "I suppose you see now?"

Fred's answer was cut short off by the heavy step of the landlord, who came up with a sympathising look in his face, and seemed eager to serve.

"The young gentleman's not worse, sir, I hope."

"You are sorry for him, then?" said the colonel, quietly.

"Sorry for him, sir? Why of course I am."

"As sorry as you were for the young prisoner he brought by here."

"Oh yes, sir, I was sorry for him, too; but he was not wounded."

"You treacherous dog!" cried the colonel, in a voice of thunder, as he seized the landlord by the throat, and forced him to his knees; "so nothing would do but you must bid that boy take the pony and ride over to Brownsand so as to betray the fact that an escort of prisoners had halted at your house and were gone on by the Brownsand road."

"No, sir; I never—I never did."

"You lie, you old villain: tell the truth before I hand you over to my men, and have you hung for a spy on the nearest tree."

"I swear, colonel, I never did anything of the kind," cried the landlord, piteously.

"No, sir, it is not true," cried a girlish voice; and the landlord's little daughter appeared in the doorway.

"Then pray who did?" cried Colonel Forrester.

"I did, sir," said the girl, undauntedly.

"And pray, why?"

"Because I heard that the young officer was Sir Godfrey Markham's son, and it seemed so horrible that he should be dragged off a prisoner."

"What do you know of Sir Godfrey Markham?" asked the colonel, sternly.

"I had heard my father speak of him, sir."

"And so you planned all this and executed it yourself?"

"Yes, sir; I sent our lad off with a message to where the king's men lay."

"I need not ask, I suppose, whether you are telling the truth," said the colonel, grimly.

"No, sir. Why should I tell a lie?" replied the girl, quietly; and she looked unflinchingly in her questioner's face.

"And at the first opportunity, I suppose, you will betray us into the enemy's hands?"

"Oh no, sir," said the girl, with the tears in her eyes, as she glanced at Fred. "I would sooner try and save you, though you are the enemies of our king."

"Silence, girl! there is no king now in England, only a man who calls himself king. A tyrant who has been driven from the throne."

The girl flushed and held up her head.

"It is not true," she cried, proudly. "God save the king!"

"What!" cried Colonel Forrester, in a voice of thunder; and for the first time the innkeeper spoke, his ruddy face now mottled with white, and his hands trembling as he placed them together beseechingly.

"Don't take any notice of what she says, sir. She's a foolish, wilful girl, sir. I've been a miserable coward to hold my tongue so long, but I will speak now. It was all my doing. I held back so as not to seem in the business, because I wanted to be friends with both sides, sir; but I could not bear to see the young squire carried off a prisoner, and I winked at it all. It was my doing, sir. Don't believe a word she says."

"Father, what have you said?" cried his child, clinging to him.

"Hush! Hold your tongue," he whispered angrily.

"So we have the truth at last," said the colonel. "You convict yourself of being a spy and traitor; and you know your fate, I suppose?"

As Colonel Forrester spoke, he rose and walked to the window, made a sign with his hand, and directly after heavy steps were heard upon the stairs, accompanied by the clank of arms.

In an instant the girl was at the colonel's feet.

"Oh, sir, what are you going to do?" she shrieked. "He is my father."

The guilty innkeeper's lips were quivering, and the white portions in his face were gradually increasing, to the exclusion of the red, for the steps of the soldiers on the stairs brought vividly before his eyes the scene of a spy's fate. He knew what such a traitor's end would be, and, speechless with terror, he could hardly keep his feet, as he looked from his child to the stern colonel and back again.

"Father!" she cried, "why don't you speak? Why don't you ask him to forgive us?"

"Mercy—mercy!" faltered the wretched man.

"What mercy did you have on my poor boy?" cried the colonel, fiercely. "Through your treachery, he was surrounded by five times the number of his own men; and, for aught you cared, instead of lying wounded here he might have been dead."

"Mercy! I did not know," gasped the miserable culprit.

"Mercy? Yes; you shall have the choice of your own trees on which to hang," cried the colonel.

"No, no; mercy!" gasped the trembling man, dropping on his knees; "for my child's sake—for Heaven's sake—spare me!"

"Father!" cried Fred, excitedly.

"Silence, boy! I am their judge," said Colonel Forrester, sternly. "Yes, man, for your child's sake, I will spare you, in spite of your cowardly treachery."

"Father, father!" cried the girl, excitedly; but he could not speak.

"Yes, I will spare you for your child's sake," said the colonel again. "There, little woman, I forgive you, for you are as brave and true-hearted as can be. I believe you—every word. Your little heart was moved to pity for the prisoner, as it has been moved to pity for my poor boy here, and for my men."

He took her hand in his, and held it.

"I have heard of all your busy nursing, and I do not blame you; I would rather praise. There, help the old man downstairs, and I am not afraid of your betraying us."

The girl raised his hand and kissed it before rushing to her father, flinging her arms about him, and helping him away, so weak and semi-paralysed by fright that he could hardly totter from the room, the colonel following to the door, and signing to the soldiers to go down.

"There, he has had his punishment," said the colonel, smiling; "and now you will be able to rest in peace."

"Thank you, father, thank you," whispered Fred, huskily.

"You see you were not to blame now."

"Not so much as I thought, father."

"Not to blame at all. There, make haste and grow strong, my boy, before we are driven out in turn by the enemy."

"Are they near, father?"

"No; as far as I know, my boy. But the victors of yesterday are the defeated to-day, perhaps to win again to-morrow. Ah, my boy, it is fratricidal work! and, though I love my cause as well as ever, I would give all I possess as one of the richest men in our county to see home smiling again in peace."

Chapter Twenty Five
Towards Home

Weeks followed of desultory warfare. One day messengers came bringing news to the little inn—which had gradually become headquarters from the coming there of General Hedley, and the centre to which reinforcements were continually gathering—that the king's men were once more in force, and preparations were made for a hasty move.

"Far sooner than I could wish, my boy," said the colonel, as he sat beside his son after a busy day.

"But I feel quite strong again, father," pleaded Fred. "You are too anxious about me."

"Too anxious, my boy? No, I think not. Well, you will have to try and sit your horse again, even if you are a non-combatant."

"Which way shall we retreat?" asked Fred.

"Retreat? Who said anything about retreat?" cried a stern voice, and General Hedley entered the room. "Oh, you, eh, boy?" he continued, shaking one of his buff gauntlets at the convalescent. "Don't you let Captain Miles hear you say that again. We may move to a different position, but we will not talk of retreat yet."

Fred felt the colour burning once more in his pale cheeks, and the general went on—

"Forrester, I want a chat with you. Come into my room. I have fresh despatches."

The colonel followed his leader out of the little parlour which had been devoted to the wounded lad by the general's command, he having insisted upon its being retained when he joined them there, and tents had sprung up in all directions upon the moor close to the inn.

Directly after, there was a hoarse cough heard outside, in company with a heavy step.

"Hem! Master Fred, sir."

"You, Samson?"

"Yes, sir. Alone, sir?"

"Yes."

"May I speak to you!"

"Yes; go on."

Samson's head appeared at the window, upon the sill of which he leaned his arms as he gazed in.

"Getting quite tidy again, arn't you, sir!" he said, in a hoarse whisper.

"Yes, quite strong; and you?"

"Never better, sir; only wind feels a little short sometimes, and I gets too hot too soon."

"You didn't come to tell me that, Samson."

"No, sir; I come to tell you there's news in the camp."

"What of?—a movement?"

"Yes, sir; that's it."

"Do you know where we're going next!"

"No, sir; do you?"

"No, Samson; and I should say that is the general's secret. We shall know when we get there."

"Start to-morrow, don't we, sir?"

"Impossible to say. What do they say in the camp?"

"Weather-cockery."

"What?"

"Well, sir, it's just like a vane in a wind: now it's east, now it's west, and when it ain't east or west, it's north or south. Everybody says everybody else is wrong. But we are going somewhere directly; that's for certain. And, I say, Master Fred."

"Yes?"

"How do you feel about mounting your horse again?"

"I long to, Samson. How are the poor beasts?"

"Lovely, sir. The farrier doctored the cuts and scratches they got in the skirmish, and they're pretty well healed up now. It's a cowardly thing to cut at a horse. Then you feel strong enough to have a try, sir?"

"You wait till we get the orders to start, Samson, and you shall see."

Samson rubbed his hands and began to smile, but the pleasant look was ousted by a grotesque twitching of the countenance.

"What's the matter?"

"I always forget, sir. Wound reminds me when I go too fast, and aren't careful. All right again soon, though. Don't hear no noos of the war being over, sir, I s'pose?"

"No, Samson, none. Tired of it?"

"Tired, sir? I don't know about tired, but I can't help thinking of the manor now and then, and what sort of a state my garden will be in. Why, Master Fred, sir, you know that bit under the north wall, where the mistress's herbs and simples grow!"

"Yes."

"Well, sir, I shan't know that bit again. That there patch in partic'lar 'll be one big touzle o' weeds, and—"

Tantara, tantara, tantara! A trumpet rang out, sending a thrill through Fred, as he grasped its meaning, and that of the blasts that followed, with the rush of feet and trampling of horses. For a messenger had come in bearing a despatch, and in an incredibly short space of time tents were struck, baggage waggons loaded, and the little force was marching slowly to the west, Fred having only time to shake hands with his little nurse, and assure the landlord for the fiftieth time that he forgave him for being the cause of his wounds, and was most grateful for the kindness he had received.

Then, to his intense delight, he was once more mounted on his horse, which gave a whinny of recognition as his master patted his neck and smoothed his velvet muzzle. The trumpets rang out the advance, and with the sun flashing from the men's arms, the array moved slowly off, and the youth's eyes sparkled as he drew in long breaths of the soft sweet air, while he gazed wonderingly in the direction they were taking, his breast filled with new hopes, in which he was afraid to indulge, lest they should prove to be false.

The longing to question his superior officers was intense, though he knew that even they would probably be in ignorance of their route; and never before had he felt so strongly that a soldier is only a portion of one great piece of mechanism moved by one—the general in command.

As they settled down at last into the line of march, Fred found himself for the present with the staff, riding behind his father, who was General Hedley's most trusted follower, but hours went on before a word passed between father and son. Such conversation as did ensue was with Samson, who rode behind, neither being considered sufficiently recovered to go back to the regiment, but settling down to the work of aide-de-camp and orderly.

And as they rode slowly on, the cavalry halting from time to time to give the infantry opportunities for keeping up and preserving their position in the column, it soon became evident that the Royalists, who had made no sign in their neighbourhood for weeks, must be somewhere near at hand. For the greatest precautions were taken, scouting parties were out, and a regiment of horse formed flankers well away on either side to guard against surprise.

Fred was riding slowly on at a short distance behind his father, thinking with all a convalescent's freedom from fever and pain, of how beautiful everything around seemed to be, and longing to cast aside the trammels of discipline, so as to be a boy in nature once more, as well as in years, when a low voice behind him made him sharply turn his head.

"Don't it seem a pity, Master Fred?"

"Eh? What, Samson?"

"Why, sir, that we should be all riding and walking along here over this moor, thinking about hoeing up and raking down people and mowing 'em off, instead of enjoying ourselves like Christians?"

"Ah, yes," sighed Fred; "it does. It is very beautiful, though, all the same."

"Beautiful, sir? Ah, Master Fred, how I should like to put away my tools—I mean this here sword and pistol—and for you and me to take off our boots and stockings, and wade up yonder stream after the trout."

"Hah!" ejaculated Fred, with his eyes brightening. "Yes."

"Or to go away north, and get out on that there short soft grass, as always looks as if it had been kept well-mown, out there by the Rill Head, and lie down on our backs, and look at the sun shining on the sea and ships a-sailing along, eh, Master Fred?"

"Oh, Samson, Samson, don't talk about it!" sighed Fred, as he gazed right away in imagination at the scene his rough companion painted.

"Can't help it, sir. Feel as if I must. Steady, my lad! you mustn't break away for a gallop. We're soldiers now."

This was to his horse, which felt grass beneath its feet and the wind blowing, and wanted to be off.

"'Member how the rabbits used to scuttle off up there, Master Fred, and show their white tails as they popped into their holes?"

Fred nodded, and let his reins fall upon his horse's neck.

"And that there hole up in the Rill, sir? 'Member how I come and found your clothes up beside it, and fetched my garden line to fish for your rope?"

"Oh yes, yes, yes!" said Fred, sadly.

"And we never went down that place again, after all, sir. Well, let's hope that we shall some day. I'm getting tired of soldiering, and feel as if it would be a real pleasure to have a mug of our cider again, and pull up a weed."

"I'm afraid I am getting tired of it, too, Samson; but I cannot see the end."

"And on a fine day like this, sir, with the blue sky up above, and the green grass down below, and the birds singing, it's just lovely. Why, I feel so well and happy this morning that I do believe, if he was here, I could go so far as to shake hands with my brother Nat."

"Why, of course, Samson," said Fred, thoughtfully.

"No," added Samson, "I don't think I could go so far as that."

"And if Scarlett Markham were here," thought Fred, "I believe I could grasp his hand, and be like a brother again, as in the past."

"Wonder where we are going, and whether it means another fight, sir?" said Samson, after a pause. "Look, sir!—the colonel. Master's waving his hand."

Fred saw the motion, and trotted up to his father's side.

"Fred, my boy, do you know where we are making for?"

"No, father!"

"Home."

"Oh, father!" said Fred, with his pale face flushing. "I am glad."

"Oh, Fred, my boy," replied his father, seriously, "I am very sorry."

"Sorry, father? Why, we may have a chance to see them all again."

"Yes—perhaps; but we are taking the horrors of war to the abode of peace, my boy."

"Yes," said Fred, thoughtfully. "I did not think of that."

"It was our duty and hope that we might keep the ruin and misery brought by war from our pleasant moors and lanes. Better not see those we love at such a cost."

"Then, don't let's go, father."

Colonel Forrester shook his head.

"A soldier's duty is to obey, Fred. Our general has had his orders, and feels that for military reasons our district will be the most suitable place for intercepting a force which is threatening the west; and our duty is to go."

"Yes, father. But shall we see my mother?"

"I hope not, Fred."

"Oh, father!"

"Not yet awhile, my boy. We must only think of those we love when our duty to our country is done."

They rode on in silence for a time, with Fred picturing, amid the trampling of hoofs and jingle of weapons, the scenes of his boyhood, but to be awakened from his dream by his father's voice.

"Do not talk about our destination. I only tell you, my boy, because it is a matter which interests us both."

"No, father. You may trust me."

"I know that, or I should not speak. Our destination is—"

"Not the Manor, father?"

"No, my boy, the Hall."

Fred sat staring wildly at his father, as bit by bit he grasped what this really meant to these who had always been their nearest friends; and then, bubbling over with excitement, he exclaimed—

"Oh, father, Sir Godfrey will think this is your doing."

"Yes, my boy."

"And is it, father?"

There was a pause.

"Oh, father, how could you?"

"Don't misjudge me, boy," said the colonel, sternly. "I have done everything I could to stop it."

"And—"

"Failed, Fred. It is a strong position for many reasons, and I have been compelled, by my duty to my country, to hold my peace. Rein back."

It was the officer speaking now, and Fred checked his steed till Samson was nearly abreast of him again, when, after quite a dozen attempts to draw his young master into conversation, Samson muttered to himself, "In the grumps;" and rode on in silence too.

Chapter Twenty Six
A Petition to the General

It seemed to Fred Forrester a strange stroke of fate, when, after three days' slow and steady advance, feeling their way cautiously, as if at any hour they might meet the enemy, he rode with the advance to take possession of the Hall, for in spite of the colonel offering his own home again, the general kept to his decision that the Hall was the more suitable place for head-quarters.

The day was bright as one of those when, full of boyish spirits, he used to run over to spend the day with Scarlett Markham; and where was he now? A fugitive, perhaps; who could say where? And Sir Godfrey, where was he?

Fred felt very sad as he rode on, with the horses' hoofs trampling deeply into the soft green turf. But how beautiful it all seemed, with the rich red-brown stone of the old house contrasting so well with the green of the stately trees. The lake glistened like a sheet of silver in the sunshine, and all seemed familiar and welcome, and yet somehow as though connected with his life long, long ago, and as if it was impossible it could have been so short a time since he was a boy, and played about there.

"I hope the men will be careful," he found himself thinking; "and that every one will be respectful to Lady Markham."

He had not much time for thought after that, for the men were halted on the level grass land in front of the terrace garden, and he found himself one of the officers who, after an advance guard had ridden up to the front, and others had been despatched to form piquets surrounding the place, rode up in the train of the general.

To Fred's surprise, Lady Markham and her daughter came to the broad step in front of the entrance, and the general touched his horse's sides with the spurs, and rode up.

Fred was so near that he heard every word, and he bent forward, looking in vain for some token of recognition from the pale, careworn lady and her shrinking daughter, who received the general.

The latter saluted Lady Markham gravely.

"I regret to trouble you, madam," he said; "but we are compelled to take possession of your house for the present."

Lady Markham bowed coldly.

"We are at your mercy, sir," she said.

"Nonsense, madam!" cried the general, shortly. "You and the pretty young lady there by your side need not talk about mercy. The stern necessities of war bring us here, so all I have to say is, be good enough to reserve such apartments as you need for yourselves. You and your servants will be perfectly unmolested."

Lady Markham bowed once more.

"The housekeeper is here," she said, "and will provide all we have. We have no men-servants now, to show where the stables and granary lie."

"Pray don't trouble yourself about these matters, madam. My men will find what they want, and I dare say," he added sarcastically, "unless General Markham comes to look us up, and forces us to make more reprisals, we shall ride away, and you will find the Hall little the worse for our visit."

A sudden change came over Lady Markham at the mention of her husband's name, and after a few minutes' hesitation, she stepped out to stand with joined hands, looking supplicatingly at the general.

"My husband?" she said imploringly, "is—is he well?"

"You ask me a question I cannot answer, madam," said the general, taking off his morion, and speaking in a quiet sympathising voice. "But there is one of my young followers who may be able to give you some information."

He turned and made a sign to Fred, who touched his horse's flanks, and rode forward with a peculiar singing noise in his ears.

"You!" said Lady Markham, looking at the young officer in a startled manner, and then turning from him with a look of disgust, while he saw that Lil shivered.

"They look upon me as if I were some one who had been the cause of all this," he thought; but his countenance lightened directly, as Lady Markham turned to him again, and said gently—

"Forgive me, Fred. This meeting brought up the past. It seemed so terrible that my boy's companion should be among our enemies."

As she spoke, she held out her hand, which Fred seized and held for a few moments before he could speak, and when he did give utterance to his words, they were in a voice broken by emotion.

"I am not your enemy, Lady Markham," he said. "I would do anything to spare you pain. Lil, won't you shake hands?"

The girl hesitated for a few moments, and then held out her little hand timidly, but only to turn to her mother directly, and cling to her as she strove to keep back her sobs.

"Ask him—ask him," she whispered.

"Yes. Tell us, Fred—my poor boy," said Lady Markham, in a low voice, so as to be unheard by the soldiers close at hand. "Where is my husband?"

"The last I heard of him, Lady Markham, was that he was with the Cornish men beyond Plymouth. They are all on the king's side there."

"But was he safe and well?"

"Yes; quite safe and well, and Scarlett—"

"Yes; pray go on. I dared not ask, for fear of hearing bad news."

"I heard that he was quite well, too, and acting as his father's aide-de-camp."

"Thank Heaven!" sighed Lady Markham, piously. "It is so long since we had heard from them. Now I can feel more at rest."

She seemed to gain strength from the news; and after a pause she went on—

"Tell your leader," she said, "that I am grateful, for my child's sake. He has been most courteous. I did not expect this consideration."

"Oh, Lady Markham, I am sure that you have nothing to fear. The discipline is so strict among our men. They will only take food and shelter for a night or two. Any act of disorder would be punished."

Lady Markham drew a breath of relief.

"You are our enemy, Fred," she said softly, "and when we meet again, I shall not forget to tell my husband of the treatment we have received. There, Lilian and I will go to our room. You know the place by heart. See that everything is done for your officers' comfort. Let them learn that Sir Godfrey Markham can show hospitality, even to his foes."

She bowed stiffly, and, taking her daughter's hand, was withdrawing into the house, when Lil snatched her hand away, and stepped quickly to Fred's side.

"I hate you," she whispered. "You are dear father's and Scar's cruel enemy; but please, please, Fred, don't let them do us any harm."

"Don't be afraid, dreadful enemy," said Fred, smiling, as he saw the depth of his old playmate's hatred. "I'll do everything I can, Lil dear, for all your sakes. Good-bye, if I do not see you again."

She gave him a quick look, which seemed in an instant to bring up sunny days when he had swung her on the lawn, rowed on the lake, and climbed the apple-trees to get her fruit; and then she was gone, and he was listening to the trampling of horses, the shouting of orders, and he was called away.

Directly after, he was making use of his knowledge of the place to fulfil Lady Markham's wishes, and over these he worked the harder, because he felt that by hastening the production of the necessaries for the troops, much waste and destruction would be spared.

The result was that in less than an hour the Hall was occupied by the little force, which was in high good humour with its pleasant quarters, while sentries were put in different directions, and every precaution taken against surprise.

"Capital quarters, my boy," said the general, as he sat with his officers in the old oak dining-room; "and I wish your father was here to share them. But you have not taken care of yourself in all this business."

"Oh, I have snatched a little food, sir," replied Fred. "I'm not hungry, but—"

"Well, what is it? Speak out. What do you want?"

Fred hesitated for a moment, as if collecting himself.

"You know that the Manor is only two miles from here, sir?"

"Eh? So near. No; I knew it was somewhere about this part," said the general, smiling. "Oh, I see, my boy. Well, it's quite right, but risky. And besides, we may stay here a week or we may stay a minute. How do I know how soon the enemy may rout us out? No, Fred, my boy, love must give way to duty. I cannot spare my young officer, even to go and see his mother, much as I should like to say 'Yes.'"

"You mistake me, sir," said Fred, colouring a little. "I would not have asked leave at this busy time for that."

"Then what do you want, my boy?"

"Lady Markham and her daughter, sir. This is no place for them."

"Humph! No. But we have no time for paying attentions to ladies."

"No, sir; but what I want to do is a little thing. We may stay here some time, and other troops join us."

"Yes, I am expecting reinforcements. What do you want to do?"

"As this may be quite a rendezvous for some time, to get them away."

"I cannot undertake such duties, my boy; but Lady Markham and her daughter are free to go anywhere."

"Thank you, sir. That is what I want; but the only asylum for them is our old home, and they would not go there unasked."

"Well, ask them."

"It would be of no use."

"My good lad, I am tired out. I want to snatch a few hours' sleep. What is it you want?"

"I want to take half a dozen men to ride over and fetch my mother here. They were once dear friends, and if my mother came, she could persuade Lady Markham, for her child's sake, to go back with her."

The general sat frowning for a few minutes, during which he poured out a little wine in a long Venice glass, filled up with water, and drank.

"Yes," he said in a quiet, decided voice, as he set down his glass, "take a sergeant and half a dozen—no, a dozen men, ride over and do the business as quickly as you can, so that the men and their horses may get back and rest. It means a double journey, you see. No; no thanks. Despatch!"

Fred looked his thanks, and retired with the promptness loved by his leader; and a very short time later, just as the turret clock was striking ten, he rode out with his little detachment, being challenged again and again by the mounted sentries placed along the road which skirted the west end of the lake.

"Only think of it, Master Fred," whispered Sergeant Samson Dee, as they rode slowly along beneath the light of the stars—"going home in this way. What will the mistress say?"

They were not long in hearing.

As they rode over the familiar ground, Samson was very silent, for he was thinking of the old garden, while Fred felt a swelling sensation at his breast as every object so well-known peered cut of the surrounding darkness. There was the pond in which Dodder took refuge one day after he had broken out of the field to escape capture, and there stuck so tightly in the mud that cart ropes had to be thrown over him, and he was dragged out looking the most drenched and deplorable object possible.

There, looming up under the stars, was the great hollow elm where the owls regularly bred and slept all day. Another minute, and the horses' hoofs were slashing up the babbling water of the stream which crossed the road — the tiny river where they had so often waded after trout and stone loaches.

There at last, calm and still in the starlight, lay the Manor, and the young officer felt a wild kind of joy, which he had to fight down, lest he should seem childish before his followers, for the impulse of the moment was to leap from the horse and rush through the garden, over the lawn, and up to the doorway, shouting for joy.

But discipline, the desire to seem manly, and a strange feeling of dread kept him calm and stern beyond his years, the feeling of dread soon dominating the other sensations. For how could he tell but that a party of the enemy had ridden up to his dear old home, as they had that evening ridden up to Scarlett's, and were perhaps behaving with far less consideration than they had shown? and how did he know that his old habitation was not a ruin, and his mother a wanderer far away.

A curious dimness came over his sight at these terrible thoughts, and he felt as if he were going to fall from his horse. His old injuries throbbed and stung, and it seemed to him that his fears were correct, for the old Manor did not look as it should be. Surely the windows were all bare of glass, the great chimney stack was down, and the ivy which clothed the front torn away and scorched by fire.

The giddy sensation increased, and he involuntarily clutched the pommel of his saddle as he bent forward, staring wildly at the dear old place, when he was suddenly brought to himself by the voice of Samson, who said aloud —

"All fast asleep. Oh, Master Fred, I wonder how my dear old garden looks."

The misty, giddy sensation had gone, and in a firm voice Fred cried, "Halt!"

For there before him, dimly seen in the starlight, lay the old Manor, quite unscathed, for the tide of war had not yet swept over that part of the pleasant land.

Fred dismounted, passed through the little oaken gate, and walking up the path, was about to rap at the door with the hilt of his sword.

But the trampling of horses and a loud neigh like a challenge had awakened those within. A well-known casement was opened, and a familiar voice exclaimed —

"Who's there?"

"Mother!" whispered Fred, hoarsely.

There was a cry of joy from the open window; then a clicking noise of flint and steel, a light gleamed blue and faint on the ivy leaves which framed the casement; then a brighter light, and in a few minutes the lower windows were illumined; there was the sound of the bolts being shot, and directly after Fred was in the little hall, clasped in his mother's arms.

"My boy!" she whispered in a deep voice. Then, in a quick, agitated manner, "Your father?"

"Safe and well, mother."

"And you have come to stay? Thank God, thank God."

"No, not to stay," he cried earnestly, "but to ask you to perform a duty, an act of kindness towards—"

"Some wounded men? Yes, yes, my boy; bring the poor fellows in."

"No, no, mother, not towards men," said Fred, holding her tightly to his side, "to one who was once your dearest friend—to her and her child."

"Lady Markham? Oh, Fred, my boy, they are still dear to me, though this terrible war keeps us apart. But they are there. Oh, why do you stop? Bring them in at once."

"No, no, dearest mother, you are too hasty," whispered Fred. "They are at their own place. But it is taken by our troops. It is to be a little camp for us, perhaps for weeks. It is no place for them. General Hedley consents, and I want you to come and fetch them here."

"Yes, yes, my boy; but Lady Markham would not leave her home."

"Yes, she will, at your persuasion, mother. You must come at once."

Mistress Forrester drew a long breath, stifled a sob, and said firmly—

"I will be ready in a few minutes."

"Shall I saddle Dodder, mistress, or will you ride pillion behind the captain?" said a gruff voice at the door.

"Ah, Samson, my good, true lad," cried Mistress Forrester, "I am glad to hear your voice again."

She ran forward, and held out her hand.

"And it's like the sweet music of the birds to hear yours, mistress," said the rough fellow, kissing the extended hand.

"Quick, my boy!" whispered Mistress Forrester. "Give your men refreshment. Saddle the pony, Samson. I will soon be down."

She ran to the staircase, and Samson tramped off to the old stable, thrust his hand in the thatch over the door, where, to use his expression, "the key always laid," and a neigh of recognition greeted him as soon as he spoke.

In five minutes he was leading the pony round to the gate, where he was in time to find a huge black jack of cider being passed round with horns to the men, one of the maids having hastily dressed and come down.

Directly after, in her dark riding-habit and hat, Mistress Forrester was at the door, was helped into the saddle by her son, and the little cavalcade was on its way back through the dark lanes, and over the stretch of moor.

Chapter Twenty Seven
How Scarlett Visited his Mother

"Oh, mother darling, how shocking it all seems!" said Lil, after a long burst of weeping, as she knelt by her mother in the darkness of their own chamber that dreary night.

"Yes, yes, my child; but we must be patient and wait."

"But it seems so terrible. These men here—our dear old home full of soldiers, and poor father and Scar—"

"Hush, hush, my darling!" whispered Lady Markham. "You do not know what pain you are giving me. Heaven's will be done, my child. Let us pray for the safety of those we love."

She softly sank upon her knees beside her child in the darkness of the sombre chamber, and through a broken casement the bright starlight shone down, shedding sufficient lustre to show the two upturned faces with their closed eyes.

The trampling and bustle had gradually died out. The loud orders and buzz of talking had ceased by degrees, and now the silence of the night was only broken by the impatient stamp of a horse, the regular tramp of armed sentries, and from time to time a low firm challenge.

Some time before Lady Markham's attention had been drawn by Lil to the gathering of a little detachment of horsemen, and she had recognised the voice of him who gave the order to advance, while from the open window, themselves unseen, they had watched the faint gleam of the men's breastplates, as they rode down the avenue, to be seen afterwards like a faint moving shadow on the banks of the lake before they disappeared.

Then all was still. The frightened servants had gathered, as it were, under the wings of their mistress, and two of them were occupying the inner room—Lil's, and had sobbed themselves to sleep.

"But you will not go to bed, mother?" Lil had whispered.

"No, my child; I will sit up, and watch by you."

"But I could not sleep, mother," said Lil; and the result was that they were keeping vigil, and sank at last in prayer for those in danger far away.

How still it all seemed as Lady Markham rose from her knees at last, and went with Lil to the open window, where they seated themselves to look out at the darkened landscape, and the faint glimmer of the star reflections in the lake.

They felt calm now and refreshed, but neither spoke. It was as if they were unconsciously waiting for something—they knew not what, but something that was to happen before long—and in which they were to play some part.

Tramp, tramp! tramp, tramp! on the terrace; and tramp, tramp the sentry, whose post was from the porch right into the great oaken-panelled hall and back.

The weary troopers were asleep, and the stillness of the old west-country home was oppressive, not a sound coming now from the undulating moorland stretching to the sea. For there is a grand solemnity at such times in the wild open country, away from busy towns, and when the sentry by the porch let his thoughts stray back to the days of peace, and some merry-making in the village from which he came, and began to hum gently to himself the air of an old ballad, it sounded so strange that he stopped short, shifted his heavy gun, and continued his tramp in silence.

He had just reached the front of the great stone porch, and was gazing out across the park, and then to right and left, before turning to resume his march right up the hall to the back, when—

C—r—r—rack!

The man turned sharply, brought his clumsy piece to the present, and stood listening and gazing before him into the dark hall.

Not another sound.

Should he fire and give the alarm?

What for? It was not likely that danger would come from within. It could not. The place was too well guarded on all sides. Besides, if he fired and gave an alarm that turned out to be false, there would be a severe reprimand from the officers, and a long course of ridicule and annoyance from the men.

Shifting his piece once more, the sentry stood listening for a few minutes, and then drawing his sword, he walked boldly into the dark hall, looking to right and left, then along all the sides, and ended by standing at the foot of the stairs, gazing up at the gallery which crossed the end, and went right and left into the two wings of the great house, where the rooms were occupied by the officers and men.

"Wonder whether one of the officers did that to see if I was on the look-out?" thought the man. "If he did, and he only came within reach, I'd let him see that I'm wideawake."

He stood, with his sword drawn, looking up that staircase for quite five minutes, but there was not a sound, and gloomy as the hall was by day, with its narrow stained-glass windows, it was almost blackness itself by night.

"Something must have fallen," thought the sentry at last, as he recalled seeing, by a light carried by one of the officers as he went upstairs, that the walls were ornamented with trophies of old weapons.

"Yes; something must have tumbled down," he said again, as he returned his sword to its sheath, changed his piece to its old position, and faced round and marched toward the door.

As he did so, something—not the something which the sentry said had fal'en down, but another something which had lain at full length in the top stair but one—moved gently. There was a faint gliding sound, and then perfect stillness, as the sentry marched in again right to the foot of the stairs and listened.

He turned, walked right round the hall, and out once more to the front of the porch, while something long and soft seemed in the darkness to rise out of the top stair but one, as from a long box, on to the stair below.

The sentry marched in again, slowly and steadily, right to the end of the hall, and back to the front of the porch; and as he went the gliding sound was heard again, followed during the next march back by a very faint crack, and then for quite five minutes the long, soft-looking figure lay on the stair motionless.

Then, when the sentry was tramping along the porch, the figure gave a quick writhe and lay still a step higher.

Again, when the sentry was his farthest, there was another writhe, and the figure was on the top of the stairs, to roll by degrees gently over and over across the landing, and lie close to the panelled wall. Then began a slow crawling motion as if some hugely thick short serpent were creeping along the polished oaken boards almost without a sound, till the end of the gallery was reached. Then all was still but the regular tramp of the sentry, who told himself that he had done wisely in not giving the alarm.

Not the first man who has congratulated himself upon making a great mistake.

Meanwhile, Lady Markham was seated at the window, with Lil's hand clasped in hers, waiting, as it were, for that something which seemed as if it would happen. No great wonder, at a time when change succeeded change with marvellous rapidity. They had neither of them spoke for some time, till suddenly Lil pressed her mother's hand.

"What is it, dear?"

"Listen!"

Lady Markham bent forward, and remained silent for some minutes before saying—

"I heard nothing, Lil."

"I thought I heard horses a long way off. Oh!"

She started violently, for there was a sharp, but faint tap on the panel of the door, as if some one had sharply loosened one finger-nail with the other.

Neither stirred for a few moments, and then the sharp cracking sound was repeated.

Lady Markham did not hesitate, but walked across to the door.

"Who is there?" she said in a low, firm voice.

There was a faint rustle, as of some one moving a hand over the door outside, and then from low down came a low—

"Hist!"

It was from the keyhole without a doubt, and stooping, Lady Markham repeated her question, placing her ear close to the keyhole, as she listened for the answer.

That reply sent the blood thrilling through her veins, as it was whispered through the keyhole, and for the moment, she felt giddy with anguish, love, and fear.

It came again, with an addition.

"Mother! Open! Quick!"

With her hands trembling so that they almost refused their office, she turned the key, felt a strong grasp on the handle, the door was thrust open softly, closed, and locked, as she stood trembling there, and a pair of arms were clasped around her neck.

"Mother, dearest mother!"

"Scar, dear Scar, me too," whispered Lil, for Lady Markham was speechless with emotion.

Brother and sister were locked in a loving embrace, and then Lil shrank away.

"Scar," she whispered; "why you are all wet."

"Yes," he said, with a half-laugh. "I had to swim across part of the lake."

"Oh, my boy, my boy, how did you get here?" whispered Lady Markham.

"Oh, I found a way, mother dear."

"But your father? Oh! There is no bad news?"

"No, no; don't tremble so. He is quite well, and not many miles away."

"Thank Heaven!" she sighed; "but, Scar, my darling, you do not know."

"Oh yes, I do, dear," he said calmly; "the house is full of rebels, and they have their outposts everywhere. I have had a fine task to get here without being seen."

"And you must not stay a moment, my darling. You must escape before you are discovered."

"Hush! don't speak so loudly; we may be heard. There is no danger, if you keep still."

"But, Scar, my boy, why have you run this terrible risk?"

"Soldiers have to run risks, mother. My father, who is at Ditton, with a strong body of horse, was terribly anxious about home. A spy came in and said the rebels were in this direction, so I said I could make my way here and get news, and he trusted me to come. That's all."

"But if you are taken, Scar?"

"I don't mean to be taken, mother. I shall go back as I came. Rebel sentinels are clever, but some people can manage to elude them."

"Oh, my boy, my boy!"

"Don't—don't fidget, dear, like that. I tell you there is no risk. But I must not stay long."

"Are you sure no one saw you come?"

"Quite certain. But I am sorry that I have such poor news to lake back. But, mother dear, they have treated you with respect?"

"Oh yes, my boy. Fred Forrester's with them."

"Ah!" ejaculated Scarlett, angrily.

"And he has been most respectful and kind."

"For a traitor."

"Do not speak harshly of him, Scar."

"Not I; but have they sacked the place?"

"No, no. Nothing has been touched."

"I'm glad of that, for poor father's sake. He will be enraged when he knows they have taken possession here."

"But he is in no danger, Scar?"

"Not more than usual," said Scarlett, grimly.

"And when is he coming home?" said Lil, thoughtfully.

"Coming home, Lil! Ah, who can say that? Well, I must soon be going. If I stay, it is to be taken prisoner."

"My darling!"

"Hush, mother! the sentries may hear you speak. They are all around."

"I will be careful, dear," she whispered. "Then you must go? So soon?"

"Yes; and it is bad news to take to my father, but he will not care when he hears that you are safe and well. What's that?"

He ran softly to the window, and they realised that he was barefooted, and only dressed in light breeches and shirt.

There was the sound of a challenge, a reply, and then the trampling of horses came through the open casement.

Lady Markham seized her son's hand as he stood listening at the deep mullioned window, while Lil clung to the other.

"A fresh detachment joined, I suppose," whispered Scarlett, as he drew back. "Perhaps I had better wait half an hour before I go back."

"Oh, Scar, Scar!" half sobbed Lil.

"And you so cold and wet, my darling," sighed Lady Markham.

"Pish! what of that. I don't mind. I would not go so soon, for it is quite delightful to be with you again, but I must be right away before it's light, and one never knows how far one may have to go round to escape notice from the enemy's men. They seem to swarm about here, mother."

Lady Markham could say nothing, only kiss and embrace her boy, torn as she was by conflicting emotions—the desire to keep him, and that of wishing him safe away.

All at once, Scar started from his mother's encircling arm, and darted to the window, but only to draw back, for there were two sentinels talking just beneath.

Then he ran to the door, but drew back, for steps of armed men were heard coming along the corridor, and escape was cut off there.

"Caught," he said grimly. "Poor father will not get his news."

At that moment there was the sharp summons of a set of knuckles on the door.

Chapter Twenty Eight
How Lady Markham Left the Hall

"Hist!" whispered Lady Markham, in her agitation snatching at the first straw that offered. "They may think we are asleep, and will go away."

Vain hope; there was another sharp rapping at the door.

"Answer," said Scarlett, in a low, firm voice. "Hear what they have to say."

"Who is there?"

"I, Fred Forrester, Lady Markham. Have the goodness to open."

"The traitor!" muttered Scar, glancing once more at the window, but the sounds from without told him that attempt to escape there was vain, for, if he dropped from the sill, the chances were that he would hurt himself, and even if he succeeded in reaching the ground unharmed, the alarm would be given by the sentinels, who would fire at him, and if they missed, there was a detachment of horse waiting to ride him down, for the steeds were stamping impatiently, and uttering a loud snort from time to time.

"Why am I disturbed at this time of the night?" said Lady Markham, trying to speak firmly and haughtily.

"I am sorry to have you disturbed, Lady Markham; but there is good reason. My mother is here."

"A ruse," said Scarlett, softly. "Never mind, dear. It is not the first time I have been a prisoner. It is madness to try to escape. I surrender."

"No, no," whispered Lady Markham. "You shall not." Then aloud. "I refuse to open my door at this time of night."

"Lady Markham, will you admit me alone to speak with you?" came now from outside.

"Hist!" whispered Scarlett. "They do not know I'm here. Open the door. It will be best."

As soon as he had spoken, he ran toward the great bedstead, but came back and whispered quickly—

"Open, dear mother, and try to invent some plan to get them all away from this room. Then I can easily escape. Quick. Open."

He darted to the bedstead, and drew one of the head curtains round him; while driven, as it were, to obey the stronger will of her son, urged, too, by his words about escape, Lady Markham went to the door, opened it, and Mistress Forrester stepped in, to pause for a moment, then, forgetful of everything but their old friendship in the happy days, she threw her arms about the trembling woman, and kissed her passionately.

"I have come to fetch you and dear Lilian," she said, "at my son's wish. He has obtained permission from the general, and horses are waiting. You are to come at once."

"Come—leave my husband's house?"

"Hush! do not oppose the plan," said Mistress Forrester, gently. "This is no longer a place for you. Perhaps for some time to come it may be the retreat of rough soldiery. My home is so near, and you will beat peace."

"I cannot leave my husband's home," said Lady Markham, firmly.

"You must," said her visitor. "It is for Lilian's sake as well as your own."

For Lilian's sake? Yes, and it was for Scarlett's sake. For what had he said? Get them away from this room, and he could escape. How or when she had no idea. All she knew was that he had said decidedly that he could, and she must believe him.

"Ah, you are hesitating!" said Mistress Forrester, tenderly. "You are thinking of enemies. What is this warfare to us? We are mothers, and our duty is toward our children. Say that you will come and stay with me in peace till better times are here."

Lady Markham hesitated no longer. It was a way of escape for her son, and protection for herself and daughter. Besides which, the old sisterly affection was as warm as ever.

"He would tell me to go, if he were here," she said to herself. "It is to save my boy;" and without another word she laid her hand in her visitor's.

Mistress Forrester kissed her eagerly, embraced Lilian, who stood there trembling and cold, and then ran to the door.

"Fred, my boy," she said quickly; "have all ready. Lady Markham will come."

There was the first sense of relief to the trembling mother's overladen heart as she heard the tramp of men in the corridor, and she glanced quickly toward the curtains which concealed her son.

"It will leave the way open for his escape," she said to herself. Then to Mistress Forrester, as she pointed at the farther door—

"Two of the servants who have remained with me through the troubles are there," she said.

"And they will accompany us, of course," said her visitor. "Will you tell them to get ready?"

"If you would not mind," said Lady Markham, appealingly; and without further parley Mistress Forrester crossed the room, tapped lightly, and passed through the door, while Lady Markham darted to the curtain and seized her son by the arm.

"Am I doing right?" she whispered.

"Quite, dearest mother," he replied in so low a tone that she could hardly hear. "Some day perhaps Fred and I may be friends again."

"Then I am to go?"

"Yes; it will give me a chance to escape."

"They are dressed and ready," said Mistress Forrester, returning. "Poor things, they have not been to bed."

At that moment there was another tap at the door, and upon its being opened, Fred was standing there.

"The horses are ready," he said quietly. "I have had your pony saddled, Lilian. Lady Markham, the two servants will have to ride pillion behind a couple of our men."

For answer Lady Markham drew her hood over her head, and assisted Lilian, who was ready to burst into a fit of hysterical sobbing; and in fear lest she should betray her brother's whereabouts, her mother hurried her to the door, but stopped to see all out before her, leaving last, and taking the precaution to slip the key from the lock, lest some one should come and her son should find it fast.

Ten minutes later, Scarlett Markham stood at the window listening to the setting off of the little party, with his head well hidden behind the curtain, and remained motionless till the trampling of the horses died away in the silence of the night.

"Ah," he said to himself, "nothing could have happened better, as the enemy is in possession. Poor mother! Poor Lil! What a pang to have to leave the dear old home; but they will be away from the tumult and bloodshed if the rebels stand. Now for my news, if I can carry it without being caught."

Chapter Twenty Nine
Scarlett Escapes under Difficulties

"Ugh! it's cold," said Scarlett, as he moved away from the window in his mother's chamber, and gave one look round in the gloom at the familiar old place, associated with his childhood and boyish life before he was forced into this premature manhood by the exigencies of the war. "But never mind; I shall soon be warm enough—hot enough, if I am seen and pursued."

He tightened the belt he wore, and drew a long breath, as if about to start running. Then crossing the room softly, he opened the door, meaning, as his mission was at an end, to make a bold quick rush for the secret stair, to open the slide and pass in. If he made a little noise there, the sentry might hear it and welcome, he would discover nothing.

A sudden thought struck him.

"Capital!" he said to himself, joyously. "Fifty men quietly introduced by the secret passage, and led right into the house. Why, we could surprise them all asleep, and the place would be taken without loss of life. What a result to an accidental discovery!"

Then a damping thought occurred.

"No," he muttered; "Fred will have remembered it, and made all safe. Perhaps let us get in, and trap us. He is too clever to leave that place open. He has not had time to secure it yet. What a pity we two are on opposite sides!"

As he thought this, he involuntarily raised his hand to his shortly cut hair, and a look of vexation crossed his face.

"Forward!" he muttered, as if giving an order, and to put an end to his musings; and at the word he was in the act of passing through the doorway, and had taken a step into the corridor when there was a sharp challenge from the sentry down in the hall. But the password was given, and by the sounds it seemed to Scarlett that two armed men had begun to ascend the stairs.

Yes, undoubtedly two, for one said something lightly, and he caught the reply.

"We'll soon see about that."

The words were in a subdued tone of voice, and passing back into the room, Scarlett drew the door after him, leaving a mere crack, so that he could listen.

"Officers going to their quarters," he thought. "I wonder which room they occupy."

He listened, and they reached the top of the stairs, turning to the left, a movement which brought them towards him.

He would have closed the door entirely, but dreading a noise that might betray him, he left it ajar, and stood waiting for them to pass, but only to flush crimson with indignation as a sudden thought struck him in answer to his wondering question.

"They would not dare!" he ejaculated in an angry whisper; and he turned to flee into the farther room, where the servants had been, and where as a rule his sister slept. But as he moved towards it quickly, it occurred to him that there were no such voluminous curtains for hiding behind, and, quick as thought, he darted to his old place of concealment, only just having time to throw the heavy hangings round him as the door was thrust back, and two men strode into the room.

"The cowardly, plundering villains!" muttered Scarlett, and his hands involuntarily clenched, and he felt ready to rush out and face these nocturnal marauders, but he checked the desire.

"Poor mother!" he sighed; "she would not value every jewel she possesses as a featherweight against my safety. They must go, I suppose; but oh, what a delight to make the rogues disgorge!"

"Plaguey dark," said one of the new-comers. "Light enough for what we want to do, my lad. Shut and fasten the door. We don't want any one to share our bit of luck."

"No. Just enough for two. It may be weeks before we get such another chance."

They were evidently well-to-do men, by their conversation, probably officers; and Scarlett bit his lip with rage as he thought of his mother's watch and chain, and the beautiful set of pearls, his father's present to her in happier days. Then, too, there was a case with rings and brooches, beside many other elegant little trifles that would be welcome to a plunderer.

Once more the desire to rush out and face these wretches was strong upon him, but a moment's reflection told him that to do so was to surrender himself a prisoner, and place himself beyond the power of giving valuable information to the general, his father, who might unwittingly come on to his old home and walk into a trap.

"Better lose a thousand times as many jewels," he muttered, "than that. Let them steal, for I suppose my poor mother would not have placed her treasures in a place of safety." He listened breathlessly behind the thick curtain, hoping that the plunderers would be quick and leave, and give him the opportunity to escape.

The chance came more quickly than he had anticipated, for it seemed from the footsteps that the men had gone into the inner chamber, leaving him free to slip out.

His hand was upon the thick fold of the curtain, for all was still in his mother's room, and he was mentally going on tiptoe to the door, when there was a loud yawn from the *prie dieu* chair close to the bed's head, and a voice almost at his elbow said —

"Well, what's it like?"

"Can't see much; but it seems a cosy little nest, as soft as can be."

"Which will you have, that or this?"

"Oh, I'll stop here," was the reply.

"Then may the trumpeter forget to blow for twenty-four hours," said the voice at Scarlett's elbow, "and the enemy never know that we are here."

"Amen!" came from the further room.

"And, I say," exclaimed Scarlett's neighbour, as he seemed to be moving about vigorously.

"Yes."

"Don't disturb anything. Poor ladies! it's like sacrilege to take possession here; but when there's a soft bed on one side and some straw on the boards of a loft on the other, one falls into temptation."

Clump went a heavy boot on the thick rug, and then another.

"Yes. Goodnight. Don't talk any more," came from the inner room.

"Not I," said Scarlett's neighbour; and there was the sound of a sword-belt being unbuckled, and the weapon laid across a table.

Then, as Scarlett stood there, hot and indignant, he heard the soft sound of stockinged feet crossing the room, and directly after a faint rattle at the door, followed by an angry exclamation, and then by a loud rumbling noise.

"What are you doing?" came from Lil's chamber.

"Pushing something against the door—big table. There's no key."

"Oh!"

The table seemed to be followed by something else heavy, and directly after the occupant of the room crossed to the bed, and it seemed to Scarlett that he threw himself upon his knees for a few minutes.

Then he rose, sighed, and yawned.

"Oh, for dear old home again, and peace," he muttered, and threw himself, all dressed as he was, upon the bed.

"By your leave, Dame Markham," he muttered again, with a sigh of satisfaction. "If you knew how dog-tired this poor soldier is, you would forgive me. Hah!"

There was a long deep sigh, and as Scarlett stood there so closely that he could have laid his hand upon his enemy's head, he felt that he was completely trapped, and that perhaps even to move was to ensure capture.

"What shall I do?" he asked himself. "It will be getting toward morning soon;" and now the necessity for escaping at once seemed ten thousand times more clear.

"He will come in search of me, for he will never think that the enemy can be at the Hall, or if he does, he will come to try and save me, thinking I am a prisoner, and there will be a battle here."

As he listened, trying hard to stifle his breathing and the throbbings of his heart, which sounded so loud that he felt sure he would be heard, the Parliamentary officer turned uneasily upon his bed, muttered something about home, and then his breathing became regular and deep.

When Scarlett had started upon his expedition to see if the enemy were near, and finding that they had taken possession of the Hall, determined to make use of the secret passage and see how his mother fared, he knew that everything depended upon quickness of movement, and that fighting would be of no avail. So he had stripped off buff jerkin and gorget, and placed them, his weapons, cavalier hat, and heavy horseman's boots in the wood where he had secured his horse. Hence he was absolutely defenceless.

He thought of this as he for a moment dwelt upon the possibility of slaying this man as he slept, and so escaping.

But he indignantly thrust from him the treacherous thought, and trusting to the possibility of getting away when his enemy should be sound asleep, he gradually let the curtain fall to his feet.

In the silence of that room the noise made as the thick material rustled down, seemed to Scarlett to be enough to awaken the sleeper, but he did not stir; and after wailing a few minutes, which seemed like an hour, the young Royalist began to move gently from his hiding-place.

The distance he had to traverse was very short, but there was a great difficulty awaiting him—the removal of the table and the other object placed against the door. But the sleeper was sound enough now, and Scarlett's hopes began to rise as, with outstretched hands, he softly touched the stand upon which lay the sword, and then his heart's pulsations seemed to stop, for he kicked against one of the heavy jack-boots in the darkness, and the great stiff leather foot and leg covering fell over with what seemed quite a loud noise, while to his horror Scarlett learned that the door between the rooms was open, so plainly sounded the other officer's voice.

"Anything the matter?" he said; and there was the rustling sound of one rising upon his elbow.

It was the saving instinct of the moment, and it had its intended effect, the boldness of the conception carrying all before it. For, as the officer in his sister's room asked that question, Scarlett covered his face with his hand, and uttered a deep yawn, like that of a half-sleeping man.

For a moment or two he dreaded lest he had betrayed himself, but to his intense delight, as he stood with every sense on the strain, he heard the questioner subside in his place, and Scarlett, with a quick appreciation of his difficulties, seized the opportunity of the man's movement to cover the sound he made as he glided quickly across the room to the door, laid his hand upon the table, and recognised it by the touch as the one which generally stood in the great embayment of the window.

But, just as he touched the heavy carved side, he broke out into a cold perspiration, for there came in a sharp, short, imperious tone—

"Halt!"

"He was not asleep," thought Scarlett; and in an instant he had seized the table to drag it away, when a loud sound from the adjoining chamber made him drop down on his hands and knees, in the expectation of a bullet from a petronel.

The sound he had heard was that of a man leaping from his bed. Then there were the dull soft steps of stockinged feet, and he could hear the second officer enter the room.

"What's the matter?" he said, as he advanced toward the bed where his companion lay.

"Left troop to the front!" came from the bed.

"Poor old fellow!" muttered the second officer. "He cannot even keep this weary work out of his sleep."

Scarlett heard him walk back to the inner room, and as soon as he felt that the door was passed, he began to feel for the second obstacle between him and liberty.

For a few moments he could not make out what it was. He tried softly to left and right, but there was nothing. All he could detect was that the end of the long table was against the door, and then as he rose and stretched his hand across it, he discovered at once what it was—nothing but a heavy oaken chest, which had been lifted up and stood upon the table, to give it weight.

Meanwhile, he could hear every movement of the occupant of the inner chamber, and a dull feeling of despair came upon him, as he knew that to attempt to stir the table, heavily laden as it was, would make so much noise that he would be detected.

"But could I get through in time to reach the stair?" he thought.

Impossible! He would be heard by the officer, and probably by the sentinel in the hall, and with his heart sinking, he determined to make for the window, and drop down from there.

The casement was still open, and crossing softly, he cautiously looked out, to find that a couple of sentinels were marching to and fro to meet every minute just beneath the spot where he stood.

"No," he said to himself, "there is but one road;" and going back to the table, he nerved himself for the effort, and began to draw it softly away by almost imperceptible degrees.

Fortunately for him, the floor by the door was covered by a thick rug, over which the table began to move; but, to Scarlett's horror, it had not passed a couple of inches before there was a sharp crack.

An impatient movement came from the far room, and Scarlett knew as well as if he were present in the broad daylight, that the officer had started up and was listening; but, fortunately at that moment, the heavy sleeper said something aloud and stirred upon the bed.

This was sufficient to satisfy his companion, who lay down again. But it was impossible to attempt more for a time, and the would-be fugitive was forced to crouch there, letting the valuable moments fly, and fretting, as he knew how impossible it would be for him to escape if he waited till day.

At last, with the feeling of despair upon him strongly, he seized the table again, and, lifting one end, drew it slowly towards him, this time finding, to his great delight, that the rug glided with it over the oaken boards, so that he knew that with a little more effort, the obstacle would be sufficiently far away for him to open the door.

Had it been light, he would have seen the danger, but, all he realised was that the table came along more and more easily, and then in the black darkness there was a loud crash, the coffer placed upon the table had, consequent upon its being inclined, glided slowly over the polished surface, till it was right beyond the edge, and then it was but a matter of moments before it overbalanced and fell.

Scarlett heard two loud ejaculations and the leaping of his enemies from their beds; but, quick as thought, he had dragged the door open, bounded into the corridor, and ran to the left to the top of the stairs.

He was in the act of seizing the balustrade, when shouts came from the door he had left. Worse still, he saw a faint spark of light below him, and heard the challenge of the sentry in the hall.

To have tried to escape by the passage would have meant the discovery of the way, for there was not time to get the stair open, so without hesitation, as he heard the alarm spreading, he dashed down the stairs, followed by the shouts of the two officers as other doors were opened, and the noise of gathering feet could be heard.

There was a sharp flash, a loud report, and Scarlett heard the thud in the wainscot beside him as he leaped the last half-dozen stairs, right on to the sentinel, who was driven backward by the force of the blow, while Scarlett darted across the hall, through the porch, and between two of the men stationed outside so closely that they touched him.

"Fire, fire!" roared a voice from the gallery, and matches were blown, and shots went whizzing after the fugitive, who was hard followed by half a dozen of the heavily armed men.

But the darkness held good, and Scarlett had the advantage of knowing every inch of the ground, every bush and clump which could give him shelter; and besides, he was dressed for running, his pursuers being heavily hindered by their thick garments, steel protections, and heavy boots.

Still the pursuit was kept up, and the piquets round, alarmed by the sounds of firing, began to close in.

It was a desperate game to play, but Scarlett played it. He made straight for the lake, and kept as near to its bank as he could for the overhanging trees, till he neared the eastern end, where, with the shouts of his pursuers ringing in his ears, he slowly lowered himself down by the steep rocky bank, stepped silently into the clear water, which looked terribly black and treacherous, waded out a short distance, with the water rapidly rising to his chest, then to his chin, and began swimming as easily as an otter for the opposite side.

It was a cold plunge, but Scarlett did not notice it in his excitement. His mind was too much taken up with endeavouring to swim steadily and quietly, so as not to betray his whereabouts by a splash.

As he swam, he could see lights moving about in the Hall, and he could tell by the shouts that his pursuers were not very far distant, while soon after he began to realise, with a profound feeling of satisfaction, that the men and their leaders had come to the conclusion that they had only to form a line across from the house down to the shore in two places to succeed in capturing him, for the lake would be an effectual bar to his escape in that direction.

"And all the time this is the high-road to freedom," Scarlett said to himself, as he swam on, thinking of how long it would take him to reach the further side, and reaping now the advantage of having acquired an accomplishment in his earlier days, whose value he little appreciated then.

The distance seemed greater than he had reckoned upon, and he had not been in the water for a long time before that night, the consequence being that after he had been swimming about ten minutes, a peculiar weary sensation began to make itself felt in his arms, and a strange aching at the nape of his neck, as if he had been forcing his head too far back so as to enable him to keep his lips and nostrils above the surface.

Then, too, he became aware that swimming without clothes was one thing, with them clinging to his limbs another; and the thought occurred to him, as unpleasant thoughts will, just when they are not wanted, that it was somewhere out here he and Fred Forrester had lowered down a weight at the end of a piece of twine, to find in one spot it was twenty feet, in another twenty-five; but all over this eastern end there was a great depth of water.

It was impossible after that to help thinking about people losing their lives. A boy had once been drowned out there through trying to cross the ice before it was sufficiently strong, and—

A curious hysterical sensation attacked Scarlett Markham just then, and for a few moments, unnerved by the excitement of the evening, he began to strike out more quickly, under the mistaken notion that he would reach the opposite side much sooner; but the fatigue of the effort warned him that he was doing wrong, and growing calmer, he turned over on his back to float for a few minutes, while he diverted his thoughts from his position by forcing himself to think about his pursuers, whom he could hear plainly enough calling and answering each other.

Then once more the thought forced itself upon him that it was terribly deep down below, that he was growing utterly exhausted, and that if he sank and was drowned, no one had seen him enter the water, and his father—his mother—

"Oh, am I such a coward as this!" he muttered angrily. "After being in battle and skirmish, and hearing the cannons roar, I will swim across."

He turned, and will did what will often does, gives to those who are determined powers that others do not seem to possess; and so it came that the rest of the task grew comparatively easy, the bank which in the gloom had seemed to be so distant suddenly loomed over him, with the pendent branches of the birches within easy reach, and a few moments later he was ashore, had climbed the bank, paused to look back, and then started off at an easy run, with the load of water he carried becoming lighter at every step.

Later on, mounted men came round both ends of the lake, and began to search on the further side, but by this time the fugitive was well on toward where he had left his horse and arms, and his dangers lay in front, and not behind.

Long before all this, Lady Markham had arrived at the Manor, with Lil weeping silently at her side. There had been a brief and formal leave-taking, a quick embrace from his mother, and Fred rode back with his detachment, to reach the Hall, take possession of the quarters assigned to him, and after thinking deeply of the events of the night, he dropped asleep. He was aroused by the noise, and heard that the sentinels had fired upon an escaping figure, which had endeavoured to break into the room occupied by two of the officers.

There were those who said it was an attempt at assassination, and others that it was a false alarm, which the ill success of the search-party seemed to confirm.

Then fresh sentinels were posted, and the day soon after began to break with its promise of a glorious morrow, and soon after the first glow of orange in the east told of the coming sun, and as it shone through the casement of a long low room where a pale slight girl was lying asleep, it illumined the handsome sad countenance of one who had not slept, but had knelt there praying for the safety of her son.

Chapter Thirty
A Desperate Gallop

To Fred's great satisfaction, the sturdy, serious-looking followers of General Hedley treated the Hall and its surroundings with a fair amount of respect.

They did not scruple to make bountiful use of the contents of the garden; and, as far as they went, revelled on the productions of the dairy, while they one and all declared the cider to be excellent.

So comfortable were the quarters, that the absence of news of the expected reinforcements gave great satisfaction to all but the general, who walked up and down Sir Godfrey's library fretting at the inaction, and shaking his head at his young follower, who was for the time being acting as his secretary, but with no despatches to write.

"It's bad, Fred Forrester—bad," he said. "When you have anything to do, let it be done firmly and well. Let there be no procrastination. Your father ought to be here by now."

"I don't think it can be his fault, sir," said Fred, stoutly.

"It's somebody's fault," said the general, angrily. "No, no; I am sure it is not his. Well, I must have the men out to do something. No rust, Fred Forrester, no rust. What are you going to do?"

"Take my place in the regiment, sir, if you have no more writing for me to do."

"Don't want to go over to the Manor, then, to see the ladies, and ask how all are?"

"Of course I should like to, sir, but I was not going to ask leave."

"You can go, my lad. There is no news of the enemy, and the scouts are well out in every direction. Be on the look-out though, and I cannot give you more than three hours."

Overjoyed at this unexpected piece of good fortune, Fred hurried to his sleeping quarters, to try and give a few touches to his personal appearance, for, after months in the field, he did not feel at all proud of his sombre and shabby uniform.

This done, he made off just as the little force of well-mounted, sturdy men under the general's command were filing slowly out, and making for the broad open park, where a long and arduous drill was to be carried out.

It was a glorious day, and the prospect of being at home for even so short a time, and seeing his mother and those who had been his best friends was delightful. There was no sign of warfare anywhere, such as he had seen in other parts, in the shape of devastated crops and burned outhouses. But as he rose one of the hills that he had to cross, a glint of steel, where the sun shone on a morion, showed where one of the outposts was on the look-out. Further on, away to the left, he caught sight of another, and knowing pretty well where to look, he had no difficulty, sooner or later, in making out where the different vedettes were placed.

"Puzzle an enemy to catch our weasel asleep," he said to himself, laughingly, as he trotted on. "Why, if all our leaders were like General Hedley and my father, the war would soon be at an end—and a good thing too."

He rode on, thinking of the reception he would get, and hoping that Lady Markham would not behave coldly to him; and then the watchfulness of the pupil in military matters came out.

It was not his business to see where the outposts were, but it seemed to come natural to him to note their positions.

"I might have to place men myself, some day," he said; "and it's as well to know."

"Yes; there he is," he muttered, as he caught sight of another and then of another far away, but forming links of a chain of men round the camp, well within touch of each other, and all ready to gallop at the first alarm.

"There ought to be one out here," said Fred, at last, just as he was nearing the Manor; and for the moment he was ready to pass him over, and think of nothing but those whom he had come to see, but discipline mastered.

The spot he was approaching was a little eminence, which commanded a deep valley or coombe, that went winding and zigzagging for miles, and here he looked in vain for the outpost.

"Strange!" thought Fred; and he rode on a little further, till he was nearly to the top of the eminence, when his heart leaped, and by instinct he clapped his hand to his sword. For there, with lowered head, cropping the sweet short grass among the furze and heath, was the outpost's horse; and this, to Fred's experienced eye, meant the rider shot down at his post.

Half dreaming a similar fate, he looked sharply round, and then uttered an angry exclamation, as he touched his horse's flanks, and rode forward to where the man lay between two great bushes.

But not wounded. The secret of his fall was by his side. By some means he had contrived to get a large flask of wine up at the Hall, and the vessel lay by him empty, while he was sound asleep.

"You scoundrel!" cried Fred, closing up and bending down to take hold of the man's piece, where it stood leaning against a bush.

As he raised it, a distant flash caught his eye, and there, winding slowly and cautiously along the bottom of the coombe, with advanced guards, came a strong body of horsemen, whose felt hats and feathers here and there told only too plainly that they belonged to the Cavaliers.

To his horror, Fred saw that some of the advance were coming up the side of the valley not two hundred yards away, and that unless the alarm were given, the little force so calmly going through their manoeuvres in the park would be surprised. At the same moment, he saw that he had been noticed before he caught sight of the approaching enemy, but he did not hesitate. Raising the heavy piece, he fired, and at the shot the grazing horse tossed its head and cantered to his side, leaving its master to take his chance.

"He'll get no wine as a prisoner," said Fred, bitterly, as he spurred his horse to a gallop, just as shot after shot from the other outposts carried on his alarm—while, following a shout to him to surrender, came shots that were not intended to give the alarm, but to bring him down.

Fred glanced back once, and saw that the advance guard of the enemy were in full pursuit, a sight which made him urge on his steed to its utmost, while as he glanced back on getting to the top of the next hill, he could see that the enemy had divided into two bodies, and throwing off all concealment, they were thundering on, so as to get up with those who would spread the alarm, intending to spread it themselves, and to a dangerous extent.

"They'll overtake me," muttered Fred, as he looked back and saw how well some of the leading men were mounted, and also that some of those in the main body were better mounted still, and were rapidly diminishing the distance between them and their advance guard.

Right and left and well ahead of him he could see their own outposts galloping in toward the centre, but, strive how he would, he felt that he must be overtaken long before he could reach the Hall.

"They will not kill me," he said to himself. "They would only make a prisoner of me, unless some fierce Cavalier cuts me down."

"But I have saved them from a surprise," he continued; and he once more tried to get a little speed out of the worn-out horse he rode.

It was a neck-or-nothing gallop, and over and over again Fred would have been glad to change his mount, and leap on to the trained horse which kept its place riderless by his side. But the enemy were thundering on in full pursuit, and to have paused meant certain capture.

On they rode, the Cavaliers behind, with their blades flashing, and their feathers streaming, and in the excitement of the race he could not help thinking of the gallant appearance they made, as they spurred one against the other in their reckless endeavour to overtake him.

He had forsaken the road, and turned on to the rough moorland, a more difficult way, but he and his horse were more at home there, and he knew how to avoid the roughest rocky portions, and the pieces of bog, while there was always the hope that the pursuers might try to make some cut to intercept him, and so find themselves foundered in the mire.

The race had lasted some minutes now, and the fugitive was in full hope that the alarm had been spread by the inner line of vedettes, when a bright thought flashed across his brain.

He glanced back, and could see about a dozen of the Cavaliers some forty yards behind, and a few hundred yards behind them a couple of regiments.

"They will follow my pursuers," he argued; and as he came to that conclusion, he drew his right rein, and bore off a little, making straight for a deep hollow where the peat lay thick, and it was impossible for a horse to cross.

If they followed him there, he could swerve off to the right again as he reached the treacherous ground, and edge safely round it, while the main body of his pursuers would in all probability plunge in.

"That would ensure their defeat," he said to himself, as in imagination he saw the gallant regiments floundering saddle deep in the black, half-liquid peat.

As he had hoped, so it seemed to be. His nearest pursuers turned off after him, so did the main body, and, almost indifferent now as to capture, so long as he could save those at the park, he turned to look back, when, just as the Cavaliers were thundering on to destruction, one horseman dashed in front, waving his plumed hat, and meeting them—sending all but about half a score round to the left, so that they skirted the morass, just as they were on the point of charging in.

"Some one who knows the danger," muttered Fred, as he galloped on. "Scarlett, of course. It must have been he."

Another five minutes, with the foremost men not half a dozen yards behind, brought Fred to the top of a hill, beyond which he could see the park, and to his horror the general's men were only then hurrying up into formation, with their officers galloping excitedly to and fro.

"Hold out, good old horse," panted Fred,—as he glanced back once more to see that capture must be certain now. "Another five minutes, and I could be with them," he sobbed out breathlessly; and, as if his horse understood him, or else nerved by the sight of his fellows so near at hand, he lay out like a greyhound, just as a trumpet blast rang out on Fred's left from the main body of the Cavaliers, a call whose effect was that Fred's pursuers who had skirted the right of the morass, turned off to the left, and rode on so as to regain their places in the ranks, where their presence would be of more value than in pursuing a few scattered outposts.

To an ordinary commander, the act of the Royalist leader seemed utter madness. The horses of his men were half-blown by a long gallop, and they were about to charge a body of sturdy cavalry, whose mounts were rested and fresh.

But there was no hesitation. As they drew near, the trumpets rang out, steel flashed, feathers flew, the horses snorted, and with a wild hurrah! the Royalist troops literally raced against the advancing Parliamentarians. There was a shock, the crash of steel, a roar as of thunder, horse and man went headlong down on the green turf of the Hall park, and to General Hedley's chagrin, and in spite of the valour of his officers, and the stern stuff of which his men were composed, the gallantry and dash of the first regiment was such that it seemed as if a wedge had been driven through his ranks, and his discomfiture was completed by the following charge of the second Cavalier line.

One minute his well-trained horsemen were advancing in good formation to meet the shock of the Royalists, the next, discipline seemed to be at an end, and the Parliamentarians were in full flight.

Chapter Thirty One
Samson to the Rescue

Unscathed, in spite of the terrible dangers of the *mêlée*, Fred, after succeeding in reaching his companions, joined them in their charge, and was driven back in their reverse, riding headlong as they rode in what was hardly a retreat, but rather a running fight, till seeing his opportunity, he made for where he could see General Hedley striving, in company with the officers, to check the retrograde movement, but striving in vain.

For there was a wild valour and dash exhibited by the Cavaliers, which for the time being carried all before them. No sooner had something like a rally been made by the Parliamentarians, than the Royalists charged at them in a headlong rush, which would have ended in almost total destruction with some troops.

But there was a sturdy solidity about the followers of General Hedley, and the result of these charges was that, while some fell, the others were merely moved here and there, and as soon as their assailants had passed on they seemed to hang together again, driven outward always, but not scattered. In fact, for mile after mile the running fight was continued, growing slower and slower as horse and man were wearied out, till, had a minute's grace been afforded them, General Hedley felt that he could have gathered his men together, and by one vigorous charge have changed the state of affairs.

But the opportunity for re-formation was never afforded, and the great crowd of mounted men of both parties rode on mingled together in confusion, right over the wild moorland countryside. The number of individual combats was almost countless, and their track was marked by the heather being dotted with fallen men, the wounded, and often the dismounted, and by exhausted or hopelessly foundered horses.

And still the fight went on, with the attacks growing more feeble, till the Cavaliers' horses could hardly be spurred into a canter, and many a one stopped short.

It was a strange flight, in which the beaten gave way slowly, and with an obstinate English tenacity of purpose, which made them cling to their enemies, and refuse to acknowledge their rout. They were broken up, and, according to all preconceived notions of cavalry encounters, they ought to have scattered and fled, but they only went on as they were driven and broken up in knots, and the Cavalier leader knew perfectly well that the moment he ceased his efforts, the other party would, as it were, flow together again and return their charge, perhaps with fatal results to his little force, for his men were growing completely exhausted.

"If I could only get a troop together!" muttered General Hedley between his teeth; and again and again he tried to rally his men. But the Cavaliers dashed at them directly, the efforts proved vain, and the *mêlée* continued—a struggle in which order was absent, and men struck and rode at each other, broke their weapons, and often engaged in a mounted wrestling bout, which ended in a pair of adversaries falling headlong to the ground. Fred would have been out of the skirmish early in the engagement from the exhaustion of his horse, but as the pace grew slower, the poor brute recovered itself somewhat, and whenever flight or attack grew more rapid, exerted itself naturally to keep as near as could be in the ranks.

The scene was terrible for one so young, as he sat there grimly, often in the middle of a confused crowd, his sword drawn ready more for defence than offence, for now that the excitement of the flight was over, and he had rejoined his regiment, there was little of the blind desire to strike and slay in Fred Forrester's breast. He contented himself with turning aside thrusts and meeting blows with a clever guard, as some Cavalier tried to reach him, while twice over he found another sword interposed on his behalf.

The fight must have lasted for half an hour, when about a dozen of the Cavaliers raised a shout, and made a dash at where General Hedley was slowly retreating, their object being evidently to take him prisoner before, from sheer exhaustion, the pursuit was given up.

But the idea was not so easy to carry out, though for the moment the general was alone. The horse he rode was strong and fairly fresh, those of his would-be captors pretty well foundered, and, in addition, there was help at hand.

Fred had just had a narrow escape, for a stout Cavalier had forced his own horse alongside, contriving, in spite of the lad's efforts, to get upon his left or weaker side, and pressing him sorely. Fred had need for all the skill with the sword he had picked up since he had been with the army, and he had dire need for more power in his muscles, for after a minute's foining and thrusting, he found his guard beaten down through his adversary's superior strength, a hand was outstretched, catching him by the collar of his jerkin, and in spite of his efforts he was dragged sidewise toward the pommel of his enemy's horse.

"I'll have one prisoner, at all events," growled the man, fiercely; and he gave Fred's horse a savage kick in the ribs, with the intention of making him start away.

Had the horse followed the enemy's wishes, his rider would have been unseated, but, instead of starting away, the well-drilled beast pressed closer alongside the horse by his side, and Fred still clung to the saddle.

"Ah, you wretched young Puritan spawn! Would you sting?" growled the man, as Fred made a desperate effort to use his sword. "Then take that."

The Cavalier rose in his stirrups, and was in the act of striking with all his might, when a fresh sword parted the air like a flash, swung as it was by a muscular arm, and the middle of the blade caught the Cavalier trooper right upon the plated cheek-strap of the morion he wore, dividing it so that the steel cap flew off, and the man dropped back over the cantle of his saddle, his frightened horse making a bound forward and carrying his master a dozen yards before he fell heavily on the heath.

"Who says I can't use a sword as well as a scythe?" cried a familiar voice.

"Oh, Samson, you've saved my life," cried Fred.

"Serve you right, too, my lad—I mean, serve him right, too. Trying to chop down a boy like you."

"I am sorry. Look, look, look!" cried Fred, excitedly.

"Eh? Look? What at?"

"Over yonder, where all those Cavaliers are crowding together to make another charge."

"Yes, I see 'em. What a state their horses are in!"

"But don't you see Scarlett Markham? And who's that with them? I see now. Your brother."

"What, Nat? Where, where? Let me get at him. There's going to be a prisoner took now, Master Fred, and he'll have to look sharp to get away."

Samson set spurs to his horse, but Fred checked him by seizing the bridle.

"No, no," he said; "keep by me, and let's close up to the general. This is no time for personal feelings, Samson. We must think only of our party."

"Ah, well, I won't hurt him, Master Fred; but how would you like your brother to be hunting you about the country, as Nat has been hunting us? Wouldn't you like to have a turn at him?"

"I have no brother, Samson," replied Fred, as he glanced in the direction where, about a hundred yards away, Scarlett was in the midst of a group of the Cavaliers, who were steadily driving the grim Cromwellian troopers before them, and effectually keeping them from combining so as to retaliate with effect.

Then Scarlett was hidden from his sight, and yielding slowly step by step, the Parliamentarians kept up a defiant retreat.

It might be supposed that at such a time the slaughter would be terrible; but, after the first onset, when men went down headlong, the number of killed and wounded were few. For there were no withering volleys of musketry, no field-pieces playing upon the disorganised cavalry from a distance; it was a sheer combat of mounted men armed with the sword, against whose edge and point defensive armour was worn; and in consequence many of the wounds were insignificant, more injuries being received by men being dismounted than by the blades.

The officers of the retreating party kept up their efforts to rally their little force, but always in vain, for the gathering together of a cluster of men resulted in the Cavaliers making that the point for which they made, and they carried all before them.

"They are more than two to one, literally," growled the general, fiercely, as he felt that there was nothing to be done but to summon his men to follow, and, taking advantage of the fresher state of their horses, put on all the speed they could, and make for a valley right ahead, where they might elude their pursuers, and accepting the present defeat endeavour to make up for it another time.

Giving the order then, the trumpet rang out, and the men sullenly obeyed, setting spurs to their horses, and for the most part extricating themselves from their pursuers, whose horses began to stagger and even stop as their masters urged them to the ascent of a slope, up which the Parliamentarians were retreating.

This being the case, their own leader ordered his trumpeter to sound a halt, and the successful party set up a tremendous cheer as they waved their hats and flashed their swords in the sunshine.

"Yes," muttered General Hedley, as he looked back at his triumphant enemies exulting over his defeat, but too helpless to pursue, "make much of it; a reverse may come sooner than you expect."

"I don't like being beaten like this, Master Fred," grumbled Samson, leaning over to smooth the reeking coat of the horse his young master rode; "and it's all your fault."

"My fault? How?"

"Holding me back as you did, and letting that brother of mine get away sneering and sniggering at me, with his nose cocked up in the air, and swelling with pride till he's like the frog in the fable."

"How do you know he was sneering at you?" said Fred, who felt stiff, sore, and as if he would give anything to dismount and lie down among the soft elastic heather.

"How do I know, sir? Why, because it's his nature to. You don't understand him as I do. I can't see him, because I can't look through that hill, but I know as well as can be that he's riding on his horse close to Master Scarlett, and going off."

"Going off?"

"Yes, sir, in little puffs of laughing. It's his aggravating way. And he's keeping on saying, 'Poor old Samson!' till it makes my blood bile."

"What nonsense! He is more likely to be riding away jaded, and sore, and disheartened."

"Not he, sir, because he aren't got no heart, and never had none—leastways, not a proper sort of heart. I can feel it, and I always could. He's a-sneering at us all, and thinking how he has beaten us, when, if you had let me have my head, I could have gone at him sword in hand—"

"And cut his head off?"

"Cut his head off, sir? Why, it aren't worth cutting off. I mean to keep my sword, which is a real good bit o' stuff, and as sharp as a scythe, for better heads than his. I wouldn't stoop to do it. No, Master Fred, I tell you what I'd have done: I'd have ridden up to him right afore 'em all, and I should have said, 'Nat, my lad, your time's come;' and I should have laid hold of him by the scruff of the neck, and beat him with the flat of the blade till he went down on his knees and said he wouldn't do so any more."

"Do what any more, Samson?"

"Everything as he have been doing."

"And suppose he wouldn't have let you beat him before all the others?"

"Wouldn't have let me, Master Fred? He'd have been obliged to. I should have made him."

"You are too modest, Samson," said Fred, laughing.

"Oh no, I'm not, sir—not a bit. I wish sometimes I was a bit more so. But you should have let me go at him, sir. I'd have made him run, like a sheep with a dog at his heels."

"Ah, Samson," cried Fred, wearily, "it's sore work when brothers are fighting against each other."

"No worse, sir, than two such friends as you and Master Scarlett was. Why, you was more than brothers. Oh, I don't like this here at all."

"What?"

"Running away with our tails between our legs, like so many dogs with stones thrown at 'em."

"It is miserable work, but better than being taken prisoners."

They rode on down into the coombe, and followed its wanderings with rear and advance guards, though they felt but little fear of pursuit, and for a long time hardly a word was spoken along the ranks. The horses were going at a foot-pace, and as they went the troopers played surgeon to each other, and bound up the slight wounds they had received, for these were many, though not enough to render them beyond fighting if necessity should occur.

Once the general called a halt, and posted scouts on the hills around, while he gave his men an opportunity to water their horses at the running stream at the bottom of the coombe, and to attend to the wounds the poor beasts had received, many a sword-cut intended for the rider having fallen upon his horse.

The surgery in these cases was simple and effectual. It consisted in thrusting a pin, sometimes two, through the skin which formed the lips of the wound, and then twisting a piece of thread round and round the pin, passing it first under the head, and then under the point, the result being that the wound was drawn close, and so retained with a pad of thread. This rough treatment generally proved sufficient, and while the treatment was in progress the poor animals stood patiently turning their great, soft, earnest eyes upon the operator with a mournful look which seemed to say, "Don't hurt me more than you can help." Sometimes, but these were the exceptions, when instead of the above a stab had to be attended to, and a plug of flax thrust in, the horse would start, and give an angry stamp with its hoof, but only to stand patiently again, as if it resigned itself to its master, who must know what was best.

The general soon gave orders to continue the march, for he knew that the longer they stayed the stiffer and sorer his force would be; and once more the retreat was continued in a south-westerly direction, while, as the afternoon began to grow old, Samson, after having been very silent for a long time, turned sharply round.

"What are you thinking about, Master Fred?"

"I was wondering whether Scarlett Markham will behave as well to my mother as I did to his."

"He'd better," said Samson, fiercely. Then, after a pause, "Oh, I don't feel afraid about that, sir. He's sure to. You see, he's a gentleman, and there's a deal in being a gentleman. He'll take care of her, never fear. That's not what I was thinking."

"What were you thinking, then?" said Fred, anxiously.

"Well, sir, to speak the plain, downright, honest truth, as a Coombeland man should, whether he be a soldier or a gardener—"

"Yes, yes. Go on. You talk too much, Samson," said Fred, pettishly, for he was faint and sore.

"Well, sir, suppose I do. But I aren't neglecting anything, and there's nothing else to do. Seems quite a rest to hear one's self speak."

"Then speak out, and say what you were thinking."

"I was thinking, sir, that I wish I was a horse just now."

"A horse? Why?"

"So as I could have a good fill of water, and keep on taking a bite of sweet fresh green grass."

"Why, Samson!"

"Ah, you don't know, Master Fred. I'm that hungry, it wouldn't be safe to trust me anywhere near meat; and not so much as a turnip anywhere, nor a chance to catch a few trout. I wish I could tickle a few; I'd eat 'em raw."

"I'm sorry, Samson, and I haven't a scrap of food with me."

"No, sir, nor nobody else. You see, we were all out for exercise, and not on the march, with our wallets full. And that aren't the worst of it. Master Fred, I could lie down and cry."

"Because you are so hungry?"

"No, sir; but when I think of what we've left behind at the Hall. Ducks, sir, and chickens; and there was hams. Oh!" groaned Samson, laying his hand just below his heart, "those hams!"

Fred was weak, tired, faint, and low-spirited, but the doleful aspect of his henchman was so comic that he burst into a fit of laughter.

"Well, Master Fred," said the ex-gardener, letting the reins rest on the horse's neck, as he involuntarily tightened his belt, "I did think better of you than to s'pose you'd laugh at other folk's troubles. Then there was the cider, too. It wasn't so good as our cider at the Manor, sir, for they hadn't got the apples at the Hall to give it the flavour, spite of old Nat's bragging and boasting; but still, it wasn't so very bad for a thirsty man, though I will say it was too sharp, and some I tasted yesterday told tales."

"What of, Samson?"

"My lazy, good-for-nothing brother, sir," said Samson, triumphantly.

"Told tales of your brother—of Nat?"

"Yes, sir. There was a twang in that cider that said quite aloud, 'Dirty barrel,' and that he hadn't taken the trouble to properly wash it out before it was used; but all the same, though it was half spoiled by his neglect, I'd give anything for a mugful of it now, and a good big home-made bread cake."

"So would I, Samson," said Fred, smiling.

"And them enemies with my brother are all riding comfortably back to feast and sleep; and while we're camping cold and miserable on the hills, they'll all be singing and rejoicing."

"I hope they are thinking more of the poor wounded fellows they will have to pick up on their way back. Hallo! Look! Steady there. Halt!"

He passed the word received from the front, for half a mile ahead, on one of the hills, a scout was signalling.

Fresh men were sent forward, and as the signals evidently meant danger ahead, the general hurriedly took up a position of advantage, one which gave him the choice of advance or retreat.

"Dismount!" was the next order, so as to rest the horses as much as possible.

"More fighting," said Samson, in a low, grumbling tone. "Well, if one don't get enough to eat, one get's enough hard knocks, and I never felt miserly over them. Look here, Master Fred, are we going to have another scrummage?"

"Hush! Yet, I think so."

"So do I, sir," said Samson, taking up his belt another hole. "Very well, then; I'm that hungry, that I'm regularly savage now, and this time I mean to hit with all my might."

"Silence, there!" said a deep stern voice, and General Hedley rode along the regiment, scrutinising his little force, and waiting the return of the men sent out before deciding whether he should make a bold advance or a cautious retreat.

The horses took advantage of the halt to begin cropping the tender growth around, and as Fred listened and watched the movements of the scouts far away on the hillside, it seemed hard to realise that he was in the midst of war, for high overhead a lark was singing sweetly, as it circled round and round, ever rising heavenward; and at his feet there was the regular tearing sound of the grass.

These recollections of home and peace came back as, with a look of boyish pleasure on his face, Samson pointed to the lovely little copper butterflies flitting here and there, their dotted wings glistening in the sun.

"Look at 'em, Master Fred," he whispered; and then stood with his hand upon his horse's withers, the stern man of war once more, as his master made a gesture bidding him hold his peace.

For quite half an hour they stood there by their horses' sides, every minute being of value in the rest and refreshment it afforded the weary beasts.

The scouts could be seen following up, as it were, the movements of some force hidden by the hills from where the regiment had halted, and by degrees they began to work over the eminence and disappeared, while the general seemed to be fretting with impatience, till all at once those near him heard him utter a low "Hah!" and he gave the order to his men to prepare to mount.

A thrill ran through the long line of men, and Fred heard his follower utter a low, adjuration to his unwilling steed.

"Leave off eating, will you? Hold your head up. Who are you, that you are to go on feasting while your master starves?"

The horse looked at him reproachfully, and had to content itself with chewing a few strands of grass off his bit.

The reason for the general's order was plain enough directly, for they could see one of the advance men coming back at full gallop down the distant hill, and long before he could reach them the other scouts appeared, retiring slowly in two lines, one sitting fast and facing the approaching force, while the other careered by them, and took up a fresh position in their rear.

There were only ten men out, at a distance of sixty or seventy yards apart, but as they drew nearer to their goal their lines contracted, and this was continued so that they could ride in as a compact little knot.

Meanwhile the first man came tearing in as fast as his horse could go, and when he was a few hundred yards away, the order was given, and the dismounted men sprang into the saddle.

"Don't seem to have a bit of fight left in me now," muttered Samson. "No dinner, and no Nat here to make a man feel savage. Wish I was back at the Manor, digging my bit o' ground. Anybody might fight for me."

At that moment a fresh order was given, and every man sat stern and ready for the advance or retreat, wondering which way they would go, and of what nature the force was, evidently advancing fast.

Chapter Thirty Two
The Hall Changes Masters Again

The cheering and triumphant congratulation amongst the Royalist party was mingled with regret at being unable to crown their little victory by taking their opponents prisoners to a man. But their horses were exhausted, and they had the mortification of seeing the little body under General Hedley ride away.

Then the order to return was given, and a strong party was told off to the painful duty of picking up the wounded, and bearing them back to the Hall.

Sir Godfrey Markham gave the order that they should be taken there, and Scarlett was deputed to see that the work was properly carried out—a gruesome task enough; but he was growing used to such scenes, and the feeling of doing good and affording help to those in need robbed the duty of much of its terrors.

In this case the task was comparatively light, for there were very few dead, and of the wounded, fully one-half were able to limp slowly back toward the Hall, the troops remaining to cover them till they had reached one of the great barns which was set apart for the temporary hospital.

To the credit of all concerned, be it said that, principally due to the action of Sir Godfrey Markham, who was in command of the two regiments which had routed the late occupants of the Hall, the wounded were treated as wounded men, no distinction being made as to whether they were Cavalier or Roundhead.

All this took some time, and at last Scarlett rode up to where his father was standing among a group of dismounted officers, whose followers were letting their tired steeds crop the grass in the same way as that practised by their enemies, when one of the outposts came galloping in with news which sent the Cavaliers once more into their saddles, when lines were formed, and Sir Godfrey gave the order to advance.

"Could you hear what he said?" whispered Scarlett to Nat, who was close behind him.

"Coming back, sir, three times as strong," whispered Nat. "Means another fight."

The hurried orders and the excitement displayed on the part of the officers endorsed Nat's words; though, had there been any doubt, the summons Scarlett had to his father's side cleared it away at once.

"Listen, my boy," said the general, as Scarlett cantered up; "the enemy are upon us, and we shall perhaps have to retreat, for, jaded as we are, they will be too much for us. Be cautious, and don't let your men get out of hand through rashness. We must give way as they did to-day."

"Run, father?"

"No; bend back right to the earth if necessary, so that the rebound may be the stronger. Now, to your place."

As Scarlett regained his troop, the young officer over him was talking loudly to his men.

"They're not satisfied with the beating they have already had," he was saying. "Let's show them now what we can do when we are in earnest. It was a mistake to show the rascals mercy this morning. Why, if I had been in command of the men, instead of Sir Godfrey, I would not have left two of the rebels together. Now you see the mistake."

"I have no doubt that my father and Colonel Grey did what was right," said Scarlett, hotly.

"And what does a boy like you know about it, sir?" cried the young officer, fiercely. "To your place."

Scarlett felt ready to retort angrily, but he knew his duty, young soldier as he was, and resumed his place without a word.

It was none too soon, for directly after there was a glint of steel over the edge of one of the undulations of the moor, and seen at the distance they were, with the western sun shining full upon them, it seemed as if a long array of armed men was rising from the earth, as first their helmets, then their shoulders, breastplates, and soon after the horses' heads appeared, and then more and more, till a line of well-mounted troops appeared advancing at a walk, while behind them, gradually coming into view in the same way, a second line could be seen.

As they approached over the moor, a third line came into view, while, in obedience to their orders, the Cavaliers retired by troops in slow order, each in turn having the duty of facing the advancing enemy.

When it came to Scarlett's turn to sit there motionless watching their approach, he could not help letting his eyes stray over the moor, every foot of which was familiar. Away behind him to the left the ground rapidly descended to the park, with its lake and woods, through which he had made his way so short a time before. There, hidden by the noble trees which flourished as soon as the moorland proper, with its black peaty soil, was passed, lay the Hall, and a feeling of sadness and depression came over him as he thought of his home being made the scene of a bloody fight, and again falling into the enemy's hands.

"May I speak a word, Master Scarlett?" said a voice behind him, in a whisper.

"Yes; what is it?" said the young officer, without turning his head.

"Hit hard, Master Scarlett, and do your best. I don't like killing folk, and you needn't do that; but do hit hard."

"For the king," said Scarlett, thoughtfully.

"Yes, I suppose so, sir," said Nat, mournfully; "but I was thinking about the old home and my garden."

"Silence, there!" came in a stern voice from the leader of the troop; and the next instant the trumpet rang out, and they had to face about and trot behind the foremost troop of all, leaving another to face the coming enemy.

This went on till the slope was reached upon which General Hedley's men had been going through their evolutions in the morning; and here, in full view of the old Hall, Sir Godfrey Markham and the colonel of the other regiment drew up in a favourable position for receiving the charge which seemed to be imminent from the action of the enemy.

This position would force the Parliamentarians to gallop up a hill, and it was the intention of Sir Godfrey to meet them half-way with the *élan* given by a rapid descent, when he hoped to give them a severe check, one which would enable him to either rid himself of his enemies or give him time to make good his retreat on one of the towns in his rear, where he hoped to find reinforcements.

All turned out as he expected, with one exception. The troop in which Scarlett rode was selected by him, naturally enough, to go on in front on the line of retreat, while the rest of his little force sat fast on the hill slope, waiting the moment when the enemy were coming up the hill for their own advance to be made.

The young officer at the head of the little troop of about forty men muttered angrily at having such a task thrust upon him, but he did his duty steadily and well, riding slowly on over the moor down toward the Manor, which, like the Hall, would be left upon their right.

As they passed over the top of the hill, Scarlett glanced back to see that the enemy were evidently about to deliver their charge; and his heart beat painfully as he felt that he would have to imagine what would take place, and pray that no harm might happen to his father.

The next minute the long slope with its dotted trees was out of sight, and he was descending steadily, his ears strained to catch the sound of the impending shock, as the notes of a trumpet, softened by the distance, fell upon his ear, and then his heart gave a sudden bound, and seemed to stand still.

For at that moment their advance guard came galloping back, and before they could more than realise their danger, a line of fully a hundred and fifty men wheeled into sight, right in their front, from behind a patch of wood a hundred yards away, and came sweeping down upon them.

To have retreated would have meant annihilation, and with a ringing cheer the little band dashed down to meet their advancing foes.

Then, in the midst of the wild excitement, as the moor seemed to quiver beneath their horses' feet, there was a cheer, a clash of steel, and amidst shouts and the blaring of trumpets, the stronger prevailed over the weaker, and Scarlett found himself in the midst of a confused group of his men being driven back upon the main body higher and higher up the hill, till he reached the summit among a scattered party of his own side, through whose ranks the Puritans were riding furiously.

One glance showed him where his leaders were, and he made for the spot, fully realising that the Royal force had been driven back by the bold charge delivered, and then in the midst of the confusion consequent thereon, utterly routed and scattered by the dashing attack on their rear, while, to fulfil the truth of the adage about misfortunes never coming singly, a fresh troop wheeled up on their flank and completed the downfall.

"Ah, quick, my boy! Here!" cried a familiar voice, as Scarlett rode up, and a party of about fifty dashed down the slope, headed by Sir Godfrey, and, hotly pursued by a squadron of the enemy, galloped round the head of the lake, leaping the stream and then the low stone wall of the Hall garden, to take refuge there.

As they reached this haven, a trumpet sounded a recall, and the pursuing squadron missed their opportunity of capturing the flying band, while, when they advanced again, it was to find that the horses were well secured within the Hall yard, whose stout oaken gates were closed, and that the old house was garrisoned by a desperate little force ready to withstand a siege.

"Better than giving up as prisoners, Scar, my boy," said Sir Godfrey, sadly; "and better than being hunted down. All was over, and it was in vain to keep up the fight. It only meant the useless loss of brave men."

"Will they attack us here, sir?" said Scarlett.

"Most likely, and if they do, we'll fight till the very end—fight for our hearth and home, my boy. But there, we must do all we can to make the place more secure before night comes."

"Look!" said Scarlett, pointing.

"Yes, I see, my boy," said Sir Godfrey, sadly; "completely scattered, and a strong body in pursuit. Ah, they are going to bivouac there, and we shall have them here directly foraging for food and shelter. Well, cheer up. These are times of reverses. They were here yesterday; it is our turn to-day."

And without another word, Sir Godfrey went into the hall, to pay the double part of commander and host, his words and example soon putting spirit in the disheartened band.

"But we shall have to surrender, Sir Godfrey, shall we not, unless we wait till dark, and then take our horses and try to get away?"

"You may depend upon one thing, gentlemen," said Sir Godfrey, "the enemy are far stronger than we think. Every path will be carefully guarded, our horses are worn-out, and we are safe to be taken."

"But we cannot defend this place, sir," said another.

"Why not? I say, defend it as long as one stone stands upon another."

"But food—ammunition."

"Plenty, sir, for a month," continued the general, "unless all was carried off by our friends. No fear. Their occupation was too short, and we took them too much by surprise. Why, look there," he said, pointing to one corner of the hall, "there are enough of their pieces there to arm us all. What is it to be, gentlemen? Surrender or fight?"

For answer, hats were tossed in the air, and the carved beams of the roof rang with the hearty cheers of the Cavaliers, and the cry of—

"God save the king!"

Chapter Thirty Three
What Fred Found in the Wood

"Why, Fred, my boy, what a long face. What's the matter?"

For answer, Fred pointed to the trampled garden, the litter in the park, and the desolation visible at the Hall, where window casements had been either smashed or taken off, and rough barricades erected; so that where all had once been so trim and orderly, desolation seemed to reign.

For the little band of devoted Royalists, under Sir Godfrey Markham, had offered a desperate defence to every attempt made by the attacking party, which for want of infantry and guns, had settled down to the task of starving them out.

The prisoners and the wounded from the barn, irrespective of party, had been sent to the nearest town; and as no immediate call was being made upon his services, and his orders were to wait for reinforcements, so as to render the men under his command something like respectable in number, General Hedley set himself seriously to the task of crippling the Royalist forces, by securing the person of Sir Godfrey Markham, whose influence in the district was very great, and whose prowess as a soldier had worked terrible disaster to the Puritan cause.

The little siege of the Hall had been going on four days, when Colonel Forrester, who had been with the relieving party, found his son contemplating the ruin.

"Yes," he said, "it is bad; but better so than that these Royalists should be destroying our home, my boy."

"Is it, father?" said Fred, doubtingly.

"Is it, sir? Of course. That is the home of our most deadly enemy, a man who has wrought endless mischief to our cause and country. Why, you do not sympathise with him?"

"I was not thinking of sympathy, father, but of the happy days Scar Markham and I used to spend here."

"Pish! Don't talk like a child, sir. You are growing a man, and you have your duty to do."

"Yes, father, and I'm going to try and do it."

"Of course. That's better, Fred. As to Markham, we are behaving nobly to him by having his wife and daughter at the Manor, and caring for them there."

"I don't see much in that, father."

"What, sir?"

"Men do not make war upon women, and I think it was our duty to protect Lady Markham, and I acted accordingly."

Colonel Forrester turned fiercely upon his son, but checked himself.

"Humph! Yes. I suppose you were right, Fred. There, we need not argue such points as these. Too much to do."

"Of course, father; but one cannot quite forget the past."

"No, certainly not. But do your duty to your country, my boy, and leave the rest."

"Yes, father," said Fred; "but are we going to attack the place again soon?"

"Yes; and this time most vigorously. The nest of hornets must be cleared out, eh, Hedley?" he said, as the general came up from the rough tent erected under one of the spreading trees.

"Of what are you talking?"

"My boy, here, asks me if we are going to attack the Hall again."

"Yes; if they do not march out by to-night, and give themselves up, I shall attack, and as I shall send them word, they must expect little mercy. By the way, Forrester, I want to talk to you." The pair marched slowly away, leaving Fred to his contemplation of the Hall and its surroundings; and he seated himself upon the mossy roots of a huge beech on the slope facing the old red stone building, and gazed eagerly at the distant figures which appeared at the window openings from time to time, wondering whether either of them was Scarlett, if he was with his father, for he was not among the wounded, or whether he had escaped among the scattered Royalists after that last fierce charge.

"He is sure to be there," said the lad to himself, as he sat on the rough buttress with his sword across his knees. "Poor old Scar! how I remember our taking down the swords and fighting, and Sir Godfrey coming and catching us. It seemed a grand thing to have a sword then—much grander than it seems now," he added, as he looked gloomily at the weapon he held.

He gazed moodily across the lake again, and then thought of his father's words about his duty to his country; and his young brow grew more and more wrinkled.

"Yes," he said; "I ought to do my duty to my country. Those people can hold us off, and there'll be a desperate fight, and some of our men will be killed, and nearly all theirs. I could stop it all and make an end of the fight easily enough by doing my duty to my country. But if I did, I should be sending Sir Godfrey and poor old Scar to prison, perhaps get them killed, because they would fight desperately, and I should make Lady Markham and poor little Lil miserable, and be behaving like a wretch. I don't like doing such duty."

"Let me see," continued Fred, as he gazed across the lake, "how should I do it? Easily enough. Get thirty or forty men, and take them in the old boat across to the mouth of the passage, ten at a time. What nonsense! March them after dark round to the wilderness, pull away the boughs, drop down, and thread our way right along the old passage into the Hall, surprise every one, and the place would be ours.

"And a nice treacherous thing to do; and I should fail," he cried joyously, "for Scar will have given me the credit of planning such a thing, and I'll be bound to say he has blocked the place up with stones.

"No; I couldn't do that, and if ever we meet again as friends, and Scar tells me he was sure I should attack them there, and that he guarded against it, I'll kick him for thinking me such a dishonourable traitor."

Fred sat musing still—wondering what the garrison were doing, and fighting hard to keep the thought of the secret passage out of his mind.

What would his father say if he knew of the secret he was keeping back? and conscience ran him very hard on the score of duty to his country.

"But," he said at last, "duty to one's country does not mean being treacherous to one's old friends. I'm obliged to fight against them; but I'll fight fairly and openly. I will not, duty to my country or no duty, go crawling through passages to stab them in the dark."

It was a glorious day, succeeding two during which a western gale had been blowing, drenching the attacking party, and making everything wretched around; and as Fred lose from where he had been seated and walked slowly along by the edge of the lake towards its eastern end, the water, moor, and woodlands looked so lovely that there was a mingled feeling of joy and misery in the lad's breast.

He thought of the besieged, then of those who were in all probability still at the Manor, from which duty had kept him absent, even his father having refrained from going across, though they had had daily information as to Mistress Forrester's welfare. Fred thought then of his own position, and all the time he was gazing down into the clear water, where he could see the bar-sided perch sailing slowly about, and the great carp and tench heavily wallowing among the lily stems, and setting the great flat leaves a-quiver as they floated on the surface. Ah, how it all brought back the pleasant old days when he and Scar used to spend so much time about the water-side!

"I wonder whether he can see me now," he muttered, as he came up to one of the little patches of woodland, and stood gazing across the lake at the ivy and bush-grown bank where the secret passage had its opening.

"No; I don't suppose Scar would know me at this distance," he said; and he took half a dozen steps forward, to be stopped short by the rattle of arms and a sharp "Halt!"

For the moment Fred thought himself in the presence of one of the enemy, and his hand darted to the hilt of his sword; but he realised directly after that it was one of their own men posted there, and he shivered as he wondered whether the sentry had noted the direction of his gaze.

"Only taking a stroll round, my man," said Fred, as he gave the password.

"Not going into the wood, are you, sir?"

"Yes; right on, towards the Hall."

"Better take care, sir. There are some clever marksmen there, and I should get into trouble if you were hurt."

"Don't be alarmed," replied Fred, smiling. "I'll take care."

He pushed on, and the sentinel remained at his hidden post, while, as if he found a certain pleasure in revisiting the spots familiar to him in the boyish adventures with his old companion, Fred wandered listlessly here and there, meeting sentry after sentry, posted so that the besieged should not have an opportunity of getting away, or sending a messenger in search of help.

"And all the time," muttered Fred, "I know how easily a messenger could be sent, and help obtained."

He stopped short at last, with his head in a whirl, wondering which course he ought to pursue, as the thought occurred to him that he should be answerable for the injury to his own party if Scarlett did send for assistance, making use of the passage as a means by which he could avoid the sentries.

"But he would not avoid the sentries, for they would catch the messenger all the same," he cried; "and I am driving myself half crazy about nothing, and— What's that?"

He stood listening, for it seemed to him that a low harsh moan had come from out of the dark shady woodland near where he stood.

He listened, but there was no further sound, and then he looked round, puzzled for the moment as to where he was. But he recognised certain features in the dense piece of forest directly after, and found that he had during his musings wandered in and in among the trees till he was in the old wilderness, close to the great fallen tree where they had made the discovery of the broken way into the hole.

He turned angrily away, for the thought of the secret passage brought back his mental struggle, as to which course he ought to pursue, and flight being certainly the easiest, he was about to hurry off, when once more the low harsh moan smote his ear.

"Two boughs rubbing together," he muttered, after listening for a repetition of the sound, recalling the while what peculiarly strange noises two fretting branches would make.

"But there's no wind," he said to himself; and directly after there came the sharp chirp of a bird, and then the low moan.

It was so unmistakably a cry of pain, that Fred took a few steps forward among the dense bushes, and then looked around.

There was nothing visible, but he was not surprised, for he was close now to the hidden hole down which he had fallen when he made his jump, and crushed through part of the touchwood trunk, and everywhere there was a dense thicket of undergrowth, through which, after another pause, he forced his way.

Nothing to see—nothing to hear; and he paused again, listening intently, and bending forward in the direction of the hidden opening, as the thought struck him that the cry might come from there.

Still, there was no further sound, and feeling convinced that he had hit upon the true source of the noise, and with a shiver of dread running through him as a dozen terrible suggestions offered themselves in connection with the sound and with Scarlett, he was about to force his way to the hole and drag away some of the broken branches which they had heaped there, and which he could now see were intact, and with the ferns and brambles and ivy growing luxuriantly, when a fresh moan met his ear, evidently from quite another direction.

It was with a feeling of relief that he turned from the way to the passage, and forcing his way on for some little distance, he paused again, and listened with almost a superstitious dread, for the sounds heard were in the midst of the gloomy wilderness, where the foot of man rarely trod, and appealed strongly to the superstitious part of the youth's nature.

In fact, after listening some time, and hearing nothing, the uncomfortable sensation increased, and he began to back away, when the sound was again heard—a harsh, wild, but very subdued cry from quite a different direction, thrilling the lad's nerves, and making him turn hastily to flee from the dark precincts.

For it was like no other sound which he had ever heard. No animal or bird could cry like that. The hedgehog, if shut up in a pit, would sometimes utter a wild strange noise, which, heard in the darkness, was startling as the shriek or hoot of an owl. But it was none of these, and giving way for the moment to ignorant superstition, Fred began to get out of the wilderness as fast as he could, till he stumbled over a briar stretched right across his way, fell heavily, and as he struggled up again, he heard the cry repeated.

"Oh, how I wish some one was here to knock me over!" he muttered angrily. "What a miserable coward I am!"

And now, fully convinced that some unhappy wounded man had crawled into the thicket to die, he went sharply back to where he had seemed nearest to the sound, and began to search once more.

It was for some time in vain, and probably he would have had to give up what seemed to be a hopeless task, had he not suddenly seen a bramble strand feebly thrust aside, and the point of a rusty sword directed toward him.

He drew his own weapon, and beat the rusty blade away, hacking through a few bramble strands, and there, deep down in a tunnel of strands and boughs, was the ghastly blood-besmeared countenance of a man, with hollow cheeks, sunken eyes, and a look of weakness that strongly resembled that which, to his sorrow, he had so often seen upon the field of battle.

The wretched man seemed to make an effort to raise his rusty sword again, but it fell from his grasp, and he lay staring wildly at his finder.

"Who are you? How came you here?" began Fred, involuntarily, though he felt that he knew; and then, with a cry of surprise and horror, he dropped upon his knees beside the wounded man. "Nat, my poor fellow," he cried, "is it you?"

The man looked at him wildly for a few moments, as if he were dreaming, before the light of recognition came into his sunken eyes.

"Master Fred!" he whispered. "You? That's right. Put me out of my misery at once."

"Are you wounded?"

"Water—for Heaven's sake, water!"

Fred started up.

Water? How could he get water?

The lake was close at hand, if he could reach it unseen, for he shrank from calling help, which meant condemning the poor fellow to a prisoner's life as soon as he grew better. So, forcing his way along as cautiously as he could, he contrived to reach one of the trees whose boughs overhung the lake, and taking advantage of the shelter, he lay down upon his chest, grasped a stout hazel, lowered himself to where he could reach the surface, where he took off his steel morion, dipped it full, and rose carefully to bear the refreshing fluid to the suffering man.

It was not an easy task, for the undergrowth seemed to be more tangled than ever; but by stepping cautiously, he managed to bear almost every drop, and kneeling down, he gave the poor fellow a little at a time, an appealing look in the sufferer's eyes seeming to ask for more and more.

"Can you speak, Nat?" Fred said at last, as the man lay back with his eyes closed, and without opening them he softly bent his head.

"Are you wounded?"

"Yes; badly," came in a faint whisper.

"You were hurt at the last encounter?"

"Yes, and crawled here. Water!"

Fred administered more, every drop seeming delicious to the fevered lips of the wounded man.

Just then Fred remembered that he had a little bread in the wallet at his side; and breaking it up, he soaked a small piece in the water, and placed it between poor Nat's lips.

This was eaten, and a few more scraps, the refreshment seeming to revive the sufferer wonderfully, and he looked up now in Fred's eyes, as he whispered faintly—

"I was dying of thirst. I hid here—after the fight—and used to crawl at night to my old garden for food. Then I grew too weak. Master Fred, it would have been all over, if you had not come."

"Thank Heaven! I heard you," said Fred, giving the poor fellow a few more scraps of the moistened bread till he signed to him to cease, and then he looked up in his benefactor's face with a faint smile on his parched and cracked lips.

"Oughtn't you to kill me, Master Fred?" he whispered.

"Oh, Nat, don't talk like that, my lad! I can't forget the past."

"Nor can I, Master Fred. But tell me, lad, Master Scarlett? Don't say he's dead."

"No, no; I believe he's alive and well," cried Fred, eagerly. And he saw the poor fellow close his eyes and lie back, with his lips moving as if he were in prayer.

But he opened them again, and looked round wildly, as if he were slightly delirious, but as his eyes rested on Fred's face he grew calm, his lips parted, and he looked earnestly at him who was playing the good Samaritan where he lay.

"Ah, that seems to put life in me!" he sighed; "but you'll get in trouble, Master Fred, for helping such a one as me. We're enemies, don't you see?"

"Wounded men cease to be enemies, Nat," said Fred, bluntly, "so don't talk about that. You were separated from your master?"

"Yes, sir, with a sword. I don't know whose it was; but it went through my shoulder and laid open my head."

"Ah, well, don't talk. Drink a little more water, and I'll go and bring some men with a litter to fetch you away, and you shall be tended carefully; rest assured of that."

"No, no, Master Fred; let me bide here. How do I know but what Master Scar will come looking for me with some of our lads. I've been expecting them every minute, ever since I crawled in among the bushes; but it seemed a long time, and no one came, and no one—"

He ceased speaking, and lay back fainting.

Fred sprinkled and bathed his face for a few minutes, and then becoming alarmed at the poor fellow's long-continued swooning, he was about to get up and run for help, when Nat slowly opened his eyes again and his lips moved.

"Where's that Samson?" he whispered faintly.

"With my regiment."

"Not hurt badly like me, is he, Master Fred?"

"No; he has escaped wonderfully."

"I'm glad of that, sir, because I shouldn't like for anybody else to give him his lesson. That's to be my job, as soon as I get better. I'm going to take him in hand, Master Fred, and weed him. He's full o' rubbish, and I'm going to make him a better man. A villain! fighting again his own brother."

"There, Nat, drink a little more water, and eat some of this cake, and then I'll go and get help to have you carried up to camp."

"What? A prisoner? No, Master Fred. Sooner die where I am, than let that Samson see me like this, and jump upon me."

"Nonsense! Samson's a good fellow at heart, and as soon as he sees you in trouble, he'll be only too glad to help you."

"Not he, sir; he's my born enemy."

"He's your brother, and I shall send him, for one, to fetch you."

"No, Master Fred, don't; don't, pray don't, sir. Let me lie here. I don't feel the cold and wet much, and if you'd come once a day and bring me a bit o' bread and a drop o' water, I shall soon get well. Don't have me made a prisoner, sir."

"But I can't leave you helpless, and —"

He was about to add dying, but he checked himself.

"And free, Master Fred? Why not? You let me alone, sir. You've saved me this time, for I was going to die to-night. Now I'm going to live. Rather strange for enemies, sir, isn't it? Hark!"

Fred was already listening to a trumpet call, and springing to his feet, he prepared to go.

"I shall send a litter for you to be borne up to camp," he said.

"No, Master Fred, please. I'm a poor helpless thing now, not strong enough to lift a spade, but if you leave me the rest of that bread, I shall do; and if you can come and look at me once or twice, that will be all I shall want. But, Heaven bless you, sir! don't have me made a prisoner."

"Well, Nat, I shall leave you to-night, as it's going to be fine. But let me look at your wounds."

"No, sir, let them bide. I did all I could to them. Come back to-morrow, sir, and if I ain't better then, you may talk of sending me away a prisoner, with my brother Samson to stand and sneer because I am so weak."

A second trumpet call rang out, and, unable to stay longer, Fred hurried back into the open, and made his way over to the little camp, asking himself whether he had not better disregard the poor wounded man's prayers, and have him fetched out, always coming back to the conclusion that he would at all events leave him for another day, when he would take him an ample store of provision, if possible, and decide then as to his future course.

Chapter Thirty Four
A Vain Appeal

That same night, an officer was sent with a flag of truce to the Hall, and bearing a summons to surrender.

To his intense delight at first, and intense sorrow afterwards, Fred found that it was to be his duty to bear the flag and the message to the officer in command of the little garrison.

He received his instructions and a despatch to Sir Godfrey Markham, and carrying a small white flag, and preceded by a trumpeter, he rode slowly through the evening mist, which was rising from the lake and the low meadows down by the stream, till he reached the path leading up to the Hall garden, where he stopped short, gave the order, and the man blew a cheery call, which echoed and re-echoed from the red stone walls.

Then, riding forward with his white flag well displayed, he advanced boldly to the front of the barricaded porch.

For a few minutes he sat there gazing up at the front, and wondering that no heed was paid to his coming. So still was everything, that it seemed as if the Hall had been deserted, till, happening to glance to his left, he caught sight of a dark eye at one of the windows, and directly after he realised that this eye was glancing along a heavy piece, the owner taking careful aim at him as if about to fire.

It was impossible under the circumstances to avoid a feeling of trepidation; but second thoughts came to whisper to him as it were—

"You are under a flag of truce—an ambassador, and sacred."

"But he might be ignorant, and fire," thought Fred, as he glanced to his right, where, to his horror, he saw a second man taking aim at him, and apparently only waiting the word.

Fred's first thought was that he ought to clap spurs to his horse, wheel round suddenly so as to disorder the men's aim, and gallop back for his life.

"And then," he said to himself, "how should I dare face the general and my father?"

Drawing a long breath, he sat firm, and then fighting hard to keep down his trepidation, he turned his head, and called to his follower, bidding him summon the garrison once more.

The man raised his trumpet to his lips, and blew another call, falling back again at a sign from the flag-bearer, and though he would not show that he knew of their presence, a glance to right and left told Fred that the two men were taking aim at him still.

"They dare not fire. They dare not!" he said to himself, as he sat fast; and directly after a group of showily dressed Cavaliers appeared at the large open window above the broad porch.

He could see that Sir Godfrey Markham was in the centre, with a tall fair man with a pointed beard on one side, a grey dark man on the other, and half behind him stood Scarlett, with some dozen more.

"Well, sir," said Sir Godfrey, sternly, and speaking as if he had never seen the messenger before, "what is your business?"

"I am the bearer of a despatch, sir," replied Fred, "for the chief officer here."

"That will be you, sir," said Sir Godfrey to the gentleman on his right. "Well, boy, pass the letter here."

"How, sir?"

"Put it on the point of your pike, and pass it up."

Fred did as he was bidden, and sticking the folded missive on the point of the pike which carried the white flag, he held it up, and it was taken.

"You had better retire while it is read," said Sir Godfrey, contemptuously. "I see there are two of our men paying attention to you. Rein back, if you are afraid."

It was a hard struggle, for with those two fierce-looking troopers watching him along the barrels of their pieces, Fred's inclination was still to turn and gallop away as fast as his horse would go.

But at that moment he raised his eyes, and could see that Scarlett was looking down at him, as if to watch the effect of Sir Godfrey's words.

This look seemed to stiffen him, and he sat perfectly erect upon his horse, with the pike-shaft resting upon his toe, as he told himself that he hoped if the men fired they would miss; that before he would run away, with Scar Markham to laugh at his flight, they might riddle him with bullets through and through.

"Well, sir," said Sir Godfrey, half mockingly, "are you going to retire?"

"I am under a flag of truce, Sir Godfrey," said Fred, quietly. "I thought the Royalist party were gentlemen, and knew the meaning of such a sign."

"Ha, ha, ha!" laughed the tall Cavalier by the general's side. "That's a good sharp retort for you, Markham. Well done, youngster! Don't be afraid."

"I am not," said Fred, stoutly; but at the same time he said to himself, "Oh, what a horrible lie, when I'm all of a cold shiver."

"I didn't quite mean afraid," said the tall officer, laughing, "I meant to say that no one here shall harm you, my young ambassador. But look here, how comes it that you, who are evidently a gentleman, are taking sides with that beggarly scum of tatterdemalions who have taken up arms against their sovereign?"

"Look here, sir," said Fred, "is this meant for flattery or insult?"

"Neither one nor the other, young ferocity," said the Cavalier, laughing. "But don't look like that; you alarm me. Here, young Markham, you had better come and deal with this pernicious enemy; he is too much for me."

But Scarlett did not move, and Fred drew a deep breath, as he prepared for the next verbal encounter, for the fair Cavalier was leaning carelessly out of the window, and looking down at him till, as if fascinated by his look, and after a long struggle to keep his gaze fixed on the stonework upon a level with his nose, Fred raised his eyes, and found that the Cavalier was regarding him with a pleasant, friendly smile.

"I did not mean to affront you," he said; "I only thought it a pity that such a stout lad as you should be on the opposite side."

"Thank you," said Fred, haughtily.

"I suppose we are enemies, are we not!"

Fred nodded.

"And next time we meet you will be trying to send the point of your sword through me, or to ride me down, eh?"

"I suppose I shall try," said Fred, smiling in spite of himself, and showing his white teeth.

"Ah, it's a pity. You're going wrong way, young man. Better come in here, and fight for the king."

"Better stand up manfully for my own side, and not be a traitor," retorted Fred, hotly. "How dare you, standing there in safety, keep on this wretched temptation?"

"Wounds and wonder!" cried the Cavalier, "what a fire-eater it is. Here, I don't wonder that we are shut up helplessly here. I say, Roundhead, will you have a glass of wine?"

"Keep your wine," said Fred. "I've come on business, not to talk and drink."

At that moment, Sir Godfrey spoke to those about him, drawing back from the window, and the conversational Cavalier followed, leaving Fred sitting stiff and fretful, with all his moral quills set up, the more full of offence that he believed Scarlett was still watching him.

As he sat there, assuming the most utter indifference, and gazing with a solidity that was statuesque straight before him, he could hear a loud buzzing of voices, following the firm deep tones of Sir Godfrey Markham, who had evidently been laying the contents of the message before his companion.

"Will they surrender?" thought Fred. "I hope they will. They are debating the question. It would be a relief; and Scarlett Markham and I— no, Scar and I," he said, mentally correcting himself—"might perhaps be together again. If he would promise not to take up arms, I dare say my father and General Hedley would let him off from being a prisoner if I asked, and he could go with me to where poor Nat lies out in the wood, and look after him."

"Huzza! God save the king!"

The shout and words came so suddenly that the little horse Fred rode started and reared, and he was in the act of quieting it down, feeling the while that his ambassage had been in vain, when the party defending the Hall reappeared at the window.

"Youngster!" began Sir Godfrey, in a stern deep voice which annoyed Fred.

"When he knows me as well as he does his own son!"

"Ride back, and tell your leaders that I have laid the contents of their letter before the gallant gentlemen who are my companions here."

There was a buzz, and an attempt at cheering, which ceased as Sir Godfrey went on.

"They all join heart and soul with me in the determination to hold my home here in the name of his majesty the king, so long as there is a roof above us and a piece of wall to act as shelter, to help us keep your rascally rebellious cut-throats out of the place."

Fred felt all of a tingle, and his eyes flamed as he gazed up defiantly at the speaker.

"Tell your leaders that if they will at once lay down their arms and return to their homes, they shall be allowed to do so in peace."

"Huzza!" came from within.

"But if they still keep in arms against his majesty, they must expect no mercy. Once more. Tell your leaders that we treat their proposal with the contempt it deserves."

"As we shall treat your silly proposition, sir," said Fred, quite losing his temper at being made the bearer of such an absurd defiance from a little knot of men, completely surrounded as they were. "Am I to fully understand that you are obstinate enough to say you will hold out?"

"Look here, insolent boy," said Sir Godfrey, sternly, "you are safe— your character of messenger makes you so—but if you stay where you are in front of this my doorstep another five minutes, one of the men shall beat you away with a staff. Go!"

Fred turned white, then red, and he felt the bitterness of the general's words the more keenly from having forgotten himself and departed from his neutral position of messenger to speak as he had. He wanted to say something angry that should show Sir Godfrey and his companions, and above all, Scarlett, that he was obliged to go, but that it was on account of his duty, and not that he feared the man with the staff. But suitable words would not come, and, bubbling over with impotent wrath and annoyance, he touched his horse's flanks with the spurs, turned as slowly and deliberately as he could, and began to move away, but only to face round fiercely as the tall Cavalier at the window said banteringly—

"Good-bye, young game-cock."

There was a roar of laughter from the careless party looking on.

"You coward!"

"Not I, my lad," came back in cheery tones. "I was only joking. Good-bye, and good luck go with you, though you are a Roundhead. Think better of it; let your hair grow, and then come and ask for Harry Grey. I shall have a regiment again some day, and I shall be proud to have you at my side."

The words were so frankly and honestly said that Fred's eyes brightened, and passing the pike-shaft into his bridle hand, he raised his steel cap to the Cavalier, replaced it, and rode off, while the Royalist officer turned to Scarlett.

"As frank and sturdy a boy as I have ever met, excepting you, Scarlett Markham, of course," he added, as merrily as if there were no danger near.

"Yes, he's as true as steel," said Scarlett, flushing. "He always was."

"You know him?"

"It's Fred Forrester, Colonel Forrester's son, from the Manor. We were companions till the war broke out."

"Three cheers for bonnie Coombeland and its boys," said the Cavalier. "Why, Scarlett, my lad, we shall have to get him away from these wretched rebels. Can't it be done?"

"No," said Scarlett, gravely. "Fred is too staunch and true."

And staunchly enough, Fred, with his trumpeter behind, was riding back to camp with his message, which he delivered to General Hedley and his father.

There was a pause after he had done, and the general sat gazing straight before him.

"Well, Forrester," he said at last, "I have done my duty so far, and I must go on. We cannot leave this little nest of hornets in our rear to act as a point to which other insects will gather for the destruction of those who are fighting for their homes. It is of no use to give them time."

"No," said Colonel Forrester, sternly. "I agree with you. They must fall, or be taken to a man."

"And their blood be upon their own heads."

"Amen," said Colonel Forrester, in a deep voice; and as Fred glanced at him he saw that he was very pale, while a cold chill of dread ran through the lad's veins as, in imagination, he seemed to see stout, handsome Sir Godfrey Markham borne down by numbers, with Scarlett making frantic efforts to save him; and then all seemed to be dark—a darkness which hung over his spirit, so that he led his horse mechanically to the improvised stabling beneath the trees, seeing nothing, hearing nothing, till a voice said—

"No, no, Master Fred, I'll see to your horse;" and he turned and found Samson there, and this set him thinking about poor Nat lying helpless in the wood.

Chapter Thirty Five
Samson Visits his Brother

No orders were given for attack that night, and Fred went to the rough shelter that served him for tent, to lie down, but not to sleep, for his thoughts were either at the Manor, which was to him as if it were a hundred miles away; at the Hall, where he knew that the little Royalist party were doing everything to resist the impending attack; or in the gloomy old patch of ancient forest they called the wilderness, where poor Nat lay helpless, and very little removed from death.

"I can't sleep," said Fred, at last, as he rose from his bed, which consisted of a pile of heather, over which his horseman's cloak was thrown, and impetuously hurrying out, he stood gazing up at the bright stars, with the cool moist wind from the north-west bearing to his hot cheeks the freshness of the sea.

"Perhaps dying," he said to himself at last. "I can't lie there thinking about it. I will go, at all costs, and he shall go with me."

He stepped back into his rough tent, buckled on his sword, threw the strap of a wallet over his head, and then took the remainder of his evening meal and a small flask, which he placed in the wallet. This done, he paused for a few moments, and then sought a scarf and a couple of handkerchiefs, which he also thrust into the wallet.

The next minute he was groping his way toward the place in a thick grove where the horses were picketed; and he had not far to look, on reaching his own, before finding Samson curled up in a half-sitting, half-lying position between the mossy buttresses formed by the roots of a huge beech.

Stooping down, he seized his henchman's shoulder, and shook him, but only elicited a grunt.

He shook him again, but though his act was more vigorous, it only elicited a fresh series of grunts.

"You idle pig!" cried Fred, angrily, as he administered a kick; "get up!"

Snore!

A long-drawn, deep-toned snore.

"Samson! I want you." No response. Samson's senses were so deeply steeped in sleep that nothing seemed to rouse him.

"I wish I had a pin," muttered Fred, as he kicked and shook again, without effect. "And there isn't a thorn anywhere near. Spurs!" he exclaimed. "No," he added in a disappointed tone—"too blunt. There's no water to rouse him nearer than the lake; and if there was, it would be too bad to let him go about drenched. What shall I do? Samson, get up; I want you. I'll prick you with my sword, if you don't wake up."

"Tell him the enemy's here, sir," said a sleepy man lying close by.

"Wouldn't wake him, if he did," grumbled another.

The men's remarks suggested an idea which made Fred smile, as he went down on one knee, placed his lips close to Samson's ear, and whispered—

"Well, I wouldn't let him meddle with my garden. Your brother Nat."

That one word, "Nat," seemed to run echoing through all the convolutions of Samson Dee's brain, and he started up at once, full of eagerness and thoroughly awakened, as if by a magic touch.

"Nat?" he said. "Who spoke of Nat? Here, where is he?"

"Are you awake?"

"Awake, sir? Yes, sir. I was dreaming about my brother Nat coming and interfering with our garden. Beg pardon, Master Fred, but I was dead asleep. Want me, sir? Your horse?"

"I want you to come with me."

"Yes, sir, of course," cried Samson, "Ready in a minute."

He was ready in less, for all the dressing he had to do consisted in buckling on the sword, which hung from a knot in the beech-tree, and sticking on his steel cap.

"Don't ask questions, Samson, but come along."

Fred led the way out of the camp and down by the lake, which he skirted till he had passed round the extreme end, when, to Samson's astonishment, Fred struck out straight for the wilderness.

"We going to surprise them up at the Hall, sir, and take it all by ourselves?" Samson whispered at last, for he could contain himself no longer.

"No; I am going to surprise you, Samson," was the reply, in a low whisper, as they went on, their way lying between two lines of sentinels, the outposts being posted further away, and those who hemmed in the little garrison being run right up as near as possible to the Hall, so as to guard against any sally or attempt at evasion.

"Nothing won't surprise me now," muttered Samson, as he tramped on slowly behind his leader in a very ill humour, which he did not display, for it was not pleasant for a heavy sleeper to be roused from his rest. "But it don't matter. I'm about ready for anything now. Why, what's he going to do up in the old wilderness? Oh, I know; after rabbits. Well, that's better. A biled rabbit for dinner to-morrow, and a bit o' bacon, will be like a blessing to a hungry man. Heigh—ho! ha—hum! how sleepy I do feel."

"Hist!"

"Right, Master Fred."

"There are sentinels a hundred yards to the right, and a hundred yards to the left," whispered Fred, in his companion's ear.

"Which as you haven't measured it, sir, you don't know," said Samson to himself. But replying in a whisper, he said, "Yes, Master Fred, but you didn't fetch me out of bed to tell me that."

"No; I tell you now, to keep you from yawning like the Silcombe bull."

"Well, I couldn't help it, sir; but I won't do so no more."

"Keep close behind me, tread softly, and as soon as we get up to the wilderness move every bough as carefully as you can."

"Rabbits, sir?"

"No, no. Silence! Follow me."

"'Course I'll follow him; but what's he going after? Well, I aren't surprised. Nothing surprises me now that the place is turned upside down. I don't believe I should feel surprised if my brother Nat was to want to shake hands, though that would be a startler."

Samson went on musing after his fashion, as he kept close to Fred's heels, and they went quickly and silently on over the soft wet grass, till a great black patch began to loom over them, grew more dark, and then, after a few moments' hesitation and trying to right and left, Fred plunged in, to force his way as carefully as possible, but making very slow progress toward the spot he sought, for to a great extent it was guess-work in the utter blackness which reigned around.

"I say, Master Fred?" whispered Samson, as a pause was made.

"Yes."

"You said something just now about the Silcombe bull."

"Well?"

"I wish he was here."

"Why?"

"So as to go first and make a way. I'm getting scratched all to bits."

"I think we are right. Come along."

"Come along it is, sir; but I'm getting so thirsty."

They went on for a few minutes more, and then Samson uttered an exclamation.

"Hush!" whispered Fred.

"But didn't you hear that, sir? It's the guytrash."

"Here, this way," whispered Fred. "I can find the place now."

"No, no, dear lad, don't go near it," said Samson, under his breath. "You never know what may happen, if you go near it. Don't, pray don't go."

Samson emphasised his appeal by holding tightly to his young master's jerkin, impeding his movements to such an extent that Fred turned upon him fiercely.

"You ought to be ashamed of yourself," he said, "with your guytrashes and goblins, and witches and nonsense."

"What, sir! Why, didn't you hear it moan yonder?"

"I heard a sigh."

"Well, sir, that was the guytrash calling to you to come, so as to get hold of you; and if it did I should never see you again."

"Not if it keeps as dark as this, you stupid old grub. I know what made that sound. Come along."

"What, are you going to risk it, sir, in spite of all I said?"

"Yes; I am going on there."

"Very well, sir. I didn't want to die like this in the dark, and I don't know whether weapons is of any use against things like that; but I'll stand by you, Master Fred, to the end."

As he spoke, there was a faint grating sound which attracted Fred's attention.

"Were you drawing your sword?" he whispered.

"Yes, sir."

"What for?"

"To cut the guytrash down, if I can."

"Put it away," whispered Fred, angrily. "What you have come to see wants no cutting down. It's a wounded man."

"Oh!" ejaculated Samson, as he thrust his sword back into its sheath. "Why didn't you say so sooner, Master Fred?"

"This way—this way," came back to him, accompanied by the rustling of branches and the sharp tearing noise made by thorns. "Yes; here we are."

Samson followed closely, with his arms outstretched, and in a minute or two he heard a sound which made him bend down to feel that Fred was kneeling, and the next moment talking to some one prostrate there in the darkness.

"Well, how are you?"

"Is that you, Master Fred?" came in a husky whisper, which made Samson start.

"Yes; I've brought you some bread and wine. How are the wounds?"

"Don't give me much pain, sir, now."

"Master Fred."

"Well?"

"Who's that?"

"Can't you hear, Samson? Your brother Nat."

There was utter silence for a minute, during which it seamed as if Samson was holding his breath, for at the end of that pause, he gave vent to a low hissing sound, which continued till it seemed wonderful that the man should have been able to retain so much air.

"Drink some of this," Samson heard Fred whisper; and there was the peculiar gurgling sound as of liquid escaping from a bottle, followed by another whisper bidding the sufferer eat.

"Look here, Master Fred," said Samson, as soon as he had sufficiently recovered from his surprise to speak.

"What is it?"

"Do you know who it is you're talking to there in the dark?"

"Yes; your brother Nat."

Samson remained silent and motionless as one of the trees for a minute. Then he caught Fred by the shoulder.

"What is it, Samson? Do you hear any one?"

"No, sir; I was only thinking about what I ought to do now. Just stand aside, and let me come."

"What for?"

"Well, sir, that's what I don't know. Ought I to—? You see, he's an enemy."

"Samson, we can't leave him here, poor fellow! He may die for want of attention."

"Well, sir, then there'd be one enemy the less."

"Yes. Shall we leave him to die?"

"No, sir; that we won't," said Samson, severely. "We've got to make him prisoner, taking him up to my quarters, let the doctor make him well, and then I've got to spend an hour with him, just to set him to rights and pay him all I owe. Here, you sir, do you know who I am?"

"Yes," said the wounded man, feebly.

"Then look here; you've got to come on my back, and I'm going to carry you up to the camp."

"Master Fred."

"Yes, my lad."

"Don't let him touch me," whispered Nat. "I couldn't bear to be moved, sir."

"Not if we carried you gently?"

"No, sir; I feel as if it would kill me. If you could leave me some bread, sir, and some water, and let me alone, I should get well in time. I'm only doing what the dogs do, sir, when they're hurt. I've crawled into a hole, sir, and I shall either die or get well, just the same as they do."

Fred refused to be convinced, but on trying to raise the poor fellow he seemed to inflict so much agony that he gave up, and felt disposed to return to his first ideas of coming to see the poor fellow from time to time, and giving him food.

"Better, after all, Samson," he said.

"What, leaving him, sir?"

"Yes. You do not want to see him a prisoner?"

"I don't want to see him at all, sir. He has disgraced his family by fighting against his brother. Did you bring anything to cover him up, sir?"

"No, Samson, I did not think of that."

"Well, sir, you mustn't let him die," muttered Samson; and there was a peculiar rasping sound.

"What are you doing?"

"Only getting off my leather coat, sir. Lay that over him. It may rain again any time, and he might be getting cold."

Fred caught the coat, laid it gently over the wounded man, and he was in the act of bending down to hear what he whispered by way of thanks, when there was a sharp report close at hand.

"Quick! An attack," said Fred, excitedly; and the next moment he and Samson were struggling out of the wilderness, just as shot after shot ran along the line, as the alarm spread, and directly after the ear-piercing call rang out on the clear night air, and was echoed again and again among the distant hills.

Chapter Thirty Six
Colonel Forrester is not Angry

It was no easy task to run the gauntlet of the sentinels, now that the alarm had spread, for they were falling back upon the camp, and twice over Fred was challenged, and had to run the risk of a bullet; but partly by knowing the ground far better than those who challenged, and partly from the darkness, the pair succeeded in reaching the little camp, to find all in commotion, horses saddled, men ready to mount, and an intense desire existent to know from which side to expect the attack.

After a time the hurry and excitement quieted down, for after scouts and patrols had done their work, the whole alarm was traced to one of the sentinels, who had heard whispering in the wood near which he was stationed, and had fired at once, his nearest fellow having taken up the signal, fired, and slowly fallen back.

"Better too much on the *qui vive* than too drowsy," said the general, at last, good-humouredly. "I was afraid, Forrester, it was an attempt on the part of the enemy to escape."

"And we could clear it all up with a word, Samson," said Fred, who was full of self-reproach.

"But don't you speak it, Master Fred," whispered Samson, who had contrived to get another jerkin. "If you tell, they'll go down to the wood, and find that brother of mine, and bring him in, and here he'll be lying in clover, and doctored up, and enjoying himself, while poor we are slaving about in sunshine and rain, and often not getting anything to eat, or a rag to cover us."

"I shall not speak, Samson, for there was no harm done," said Fred, quietly; "but I wonder at your covering your enemy from the cold."

"Needn't wonder, sir. Didn't I always cover my tender plants from the cold? It wasn't because I liked them, but so as they'd be useful by-and-by. My brother Nat will be useful by-and-by. I want him. I shall give him such a lesson one of these days as shall make him ashamed of himself."

A trumpet rang out again on the night air, and men dismounted, picketed their horses once more, and some lay down to snatch a few hours' rest, while others sat together talking and asking one another questions about the attack they foresaw would most probably take place that day, for the night was waning, and they knew that before long the dawn would be showing in the east, and that it would be morn; while, in spite of plenty of sturdy courage and indifference to danger, there were men there who could not refrain from asking themselves whether they would live to see the next day.

It was somewhere about sunrise when Fred fell asleep, to dream of being in the dense thicket, carrying Nat, the Hall gardener, on his back to the hole broken through into the secret passage, where he threw him down, and covered him up with bushes to be out of the way till he got better; but, as fast as he threw him down, he came back again, rebounding like a bladder, till Samson came to his help, drew his sword, and pricked him, when he sank down to the bottom and lay still. Then Scarlett seemed to come out of the hole and reproach him for being a coward and a rebel, seizing him at last and shaking him severely, and all the while, though he struggled hard, he could not free himself from his grasp. So tight was his hold that he felt helpless and half strangled, the painful sensation of inability to move increasing till he seemed to make one terrible effort, seized the hands which held him, looked fiercely in his assailant's eyes, and exclaimed, "Coward, yourself!"

"Well, sir, dare say I am," was the reply; "but what can you expect of a man when you take him out of his garden and make a soldier of him all at once."

"Samson!"

"Yes, sir. Breakfast's ready, sir, such as it is. What's the matter with you? I never had such a job to waken you before."

"I—I was very sound asleep," stammered Fred, rising hastily. "Did— did I say anything?"

"Pitched an ugly word at my head about not being so brave as you thought I ought to be, that's all."

"Don't take any notice of what I said, I must have been dreaming."

"That's what I often wake up and feel I've been doing," said Samson. "I often don't know whether I'm on my head or my heels; it seems so strange. Wonder how that Nat is. He always gets the best of it. Lying there with nothing to do. Just his way, sir, curling himself up snug, and letting other people do his work. There you are, sir, bucket of clean water from the lake. Have a good wash, and you'll feel like a new man. What a difference it must make to you, sir, dressing yourself out here, after having your comfortable room at home, and you so near it, too. Why, sir, the colonel might have told you to go home to sleep. Say, sir!"

"Well?" said Fred, taking his head out of the bucket of clear cold water, and feeling afterwards, as he rubbed himself dry, that new life was running through his veins.

"Wouldn't it be nice for you to run down to the Manor to breakfast, sir, and bring back a few decent things to eat? I wouldn't mind coming with you and carrying the basket."

Fred looked hard at Samson, whose face was perfectly stolid for a few moments; but a little ripple gradually spread over his left cheek, and increased till it was a broad grin.

"Well, sir, you see it is so tempting. I'd give anything for a bowl of new warm milk. When are we going to have a good forage again, so as we might catch some chickens and ducks or a young pig?"

"I'm afraid there'll be other work on hand to-day, Samson," replied Fred, sadly, as he glanced in the direction of the Hall. "There, take away that bucket."

"Yes, sir. Done you good, hasn't it? and you can dry your head. Puzzle some of them long-haired chaps to get theirs dry."

Samson went off with his young master's simple toilet arrangements, and Fred joined his brother-officers in their frugal meal, after which he spent the morning in a state of indecision.

"I will do it," he said, when afternoon had come; and, giving his sword-belt a hitch, and thrusting his morion a little on one side, he began striding forward, planting his boots down heavily on the soft heather, in which his great spurs kept catching till he at last nearly fell headlong.

Recovering himself, he went on, hand upon hip, and beating his gloves upon his thigh, till he came to where Colonel Forrester was slowly pacing up and down, with his hands clasped behind his back.

As Fred drew nearer, an orderly came up to the colonel, and presented a letter, which brought the lad to a standstill. He had been having a long struggle with self, and had mastered his shrinking, but he was so near the balance of vacillation still, that he felt glad of the excuse to hang back, and walked aside, feeling like one who has been reprieved.

"How do I know what he will say?" thought Fred, glancing back at his father's stern, wrinkled countenance as he read his despatch. "It isn't like the old days, though I used sometimes to feel shrinking enough then. It is not between father and son, but between colonel and one of his followers."

Fred felt as if he would like to walk right off; but there were those at the Hall occupying his thoughts, and he made an effort over his moral cowardice and stopped short, meaning to go to his father as soon as the messenger had left.

He had not long to wait, for the orderly saluted and rode off, but there was something else now to check him. His father looked so very severe, and as if there was something very important on his mind.

"I have chosen a bad time," thought Fred. "I'll go away and wait."

"No, no," he said, half aloud; "how can I be so foolish? I will go up and speak to him like a man. It is mean and cowardly to hang back."

He stepped toward the colonel again, but there was another reprieve for him, the general riding up; and for the next quarter of an hour the two officers were in earnest converse.

"Yes," said Fred; "I have chosen a bad time. I'll go."

But he did not stir, for at the same moment he felt that the general might be planning with his father that which he sought to prevent.

"I'll go and speak now they are together," he said to himself, desperately. "General Hedley likes me, I think, and he could not be very cross."

"No, I dare not," he muttered; and he paced to and fro again till the general touched his horse's flanks, and rode slowly away, Colonel Forrester following him thoughtfully for some distance, till in a fit of desperation Fred hurried to his side.

"Want me, my boy?" said the colonel, gravely.

"Yes, father. I want to ask you something."

"Yes; go on. I am very much occupied just now."

Fred looked at him piteously, his words upon his lips, but refusing to be spoken.

"Well, my boy, what is it? Are you in some great trouble?"

The words came in so much more kindly a tone, that Fred made a step toward his father, and the barrier of discipline gave way, and it seemed to be no longer the stern officer but the father of the old Manor house days he was longing to address.

"Well, my boy, what is the trouble?" said Colonel Forrester, kindly.

"It is about—"

Fred did not finish his sentence, but pointed across the lake.

"Ah, yes, about the Hall!" said the colonel, with a sigh. "Well, my boy, what do you wish to say?"

"Are they keeping to what was in Sir Godfrey's message, father?"

"Yes, my boy," sternly.

"But don't you think they could be persuaded to surrender?"

"Yes, Fred."

"Oh, father, I am glad," cried the boy, joyously.

"Yes, persuaded," continued Colonel Forrester, in measured tones, "with sword and gun, not till they are utterly helpless. Then they may."

"Oh, father!"

"Yes, my boy; it is very sad, but they will not see that their case is desperate."

"Is the attack to be made to-day, father?"

"I am not the general in command, my boy. That is a matter for another to decide."

"Yes; but you know, father, and you can trust me."

"Of course I can, Fred, and I will. Yes; the attack is to be made directly."

"And will it succeed?"

"It must. It shall. No. I will not interfere," he added to himself a moment later.

"And you, father?" said Fred, anxiously.

"Well, my boy, what of me?"

"You— Oh, father. Must I speak out. Don't be angry with me. I have no right to say such things to you, but I always looked upon Scar Markham as a brother, and they always treated me at the Hall as if I was a son; and it does seem so terrible for you to be going up at the head of armed men to attack our dear old friends."

Colonel Forrester stood with his brow knit.

"You are angry with me, father; but I can't help speaking. I say it seems so terrible. You ought not to do this thing."

Fred's hesitation had gone. He had taken the plunge, and now he felt desperate, and ready to speak on to the end. He gazed full in the stern face with the lowering brows, but it checked him no longer. His words came fast, and he caught his father by the arm.

"If you speak to General Hedley, he will listen to you, for Sir Godfrey is your oldest friend; and think, father, how horrible it would be if the Markhams were to be killed."

The brows appeared to be knit more closely, and Colonel Forrester's gaze seemed fierce enough to wither his son.

But Fred kept on, begging and importuning his father to do something to change the general's purpose, without obtaining any reply.

"Then you are going to lead the attack on the Hall, father?" said Fred at last.

The colonel turned upon him sharply.

"You must not, you shall not," cried Fred, excitedly. "Yes; I see you are angry with me; but—"

"No, my boy, not angry," said the colonel, gravely; "but very, very proud of you. No, my boy, I am not going to head the fight."

"Father!" cried Fred, joyously.

"And I have done more than beg General Hedley to excuse me from all participation in to-day's work."

"Then it really will be to-day?"

"Yes, my boy, it really will be to-day, and I'd give anything for this day to be past, and the worst known."

"But they will give them quarter, father?"

"Yes, my boy, of course, but who can say what may happen in dealing with fierce, reckless men, fighting as they believe for their lives. Those with whom they are engaged may be willing to take them prisoners, but they will fight with terrible desperation, incited by Sir Godfrey's example, and no one can say how the attack will end."

"Yes, father, I see," said Fred, sadly, "but could you not persuade General Hedley to give up the attack?"

Colonel Forrester was silent for a few moments, and then said sadly—

"No."

"Oh, father! think of Lady Markham and of little Lil."

"I have thought about them, my boy," said the colonel, speaking in a slow, measured voice, "and I have three times over begged of the general to spare the Hall and its defenders, and to let us go on at once."

"And what did he say?" cried Fred, eagerly.

"He asked me if it was the voice of duty speaking, or that of friendship, and what could I say?"

Fred looked at him piteously.

"How could I leave that nest of hornets to harass our rear, and gather a fresh and stronger force together, so as to be ready for the next detachment which comes along west. No, boy, I am obliged as an officer to agree with my superior that every man must be cleared out of that Hall before we can stir. Sir Godfrey Markham has his fate in his own hands."

"What do you mean, father? Surrender?"

"Of course. He shall have due respect paid to him and his followers; but it is madness to expect it of him, even for their sake."

"For their sake, father?"

"Yes, my boy. There, I may as well tell you. I am not the stern, implacable enemy you think me. I wrote to Sir Godfrey last night, asking him to surrender for his wife and daughter's sake."

"You did this, father?" cried Fred, eagerly.

"I did, my boy."

"And what did he say?"

"He sent a stern, insulting message, similar to his last, and those who were with him threatened to crop the next ambassador's ears if he dared present himself at the Hall."

"Let me go and make another appeal to Sir Godfrey."

"You heard the threat?" said Colonel Forrester, looking at his son curiously.

"Yes, I heard, father."

"And will you risk it, if I give you a message to take?"

"Yes, father, it was a vain boast. They dare not insult a messenger."

"No, my boy, you shall not go," said Colonel Forrester, laying his hand upon his son's shoulder. "It would be courting injury for no good purpose."

"But if it would save Sir Godfrey and poor Scarlett?"

"It would not, Fred."

"Don't say that, father. If I could see Scar Markham, he would perhaps listen to me; and if he did, he might have as much influence upon Sir Godfrey as I have upon you. Father, let me try."

"No, Fred, it cannot be," said the colonel, sternly. "I am not in command here. The general has sent twice, the second appeal being made through my request, and in each case the answer was an insult."

"Bit, father—"

"It is useless, my boy, so say no more. Sir Godfrey brings the assault on himself. I have done all I can. General Hedley acknowledges it, and you see I have ceased to be the stern officer to you, and have spoken kindly and in the spirit you wish."

"But one moment, father. Do you think we could persuade Sir Godfrey through Scarlett?"

"No, my boy, and I am afraid I should act precisely the same were I in his place. No more now."

"But, father, shall I be expected to go forward with the troops?"

"No. I have provided against that, Fred. You and I will not be combatants here."

"Why, father!" cried Fred, excitedly. "Look!"

"Yes," said Colonel Forrester, sadly. "They have begun. I thought it would not be long. I dreaded being in the general's confidence over this."

Chapter Thirty Seven
Watching the Attack

That which Fred had dreaded had indeed begun, for about a hundred and fifty men had been told off for the attack, and these had prepared themselves by picketing their horses, arming themselves with stout axes for the barricades, and dragging after them stout scaling-ladders.

The advance had seemed to be dilatory before, and the generally received opinion in the camp had been that the defending party, to save risk, was to be starved into submission.

But those who judged did not know the general. He had been waiting his time, for sundry reasons: respect for Colonel Forrester, and mercy, being among these; but now that he found it necessary to adopt strong coercive measures, he was prompt and quick in every step.

Fred Forrester was freed from the terrible necessity of taking part in the attack, but that did not lessen his eagerness to see what would be the result, and in consequence he hurried to the top of the nearest woodland summit, and from thence prepared to witness the issue of the fight.

As he reached the clump of beeches which crowned the hill, he caught sight of the back of some one lying at the very edge of the wood, in the commanding spot he had selected for himself, and where he had often stood to make signs to Scarlett in the old boyish days. For a moment or two he hesitated, and then approached, wondering who it could be, and taking the precaution to draw his sword, for it was not likely to be one of their own men.

It was disconcerting to find any one there, and for the moment he was ready to draw back. But, on the other hand, it might be a spy of the enemy, who had crept up there to watch their proceedings; and under these circumstances, Fred felt that there were only two courses open to him, flight or bold attack.

To make such an attack in cold blood required consideration. It was not like taking part in an exciting charge, amid the stirring din of battle, when the pulses were bounding, and the bray of the trumpet called them to advance. He, a mere youth, had to go single-handed to an encounter with a great broad-backed fellow, who, at the first brunt, might turn the tables upon him.

"But he is a spy," said Fred to himself; "and he is sure to be half afraid;" and without further hesitation, the lad advanced softly, keeping well behind.

As he drew nearer he could see that the man was upon his chest with his arms folded for a support; his morion was tilted back over his ears, so that it covered his neck, and as he watched the advance, he slowly raised first one and then the other leg, crossing them backwards and forwards, and beating the ground with his toes as if they were portions of a pick-axe.

A peculiar feeling of hesitation came over Fred again, and he found himself asking whether he ought not to go down for help, and whether there were any of the man's companions near.

This he felt was only common prudence; and, stepping back, he carefully searched among the trees and round the edge of the hill. But no, the man seemed to have come up quite alone; and, gaining confidence from this, he went softly back, taking care not to trample upon any dead twig, so as to give the alarm.

In a few minutes he was again at the edge of the wood, near enough to see that the man wore a backpiece, and that the hilt of his sword was quite near his hand.

The hesitation was gone now. A glance showed that the attacking party were near the end of the lake, and that outposts of three or four men were dotted here and there, ready to drive back or capture any of the Cavaliers who might try to make their escape.

"I'll do it," said Fred to himself; and, stooping down, he crept nearer and nearer, holding back any twig or obtruding branch with his sword, and wincing and preparing for a spring, when a bramble grated against the edge of his blade.

But the man was too intent upon the scene below, and paid no heed to a warning which, had he been on the alert, would have placed Fred at a terrible disadvantage.

The lad's eyes, as he crept on with sword in advance, were fixed on the back of the man's half-hidden neck; and he had made his plans, but for all that he could not help glancing down at the advancing men, and pausing to note that the Cavaliers were at the barricaded windows, ready for their enemy.

And now for a moment Fred again wondered whether he was doing right, and whether his more sensible plan would not have been to go down to the camp and spread the alarm.

His answer to this thought was to set his teeth, which grated so loudly that his grip tightened on the hilt of his sword, and he felt sure that he must have been heard.

But no; the man lay perfectly still, watching intently, as motionless, in fact, as if he had been asleep; and Fred crept step by step nearer and nearer, till he felt that he was within springing distance, and then stopped to take breath.

"How easy it would be to kill him," he thought, "and how cowardly;" and he was about to put his first idea into action, namely, to make one bold spring forward, and snatch the man's sword from the sheath.

But the sword might stick, the sheath clinging to it tightly, as it would sometimes; and if it did, instead of the man being helpless, it would be he who was at the mercy of one who might beat him off with ease.

So, giving up that idea, he paused a few moments, till the man raised his head a little higher, so as to get a better view of those below, and then with one bold spring, Fred was upon his back, with the point of his sword driven in a peculiar way into the soft earth.

That idea had occurred to him at the last moment, and even in the intense excitement of the moment he smiled, as he saw in it success, for it effectually baffled the man in what was his first effort—to draw his sword, which was pinned, as it were, to the ground by Fred's weapon being passed directly through the hilt.

There was an angry snort, as of a startled beast, a tremendous heave, and a coarse brown hand made a dart at the sword-blade, and was snatched away with an exclamation of pain. Then in fiercely remonstrant tones a harsh voice shouted—

"You coward! Only let me get a chance!"

"Samson!" cried Fred, starting back as he removed his knee from the back of the man's head, and the ex-gardener's steel cap rolled over to the side.

"Master Fred!" was the answer; and Samson turned over and sat up, staring in his assailant's face.

"You here?"

"Here, sir, yes; and look what you've done. Don't ketch me sharping your sword again, if you're going to serve me like that."

He held up his hand, which was bleeding from the fact of his having seized hold of the blade which had pinned down his hilt.

"But I thought you were one of the enemy—a spy."

"Then you'd no business to, sir. I only come up here to see the fight."

"But I thought you were down in the ranks—gone to the attack."

"Me? Now, was it likely, sir, as I should go and fight against the Hall? No, sir, my bad brother Nat, who is as full of wickedness as a gooseberry's full of pips, might go and try and take the Manor, if it was only so as to get a chance to ransack my tool-shed; but you know better than to think I'd go and do such a thing by him. Would you mind tying that, sir?"

Samson had taken a strip of linen out of his morion, and after twisting it round the slight, freely bleeding cut on his finger, held it up for Fred to tie.

"Thank ye kindly, sir. I meant that for a leg or a wing, but it will do again for them."

"I am very sorry, Samson," said Fred, giving the knot a final pull.

"Oh, it don't matter, sir; only don't try any o' them games again. So you thought I was a spy?"

"Yes."

"And what was you going to do with me?"

"Make you a prisoner, and take you down to camp."

"Well, you are a one!" said Samson, looking at his young master, and laughing. "Think of a whipper-snapper like you trying to capture a big chap like me."

Fred winced angrily.

"Well, not so much of a whipper-snapper as Master Scarlett, sir; but you haven't got much muscle, you know."

"Muscle enough to try."

"Yes, sir," said the ex-gardener, thoughtfully; "but it isn't the muscle so much as the try. It's the thinking like and scheming. You see a bit of rock stands up, and you can't move it with muscle, but if you put a little bit of rock close to it, and then get a pole or an iron bar, and puts it under the big rock and rests it on the little, and then pushes down the end, why, then, over the big rock goes, and it's out of your way."

"Yes, Samson," said Fred, thoughtfully, as he watched the advance; "and so you didn't care to go to the attack?"

"No, sir, I wouldn't; but it was tempting, though; ay, that it was."

"Tempting?"

"Well, you see, Master Fred, Nat has got some chyce cabbage seed, and he'd never give me a pinch, try how I would; no, nor yet sell a man a pen'orth. He kept it all to himself, just out of a nasty greedy spirit, so that his cabbages might be bigger and heavier than ours at the Manor. I'd have had some of that seed if I'd gone, for he couldn't have come and stopped me now."

"No, poor fellow! I wonder how he is?"

"Getting better, sir. He's as tough as fifty-year-old yew. Nothing couldn't kill him; but look, sir, look! See how they're getting up to the terrace. Ah!"

This exclamation was made as a white puff suddenly seemed to dart from one of the windows of the Hall, and then there was another, and another, the reports seeming to follow, and then to echo from the next hill.

But no one in the attacking force seemed to fall, neither did it check them. On the contrary, they appeared to be spurred into action, and instead of creeping on as it were in a slow steady march, they broke up into little knots, and dashed forward, while a second line kept steadily on.

"Look at them! look at them, Master Fred! Don't it make you feel as if you wished you was in it?" cried Samson, excitedly. "That's it; fire away; but you won't stop 'em. All Coombeland boys, every man-jack of 'em, and you can't stop them when they mean business."

"No," said Fred between his teeth, as he tried to keep down the feelings of elation engendered by the gallantry of the attack, by forcing himself to think of how it would be were he Scarlett Markham, and these men enemies attacking his home. "Look, look, Samson!" he whispered, with his throat dry, his tongue clinging to the roof of his mouth, and the scar of his worst wound beginning to throb.

"Yes, I'm a-looking, sir," said Samson, in as husky a voice. "There, they've got a ladder up against the big long window, and they're swarming up it. They'll be indirectly, and drive the long-haired gentlemen flying like leaves before a noo birch broom."

"No," said Fred, shading his eyes with his hands; "no. Ah, did you hear the crash? How horrible! Some of them must be killed."

"Not they, Master Fred. But I don't see how they did it. Fancy turning the ladder right back with seven or eight lads running up it! But it was well done."

"Can you see whether any one is hurt?"

"Not at this distance, sir. Not they, though, unless they've got any of those long thin swords skewered into them. I've tumbled twice that height out of apple-trees, and no one to fall upon. They'd all got some one to tumble on, except the bottom one, and I don't suppose he's much hurt."

"Hurt, man? He must be killed."

"Tchah! not he, sir. T'others would be too soft. Look, sir; don't lose none of it. You may never have such a chance again. Yes; there, they've got the ladder up once more, and some's holding it while the others goes up. Yes. Huzza! they'll do it now. No. If they haven't overturned it again."

"Yes," said Fred, sadly, and yet unable to help feeling pleased, so thoroughly were his sympathies on both sides. "They're giving it up, Samson; they're retiring."

"No, sir; only carrying some of the hurt ones out of the fight. There goes another ladder up—two. Hah! look at that!"

Fred's eyes were already riveted on the fresh scene, for, plainly seen even at that distance, the strong oaken-boarding screen nailed over the window at the end of the terrace on the ground floor was suddenly thrown down, and with a shout which was faintly heard on the hill, a party of about five and twenty Cavaliers rushed out, sword in hand, taking the attacking party in the flank with such vigour that they gave way, the two scaling-ladders were overturned, and for the moment the Puritans took to flight, and the attack seemed to have failed.

"Beaten, Samson," said Fred, unable to crush down a feeling of satisfaction, even at the reverse of his own party.

"Beaten, sir? Not they. Only driven back. It's just like the waves down by the cave, yonder; they come back again stronger than ever. Told you so, sir. Look at that."

Samson Dee was right, for a solitary figure had suddenly stepped forward from the second rank, rallied the beaten men, and advanced with them slowly and steadily. There was a desperate *mêlée*, as the Cavaliers, reinforced by more from within, tried to complete their rout, and then, as it seemed to the excited watchers, the Royalists were driven back step by step, by sheer force of numbers. Then in the midst of a seething confusion, all swayed here and there along the terrace, and on and on, till the barricaded windows and porch were reached, and then, as they were checked by the stubborn walls as water is stopped by a pier, they struggled fighting ever sidewise, a stream of mingled men along the front of the house and over the broken-down boarding, till the tide of confusion set right through the open window into the Hall.

At first this human current was a mingling of both sides; then the Cavalier element seemed to disappear, and as Fred watched with starting eyes, he could see at last that it was a steady stream of their own men which flowed through the opening.

"They're in, Master Fred! The day's ours. Hark! Hear them firing inside? Look! Look!"

It was plain enough to see: from the window, whence the scaling-ladders were thrown down, men come dropping forth sword in hand, Cavaliers evidently, to be encountered by those of the Puritan party still without. Then out came other Puritans, to take the Cavaliers in the rear, as they fought together in a knot facing all round, with their swords flashing as they made their gallant defence.

Then a rush seemed to take place, and they were overpowered, while the smoke came slowly rolling out from the open window, though the firing had ceased.

The fighting still went on within for a few minutes; then a rush as made out from door and window, and a tremendous cheer arose, loud enough to strike well upon the spectators' ears, helmets were seen flashing, swords flourished in the air, and it was plain enough that resistance had ceased, while the attacking force were gathering together once again.

"Smoke seems long while rolling out, Master Fred; must ha' been a deal o' firing we did not hear."

"Oh!" shouted Fred, as like a flash the truth came home to him.

"What's the matter, lad? Are you hurt?" cried Samson.

"No, no; look! The dear old Hall!" cried Fred. "Don't you see?"

"Smoke, sir? Yes."

"No, no, my good fellow, not smoke alone; the poor old place is on fire."

And without another word, Fred, followed closely by Samson, dashed down the hill.

Chapter Thirty Eight
"Is there nothing we can save?"

It was too true.

Whether started by some smouldering wad, or by a piece of furniture being driven into one of the fire-places, or, as was more probable, by the wilful act of one of the Royalist party, who was determined that the victors should not profit by their success, the Hall was on fire, and the smoke, which rapidly increased in volume, showed that the danger must be great.

"Don't run quite so fast, Master Fred," panted Samson. "You can't keep up at that pace. Better take it a bit more coolly."

There was wisdom in the hurried words, and Fred slackened his speed a little, so as to allow his follower to come alongside; and in this way, taking in the whole proceedings as they ran, they continued their course down the park slope, toward the lake.

There before them in the evening glow was the fine old house, with the dense cloud of smoke slowly rising, and shouts reached them as men were seen running to and fro in obedience to the orders, but what those orders were it was impossible to tell.

In front of the building a strong body of the general's men was drawn up, and in their midst the prisoners stood in a knot, while from time to time horsemen came slowly in, leading other prisoners, who had evidently been captured in efforts to escape.

But though Fred strained his eyes eagerly, the distance kept him from recognising any familiar faces, and a terrible sense of heart-sinking increased as he hurried on.

All at once the thundering of horses' hoofs was heard behind, and a familiar voice shouted Fred's name.

He turned to see that it was his father, who slightly checked his powerful horse as he came up.

"Quick! you two," he cried; "lay hold of the mane, and run."

Fred grasped the idea in an instant, seized the horse's thick mane, and dropped into step as the sturdy beast trotted on. But the mane was all on Fred's side, and Samson missed his opportunity, but as the horse passed on, he made a snatch at the tail, twisted his hand in the thick hair, was nearly jerked off his feet, but recovered himself, and held on, improving his position by degrees, and contriving to keep up.

"They must have done this themselves, Fred," said Colonel Forrester, in a deeply troubled voice. "Hah! that's right. We must save the place."

"What are they doing, father?"

"Our men are joining line toward the stable yard, and getting buckets, I think. Hold on tightly."

"I'm quite right, father," panted Fred; and he kept up till they reached the men who surrounded the prisoners, and who burst into a cheer as the colonel came up.

Fred's position prevented him from seeing exactly who were numbered among the prisoners, and at that moment the general drew rein at their side.

"You shouldn't have let them fire the place, Hedley," said Colonel Forrester, in a voice full of reproach.

"It was not our doing, man. Some of their own party started it. There was a fire in the big dining-room. Hangings, chairs, and linen were thrown upon it. The fire blazed up the oak panellings, and the open windows fanned the draft."

"We must save it. Come on."

"We are doing everything possible, man; but the water is in a well, and what can we do with three or four buckets?"

"Give me a score of men to try and tear down the burning part," cried Colonel Forrester, who had leaped from his horse, and thrown the reins to the nearest soldier. "Here, quick! fifty of you come on."

He was close up to the porch, from which the men were tearing down the barricade, but the general was bending over him directly.

"Look at me, Forrester," he said.

The latter gazed up at him sharply, to see that his face was blackened with smoke, and the general's lips parted to speak.

"I stayed in yonder till I was driven out by the fire. It is not safe to go."

"But we must save the place," cried the colonel; and he dashed through the opening the men had made, followed by Fred and Samson, a dozen more, including the general, influenced by his friend's example, rushing after them.

They reached the Hall, but only to find that the flames were literally rushing out of the great dining-room door, on the one side, and running up the panelled walls, setting the beautiful ceiling ablaze, while from the library, on the other, there was a furnace-like roar, as the flames literally charged up the oaken staircase, whose balusters were already glowing, and the gallery and corridor were fast flaring up as the fire licked and darted and played about.

"You see," said the general, as he seized the colonel's arm again, "if we had ample water and the proper means, we could do nothing."

Colonel Forrester groaned as he saw the fire darting up the panels, the carved beams of fine old oak already well alight, and the various familiar objects falling victims to the flames. Even as he gazed, with the cool air of evening rushing in behind them through the porch, and wafting the clouds of smoke upward to pass rapidly along the corridor as if it were some large horizontal chimney, he saw the canvases of the old family paintings heave and crumple up, while the faces of Sir Godfrey's ancestors seemed to Fred to be gazing fiercely through the lurid light, and reproaching him for helping to desolate their home.

Frames, panelling, the oaken gallery rails, blazed up as if they had been of resin in the tremendous heat; the stained-glass in the various windows crackled, flew, and fell tinkling down.

"Well," said the general, quietly, "you see, the place was fired in two places. We can do nothing?"

"No," groaned Colonel Forrester, as he looked wildly round. Then, in a despairing tone, as he gripped his son's arm, "Fred, is there nothing we can save?"

As he spoke, a great burning fragment of the gallery balustrade fell with a crash on to the oaken floor, the embers scattering in all directions, the gallery floor rose in the intense heat, as if a wave were passing through it, and as all backed involuntarily toward the door, one of the suits of armour fell forward with a crash.

"It would be utter madness," said General Hedley. "At least here. We could not have stayed a minute but for the cool air rushing in behind. If you wish to try and save anything, we must break in through the windows from outside."

The argument was unanswerable; and after a last wild gaze round, the little party gave way step by step, and were literally driven out by the tremendous heat, Fred's last look back being at the splendid staircase, now one raging mass of fire, which was spreading upward with terrific speed.

As they stood outside once more, the dense clouds of smoke were pouring through the upper windows, and directly after, from the broad casement above the porch, where Fred had held converse with the Cavaliers in his character of ambassador, a great billowy wave of lurid smoky flame lapped and flapped like a fiery banner, and then floated upward into the soft cool air.

The afternoon had been calm and windless, but now it seemed as if a sharp breeze was setting in toward the doomed house, fanning the flames and making them roar, while overhead, and rapidly increasing in volume, floated a huge cloud of smoke, spreading and spreading till it resembled the head of a gigantic tree, whose black and purply grey foliage brightened from time to time with a lurid glow.

But by this time axes were at work breaking down the stout boarding from the wide drawing-room window to the right of the porch. This great wide window had been completely covered, as a means of defence, save that here and there slits had been left to enable the defenders to fire on their enemies.

So stoutly was this work done with boards torn from stabling and barn at the back of the house, that it took some time to clear an opening and dash in a portion of the casement, and the fire had been gaining strength so potent, that as the first casement was driven in a volume of hot stifling smoke shot out, was apparently driven in by the air which rushed toward the house, there was a dull report, and the interior, that had been black the moment before, suddenly glowed with dull red, which was brightened by flashes.

Colonel Forrester was checked for the moment, as he tried to climb in, but calling on Samson and his son to follow, he rushed on.

Samson was second, and Fred had reached the sill, when there was a bright flame, which illumined the smoke-filled room, and he uttered a cry for help, and hesitated, for he had caught a glimpse of those who had preceded him lying prone upon the floor.

The help was quickly rendered, a dozen stalwart troopers dashing in, half to come struggling out choking and blinded.

What followed, Fred hardly recalled. He knew that he had leaped down to try and drag his father out, when something seemed to seize him by the throat, a terrible dizziness robbed him of sense, and the next thing he comprehended was that he was lying on the grass, with a man bathing his face, and that for a few minutes he could not speak or make out what it all meant.

"Better, my lad?" said a well-known voice; and he recognised the face of the general bent down over him, and saw that the morion he wore gleamed in the bright light cast upon it.

"My father!" cried Fred, as his understanding grew more clear.

"Safe. He has just recovered a little. Your servant, too. Yes; here he is."

"Fred, my boy," said a husky voice. "Thank Heaven! he is safe."

"Safe? Yes, father; only a little giddy. You have escaped?"

"Yes; they dragged us out in time. Look at the poor Hall."

Fred turned to see that from half the windows the flames were rushing out with a fearful violence, the centre of the old building being now a glowing furnace, whose flames fluttered and roared and leaped, while the wings were rapidly being eaten into by the flames.

"And we can save nothing, Hedley," said the colonel, sadly.

"Yes, sir, our lives. We can do no more. Pretty well that we got you out, and that the prisoners left the place."

Fred had risen, and was standing by the general's side, looking at him wildly.

"Well?" said the latter. "What are you thinking?"

"The wounded, sir—the dead?" said Fred, huskily.

"There were no dead. The wounded were all brought out, I feel sure. My boy, we have done our best. Forrester, are you well enough to move?"

"Yes; better now."

"You see the place is doomed. It is a sad affair; but we are guiltless. I will place the prisoners in your hands. See that they are courteously treated, and send them off under the escort of a troop to Barnstaple—at once. You can go and help."

This last was to Fred, who accepted the duty eagerly, and the next minute he was making his way with his father in the direction of the knot of prisoners, whose armour shone in the light of the glowing pile.

Chapter Thirty Nine
A Fruitless Search

As Colonel Forrester and his son approached the prisoners, who were lying about on the grass in a variety of easy, careless attitudes, gazing at the fire, which had now assumed terrible proportions, Fred became aware of the fact that in place of being despondent, the Cavaliers were chatting away in the most indifferent manner.

But their conversation ceased, for from behind came a loud crashing noise, caused by some floor falling, and a buzz of wonder and admiration arose as the glowing windows suddenly belched forth flame, spark, and glowing flakes of fire, in so many eddying, whirling columns, which rose up and up to mingle and gild the lower surface of the cloud of smoke which glowed with orange and purple and red, while sparks flashed and glittered as they darted here and there like the flakes of a snowstorm suddenly changed to gold.

The scene was glorious now, for after a moment's pause, the burning wood which had fallen formed fresh fuel to the mighty furnace within the thick walls, and the flames rushed up with renewed violence, illumining the scene far and near. Great sombre trees grew visible, brightened by the wondrous glow; the lawn seemed to be cut up into paths of light, and further away, ruddy reflections flashed from the lake; while the noble old Hall seemed to stand out against a dark background, with every angle, battlement, and vane clearly cut, till the smallest carving was plainly defined.

But for the horror of the scene, Fred could have stood and gazed with delight at the wondrous series of changes that were taking place; the clouds of smoke, which seemed to form vast spirals, ever turning, and rolling over, now dull red, now bursting into light, as if from fires therein; the eddying scintillations which crackled and exploded, and disappeared; the ruddy tongues of flame which darted in and out as if the long low windows were monstrous dragons' mouths, from which the darting forks came to play over golden stony lips, and lick the mullions and buttresses around. Then came a fresh explosion, as pent-up gases, generated by heat, burst forth to augment the fire with hiss, crackle, and flutter, as it seemed to gain its climax, and then sank down with a low dull roar.

From time to time there was a sharp tinkling, as the higher windows cracked, broke, and fell upon the stones. Then came pouring down a spouting torrent of silver fire, shooting right out of a stone gargoyle-mouth as the molten lead from one part of the roof, dammed up by other lead which had not melted, at last forced its way spattering on to the paved terrace below.

But after these brilliant bursts, which had enchained Fred's attention for a time, he turned once more toward the group of prisoners, whose loud, careless talking had begun again, and he passed between two of the guard stationed round them in a circle, while lying outside, in a confused heap, just as they had been thrown, were the weapons of which the Cavaliers had been deprived.

As Fred drew nearer, he could see that the careless attitudes of some of the party were assumed, for in spite of the glow shed by the fire, it was plain enough that the cheeks of several were of a deathly pallor, and that they were suffering intense pain. One had a scarf tied tightly round his arm; another had a broad bandage about his brow; hardly one seemed to have escaped some injury in the desperate sally and defence. But the aim of all was to carry their defeat with an air of the most careless indifference—as if wounds were nothing to them, and they held their Puritan captors in the most profound contempt.

"Hallo!" shouted a voice Fred had before heard, "here's my fire-eating young ambassador. Why, hang it all, sirrah! How is it you were not to the front before? I'd rather have given up my sword to you than have had it knocked out of my hand by the ugliest crop-eared knave I ever met."

Fred, the moment before, was eagerly scanning the group in search of Sir Godfrey and his old companion; but he had searched in vain, and he was anxiously debating within himself as to whether that meant bad news or good. Had they escaped? and were they now safe, or—?

He was checked by the greeting of the tall, fair Cavalier, and advanced to him at once, the high-spirited officer continuing his bantering speech the while.

"Why, you heinous young rebel," he cried, "have you come to trample on your poor prisoners now you have taken them; or are we to be shot, or hung, or what?"

"Don't talk to me like that, sir," said Fred, eagerly, as he paused by where the Cavalier lay; and now he could see that his jerkin was darkened in one spot with blood.

"How do you want me to talk, then, eh?"

"Sir Godfrey?—Scarlett Markham? Where are they?"

"Escaped," said a gentleman lying by, with careless levity. "Run for it—broken through your lines, and got clean away."

"Not they," said the tall Cavalier, warmly. "Sir Godfrey Markham was not the man to leave his friends in the lurch; and as for my young friend Scarlett, he would have stood by us to the end."

"But they are not here?" said Fred, anxiously.

"Here, sir? No. They must be with your other prisoners."

"Other prisoners?" faltered Fred, turning pale, as a horrible thought assailed him, and he darted a frightened glance at the burning Hall; "there are no other prisoners but these."

"What!" cried the Cavalier, starting to his feet, and then turning faint, so that he would have fallen, but for Fred's arm. "Thank you, my lad," he said frankly; "a little weak, I suppose. Yes; I will lie down."

Fred helped him into a reclining position again upon the turf.

"Tell me all you know about them, sir," said Fred, going down on one knee to help the wounded officer. "Scarlett and I used to be great friends. Did they escape right away?"

The Cavalier seemed at first to be about to respond in his old careless, bantering, half-mocking way, but as he saw the eagerness of manner, and the anxiety in the lad's eyes, his manner changed.

This was no ruse, he saw; no cunning trick to find out which way the Markhams had gone, but a true honest feeling for one who had been a friend, but was now transformed by political troubles into an enemy.

"Shake hands," he said warmly. "I like you, boy. I'll tell you all I know."

Fred eagerly took the prisoner's hand, as the others looked on curiously, their assumption of carelessness gone, and a dull look of despair making its appearance in their eyes and at the angles of their mouths. And as Fred took that hand, it was cold and damp, and the grip was feeble, as its owner said slowly—

"Sir Godfrey Markham and I divided our little force, after drawing lots for choice; I won the choice, and selected the task of making the sally. It would have been too irksome to me to stay behind a barrier and wait to be attacked. I suppose you know—your people were too strong for us, and we were beaten back, followed by your men, till we were all together struggling in the dining-room, from there into the hall, and then on the great staircase. I saw Sir Godfrey and young Scarlett several times during the struggle; then we were all pell-mell, here, there, and everywhere, and I recollect no more."

"But where did you see them last?"

"I cannot say—in the drawing-room, I think."

"Yes. What were they doing?"

"What do you think they were likely to be doing, boy? Fighting bravely for their king."

There was a pause.

"You do not think that—"

Fred did not finish his sentence. "That they set fire to the Hall? No; Sir Godfrey was too proud of his old home to destroy it."

"I did not mean that," said Fred, hoarsely; "I meant—"

"Wounded—killed?" Fred bowed his head. He could not speak, for there was a horrible idea tugging at his brain, one which he could not shake off.

"Wounded? Perhaps. Killed? Heaven forbid! No; I hope and believe that they fought to the last, and then escaped, or else, far more likely, they are—"

He stopped short, for the idea that troubled Fred had now been communicated to him, and he drew in his breath with a look of horror. Then, as if unable to control himself, he glanced sharply at the burning building, while, giddy and weak with emotion, Fred walked slowly back, to make his way to his father, who met him and took his arm.

"Have you heard any news of them?" said the colonel, hoarsely.

"No, father," half whispered Fred; and he repeated the Cavalier's words.

Colonel Forrester glanced at the burning Hall, nearly every portion of which had now been seized upon by the flames, and he drew a deep hissing breath, as he whispered to himself—

"No, no; impossible! They must have escaped. Fred," he said aloud, "they will not tell us if we ask—it is quite natural; so we are quite in the dark as to how many the defenders were. There were none killed, and I find that the wounded were all carried out. Sir Godfrey and his son must have escaped, or if not, they will be brought in by some of the outposts."

Fred made no answer; he could not speak, for a terrible picture was before his eyes—that of Sir Godfrey, wounded to the death, unable to stir, and Scarlett trying to bear him out to safety, but only to be overtaken and beaten down by the flames.

He walked on by his father in silence, while the latter gazed straight before him, thinking to himself of the past, when he and Sir Godfrey were the fastest of friends.

"This cruel war!" he said to himself. "Friend against friend, brother against brother. Poor Godfrey! Poor Scarlett! So full of brave manliness and courage. Fitting end for two brave spirits; but I feel as if I had assisted at their death."

But at that moment Fred made a mental effort.

"I will not believe it," he said, with a shudder. "It is too horrible." Then aloud, "Father, may I take something to the prisoners, and help them? They look very bad."

"Yes, yes; of course," said the colonel, starting as it were back to the present. "Poor fellows! The surgeon must be with them now; but go and do your best."

But hard as Fred worked by the light of the burning house, he could do little to assuage the pains, mental and bodily, of the prisoners. They assumed a careless indifference, a good-humoured contempt for their captors. They were Cavaliers—gentlemen who did not scruple to serve as ordinary soldiers for the benefit of their country; and they smiled at the rough stern men of the Puritan ranks. But deep in their hearts there was a despairing rage at being conquered, which bit and stung, and made them writhe more than the throbbings of their wounds.

The refreshments Fred took to them, helped by Samson, were simple, but most welcome; and more than one eye brightened and directed a friendly grateful look at the lad who busied himself on the captives' behalf.

"No; no more, my boy," said the tall, fair Cavalier, smiling at Fred, as he pressed him to eat. "I have a wound here that throbs as if some one were thrusting a red-hot iron through my shoulder. I suppose it is all right, but your surgeon has not hands like some delicate lady."

"Can I do anything?" said Fred, eagerly. "Shall I bathe the wound?"

"No, my desperate and deadly enemy, no," said the Cavalier, smiling as he look Fred's hand; "and look here: some of these days the war will be over, and if you and I are not sleeping too soundly, you must come and see me, and I'll come and see you. At present our duty is to kill each other, or take one another prisoner. By-and-by we shall have more time. There," he said, drawing a ring from his finger; "you wear that, and remember that Harry Grey always feels respect and esteem for a brave enemy, while for you— Oh, curse it! We are not enemies. God bless you, my lad! You and Scar Markham ought to be working together as a pair."

He turned impatiently away, laid his head upon the folded cloak, of which Fred had made a pillow and closed his eyes, as if annoyed that he should have seemed weak; while, after pressing the ring tightly down in its place, Fred stood back watching the group of wounded and captive men for a few minutes, before turning away, and then stopping short by the little heap of swords of which they had been deprived.

As it happened, one with a peculiarly shaped guard took his attention, for he remembered having seen it hanging to the belt of the Cavalier he had been tending.

Stooping down, he was in the act of drawing it from among the others, when the sentinel made a movement to arrest his hand.

"Don't interfere," said Fred, sharply. "I will be answerable to Colonel Forrester for what I have done."

The man drew back, and stood resting upon his clumsy firelock again, while, as the lad stood with the sword in his hand, he raised his eyes from the hilt, and found that the Cavalier was watching him, and making a sign to him to approach once more.

Fred stepped to his side.

"No," he said; "you cannot have it. You are a prisoner."

"Of course," said the wounded man, smiling; "though if I had it, I could not use it. I was going to say I am glad you have taken it. A capital blade, my boy. Here, unbuckle the belt, and take it and the sheath. Yes, I insist. That's right. Keep it, lad, and don't, if we meet again, use it on me. No, no thanks; it is yours by right of capture. Now I want a nap."

Chapter Forty
A Sad Report

The Cavalier let his head sink once more upon his pillow, and Fred went slowly away, to go and watch the flames rising and falling as the Hall burned rapidly, sending forth a glow of heat that could be felt far away.

And now that the hurry and excitement were at an end, Fred had time once more to think of those of whose fate he was still uncertain.

Just then a prisoner was being brought in, and he hurried to the spot, but only to turn away disappointed, to go and gaze once more at the burning pile, musing sadly on the times when he had passed such pleasant hours about the place which had been to him as a second home; and thinking, as he gazed through the open windows into the furnace within, of the various rooms where every object was so familiar—picture, ornament, carved cabinet, trophy—and now all turning to glowing embers.

"Seems a pity, Master Fred, don't it?" said a voice at his elbow.

"You here, Samson?"

"Yes, sir; just come from round at the back."

"Has the fire made its way there?"

"Oh, bless you, sir, it's been creeping and rushing and leaping over everything! Even the big tool-house and fruit-room's burned. Such a pity. Nice lot of tools all destroyed; and, not that I want to find fault, but a deal better set than we ever had at the Manor. Why, there was a barrow, sir, as run that light in your hands, no matter how you filled it, as made it a pleasure to work."

"And all burned, Samson?"

"All burned into ashes, sir. I never could understand it, but it always did seem hard as a man like brother Nat should have such a barrow as that, while I had one as I was ashamed of."

"We must get to the wilderness to-night, Samson, somehow."

"Oh, he won't hurt, sir," said Samson, roughly. "He's right enough; but I've got a bottle o' cider, and three bread-cakes, and half a roast fowl to take with us when we go."

"That's right," said Fred, smiling in spite of himself; but only to turn serious as an agonising thought shot through him, for a portion of the roof of the Hall fell just then, and a whirlwind of sparks sprang into the evening sky.

"Have you heard any news, Samson?" whispered Fred.

"News, sir?"

"Of Sir Godfrey and Scarlett?"

Samson stood gazing straight at the fire, his eyes half shut, and his forehead a maze of puckers and wrinkles, and he seemed not to have heard in the intentness of his watching the progress of the fire.

"Do you hear what I say?" reiterated Fred. "Is there any news of Sir Godfrey and Scarlett?"

"Yes, I hear what you say, sir."

"Then why don't you speak?"

"'Cause I haven't nothing good to say."

"Oh, Samson, there is no bad news?"

"No, sir; there's no bad news at all."

"Then what do you mean? What have you heard?"

"Don't, don't ask me, my lad."

"But I do ask you, and I will know."

"I only know what the men think, and of course that may mean nothing."

"What do they think?"

"Now, look ye here, Master Fred," cried Samson, appealingly, "what's the good of your bullying me into saying things which will only make you cross with me, and call me a thundering idiot, or some other pretty thing like that?"

"But anything's better than suspense, and I want to know the worst."

"Well, then, you can't," said Samson, gruffly. "There aren't no worse, because it's all guessing."

"Well, then, what do they guess?"

"Now, look ye here, Master Fred—is it fair to make me tell you, and put you in a passion; and you a-standing there with a sword by your side, and another in your hand?"

"Speak, sir—speak!"

"Very well, sir; here goes. And if you fly in a passion, and do anything rash to me, it will only be another triumph for my brother Nat."

"Will you speak, sir?"

"Yes, I'm going to, sir; but one must make a beginning. Well, then, Master Fred, it's only hearsay, and you know what hearsay is. Some one heard one of the prisoners say that he saw Sir Godfrey go down wounded, and young Master Scarlett jump across him, fighting like a madman; and then people were driven all sorts of ways, but not before there was a regular burst of fire sweeping along; and they think that Sir Godfrey and poor Master Scarlett was overtaken by the flames. Master Fred! Master Fred! don't take on like that. It's only what they say, you know, dear lad, and it may be all wrong."

The rough fellow laid his hand upon his master's arm, as Fred turned away.

"But it's what I fear—it's what I fear," he groaned. "And my father thinks the same; I know he does. Oh, Samson, how horrible! how horrible! If I only knew who fired the place!"

"Oh, I know that, sir," said Samson. "One of the prisoners boasted about it—not one of the gentleman Cavaliers, but one of the rough fellows like me. He says he set the place a-fire in two places, when he saw the game was up; and he said that it was so as we shouldn't have comfortable quarters—a mean hound!"

"Poor Scar! poor old Scar!" groaned Fred, walking slowly away, to try and get somewhere alone with his sorrow, as he thought of his brave, manly young friend.

He walked on till he was right away down by one of the clumps of trees at the west end of the lake; and as he groaned again he started, for he thought he was alone, but Samson had followed him softly.

"Don't 'ee take on, Master Fred, lad. Be a man. I feel as if I should like to sit down and blubber like a big calf taken away from its mother, but it won't do, lad, it won't do; we're soldiers now. But if I could have my way, I'd just get them all together as started this here war, and make 'em fight it out themselves till there wasn't one left, and then I'd enjoy myself."

"Don't talk of enjoyment. Samson, my lad."

"But I must, for I just would. I'd go and get the sharpest spade I could find, and take off my jerkin, and bury what was left of 'em, and that would be the finest thing that could happen for old England."

"Nonsense, man! You don't understand these things," said Fred, sadly.

"And I don't want to, sir. What I understand is that instead of fighting the French, or the Spaniards, or any other barbarous enemies, we're all fighting against one another like savages; and there's the beautiful old Hall burning down to the ground like a beacon fire on a hill, and who knows but what it may be our turn next?"

"What, at the Manor, Samson?"

"Yes, sir. Why not?"

"Heaven forbid, man! Heaven forbid!"

"And I say 'Amen,' sir. But come back to camp, and let's get you a bit of something to eat; and, I say, sir, you did give my hand a deep cut. Think that new sword you've got's as sharp as the one I whetted for you?"

"I don't know, Samson," said Fred, drearily. "I hate the very name of sword."

"And so do I, sir, proud as I was the first day I buckled mine on. I aren't much of a smith, but I can blow the bellows like hooray, and when the time comes, as it says in the Bible, I'll make the fire roar while some one hammers all the swords and spears into plough-shares and pruning-hooks, and cuts all the gun-barrels up into pipes. That's right, sir; come along."

Fred said no more, but, with their shadows darkly shown upon the trampled grass, the pair walked back to camp.

Chapter Forty One
Nat is Lost

"Have I been to sleep, Samson?"

"Yes, sir, sound as a top. You dropped off after you had that bread and cider."

"And the Hall?—is it still burning?"

"Yes, sir; a regular steady fire down at the bottom, with the walls standing up all round."

"And the prisoners?"

"All gone, sir. They packed 'em off to the west'ard in a couple of waggons, and a troop of our men as escorts. Fine fellows, sir, all but that one as fired the Hall. I couldn't help being sorry to see how wounded and helpless they were. But how they carried it off, laughing and talking there till they'd been seen to, and were tired and got stiff! Then it began to tell on 'em, and they had to be lifted into the waggons and laid on the straw almost to a man."

"I hope they'll all recover," said Fred, sadly.

"So do I, sir, even if we have to fight 'em again. But we shall see no more of the poor lads for a long time, unless some of their party rescues them, cures them, and the game begins over again. Feel ready, sir?"

"Ready?"

"Yes; it's about twelve o'clock, and I thought you might like to come and help me bully that ugly brother of mine."

"Why, Samson," said Fred, with a sad smile, "every one says you two are so like."

"So we are, sir, to look at," replied Samson, grinning; "but I never said I was good-looking, did I?"

"Yes, I'm ready," said Fred, rising from his heather couch. "Oh, how stiff and cold I am!"

"You've just wakened; that's why. You'll be as fresh as fresh soon. Come along, sir, and we'll give that rascal such a bullying."

"With care and chicken," said Fred, with a miserable attempt at being jocose.

"Now, don't I keep telling you it's only to make him strong, so as he can feel it all the sharper when I give him the big beating I've promised him? Come along, sir."

Fred made a few inquiries as to the state of affairs; learned that the camp was quite at rest, and that he was not likely to be called on duty, and then, with a terrible depression of spirits, increasing at every step, he walked on beside Samson on as dark a night as he could recall.

"Dark, sir?" said the ex-gardener, in response to a remark. "Well, yes, sir, it is; but it don't make any difference to us. We could find our way where we are going with our eyes shut."

The darkness was not their only difficulty: they had to avoid the sentinels again, and neither could say for certain whether any changes had been made.

Still, both had been on moorland, over bog, and through the deepest woods in the dark on trapping expeditions times enough. They had even been in the darkness on the dangerous cliff slopes again and again, so that they had no hesitation in going rapidly on till the lake had been skirted and the wilderness reached, without their being challenged. Then the dense undergrowth was entered, and they stood listening for a few moments.

There were distant sounds—the snort of a horse where it was picketed, a low humming as if some sentry were cheering his dreary watch by recollections of an old west-country ditty, and then from a little distance there was the half-hissing, half-grating cry of a white owl, as it flapped along upon its downy, silent pinions, while, through the trees at the edge of the wood, there was a dull red light, which showed where the embers of the great oaken beams of the Hall sent forth their dying glow.

"Let's go on," whispered Fred, just as something came gliding along the edge of the wilderness, and as they moved it uttered a piercing screech, turned, and swept away.

"Ugh!" ejaculated Samson; but Fred's hand was upon his lips, and they stood close together with throbbing hearts, wondering whether the two cries would alarm the nearest sentinel.

But they heard nothing, and as silently as possible stole in among the trees, it being impossible to make any selection of route.

"How them owls do chill one, like, in a unked place like this! 'Member that one as come out of the wood shed as we went in last winter? Always scares me."

"I dare say it scares them more than it does us," whispered back Fred. "Now don't speak."

"Right, sir."

Fred led on, moving more by instinct than sight, and seeming to feel which was the way to the spot where they had left the injured man; but it was a long and arduous task, and not till after he had gone astray three times did he pause in perplexity.

"If I could get any idea of where the Hall lay, perhaps I could find him," whispered Fred; "but we have turned about so, that I don't know which way we are looking now."

"More don't I, sir; for aught I know we might be somewhere hundreds of miles away. It's so plaguey dark."

"Look! Isn't that the reflection of the fire?"

"No, sir; there's nothing there. Ah, look there!"

A dull low sound fell upon their ears, and simultaneously there was a flash of light in quite a different direction to that in which they had been straining their eyes.

"What's that, sir?"

"Some part of the Hall fallen in."

"And made the fire flash up just as it does when you're burning rubbish. That's right, sir."

"Yes; and I can find it now," whispered Fred.

The struggle through the undergrowth was resumed, every step having to be taken with the greatest caution; and at last, after making endless diversions to avoid tree-trunks and masses of tangled growth that they could not force their way through, Fred stopped short.

"What is it, sir?"

"This is the place."

"No, sir, I don't think it is."

"Yes; I can tell by the touch. I am close up to the fallen tree. There, I can feel the touchwood. Be quiet. Hist! Nat! Nat!"

There was no reply, and after a pause, Fred called again, as loudly as he dared.

"No, sir; I thought it wasn't," said Samson, softly. "It's further up."

"Be silent, man," said Fred, impatiently. "I am sure we are right. It may be a little to the left or a little to the right, but its close here."

He called again and again softly, but without result.

"Let me try, Master Fred, as you are so sure."

Fred gave his consent, whispering to his companion to be careful.

"Nobody won't take any notice of what I do, Master Fred," whispered Samson. "I'll give him an old cry we used to have on the moor, when we were boys;" and directly after, sounding distant and strange, and as if it could not possibly have been given by his companion, there rang out a peculiar low piping whistle, followed by a short jerky note or two.

"That's oyster-catcher, Master Fred, as you well know. If he hears that he'll answer and know it's friends—I mean enemies."

Fred made no reply to his follower's paradoxical speech, but listened intently.

"Again," he said, after a time; and the cry rang out, to be followed by a dull thud as of footsteps, and a clink of steel against steel.

Fred felt his arm grasped, and Samson's hot breath in his ear.

"Keep quiet. There's a sentry close by, and they're going the rounds."

The dull sound of footsteps died away, and not till then did Samson venture upon another call, that proved to be as unavailing as those which had preceded it.

"P'raps he's asleep," said Samson, softly; "but that ought to have roused him."

Fred drew a long breath, as in imagination he saw the poor wounded fellow lying there in the dark and cold; and as a chilly perspiration bedewed his face, he felt a horrible feeling of reproach for not having given notice of an injured man lying in the wood. For he told himself, and the thought gathered strength, that perhaps they had come too late.

For a few minutes he could not speak, and when he did, his heart was beating heavily, as he whispered—

"Samson, do you think—?"

He could not finish the terrible sentence, one which his companion misconstrued.

"Of course I do, sir. I told you so. This aren't the place, I'm sure."

"It is! it is!" said Fred, with passionate energy, "Here, I am touching the old tree; and, yes—I know. Here is the place where he must be lying."

"Very well, then, sir, stoop down and lay hold of his leg gently, and give it a pull. Be on the look-out, for he can be very nasty at being woke up. Maybe he'll kick out. He used to when we were boys."

Fred felt dizzy as he listened to his companion's careless utterance, and he asked himself whether he should tell him what he thought. Twice over he was on the point of speaking, but he clung to the hope that his ideas might be only fancy, and he stood there turning icily cold.

The idea seemed so terrible—to stoop down there in that utter darkness and touch the form of the poor fellow who had been left in despair and loneliness to die, untended and without a soul to whom he could say a farewell word. No; he could not do it, and he felt as if he must turn and rush out of the wood.

"Feel him, Master Fred?" whispered Samson.

Again the sensation of cold and dread came over Fred, and he was about to yield to it and hurry away, when his determination mastered, and, setting his teeth fast, he bent down, went upon hands and knees, and felt on before him, letting his hand sink slowly so as to reverently touch him who he felt must be lying dead.

"Well, sir—got him?"

"No!" whispered Fred, hoarsely, as his hand touched the twigs and leaves.

"Try again, sir."

Fred crept on, and again stretched out his hand.

"Now you have him, sir?"

"No," said Fred, with a throb of excitement sending a thrill through him; "he is not here."

"There, what did I tell you!" said Samson, in a satisfied tone. "You would be so obstinate. This aren't the place."

"But it is," whispered Fred. "I can feel where he laid. The twigs are all levelled down."

"Nonsense, sir!"

"I tell you I am right; it's the hole he made for himself. This is the place, and— Hah!"

"Got him?"

"No; but here is your jerkin that you left to cover him."

"Then you are right, sir. Well, feel about more."

"I cannot get any further. This is the place, and he has either been found, or he has crept away, and— Yes, that's it; he hasn't had strength to creep back."

"Then we must call again."

"Yes."

Samson repeated his cry, over and over again, without result, and then, Fred having rejoined him, they stood listening.

"We cannot find him to-night, Samson."

"No, sir. Well, it doesn't much matter. He's ever so much better, or he wouldn't have gone out for a walk. Here, let's sit down and eat this here bread and chicken, and drink the cider, sir. I feel as if I hadn't had anything for a week, and the food has been bumping about my lips and asking to go in ever since we started. I'm glad now I brought it, but I've been sorry I was so stupid all along."

"Do you think we could find him if we searched?" said Fred, ignoring his companion's remark about the food.

"Sure we couldn't, sir, without a lanthorn; and if we had one we durstn't use it. Let's set down and have a bite."

"No, no. Look here! If he has crept away, he is sleeping somewhere not far off, and he is sure to come back. Give me the food, and I'll lay it in there ready for him. He'll find it when it's light."

"Put it there, sir?"

"Yes."

"But the slugs and snails and beetles and things 'll come and eat it all before morning. Don't let's waste good food, sir, like that."

"Do as I bid you, sir. Give me the food."

Samson sighed and obeyed. The bread and fowl were placed with the bottle on the jerkin at the far end of the little tunnel where Nat had lain, and Fred backed out.

"Come," he said laconically.

Samson grunted dismally, and followed his leader; and after they had struggled out of the wilderness, they made their way back to camp without any further check than a challenge or two, the password enabling them to reach the tent not long before morning dawned.

Chapter Forty Two
Baiting a Trap

"Yes, my boy; sad, sad indeed," said Colonel Forrester. "I would have given anything to have prevented it."

Father and son were walking round the ruins of the Hall, which were still too heated to allow of approach, while from the heap of *débris* within a thin filmy smoke arose.

"Do you think there is any hope, father?" said Fred, after a long pause.

Colonel Forrester looked at him quickly.

"I mean of Sir Godfrey and poor Scar being alive?"

Colonel Forrester did not reply, but turned away with his brow full of deep furrows; and feeling as if everything like happiness was at an end, Fred turned away from the scene of desolation, and walked up toward the little camp on the hill, wondering how it would be possible to convey the terrible tidings to the two who must be suffering a very martyrdom of anxiety at the Manor.

"I could not do it. I dare not," muttered Fred. "And besides, it is too soon. There may be hope."

But as he said those last words to himself, he pictured the wounded father defended by his son, and then the rushing flames, and he groaned in spirit as he felt how hopeless it all seemed.

"Heard all the news, Master Fred, I s'pose?"

Fred started, for he had not heard the approach of Samson.

"No; I have heard nothing. I have been with my father at the ruins."

"I was there at 'bout six o'clock, sir. Couldn't have thought the old place would have burnt so fast."

"But you said news, Samson?" cried Fred, eagerly. "Not news of them?"

"No, sir; not news of them," replied Samson, sadly. "News of our stopping here for the present."

"No."

"Well, sir, I hear that's to be it, unless a stronger party comes and drives us away. Seems to me as we're like the little ones playing king o' the castle; and no sooner is one up a-top than another comes and pushes him down. But, Master Fred; had your breakfast, haven't you?"

"Yes," said Fred, whose thoughts were at the ruins.

"So have I, sir. Well, look here, sir; I want to see whether the slugs and snails have been at that there food in the wood. What do you say to going to see?"

"We cannot go till night, Samson," said Fred, sadly.

"Yes, we can, sir. Look here; I'll cut a couple o' long willows, and get some worms in the Hall garden, and I dare say I can find a basket. Then let's you and me go careless like to the far end of the lake, just as if we were going to try for a fish or two, and nobody will notice us then. Once we are there, we can creep up through the bushes to the wilderness, and get that bit o' food."

"And see if your brother is better?"

"Nay, nay; I'm not going to take all that trouble 'bout such a fellow as him, sir. 'Tis 'bout that food I'm thinking. Shall we go, sir?"

"Yes, Samson, yes; and look here: don't try to deceive me like this, because it will not do."

"Oh well, it never was no use to argue with you, sir, when you was a schoolboy. Now you're a young officer, you're harder still. There, I'm not going to say any more; but is it likely I should do all this 'bout an enemy, unless it was to make him a prisoner? There, I'm off to get them rods and worms."

Samson went across to the Hall garden, and shortly afterwards reappeared with a pot and basket.

"We can get the two rods somewhere down by the lake," he said; and one of the sentinels as he stood, firelock in hand, smiled grimly, and thought of how he would like to leave his monotonous task, and go down to the lake side to fish, after the fashion he had so loved when a boy.

This man watched them right to the edge of the water, where he saw Samson select and cut two long willow rods, and strip them clean of leaf and twig before shouldering them, and marching on beside his master.

"It's well to be them," grumbled the man, "for who knows whether in these days of bloodshed a lad may ever have a chance to fish again?"

He shouldered his firelock, and continued his slow tramp to and fro, looking out for the enemy, but more often turning his gaze toward his fishing friends.

"Bring the hooks and lines, Master Fred?" said Samson, as they went on toward the west end of the lake.

"Hooks and lines? No."

"Well, sir, we can't fish without lines. Didn't I tell you to get 'em while I got the worms?"

"No."

"Well, now, that's strange. But I did mean to, sir. What are we to do? Go back?"

"No, no! Don't let's waste time."

"But we can't catch no fish without a hook."

"We don't want to catch any fish."

"But we want people to think we do."

"Yes; and if they see us with rods down by the water, they will think so."

"More stoopids they, sir. I needn't carry this here ugly pot o' worms and the basket, then, no longer, sir?"

"Yes, you must. Don't throw them away. We had better keep up the look of being fishermen."

"Very well, sir; just as you like. But I say, Master Fred, what's the good of all this? Don't let's go."

"Not go?"

"I don't see why we should take the trouble to go and look after a fellow like Nat. He never was any credit to me, and he never will be. Like as not, if he gets better, he'll give me a topper."

"Come along, and hold your tongue, Samson. Do you suppose I can't see through you?"

"Yes, I do, sir," said Samson, with a chuckle. "Chap did try to make a hole through me just after we turned soldiers, but it's all grown up again. I say, Master Fred, though, ser'us—think Nat is alive?"

"Yes, of course, poor fellow! No, don't hurry now. Some one may be watching us. Let's pretend to be picking out a good place."

"Poor fellow!" grumbled Samson, as he obeyed, and began holding overhanging boughs aside and leaning over the water. "Don't suppose you'd say, 'Poor fellow!' if I was to be lying wounded there, Master Fred."

"No, of course not," said Fred, angrily; "I should say I was very glad to get rid of you, and I wouldn't stir a step to bring you bread or water or anything."

Samson stopped short, and burst into a roar of laughter.

"What's the matter, now?" cried Fred, wonderingly.

"Oh, you can tell 'em when you like, sir," cried Samson. "Haw, haw, haw! No, no, no; you won't get me to believe that. But let's get on, sir; we're 'bout out o' sight of the sentries. No; there's one looking at us over the hill. Let's sit down just yonder, and seem to begin."

A glance casually taken showed the wisdom of this proceeding, and one chose a spot by a tree, the other went twenty yards further toward the wood, and they began to go through the motions of people fishing, changing their places from time to time, Samson passing right on beyond Fred, and the latter after a few minutes going on past Samson, till they were well in among the trees, and not far from the steep rocky bank where the passage came down to the lake.

For the first time since the discovery, Fred went on without recalling that day when they drained the place, for he was too eager to go in search of Nat, who must be, he felt sure, lying somewhere in the wood, weak and suffering, and praying for their help.

"Now," said Samson, at last, "let's carry our rods a little way in and hide 'em with the basket, ready for us when we've done. I may pitch the pot o' worms away now, sir, mayn't I?"

"No, no; put them with the basket. There, in that bush—that's the place."

The rods were thrust in amongst the thick undergrowth, and then Fred took a final look round, seeing nothing, and then leading the way, easily enough now by day, for the displaced twigs showed to their practised eyes where they had passed before.

But even now it was no easy task to achieve before they came to the fallen oak, with its two mighty trunks, the one living, the other dead.

Then they stopped—startled; for there was a loud rustling, the leaves and twigs were forced apart, and for the moment they felt that they were discovered.

"Only a rabbit," said Samson, coolly, as the sound died away. "What a noise them little chaps can make, Master Fred! Go along."

"No, no; stop," cried Fred.

"It was only a rabbit, sir."

"Yes, I know; but don't you see?"

"See what, sir?"

"If there have been rabbits here, it's a sure sign that Nat is not in his hiding-place."

"Yes; I didn't think of that," said Samson, taking off his steel cap to give his head a scratch. "Never mind, sir; go on. He may have been back and gone out for a walk. It's just like him; being as awk'ard and contrary as can be."

Fred hesitated a moment or two, and then, feeling depressed and disappointed, thinking that the poor faithful follower of the Markhams was sharing their misfortunes, and perhaps lying dead hidden among the bushes, he took a step or two further on, pressed the twigs aside, and peered into the verdant tunnel Nat had made his temporary home.

"He is not here," he said sadly, as he crept in.

"Nor yet been there, sir?"

"No! Yes," cried Fred, changing his tone from one full of despondency to the very reverse. "He has been here, Samson. The food is all gone."

"Don't shout, sir. We may be heard. But that don't prove nothing. Rabbits and rats and field mice and all sorts of things may have been and eaten it. Cake and chicken! What waste! I might as well have eaten it myself," he muttered. Then, once more aloud, "We may as well drink what's in the bottle, sir."

"But it's gone, Samson," cried Fred, from the end of the tunnel.

"Gone, sir? The rabbits couldn't have—"

"And your jerkin is gone, too."

"Hooray! Then the poor old—"

Samson checked his jubilant speech before it was half ended, and continued, in a grumbling tone—

"That's just like Nat I told you how awk'ard he could be."

Fred came struggling back out of the verdant tunnel, and rose to his feet. Then, looking round, he said—

"We must try and follow his track, Samson. Which way is he likely to move—"

He, too, stopped short, staring wildly before him; and then he caught Samson's arm, unable to speak, so sudden was the hope which had flashed in upon his brain.

"See him, sir?" whispered Samson, as he stood gazing in a startled fashion in the same direction. "Oh, Master Fred, sir," he burst out, "don't, don't say the poor lad's dead. Nat, Nat, old chap, not without one good-bye grip of the hand."

"No, no, no," gasped Fred, half dragging his companion back.

"Not dead, sir?" panted Samson.

"No, no, no!"

"And you couldn't see him, sir?"

"No."

"Then what do you mean by serving a fellow like that?" muttered Samson to himself. "I didn't think I could make such a fool of myself— about an enemy, too."

"Samson," whispered Fred, excitedly, "can I trust you?"

"No, sir. 'Tarn't likely," growled the man, morosely. "I'm sartain to go and tell tales everywhere, and blab it all out, whatever it is."

"No, no; I don't believe you, lad. You always were true as steel, Samson."

"Master Fred, lad, I'd die for you!" half sobbed Samson, with his face working; and he clung now to the hand extended to him. "But do, do speak, sir. Poor Nat aren't dead?"

"No, no! How could I have been such an idiot!"

"Such a what, sir? Here, who says so?" cried Samson, truculently.

"I can't think how it was I never thought of it before."

"Here, sir, 'pon my head, I don't know which hole you're coming out of. What do you mean?"

"They're alive, Samson; they're alive!"

"*He's* alive, sir—*he's* alive, you mean."

"No; I mean they must be alive."

"But there never was but one Nat, sir; and that was quite enough."

"You don't understand me, man."

"No, sir, and nobody else could, talking like that."

"No, of course not. That's why I said could I trust you. Scar and Sir Godfrey and Nat must be all safe."

"Do you know what you are talking about, sir, or are you a bit off your head?"

"I'm as clear-headed as you are, man. Look there!"

"Yes, sir, I'm a-looking, and there's a heap o' sere 'ood with a bit of a hole in it."

"Yes; some one has been through there."

"What, do you think he has made himself another hole?"

"Yes, Samson."

Fred gave a quick, excited look round, but they were alone in the patch of forest.

"Yes, sir, I'm a-listening."

"There's a secret passage leads from there right up to the Hall."

"Secret grandmother, sir!"

"There is, I tell you," cried Fred, with his voice trembling from excitement. "Scar and I found it one day, and traced it right to the edge of the lake."

"Not gammoning me, are you, sir?"

"No, no, Samson."

"You didn't dream all this?"

"No, I tell you. We found it by accident, and when we were looking for the end we found that hole where that fallen tree had broken a way into the passage. We piled up all those branches to hide the place."

"Well, you stun me, Master Fred. And you think our Nat heard 'em there, and has gone to jine 'em?"

"He found them, or they found him. Hist!"

Fred crept close to the heap of dead wood, a portion of which, sufficient for a man to creep through, had been removed, and pressing as far in as he could, he made a trumpet of his hands and cried softly —

"Any one there?"

Samson had followed close to him, and he listened to his master's voice as it seemed to go in a hollow whisper echoing along under the earth.

"Well, it do stun me," he said, taking off his morion for a fresh scratch.

"Is any one there?" cried Fred again, as loudly as he dared; and there was no response. "Scar! Nat! Sir Godfrey!" he cried again; and after pausing to listen each time for a reply which did not come, he turned at last to encounter Samson's dubious face.

"Hope you're right, sir!" he said.

"Yes, man, certain. You see? You can hear?"

"Yes, sir, I can hear; and I suppose there's a sort of drain there."

"Drain, man? I tell you it's a secret passage."

"Maybe, sir; but that don't prove they are hiding in it."

"But they must be," cried Fred, excitedly. "Scar knew of it. They were cut off by the fire. They took refuge there, and I am sure they are hiding now; and, thank Heaven, safe."

"Well, sir, they're all mortal enemies, but I'm so glad to hear it that I say *Amen* with all my heart; but is it true?"

"Oh, yes, I am sure; it's true enough!" cried Fred, with his eyes full of the joy he felt. "Samson, I don't know how to contain myself—how to be thankful enough! Poor old Scar! I should never have felt happy again."

Samson's iron pot-like cap was tilted off again, and he scratched his head on the other side as he looked at Fred with a quaint smile upon his countenance.

"Well, sir, all this here puzzles me. It do—it do really. These here are our enemies, and we've been taught to smite 'em hip and thigh; and because we find they're living, instead of dead, here's you ready to jump out of your skin, and me feeling as if I could shake hands with old Nat. Of course I wouldn't; you see, I couldn't do it. Indeed, if he was here I should hit him, but I feel as if I should shake hands all the same."

"What will be best to do, Samson?"

"Do, sir? If you're right, get off as soon as we can."

"And them wanting our help."

"Tchah! They don't want our help. They want us to be out of their way. If they come and catch us here, sir, how do we know but what they may turn savage, and try to serve us out?"

"Samson, you are talking nonsense," said Fred, angrily; and he ran to the hole again and called aloud the names of those he believed to be in hiding, his words echoing and whispering along the dark passage, till Samson made him jump by touching him on the shoulder just as he was listening vainly for a reply.

"Don't do that, sir."

"Why not?"

"If that there passage goes right up to the Hall, the men yonder by the ruins on dooty will hear you hollering and find out all about it."

Fred started away as if he had been stung.

"You are right, Samson," he said; "I did not think of that."

"You didn't, sir?"

"No."

"Then that shows you that I am not so stoopid as you tell me I am sometimes."

"Oh, but I don't always mean it."

"Then you shouldn't say it, sir. Well, hadn't we better get back now?"

"But I want to make perfectly sure that they are hiding there, Samson, my good fellow; and how can we find out without waiting and watching?"

"Oh, I can soon do that for you, sir."

"How?"

"Set a trap."

"What?"

"Set a trap, and bait it same as you would for a fox, or a polecat, or one of them big hawks we see on the moor."

"I don't understand you. Pray do speak out. What trap could we set?"

"Oh, I'll soon show you that, sir. Here's the bait for it."

Samson opened his wallet, and drew therefrom a round flat cake, which had been cut open; and as he held it on his hand he raised the top, treating it as if it were the lid of a box, and grinned at Fred as he showed him within four slices of boiled salt pork.

"There, sir," he said, as he shut the top down again, "there's a bait for a trap as would catch any hungry man."

"Yes; but what are you going to do?"

"I'll show you, sir. I'm just going to hang that inside yonder hole; and if my brother Nat's there he'll smell it half a mile away, and come and take it. I know him like a lesson. We'll leave it there, go away, and come back again; and if the cake's gone we know they are there."

"We shall know some one is there," Fred said thoughtfully. "Yes, we shall know that Scar is there," he added with more show of animation, "for no one but us two know of the existence of that hole. He must have come out and found your brother."

"Shall I bait the trap, then, sir?" said Samson.

"Yes, of course."

"Ah," said Samson, placing the cake in a fork of one of the dead branches right in the hole, "you often laugh at me, sir, for bringing a bit o' food with me, but now you see the good of it. There!"

He drew back to look admiringly at his work.

"That'll catch him, sir," he said.

"Yes, they'll see that," cried Fred, eagerly. "Now let's get back to the lake, and fish for an hour."

"But we aren't got no lines, sir."

"Never mind; we must pretend, in case we are watched. Come along quickly."

Fred spoke in a low excited whisper, just as if he had helped in the setting of a gin for some wild creature; and as he hurried Samson back toward the lake he turned once, full of exultation, and shook his follower warmly by the hand.

"What's that there for?" said Samson, feigning ignorance, but with his eyes sparkling and his face bright with satisfaction.

"Because I feel so happy," cried Fred. "It's a long time since I have felt so satisfied as I do now."

"Ah, I gets puzzleder and puzzleder," said Samson, grimly, "more than ever I was. I never knowd why we all began fighting, and you don't make it a bit clearer, Master Fred. I believe you're a reg'lar sham, sir, pretendin' that Master Scar's your enemy, and all the time you seem as if you'd go through fire and water to help him. Why, we shall be having your father and Sir Godfrey shaking hands and dining together just as they did in the old times."

"And you and Nat quarrelling good-temperedly again as to which is the best cider, that at the Manor or theirs at the Hall."

"No, Master Fred; that's going a little too far, sir. Eh? What say?"

"Look here; I'll show you where the proper entrance to the passage is. That hole, as I told you, was only broken through."

Fred turned off a little, and made his way down to the edge of the lake by the rocky bank where the birches drooped down till their delicate leaves nearly dipped in the water; and as they hung over, after a careful look round, Fred pointed out the opening.

"What! that little bit of a hole, sir?"

"That's where Scarlett kicked out a stone or two. The whole of the rest of the arch is built up."

"Well, sir, I s'pose it's true, as you tell me it is," said Samson, thoughtfully; "but if anybody had told me all this without showing me the place, I should have said, 'Thank ye; now see if you can tell a bigger story.'"

"You know now it's true," said Fred, thoughtfully. "And look here," he continued, after he had related in full how he and Scarlett discovered the place, "let's go up to the Hall, and see if there is any sign of the opening there. Think the ruins will be cool?"

"No, sir, nor yet for another week. Why, some of the men was roasting meat in the hot embers, and cooking bread there this morning."

"Never mind. I had not the heart to go there when I woke. I am eager to see everything now, and I tremble for fear that the way may have been laid open. Come along."

Samson followed, nothing loth, the rods and basket being forgotten, and they made their way round by the edge of the lake on the side nearest to the Hall, Fred having hard work to keep from gazing back at the patch of the old forest which concealed the passage where he felt certain now his friends—he mentally corrected himself—his enemies, must lie.

A sad feeling came over the lad, though, once more, as he led the way through the hazel wood, where Sir Godfrey had had endless paths cut, every one of which was carpeted with moss; for there were the marks of hoofs, hazel stubs had been wantonly cut down, and the nearer they drew to the ruined Hall, the more frequent were the traces of destruction, while, when at last they came from the shrubbery and stood in full view of the place, the picture of desolation was so painful that Fred stood still, and his eyes felt dim.

"Poor Lady Markham! poor little Lil!" he said in a low voice. "What will they say?"

"Yes, and your mother, Master Fred, sir; she'll be terribly cut up too."

"Well, Fred, my lad," said a grave voice, "have you, too, come to see?"

Fred started round, to find that his father was leaning against one of the fine old beeches with his arms folded, gazing at the still smoking ruins.

He did not wait to be answered, but sighed deeply, and walked slowly away.

"Don't he know?" whispered Samson.

Fred shook his head, and stood gazing after his father till his follower touched his sleeve.

"Aren't you going to tell him, Master Fred?"

"I was wondering whether I ought."

"So was I, sir; and you oughtn't."

"You think that?"

"Yes, sir. If you tell him, he'll feel it's his duty to send in search of them, and make 'em prisoners."

"Yes," said Fred, thoughtfully.

"And that's just what we want done, of course, Master Fred; only they ought to be our prisoners, and we want to do just what we like about 'em, not be enterfered with—eh?"

"Don't talk to me, please," said Fred, as he watched his father go where his horse was being held, and saw him mount and ride thoughtfully away.

"Now, Samson, quick! and don't point or seem to be taking any particular notice."

"I understand, sir."

"Let us look as if we were walking round just out of curiosity, and do nothing to excite the attention of any sentinel who may have us under his eye."

Fred led the way, and Samson followed, as he walked completely round the ruins of the old building, apparently indifferent, but taking in everything with the most intense eagerness. But, look as he would, he could see no trace of any opening in the skeleton of the fine old Hall. Every vestige of roof had gone, and in its fall parti-walls had been toppled over, and where they still stood it was in such a chaos of ruins that the eye soon grew confused.

As to finding the entrance to the passage, that was impossible. It was easy enough to trace the entrance hall, but the carven beams of the roof had entirely gone, and there was not the slightest trace visible of the grand staircase or the corridor which ran to right and left. Smouldering ashes, calcined stone, and here and there the projecting charred stump of some beam; but no sign of a passage running between walls, and at last Samson, who had edged up closely, whispered—

"Are you sure you are right, sir? I can't see aught."

"I am certain," was the reply. "But let us go now. No one is likely to find the entrance here."

"And no one is likely to get out of it here," said Samson to himself, as they walked slowly away, to be hailed directly after by one of the officers.

"I thought you two had gone fishing?"

"Yes, sir," said Samson; "and we've left our rods by the lake. We're going down again by-and-by to see if there is a bite."

The officer nodded, laughed at them, and went on.

"You let your tongue run too freely," said Fred, angrily.

"Well, sir, you wouldn't speak; and it's quite true. When shall we go down and see if we've got a bite?"

"This evening," said Fred, shortly; and they went back to the camp to stay a few hours, and then get leave to go down again, making their way round the east end of the lake, up through the scattered woodland to the old patch of forest, and then in and out till they gained the broken-in entrance hidden by the dead blanches of the oak.

"It's all right, sir," said Samson, drily, as he caught sight of the opening at the same time as his master.

Yes: it was all right; for the bait Samson had placed there to test the presence of his brother was gone.

"Samson," whispered Fred, "this is our secret. I want to be loyal to my party; but I feel as if I must help these poor fellows."

"That's very sad, sir," replied Samson; "and I feel as if I ought to go and fetch a dozen of our men to search this place; but whatever you tell me to do, I shall do—that is to say, so long as you don't ask me and Nat to make it up."

"I will not ask you, Samson," said Fred; "I'll leave you to ask me if you may."

Chapter Forty Three
Through the Fire

That fight within the Hall was more desperate than Fred had imagined, for until overpowered by numbers, Sir Godfrey, his son, and the brave and reckless Cavaliers by whom he had been surrounded, had fought in a manner that kept their enemies at bay.

In the rush and noise and confusion of the struggle, Sir Godfrey had not at first noticed the smoke, and when he did he was under the impression that it was merely the result of the firing, and caused by the heavy powder of the period. It was not until the flames had gained a hold on either side that he realised the truth; and when it did come home to him, he had staggered forward to strike at a couple of the many enemies by whom he was surrounded, and whose swords had wounded him severely in four places.

That blow was the last he could give, for, faint from loss of blood, the effort was too great; he overreached himself, stumbled and fell prone upon the polished floor. The moment before, his enemies were retiring, but at the sight of the fallen officer one of the men raised a joyous shout, and half a dozen charged back to make him prisoner.

It was at that moment Scarlett saw the great danger, and boy as he was, rushed to the rescue, striking out boldly as he leaped across his father, and keeping the enemy at bay.

The odds were absurd, and the men were only kept back by the suddenness and dash of the youth's attack. Then, with a laugh of derision, they were about to seize both, when a warning shout reached them, and they rushed away to avoid the onslaught of the terrible enemy against which their weapons were of no avail.

Scarlett saw the danger, and cowered down over his father as a wave of flame was wafted above their heads, fortunately for them a current of air keeping off the next just long enough for him to seize Sir Godfrey by the wrists and drag him back into the centre of the hall, the polished boards rendering the task an easy one.

"Escape, Scarlett. I am spent," said Sir Godfrey, faintly.

"What! and leave you, father?" cried Scarlett, excitedly.

"Yes. You cannot get away here for the fire. Run upstairs, my boy, quick—leap from one of the windows."

"If you will come with me, father," said Scarlett.

"No, no, my boy; I am helpless. Make haste. The fire—for Heaven's sake, make haste!"

The flames and their accompanying suffocating fumes advanced so fast that for the moment the terrible peril unnerved Scarlett. The natural inclination was to flee, and he received an additional impulse from his father's words, which in their tone of urgent command made him dash halfway up the broad staircase before he checked himself, turned sharply, with one bound leaped down again to the floor, and ran to Sir Godfrey's side.

"Father, I can't leave you to be burned to death," he cried. "It is too horrible."

"Horrible? Yes," panted the wounded man; "but I can do nothing, my boy; and you—you are so young. The poor old Hall—the poor old Hall!"

For a few moments Scarlett knelt beside his father, suffocating in the gathering smoke, and looking about wildly for a way of escape, but finding none; for the defenders had taken such precautions to keep the enemy out, that in this time of peril, they had kept themselves in. Even now Scarlett felt that, by making a bold rush through the fire and smoke gathering in force to right and left, he might escape, singed and scorched, perhaps, but with life. To attempt this, however, with a wounded man, was impossible; and, with the strong desire for life thrilling every fibre, he uttered a despairing groan.

As the mournful sound escaped his lips, he caught tightly hold of his father's hands, to cling to them as if seeking strength, and asking him to keep his weak nature from repeating its former act and taking refuge in so cowardly a flight.

The hands he grasped felt wet and cold, and in the misty choking gloom Scarlett could see that his father's eyes were nearly closed, and that there was in them a fixed and glassy stare.

"He's dying!" he groaned; "he's dying!"

His son's cry seemed to rouse Sir Godfrey to a knowledge of his danger, for his eyes opened wildly, and he gazed before him, and then struggled to rise, but sank back against his son's arm.

"You have not gone!" he groaned. "Scarlett, my boy, escape!"

"I cannot leave you, father. Let me try and help you. If we could get to the upper windows!"

"And ask our enemy to take us prisoners! No, no; my poor old home is crumbling around me—where could I die better?"

"Oh, father!"

"But you, my boy, with all your young life before you! There is yet time. God bless you, Scar! Good-bye!"

He made a faint effort to thrust his son away, but Scarlett still held his hands, while the fire crackled and roared in the rooms on either side, and kept on narrowing the space they occupied, as the great smoke wreaths, pierced by ruddy tongues, rolled heavily overhead.

Scarlett set his teeth and closed his eyes for a moment, as a feeling of horror ran through him, and there before him, beyond the smoke of the burning woodwork, he saw in a instant the bright sunshiny paths of life inviting him on and on for a long career, such as youth may look forward to in its growing vigour; but he made a desperate effort to crush out the temptation, clinging frantically to his father's hands as he groaned despairingly—

"I cannot leave him. It would be too base."

Till that moment the shock of their position had robbed him of energy, but no sooner had he come to the brave determination to stop and die that horrible death by his father's side, than the strong current of life seemed to bound again in his veins, and, with a feeling of wonder that he could have been so supine—

"Father!" he cried; but there was no reply. "Father!"

Still no response, and he could just make out that the wounded man's eyes were closed. But Scarlett was full of energy now, and, leaping up, he seized Sir Godfrey by the arm, and dragged him by main force to the foot of the great staircase.

"I must get him to the corridor somehow," he thought; and, stooping down, he clasped his arms about him, terribly impeded by the breastplate and backpiece he wore, and then, panting and suffocating, he dragged him up step by step, every one being into a more stifling atmosphere. The increasing heat bathed him with perspiration, and a growing sense of languor made him feel as if each step would be the last.

But, raging and grinding his teeth in his efforts, he toiled on till the topmost step was reached, and there he paused, chilled now by a terrible and despairing sense of his position. The fire had eaten its way upwards, and to drag his insensible burden to the right through the door leading to the servants' apartments, or to the left along the corridor, was on either hand into a burning furnace.

Scarlett Markham sank upon his knees beside his father on the polished oaken floor of the gallery, and giddy now with the heat and exhaustion, his lips cracking, and every breath he drew laden with the poisonous fumes, he felt that all was over, and, with a prayer coming confusedly to his mind, he made a snatch at his father's hand, missed it, and fell sidewise.

But even then there was the natural involuntary effort to save himself from falling headlong backwards from top to bottom of the stairs, and one hand grasped at the balustrade, caught one of the carved oaken pilasters; there was a sharp cracking sound, the stair by his shoulder shot back an inch or two, and a draught of cold revivifying air literally rushed whistling through the orifice.

It was life, energy, hope, renewed courage, all in one, as he gasped and panted and wildly thrust back the loose stair till the way was open; and, gathering strength as the fresh air rushed up into his nostrils on its way to fan the growing flames, he seized his father where he lay on the top of the staircase, drew him towards his breast, and let him drop right into the opening, whose sloping floor made the rest comparatively easy.

But Scarlett worked manfully, lying down beside his father, and edging him along a few feet, before going back to close the opening in the stairs.

He paused for a few moments, feeling now that he was safe, and gazed upon the ruddy smoke clouds, listened to the roar and crackle of the flames, which were now within a few feet; and as he gazed, he could see that the sharp draught rushing by him drove the flame and smoke back, and fanned the former till it glowed more brightly.

But there was no time to lose. Seizing the woodwork, he drew it over his head, to find to his horror that already the heat had warped the wood so that it was hard to move; and, feeling that no time was to be lost, he rolled himself along, forced his father on and on, till the horizontal shallow passage was at an end—a passage already growing heated above where the fire licked the boards, and then, standing upright and breathing freely, he paused to think of his next proceeding.

Chapter Forty Four
In Utter Darkness

It was not easy to think and lay plans in such a position as that in which Scarlett Markham found himself. His temples throbbed painfully, his head swam, and at every exertion it seemed to him as if hot molten lead were rolling from side to side of his head. But the cool damp air came by him in a continuous draught, and feeling now that before long the narrow passages and the little chamber beyond must certainly grow heated in the conflagration, perhaps be swept away in the general destruction, he set himself the task of getting Sir Godfrey upon his back, and, after several failures, found that his first step in that direction must be to unbuckle and cast aside the defensive armour his father wore.

This done, the steel falling on the stone floor of the passage with a heavy clang, he once more tried, successfully, and, bending beneath the weight of his load, traversed the narrow passage, with a dull low roar sounding in a muffled way on his left.

The air came fresher and fresher as he pressed on in the intense darkness, till, recalling by an effort of memory every step he and Fred had formerly taken, he felt his way into the little chamber, having drawn his sword and used it for a staff, and to guide his way.

How well he recalled the shape of that little hiding-place, with its dust and cobwebs, and the colourless strands of ivy hanging down! And as he paused here, asking himself whether he should stay for the present, a silent answer was given to his question, for the hand which rested upon the wall felt that the stones were, growing sensibly warm, sufficiently so to suggest that the fire was raging on the other side.

Taking a long breath of the cool fresh air, he had no difficulty in telling which way to turn for the further door, whose half-open edge the extended sword touched directly. Then, grasping it with his hand, it grated heavily as he drew it towards him, passed through the low opening, and knew that he he was at the top of the long narrow descending stairs.

What a terrible depth it seemed as he went down very slowly step by step, but heartened each minute by the feeling that every step took them more out of the reach of the fire, while the steady current of air drawn in from the wilderness and the lake side by the fire within the building, rendered it certain that no flame or suffocating fume could reach them there.

The bottom at last! and Scarlett paused to rest. He was bathed in perspiration, and a curious dull feeling of exhaustion was setting in, but he did not speak; he had set for himself the goal which he must reach, and at which they would rest for the present. After he had bound up his father's wounds, he might recover somewhat, so as to walk a little with assistance; and then the opening at the end of the passage was there, and freedom for them both, if the enemy had gone.

But he had not reached that vault-like refuge yet, and the way seemed to be interminable. The excitement and effort had produced a dull, half stupefying effect upon his senses, and this was growing rapidly now, so much so, that with legs bending beneath him, he dropped his sword, which fell with an echoing clamour upon the stones, and supported himself by the wall.

And now in that pitchy darkness he crept slowly along, with a singular nightmare-like sensation growing upon him; he ceased to have any command of the power of thought, and went on and on, inch by inch, ever ready to sink beneath his burden, but always at the last moment making a desperate effort, and regaining enough strength to go on.

How long it took, how he ever got through his terrible task, he never knew. All that he could ever recall was a feeling of journeying on and on beneath an ever-increasing load, till suddenly the support on either side ceased; he made a desperate effort to save himself, but went down upon his hands and knees, felt that the burden he bore had suddenly rolled from his back, and that his face was resting on the cool damp stones.

Then all was darkness, mental as well as visual, and he sank into a stupor, which lasted he could not tell how long.

The awaking was strange.

Scarlett opened his eyes involuntarily, and looked above him and to right and left. He closed his eyes, and the effect was the same. Then he lay for a time thinking that he must be asleep, and that this was some portion of a dream.

But the sensation of faintness, his aching head, and the sore stiffness of every muscle—so painful that he could hardly move—soon warned him that he was awake, and he set himself to battle with his confused brain, to try and make out where he was, and what it all meant. For, as far as the past was concerned, it was as if a dense black curtain were drawn across his mind, and this great veil he could not thrust aside.

He was cold—he was stiff and sore—he was hungry and feverishly thirsty,—he could realise all these things, but that was all, and he lay thinking and asking himself again and again, "What does it all mean?"

The first hint which his brain seemed to seize upon was given by a low deep sigh which came from close at hand.

Scarlett started up, staring wildly in the direction from which the sound came, while his hands and brow grew moist with terror—a terror which passed away, as a flash of mental light illumined his obscured brain, and he cried aloud—

"Father!"

There was no reply, and Scarlett's horror and dread grew more intense, not from weak foolish imagination, but from the feeling that his father was lying wounded there, perhaps at the point of death, while he, who ought to have been aiding him in every way, must have been selfishly asleep.

The self-shame was not deserved, for nature had been too strong for Scarlett Markham, and it was more the stupor of utter exhaustion to which he had succumbed than sleep.

He crept to where Sir Godfrey lay, and felt for his face, which was cold and clammy, sending a shudder through the fingers which touched the icy brow, and then sought for the region of the heart.

Incongruous ideas of a trivial nature occur to people even in the most terrible times, and it was so here, for as Scarlett's hand sought for his father's breast, he found himself thinking of how good a thing it was that he removed the armour when he took him upon his back.

The heart was beating faintly, but the pulsations could be plainly felt, and this gave Scarlett some little hope, such as was badly needed at this crucial time. But what was he to do? How could he help him? For aught he could tell, they must have been there many hours, and once more a terrible chill ran through the youth, as the thought struck him that his father might be bleeding to death.

And what could he do? He was in utter darkness, and could not tell where the wounds might be.

There was comfort once more in the fresh thought which came, suggested by his experience in the skirmishes in which he had been engaged, and by his duties in tending the wounded.

For he recalled how, in the majority of cases, unless some important vessel was divided, Nature interposed as the great surgeon for the preservation of her children's lives, causing the veins to chill and contract, and the bleeding to cease; and as Scarlett Markham knelt beside his father, and pressed his lips to the icy brow, he prayed that it might be so now, and that his life might be spared.

"Now, what is to be done?" he said to himself, half rising, as if the act he had done had given him refreshment and a new access of thought.

He stood for a few moments thinking, and then, feeling his way about the place, he satisfied himself where the openings out of the little vault lay, his doubt as to which led to the lake being solved by the steps down to where it was formerly water, but which on testing he now found to be firm floor, and by the little heap of rusty arms over which he nearly fell as he crept about.

His first need was light and help for his father, and to obtain these he felt that perhaps it would be best to surrender.

With this aim in view, he made his way back along the passage, kicking against and recovering his sword, and up the flight of narrow stone steps, becoming conscious that the air was growing warmer as he proceeded, and finally that the walls were hot, while straight before him, as he reached the top and tried to penetrate into the chamber, there was a confused pile of heavy stones leaning towards him, as if some party wall or portion of the roof had fallen in that direction, and blocked the way.

He could not stay to investigate, the heat was too great; but the freedom with which he breathed taught him that the ruins had not completely stopped all the chamber, for a steady current of air was flowing past him from below.

He felt instinctively that the fire must have done its work, and that the greater part of the secret passage had been obliterated by the falling ruins, so that he must not look for help from that direction.

Retracing his steps, then, he once more reached the vault, whose coolness was pleasant after the stifling heat above. Then, crossing the dark place, he slowly descended the steps, and went onward with extended hands, feeling his way toward the two entries—the original, and that which had been broken through by the fallen tree.

He had not far to go before a faint light stole down to guide his way, and he reached the spot where the passage was roofed in with dead branches and twigs, and as he reached it, just faintly heard, came the shrill cry of a blackbird—*Pink-pink-pink*!—from somewhere in the wood above.

A trifle that he would not have heeded at another time, but which now sent a thrill of hope through him, for it told of light and liberty, and help for the sufferer lying in that gloomy vault.

But he wasted no time, passing over the crackling refuse of broken wood and stones which here impeded his way, till almost directly after he had cleared all this, and made a turn, catching sight of the bright star-like light low down by the floor of the passage—the opening that he had made, and by which the water which had been gathering probably for generations had been drained away.

He was soon at the rough wall which stopped the arch, and, going down on one knee, he listened, for peril had made him cautious, besides which the lessons of life he was receiving in his regimental work taught the necessity for being prepared for enemies at every turn.

All seemed to be perfectly still, and as far as he could judge it was early morning, soon after daybreak. The first rays of the sun appeared to be brightening the surface of the lake as he tried to peer through the orifice, and every now and then the cry of the water-fowl and the splash of water endorsed his belief in there being no danger near.

Feeling satisfied that there was no danger, he returned to the broken opening and stopped short as he heard a sharp rustling, followed by a sound that was evidently the sharp utterance of some one impatient at his position, or because one expected did not come.

Did whoever it was know of the existence of the hole through which the faint light streamed down, showing the configuration of the rough branches which covered the broken place? It seemed only probable, and, feeling the necessity for the greater caution, Scarlett stepped slowly and carefully among the broken fragments till he had passed the risky spot, and then hurried on as rapidly as he could till he reached the steps, and, mounting them cautiously, he stood once more in the chamber.

Feeling rapidly about, he uttered a cry of joy, for his hand touched his father's brow; and as it did so, he felt it raised by the burning fingers of the sufferer, who began talking quickly.

"Quick! Which way did they go—Lady Markham—my child Lilian? Why do you not speak? Tell me; they are not in the burning house?"

"Father! don't you know my voice?" whispered Scarlett.

"Know your voice—know you? Yes, yes, my boy. Scar, lad, help me. They must be somewhere here. I am looking for them. Yes, somewhere in the house."

"No, no, father; they are in safety down at the Manor."

"Here, I tell you, sir. Help me to find them. Quick! They are in the burning house and Scar, my boy, is that you?"

Then, seeming to drop off to sleep as his son knelt by him, there was a sigh or two, and then he was breathing regularly, although the inspirations sounded faint and low.

Scarlett could contain himself no longer, but, rising from his knees, he hurried down the few steps and along the lower passage, pausing for a moment before stealing carefully beneath the broken portion of the arched tunnel. For there could be no doubt about the matter: there was a rustling sound somewhere above that did not seem such as would be made by any wild animals likely to haunt the forest, and a certainty was given to his ideas by a low-muttering arising, followed by a hasty ejaculation as of impatience or pain.

So near did this sound, that Scarlett remained motionless in the obscurity of the tunnel arch, afraid to stir for quite an hour, during which he listened, feeling assured that this opening had been discovered by the enemy, and that they had placed a sentry there to trap any one who attempted to escape.

"Oh!" ejaculated Scarlett at last, softly, as what he believed to be enlightenment flashed across his brain. "Why did I not think of that before? Fred Forrester, of course! He remembered our discovery, and he has explained all to his father, with the result that there are sentinels all about, waiting to take every poor wounded wretch who seeks to escape."

It was a painful thought, for it troubled him to think that Fred had been so unprincipled as to betray their old boyish secret.

"He might have been content to fight with his party against ours, and not make use of his knowledge to do his old friends an evil turn."

The feeling of bitter anger mingled with scorn increased as he stood there in weary inactivity, longing to rejoin Sir Godfrey, but dreading to stir, for fear he should bring danger upon his father's head.

And all this time he might be awake, and in grievous suffering; perhaps dying, and feebly stretching out his hands for help, even believing that his son had left him there to die.

Scarlett could bear the agony of his thoughts no longer; at any cost he must pass beneath that opening, and rejoin his father, and to this end he stepped forward softly, to find that he had planted his foot upon a rotten stick fallen from above, and lightly as he trod, the dry, decayed piece of wood parted with a loud noise.

Scarlett turned cold, and the chilly moisture gathered upon his brow and within the palms of his hands.

"It is all over!" he muttered, as his hand went involuntarily to the hilt of his sword; and then he dragged it from its sheath, and raised the point, thinking of how strong his position was, and how few men would dare to descend with that sharp point awaiting the first enemy who came.

Then, half stifled by holding his breath, he began to breathe freely once more, for there came a low sigh from above, then a faint rustling, and then the regular, low breathing of some man asleep.

Scarlett stayed no longer, but stepped quickly across the wood-strewn patch of the floor, and then hastened along the passage, and up the few steps in the total darkness; and after a very little groping about, found himself beside his father, who was sleeping peacefully, while his head was cool, telling how the fever of his wounds had gone down.

Chapter Forty Five
Companions in Misfortune

Scarlett Markham passed some hours by his father's side, listening to his breathing in the darkness, and from time to time taking his hand as a low moan was uttered, accompanied by a restless movement; but as the time passed on, in spite of anxiety and his own weariness and pain, an intense desire for food of some kind kept on attacking him, and each time with more force.

What was he to do?

Had he been alone the task would have been simple. He would have gone at once to the broken archway, waited his opportunity, and crept out. Then he would have done his best to escape, and the worst that could have happened to him would have been seizure by the enemy, who, in spite of paity hatred, would have given their prisoner food.

But he felt that he could not take this course, and risk capture, which would mean imprisonment to his father as well.

The difficulty was solved at last by an uneasy movement on Sir Godfrey's part. He seemed to start suddenly from sleep, and, after listening for a few moments, Scarlett said gently—

"Are you in pain, father?"

"Ah, my boy, you there?" said Sir Godfrey, feebly. "I was puzzled and confused. I recollect now. Have I been asleep long?"

"Yes, father, I think so. I cannot tell, for I have been asleep too."

"Where are we?"

Scarlett explained, and from time to time Sir Godfrey uttered a few words of surprise and wonder, till his son had finished.

"I could hardly have thought it possible," he said, as Scarlett ceased. "Then we are so far safe?"

"Yes; but your wounds, father? What am I to do about getting help?"

Sir Godfrey remained silent for a few minutes, and then said quietly—

"I am terribly weak, boy, and in a good deal of pain; but from what I know of such things, I do not think my wounds are either deep or dangerous, and if this is so, nature is the best chirurgeon. But you say there is a way out?"

"Yes, father; and I am afraid that Fred Forrester has given notice, and that it is watched."

"The young villain!" muttered Sir Godfrey, and somehow those words seemed to send a sting through Scarlett's brain.

After a silence, Sir Godfrey went on.

"Well, my boy," he said, "I shall not be able to escape for days to come. You must go and try and make your way to our friends."

"And leave you?"

"Only for a time, my boy, of course. You must find some of our men, and come and get me away."

"I cannot leave you, father;" said Scarlett, firmly; and Sir Godfrey remained silent for a time.

"Thank you, Scar," he said at last; "and of course I do not want to be left. Can you propose any better way, for my thinking powers are very weak?"

Scarlett was silent in turn, and then he said quietly—

"Yes, father; I will wait my chance, steal out, and then contrive to make my way to some cottage where I can get food. I can bring it back, and we can continue to remain here in hiding till you are strong enough to go."

"Not a very pleasant prospect, Scar," said Sir Godfrey, "but I can propose no better."

"I might be able to make my way to the Manor."

"No, no; you must not get help from there, my boy," said Sir Godfrey, hastily.

"Why not, father? My mother and Lilian are there."

"True, Scarlett, but—"

"Mrs Forrester would be only too eager to help us."

"Her husband's enemies?"

"She is affording protection to my mother. Yes," added the lad, after a pause, "I must go there."

Sir Godfrey remained silent.

"Father."

"Yes."

"You frightened me by being so still."

"I was only thinking, Scarlett," replied Sir Godfrey, sadly—"thinking I was wrong to speak as I did. There, I have fought my best, and it is my turn to lie down. I would we were both prisoners in such good hands."

"Then you consent to my going, father?"

There was another pause before Sir Godfrey said in a low, weary voice—

"Yes, my boy; you must throw yourself upon their mercy. This is no time to nurse one's hatred against one's foes. When shall you start?"

"Directly I can get unseen from the opening, for you must have refreshment, father, and it is absolutely necessary that I should be back to-night."

"Heaven's will be done," said Sir Godfrey, softly; and, after a long firm pressure of the hand, he added, "Be careful, my boy; keep your liberty if you can. The king wants the help of every loyal hand."

"And you will not mind my leaving you?"

"No, my boy. I dare say, in my weak state, I shall pass many hours in sleep."

Even then Scarlett felt that he could not go, and it was not until long after, when he felt the absolute necessity of obtaining food and help, that he at last tore himself away, but with the one satisfaction of knowing that Sir Godfrey had dropped into a heavy sleep.

It was while he was once more making his way to the opening that Scarlett realised how faint and weak he, too, was. But, summoning all his energy, he stood at last beneath the opening, trying to make out where the sentinel or sentinels might be.

He drew his sword ready for action, and then, with an impatient movement, restored the weapon to its sheath, realising fully that if he was to succeed, it must be by cunning stratagem, not by blows.

All was silent, but the occasional twitter of some bird. If a watcher was there, he gave no sign of his presence, and quite a couple of hours must have passed away before, utterly tired out, and hearing not the slightest sound, Scarlett determined to venture so far as to get his head above the top of the opening.

No; he felt that would be only to court seizure, for his position would be so disadvantageous that he could not defend himself if he were seized. Besides, he would be betraying his father into the enemies' hands.

In spite of his trouble and anxiety, a smile came upon his lip, as he thought of a plan by which he might make the watcher or watchers discover their presence. He believed thoroughly that he had not so far been heard, and, under that impression, he took hold of one of the hazels above his head, and, trusting to old forest recollections in the days when he had hunted rabbits with Fred Forrester, he shook the bough above him so as to make a sharp rustling noise, and uttered with his compressed lips a sharp screeching sound such as is made by the little white-tailed furry denizen of the wood when trapped or chased by a stoat.

"That will bring him to see," thought Scarlett, as he felt that such a sound would suggest to a foraging soldier a capital addition to his camp-fire supper.

But there was not a sound in reply, and, beginning to doubt his belief that there was a sentry watching, he uttered the shrill squeal again. Then his heart gave a bound, for there was a movement close at hand, as of some one trying to pass through the bushes, but it was not continued; and, while the lad was wondering, there came a low groan.

"No sentinel! Some poor wounded fellow who has crept into the old wilderness for safety," thought Scarlett.

"But will it be an enemy?" he asked himself.

"No; one of ours," his heart replied. "An enemy would have called for help."

"Ah, if I was only as I used to be!" came in a low-muttering tone. "Is he in agin?"

"Nat!" cried Scarlett, the word starting from his lips involuntarily, and without his seeming to have the power to stay it.

"Eh!" came from close by, "who called? Master Scar, that you?"

"Yes, yes," cried Scarlett; and, leaping up, he caught at a bough, which snapped in two, and he dropped down again. But his next attempt was more successful, for he drew himself out, and the next minute was kneeling by his old follower, as Nat lay nearly hidden among the undergrowth.

"I say, don't play tricks, sir," said Nat, feebly. "I aren't dreaming, are I?"

"Dreaming, Nat?"

"I mean, I've been all in a squabble, with things mixed up in my head, and people talking to me, and rabbits squealing, and Master Scar shouting 'Nat,' I aren't asleep now, are I?"

"Asleep now, Nat? No, no, my dear old fellow," cried Scarlett, whose voice sounded thick with emotion. "But you are badly hurt eh?"

"Well, tidy, Master Scar, tidy. They give it to me pretty well. But I'm better now, dear lad; I'm better now. Oh, oh, I say, Master Scar, lad, hit me in both eyes hard. I'm so weak I'm going to blubber like a gal."

"No, no, my dear old Nat," whispered Scarlett. "Keep up, man, keep up. I want you to help me."

"Help you, Master Scarlett? Why, I don't believe I could even pull my sword out of its sheath!"

"But you will soon, Nat," whispered Scarlett, eagerly. "I want your help. My father is wounded, and in hiding close by here."

"The master?"

"Yes, yes."

"Sir Godfrey?"

"Yes, yes, Nat; badly wounded. We were nearly burned in the fire, when the Hall was in a blaze; but we got out, and he is badly wounded, and I was going to try and get food."

"Oh, if that's it," said Nat, feebly, "it's time there was an end to all this nonsense. Here, give's a hand, Master Scar. I must get up."

The poor fellow made an effort, then sank back with a groan.

"Pitchforks and skewers!" he muttered. "Didn't that go through one."

"Lie still, Nat."

"Needn't be afraid, Master Scar," groaned the poor fellow, with a comical look in his young master's face. "I don't think I shall get up yet."

"No; lie still. I'm going to try and steal away to the Manor."

"Eh? Then if you come across my brother Samson, you knock him down, sir. Don't you hesitate a moment. Knock him down."

"Nonsense! Now look here."

"Oh yes, sir, I'm a-looking," said Nat, dismally; "and a pretty dirty face you've got."

"What do you mean?"

"Why, it's all black, as if you'd been—"

"Why, Master Scar, what yer been a-doing to your hair?"

"Hair? My hair?"

"Yes, sir. Them Roundhead vagabonds cut it all off before, but now it's all scorched and singed away."

"Eh? Yes. I suppose so," said Scarlett, sadly. "I did not know, Nat. I suppose it was in the fire."

"And your face all scorched too."

"Is it, Nat? I did feel that it smarted and was sore."

"Why, my poor dear lad, what have you been a-doing of? And me not with you, but lying here like a pig in a sunny hole, pretending I was bad!"

"Hush! not so loud. Never mind the singeing, Nat. There, keep quiet till I come back with some food. Do you want a drink of water?"

"Food? What did you say about some food?"

"I'm going to try and get some, Nat. I am starving."

"Think of that now!" cried Nat, feebly. "Why, I've got some here. Master Scar! Now, let me think. I'm all in a muddle like in the head, and can't tell what's been dreaming and what isn't; but I've got a sort o' notion that some one come in the dark, and talked to me or talked about me, and then said they'd leave me something to eat."

"Dreaming, Nat, my poor fellow! Your loss of blood has made you a little off your head."

"Well, then, if I was dreaming, there aren't nothing to eat, Master Scar. But if I warn't dreaming, there's something close by me here, and— There, Master Scar, it warn't a dream!"

"Nat!" cried Scarlett, joyfully, as the poor fellow feebly brought forth the food Fred and Samson had left. "May—may I take some?" he faltered.

"Take it all, my dear lad, take it all, and yeat it. I couldn't yeat anything now. Shouldn't mind a big mug o' water. That's about my tune."

In spite of himself, Scarlett broke off a piece of the bread cake, and began to eat ravenously.

But he recollected himself directly, and placed some to the wounded man's lips.

"Thank ye, lad, no," said Nat, sadly; "but if you could get me a drop o' water, I'd be 'bliged, for I feel just like a flower a-drying up in the sun."

Poor Nat did not look it, whatever he might feel; but almost before he had ceased speaking, Scarlett had slipped through the hole as the safest way, gone to the opening by the lake, dipped his hat three-parts full of water, and borne it back, placing it safely between two boughs at the side of the top, while he climbed out; and the next minute he was holding the dripping felt to Nat's lips.

"Hah!" ejaculated the poor fellow, feebly; "it's worth being chopped a bit and lying here for the sake of the appetite it gives you."

"Appetite, Nat?" said Scarlett, taking up the bread.

"'Tite for water, lad. That's the sweetest drop I ever did taste, I will say."

"Drink again?"

"Ay, that I will, hearty," whispered Nat; and he partook of another long draught. "There," he said, "now you give me one bit o' that cake to nibble, and you may go. To get food, didn't you say, sir, just now?"

"I want some—for my father, Nat, but—if—I can have some of this?"

"Take it all, my dear lad, take it all. Where is the master, sir?"

Scarlett told him in as few words as possible, and Nat stared at him.

"No, it's of not a bit o' good, Master Scar," he said sadly. "I know you're telling me something, but I bled all the sense out of me, and I can't understand what you mean. Never mind me. I dare say it's all right."

"But, Nat," cried Scarlett, eagerly, as a thought struck him, and he realised that it was useless to try and impress upon the poor fellow about the secret passage, "you are lying out here."

"Yes, sir; not a nice place, but cool and fresh."

"Could you, if I helped you, get down that hole, where my father lies?"

"Sir Godfrey?"

"Yes."

"But you said you were going away somewhere, sir."

"Only to get some food, and you have enough for the day. To-night I'll go out and get more. Do you think you could crawl down?"

"I think I could try, sir, if it comes to that."

"And trying is half the battle, Nat."

"Right, sir; I'll try. That drop o' water seemed to put life in me."

"But—"

Scarlett stopped short, thinking. Some one had been and brought Nat food, for there it was in solid reality, tempting him to eat; and if he took the poor fellow down into the secret passage, it would no longer prove to be a secure hiding-place, for those who missed the wounded man would search perhaps and find.

That did not follow, though. They might think that he had crept away; and besides, the case was desperate, and he must risk it.

"You said, 'But,' Master Scar," said Nat, feebly, after waiting for his young master to go on.

"Nothing, nothing," said Scarlett, hastily, for his mind was made up. "Now then, pass your arms round my neck, clasp your hands together, and hold tightly. I'll draw you out of that place."

"Take the food first, Master Scar. There, stuff it in your wallet, lad."

Scarlett did not hesitate, but placed the precious treasure in the receptacle, and then bent down. Nat obeyed his instructions, and by a strong effort he was drawn out.

"Have I hurt you much, Nat?" said Scarlett, as he gazed through the dim light at the pallid face so close to his.

"Well, sir, not to make much bones about it, tidy, pretty tidy. What next, sir?"

"I want to lower you down through the branches into that hole."

"Eh?" ejaculated Nat, forgetting his weakness and the aching pain he suffered, as he gave quite a start. "No, no, Master Scar, don't do that."

"But you will be safe there for the present, Nat."

"Safe enough, I suppose, sir," groaned the poor fellow.

"Well, let me lay your legs here, and I can slide you down."

"But I aren't dead yet, dear lad. Don't hurry it so fast as that."

"What do you mean?"

"Going to bury me, aren't you, sir?"

"What nonsense, man! There's a long passage there leading to a vault."

"Yes, sir; that's what I thought. Don't do it till I'm quite gone."

In spite of hunger, misery, anxiety, and pain, Scarlett Markham could not refrain from laughing at Nat's perplexed countenance, with so reassuring an effect that the poor fellow smiled feebly in return, took heart, and allowed himself to be slid down through the opening, the task being so well managed that Nat sank on the stone floor, and when Scarlett loosened his hands, he subsided gently against the wall.

Then, after removing a few of the tracks of his passage, the elasticity of the undergrowth and its springing up helping the concealment, Scarlett descended to his henchman's side, and after a pause helped him along the passage right to the vault, where, as soon as he had got rid of his burthen, the lad found his father sleeping calmly.

"Aren't it a bit dark, Master Scar, or be it my eyes?" said Nat, feebly.

"Dark, Nat, quite dark. But you will, I hope, be safe here till we can escape."

"Right, sir. I'll do what you tell me, for I feel just like a big babby now with no legs, and my head all of a wobble, 'cause there's no bone in the neck. Yes, sir, thank ye, sir. Ease my head down gently. That's it. That's it. That's it. That's it. Ah!" the poor fellow kept on repeating to himself, and ended with a low sigh of relief; and when spoken to again there was no reply.

Scarlett's heart seemed to cease beating, and then it gave a leap.

Had he done wrong in getting the poor fellow down there, exhausted as he was? How did he know but that he might have caused the wounds to bleed again?

There was consolation directly after, for he could hear Nat's calm, regular breathing, and, satisfied and relieved, Scarlett stepped now to his father's side to touch him, but found that he too was still sleeping calmly, while for the present it seemed that his duty was to keep guard.

He seated himself on the stone floor, with his back in one of the angles, and listened for a time to the regular breathing; then his ravenous hunger made itself known to such an extent that, after comforting himself with the promise that he would get food that night, he took out and broke a piece off the bread cake, put it back, thought that those by him might require it, and determined to fight down his hunger.

Hunger won the day.

Scarlett made a brave fight, but he was weak; and, try how he would, his hand kept on going to the pocket wallet, and at last he did what was quite necessary under the circumstances—he ate heartily and well; and then, with a guilty feeling; troubling him, he yielded to a second kindly enemy.

The breathing of his two patients was as regular as clockwork, and the silence and darkness seemed to increase, with the result that they acted in a strangely lulling way, and with such potency that, after a time, Scarlett started up, and stared about him at the dense blackness around.

"Have I been to sleep?" he muttered, as he drew himself up a little more tightly, and prepared to keep his black watch firmly and well to the end — that is to say, till the time when he would start at dusk for the Manor.

The next instant he was on his way there, creeping cautiously through the undergrowth, listening to the crackling of the wood he pressed with his feet, and finally making his way to the old house, where he was able to embrace his mother and sister, feeling his cheek wet with their tears, while Mistress Forrester made him up a basket of dainties, such as would invite the appetite of a wounded man.

How delightful it all was! only he had to start back so soon, and as he hurried away, his mother called him back. "Scarlett! Scarlett!" How the words rang in his ears, as he looked back through the darkness —

Scarlett leaped to his feet, with a feeling of shame and contrition.

"I must have been asleep," he exclaimed; and he listened to the breathing once more. "And what a vivid dream that was! How real it seemed!" he added. "I'll go along to the opening, and look out. That will keep me from going to sleep again."

He started down the steps, and climbed out, wondering whether he had slept a minute, an hour, or a day, and to his delight he found and took back with him the provision lately placed there by Fred and Samson.

"Well, we shall not starve," said Scarlett, thankfully, as he began thinking of his dream; but all the same, the voice which had broken in upon him calling his name sounded wonderfully real.

Chapter Forty Six
Samson Disobeys Orders

"Ho! Scar!"

No answer.

"Hoi! Scar Markham!"

The second call was louder, and this time Fred Forrester had thrust his head down the hole, so that his voice went echoing along the passage, and died away in a whisper; but the only effect it had was to produce a low chuckling sound from Samson.

"What are you laughing at, sir?" cried Fred, angrily.

"Only at you, Master Fred, sir."

"How dare—"

"No, no; don't be cross with me, sir. I only felt as you'd have felt if you'd been me, and I'd been you."

"What do you mean?"

"Why, it seemed so rum for us to have slipped down here again, pretending to fish, so as to be laughed at because we hadn't caught any, and for you to turn yourself upside down, with your head in the hole, and your legs up in the air, shouting like that!"

"Don't be a donkey, Samson."

"No, Master Fred; I'll promise you that, faithful like; but it do seem rum. 'Tarn't likely, you know, sir, 'tarn't likely."

"What isn't likely?"

"Why, that aren't, sir. Even if Master Scar is hiding there."

"If? He must be. Nobody else knows of the existence of the place."

"Wouldn't our Nat, sir?"

"No. How could he?"

"Well, sir, I can't say how he could; but he always was a nasty hunting-up-things sort of boy. So sure as I hid anything in my box at home, or anywhere else, he'd never rest till he found it; and as he was hiding away here, he may have hunted out this hole, and took possession like a badger."

"It might be so," said Fred, thoughtfully; and he approached the hole once more.

"'Tarn't no good, Master Fred," said Samson, chuckling. "You might just as well go to a rabbit's hole, and shout down that, 'Hoi! bunny, bunny, come out and have your neck broken.'"

"Don't talk so," said Fred, angrily.

"No, sir, not a word; but you forget that we're enemies now, and that it's of no use to call to Master Scarlett or our Nat to come, because they won't do it. There's two ways, sir, and that's all I can make out, after no end of thinking."

As Samson spoke, he held up his hand, and went back a few yards to reconnoitre.

"Don't see nor hear nothing, Master Fred," he said, as he returned; "but we're making a regular path through the wilderness, so plain that soon every one will see."

"Then we must go for the future to the opening by the lake, and try what we can do there."

"And get wet!"

"What did you mean by your two ways of finding out whether they are there?"

"Well, sir, one's by putting bread and meat bait afore the hole, and coming to see whether it's been taken."

"But we've tried that again and again, and it is taken," said Fred, impatiently. "What's the other way?"

Samson chuckled, and thrust his hand into his wallet, where he made a rattling noise.

"Don't be stupid, Samson," cried Fred, angrily. "What do you mean?"

"These here, sir," cried Fred's follower, drawing something out of the wallet.

"Well, what's that—flint and steel?"

"Tinder box and bit o' candle, Master Fred. That's the best way, after all."

"Samson!" cried Fred, joyously. "I did not think of that. Come along."

"Stop a moment, my lad; don't let's do nothing rash. Just think a bit."

"I've no time to think."

"Ay, but you must, sir. That there's a long hole, and you're thinking of going down it."

"Yes, of course."

"Suppose there's somebody at home?"

"That's just what I hope to find."

"But we shall be like a couple of rabbits running into a fox's hole, and he may bite."

"Not if he knows that we come as friends."

"No, Master Fred, p'raps not; but we're enemies."

"No, we're not, Samson, and you are wasting time."

"Which I don't want to contradict you, Master Fred; but enemies we are by Act o' Parliament, and that you know as well as me."

"Then you are afraid of the adventure?"

"Who says so?" growled Samson.

"I do, sir. So you had better go back, and I'll make the venture alone."

"I wish you was somebody else, Master Fred."

"Why?"

"Oh, I'd know, sir."

"Give me the flint and steel and the candle."

"What for, sir?"

"To light," cried Fred, impatiently.

"Nay, I'm going to light that candle, and I'm going along with you, Master Fred. Why, what would the colonel say if he found out that I'd left you in the lurch?"

"Better leave me than give me a coward for a companion."

"Well, I do call that cruel to a man as only wanted to tell you what a risk it was. Never know'd me to be a coward yet, Master Fred, never! I only wanted you to understand the worst. Come along, sir."

Before Fred could interfere, Samson had taken two or three strides, and then made a leap right on to the dead branches which masked the entrance to the hole. The result was as might be expected; he crashed through feet first, and disappeared.

"Samson!" exclaimed Fred, as he dashed to the opening.

"I'm all right, sir, so far," said the rough fellow, looking up with a grim smile on his face. "That's the worst of being a coward and afraid. It makes you rush at things, instead of taking 'em coolly. Here, let me help you down."

"I can manage," replied Fred, quietly, as he felt annoyed with himself. "Better draw your sword."

"No, sir," said Samson, coolly; "if I do they'll think I'm afraid; and besides, there's no room to give it a good swing for a cut, and the point's blunt since I used it for digging up potatoes."

"No, no; I can get down," said Fred, quickly, as Samson once more offered his help, and the next moment he was also standing in the old passage, peering before him, and listening.

All was as silent as the grave, and a chilly feeling of dread came over the lad, as he wondered whether poor Nat had, after all, only crawled in there to die, just as some unfortunate wounded creature seeks a hole to be at rest.

"What nonsense! when he took the food we put there," he muttered the next moment.

"What say, sir? Shall I strike a light?"

Samson did not wait for an answer to his first question before propounding the second.

"Yes. Go a few steps forward out of the light," whispered Fred, "and then we are not likely to be heard."

"Not from outside," grumbled Samson; "but how about them inside? They'll come down and spit us like black cock on a big skewer."

"What are you muttering about?" whispered Fred, as his companion went forward and knelt down.

"I was only saying, don't blame me if they come down on us with swords that hasn't been used to dig potatoes, Master Fred."

"Let me come by you, and I'll stand on guard while you strike a light."

"No, sir; I shan't," said Samson, gruffly.

"What's that?"

"You heared, sir."

"Yes, I did hear," whispered Fred, angrily; "and please remember, sir, that I am your officer."

"Can't remember that now, Master Fred, only that you're to be took care of. I had strict orders to be always ready to shove my big body in front of you when anybody was going to" (*nick, nick*) "cut at you" (*nick, nick, nick*)—"Look at that!—with a sword."

"Who gave you those orders?" said Fred, sharply.

"Your mother, sir, 'fore we" (*nick, nick*) "started for the wars at first." (*Nick, nick*) "I shall never get a light."

Samson was down upon his knees, striking a piece of flint sharply upon a thin bar of steel turned over at each end, so as to form a double hook, which the operator grasped in his left hand, while Fred stood gazing straight before him, sword drawn, and the point held over his man's head, ready to receive any attack.

At every stroke with the flint, a number of sparks shone out for a moment, lighting up the striker's face, but though he kept on nicking away, there was no result.

"Why, Samson," whispered Fred, as he mastered a curious sensation of emotion at the man's words, which brought up the memory of a pair of tender, loving eyes gazing into his at the moment of farewell, "you have forgotten the tinder!"

The nicking sound ceased on the instant, and Samson began indignantly—

"Well, I do like that, Master Fred. I mayn't be a scholar, and I never larnt Latin, and that sort of stuff, but I'll grow vegetables and make cider with any man in Coombeland."

"What has making cider to do with tinder, you great oaf!" cried Fred, angrily, so as to hide his emotion.

"Nothing at all, sir; only you seem to think I'm such a bog-walker that I haven't sense to know how to strike a light."

"Well, where is the light? and how can you expect to get one without tinder?"

"I don't. Here's the tinder in a box, but all the sparks are blown over it by the draught."

"Then strike lower man."

"There, then," cried Samson, viciously, as he nicked harder, with the result that one of the tiny sparks, instead of fading out, seemed to remain motionless on the floor. This spark Samson blew till it increased and glowed more brightly, showing his face close to the light, and the point of something yellow being applied to the red glow.

That something yellow, being a pointed match dipped in brimstone, began to melt, and then boil and burst into a blue fluttering flame, which ignited the match; and the next minute Samson held up the lighted candle close to the arched roof of the passage, exclaiming, "There!" in a triumphant tone; and then, "Why, this is only a big drain, Master Fred!"

"Hist! Give me the light," said Fred, as he listened intently.

"Going along here, sir?"

"Yes, of course."

"All right, sir; I'm candlestick," said Samson, making a rattling noise as he replaced the light-engendering apparatus in his pouch.

"No, no; I'll go first," said Fred, impatiently.

"Yes, sir; you shall go first after the light."

"Samson!"

"Yes, sir. What would your mother say, if I let you go straight into danger like this, with me here?"

"Will you recollect that you are a soldier, sir?"

"Of course I will, Master Fred. How is a man to help it, with an iron pot on his head rubbing him bald? Ready, sir?"

"Ready? Yes."

"Then here goes!" said Samson. "Can't expect a man to obey orders when he's underground."

Samson strode on with the candle in his left hand and his sword now in his right, leading the way, with his young master close behind, and their shadows following and seeming to dance on the floor and walls, which glistened here and there with moisture.

They proceeded slowly, Samson twice over hazarding a remark on the dampness, but only to be sternly told to proceed, till at last the little flight of steps appeared leading into the vault, where they came to a sudden halt, for something suddenly flashed in the light of the candle, and a harsh voice cried—

"Stand!"

Chapter Forty Seven
At the Point of the Sword

Fred Forrester had been expecting the challenge from the moment they began to move, but so suddenly and unexpectedly did it come at last, that he remained for the moment speechless, gazing at the dimly seen figure framed in the arched way, with the light playing upon the sword extended toward his breast.

Samson was the first to speak.

"Take hold of the candle now," he whispered, "and I'll rush him. There isn't room to strike, sir; and I can put aside his point."

"No, no," said Fred, forcing himself to the front, and addressing him who barred the way. "Put up your sword; we are friends."

"Friends!" came back mockingly. "Then put up your own weapon."

"Of coarse," said Fred, quickly sheathing his sword. "I didn't know who might be here. Scar Markham, we're come to help you."

"To help?" said the guardian of the vault, in a voice which sounded strangely hollow in the narrow place. "Is this some fresh treachery?"

"What!" shouted Fred, angrily, as he stepped forward and pressed right up to the point of the sword. Military life and training both were forgotten, and in an instant the lad felt back in the old boyish days sit home, when some sharp contention had taken place between him and his companion.

"Stand back, sir!" said Scarlett, sternly, "or—"

"No, you wouldn't," cried Fred. "Put down your sword. You wouldn't be such a coward. How dare you accuse me of treachery?"

Without a moment's hesitation, the sword-point was dropped, and Fred cried eagerly—

"Now, then, come out into the daylight, and— Oh, what a fool I am! Scar Markham, we've come to help you. I say, where's Sir Godfrey? Is he safe?"

Scarlett tried to answer, but his feelings were too much for him. Hunger, misery, confinement in that dark, depressing place, and the mental agony he had been called upon to bear, rendered him speechless, and he half turned away.

Fred sprang at once to his side, and his quick movement excited Scarlett's suspicion for the moment; but he thrust his sword back into its sheath, and stood there motionless.

"Look here," said Fred, excitedly, "of course, we're enemies, Scar; but we want to help you all the same."

"I suppose we must surrender now," said Scarlett, sadly. "I can do no more. Have you your men outside?"

"No; I haven't got my men outside," cried Fred, in a boyish, petulant way. "Can't you believe me? What am I to say?"

"Nothing, Fred Forrester," replied Scarlett, mournfully. "I believe you, though we can't shake hands now."

"Can't we?" said Fred, in a disappointed tone.

Scarlett shook his head.

"I have held out as long as I could. I thought we might escape; but it was impossible with two wounded men, and I could not get through the lines in search of food."

Fred raised the light above his head, and then bent down over where he could see some one lying on the stone floor.

"Yes; he is asleep," said Scarlett, sadly.

"Is he much hurt?" whispered Fred.

"Terribly; but he is better now, and—"

"Here he is, Master Fred," whispered Samson, as he knelt beside the grim-looking figure of his brother, who seemed to be smiling mockingly in his face. "Nice object, isn't he? Brother to be proud on!"

"Silence!" said Fred, sternly; and at that moment there was an ejaculation, a hasty movement, and Sir Godfrey made an effort to raise himself upon his arm, the light, feeble as it was, dazzling him so that he could not see.

"Scarlett! My boy! Are we prisoners, then?"

"No, Sir Godfrey," cried Fred, hastily; "right or wrong, I'd sooner go and jump off Rill Head into the sea than give you up."

"Ah, my lad," said Sir Godfrey, faintly, "these are sad times; but, for pity's sake, tell me—my wife and child?"

"Quite, quite safe, Sir Godfrey."

"Ah!" ejaculated the wounded man; and then, as he stretched out his hand to Fred, "God bless you for that news!"

Fred eagerly grasped the extended hand, and wrung it, to turn directly after in a shamefaced way toward Scarlett, as if apologising to him for letting his father grasp hands with so bitter a foe.

Scarlett stood gazing sadly at him for a few moments, and then slowly raised his own cold, thin hand, which was literally snatched by Fred, and the lads stood together in silence, neither daring to trust himself to speak.

Fred was the first to break the silence.

"What would it be best for me to do, Sir Godfrey?" he said at last.

"Send for some of your men, my boy, and I will surrender."

"Father!" cried Scarlett, in anguished tones.

"It is not fair to you to keep you shut up in this dreadful place. Let us give up, and— No, you can leave me safely in Fred Forrester's hands. He will not hinder your escape."

"No, father," said Scarlett, sadly, "he will not."

"What do you mean, my boy?"

"You know, father."

"Yes," said Sir Godfrey, after a pause; and his voice sounded sadly weak and broken. "I have prayed to him to escape, Fred; but he would never leave me, and he will not go now."

"No, father! I will not go now," said Scarlett, turning away.

There was silence for a few minutes, and then Fred said slowly, and in a discontented way—

"I'm very sorry, Sir Godfrey, but I'm too stupid to think of anything better. This is a terrible place; but I suppose you must be here till you grow strong enough to walk or ride. We shall have to bring you food and things as well as we can."

"No, my boy," said Sir Godfrey, sadly; "you must not compromise yourself by helping the enemy."

"But, then, I don't feel as if you are an enemy, Sir Godfrey. There, it's of no use; come what may, I will help you."

"Don't want to speak without leave, Master Fred, sir," said Samson, in his gruff tones; "but I've been thinking about my brother here."

"Yes, Samson; quite right," said Fred.

"No, sir, it ain't quite right. He'll be no end of time getting well in a place like this."

"I'm afraid so, Samson."

"Well, sir, why not you and me and Master Scarlett there set to work first dark night, and get 'em away, one at a time, on old Dodder?"

"The pony?"

"Yes, sir."

"But where to, man—where to?"

"Well, sir, I've been thinking about that, and I thought of the Manor, where they'd be comfortable; but that place wouldn't be safe, nor the barns nor stables, nor none of the cottages round."

"No; it would be madness to attempt it."

"But it wouldn't be, if we got 'em to the Rill caves."

"Samson!" cried Fred; "the very place."

"Hah!" ejaculated Samson, drawing along breath, as if perfectly satisfied with himself.

"What do you say, Scarlett, to that?"

"Yes," replied Scarlett, thoughtfully, "if you think it could be done."

"If it could be done," said Sir Godfrey, faintly. "I might live if you could get me there, Scar, my boy. For their sake—for their sake," he added sadly to himself.

"Oh, I know it could be done," said Samson. "If Master Fred makes up his mind to do it, and asks me to help him, it's as good as done. Hear that, you ugly Coombeland ruffian?" he added in a whisper, as he pressed his doubled first in the semi-darkness against his brother's nose.

"Just you wait till I get well," whispered back Nat, doubling his own fist and holding it against Samson's nose in return.

"Yes, and just you wait till I get you well," whispered Samson. "I'd give it to you now, only it would be like hitting at a bit o' clay. Why, you're as soft as boiled bacon! I'd be ashamed to call myself a man!"

"Just you say all that again when I get well," whispered Nat.

"Yes, that I will a hundred times over.—Yes, sir?"

"We must be going now, Samson. Leave what food you have."

"I stood it in the corner there, sir."

"And the flint, steel, tinder, and matches. I wish I had thought to bring more candles. This one will not last very long."

"So you did, Master Fred. Leastwise, I did. There's five there, and one before makes six."

"Hah! that's right," cried Fred, joyfully. "Then, now you can have a light sometimes: and look here, Scar Markham—to-morrow I'll go and look at the Rill caves, and see what can be done, so be ready to escape at a moment's notice. We may come any time now. Good-bye, Sir Godfrey. Lady Markham shall know that you and Scarlett are safe."

"It is compromising yourself, my boy," said Sir Godfrey; "but I cannot say to you forbear."

"Good-bye!"

"God bless you, my lad! and may this war soon cease," added the knight to himself, as his son followed their two visitors to the opening.

"Till we meet again, Scar Markham," whispered Fred, as Samson climbed out first to reconnoitre.

"Till we meet again, Fred," said Scarlett, once more holding out his hand.

"As friends?"

"As enemies in name. Thank you, for my father's sake."

"It's all clear, Master Fred," was whispered down the hole; and, after another word or two of warning to be prepared for a sudden move, Fred seized Samson's extended hand, leaped up out of the hole, and they made their way back to camp unquestioned, while Scarlett Markham crept back to his father's side, to sit there, listening to his breathing, and to think of the possibility of escape to the cavern beneath Rill Head, where perhaps they might end by obtaining a boat to go right away.

Chapter Forty Eight
How Samson Tried to Pass the Sentinels

"Samson!" cried Fred, the next morning, in a fit of excitement, "oh, if we had properly looked over that cave in the old days, and seen what it was like!"

"Well, sir, I s'pose it would have been better, sir. All the nicer, too, for Sir Godfrey, if we'd reg'larly furnished it, and set up a couple of four-post bedsteads, and had down carpets and such."

"Do you mean this for banter, sir?"

"No, sir; I was only thinking it was stoopid of you to talk in that way."

"Samson!"

"Master Fred! How are we to know what's going to happen so as to be prepared? Human folks aren't seeds, as you know what they'll do. If I puts in a bean, it comes up beans; but you never know what we're going to come up."

"Don't ramble on like that. Now, listen to me. We must get them to the cave at once."

"Right, sir."

"Then what shall we do first?"

"First thing's wittling the place, and putting in some stores."

"Now, that sounds sensible. Quite right. We must get some blankets."

"From the Manor, sir?"

"Right again, Samson. And all the food we can. Why, Samson—"

"Yes, sir; I know what you are going to say. We've got to tell the ladies at the old home to hold their tongues, and say nothing to nobody, but go up to the Rill Head with a basket o' wittles, and enjoy themselves, looking at the ships sailing by on the sea, and not eat nothing themselves, but tumble everything down that hole, with blankets and pillows, too, if they like, and do it every day."

"Samson," said Fred, joyously, "I did not think of half that, and I'll never call you a stupid again. The very thing."

"Ah, I am a clever one, I am, sir, when you come to know me. But how are you going to get to the Manor?"

"You will have to go with a message from me to my mother. Yes, this very day; but don't tell them whom the provisions are for, and bid them be very cautious."

"You leave that to me, sir," said Samson. "And now, how are you going to get them to the cave?"

"We shall want a rope."

"I'll have it ready, sir. When?"

"This very night."

"Yes, sir."

"And we'll take them some of our men's caps and cloaks."

"Good, sir, and a pair of shears."

"What for?"

"No use to dress 'em up as our men when they've got long hair. Did you see our Nat, sir?"

"Yes, of course; but what do you mean?"

"Hair sprouted all over his head like a badly cut hedge, sir. He's been trying to grow like a Cav'lier, and he looks more like a half-fledged cuckoo."

"Don't waste time in folly. Can you get over to the Manor this afternoon?"

"Yes, sir, if you get me leave."

"And I will get the caps and cloaks."

"Don't want a donkey, I suppose, sir?"

"No, Samson; we must risk getting our horses there behind the Hall."

"Risky's the name for it, sir."

"Yes; but the poor wounded men cannot walk. We can do it no other way, and at any cost it must be done."

"Will they shoot us if we're caught, sir?"

"Don't talk about it. Leave the consequences, and act."

"Right, Master Fred; but I hope they won't catch and shoot us for being traitors."

"Don't call our act by that ugly name."

"Right, sir; but if we are caught and I am shot, you see if my brother Nat don't laugh."

"Why, man, why?"

"Because he'll say I was such a fool."

"So shall I, Samson, if you talk like that. Now, I cannot ask my father for leave to go across to the Manor without his questioning me as to why I wish you to go. You must get leave to go, so do what is necessary and get off at once."

"Don't you fear about that, Master Fred. And about poor Sir Godfrey, Master Scar, and that brother of mine? They must be terribly hungry."

"They must wait. We cannot go near them to-day. What we left must do, and they will be watching the more eagerly for us, all ready?"

"Then you mean it to-night, sir, without fail?"

"Without fail, Samson. Sir Godfrey must be got away to-night."

"Rope, wittles, blankets, and anything they like," said Samson, as he parted from his master; and after hesitating a little about asking leave to quit the camp, he came to the conclusion that it would be wiser to get permission from his officer to fish, and then, after selecting a spot where the trees overhung the water, steal off through the wood.

This he proceeded to put in force at once, to be met with a stern rebuff from the officer in question, a sour-looking personage, who refused him point-blank, and sent Samson to the right-about, scratching his head.

"This is a nice state of affairs, this is!" he grumbled to himself. "Here's Master Fred, thinking me gone off to carry out his orders, and I'm shut up like a blackbird in a cage. Whatever shall I do? It's no use to ask anybody else."

Samson had another scratch at his head, and then another, and all in vain; he could not scratch any good idea into it or out of it; and at last, in sheer despair, he walked slowly away, with the intention of evading the outposts, and, being so well acquainted with the country round, dodging from copse to coombe, and then away here and there till he was beyond the last outpost, when he could easily get to the Manor.

Now, it had always seemed one of the easiest things possible to get out of camp. So it was in theory—"only got to keep out of the roads and paths, cross the fields and keep to the moor, and there you are."

But when, after making up his mind which way to go, Samson tried to practise instead of theorise, he found the task not quite so easy. His plan was to go out of the park to the south, and then work round to the west; but he had not gone fifty yards beyond the park, and was chuckling to himself about how easy it was, and how an enemy might get in, when, just as he was saying to himself, "Sentinels, indeed! Why, I'd make better sentinels out of turnips!"

"Halt!" rang out, and a man appeared from behind a tree.

"Halt? What for? You know me."

"Yes," said the sentry. "I know you. Can't go out of the lines without a pass."

"What! Not for a bit of a walk?"

"Where's your pass?"

"Didn't get one. No pass wanted for a bit of a ramble."

"Go back."

"Nonsense! You won't turn a man—"

"Your pass, or go back."

"Go back yourself."

Samson took a step forward, and the man blew the match of his heavy piece, and presented it.

"Back, or I fire!" he cried.

"Yes; you dare, that's all!" cried Samson. "Such nonsense!"

But the man was in earnest, that was plain enough; and, seeing this, Samson went growling back, made a long *détour*, and started again.

This time he thought he had got through the chain of sentinels, and, congratulating himself on his success, he made for a little grove of birch-trees.

"Only wanted a little trying," he said.

"Stand!"

He started back in amazement, for he had walked right up to the muzzle of a firelock, the man who bore it proving more stern and severe than the one he had before encountered.

Samson went back, growling savagely; and this was the first line of sentinels! A second would have to be passed, and beyond that there were patrols of cavalry guarding the camp in every direction.

"Well, Master Fred shan't say I didn't try," he muttered, as he made now for the back of the Hall, where the great groves of trees sheltered the place from the north and easterly winds.

Here he again hoped to be successful, and, feeling assured at last that he had avoided the the sentries, he was about to make for a narrow coombe on ahead, when once more a man stood in his path, and asked for his pass.

"Haven't got it here," said Samson, gruffly.

"Then go back."

"Go back yourself," growled Samson; and, putting in effect a west-country wrestling trick, he threw the sentry on his back, and dashed down the slope toward the coombe. "He daren't go and tell," muttered the fugitive, "for he'd get into trouble for letting me go by."

Bang!

Samson leaped off the ground a couple of feet, and on coming down upon the steep slope, staggered and nearly fell. Not that he was hit, but the bullet sent to stop him cut up the turf close to his legs, and startled him nearly out of his wits.

"I'll serve you out for that, my lad," he muttered, "I shall know you again."

He ran on the faster though, and then to his disgust, found that another sentry was at the bottom of the coombe, and well on the alert, running to intercept him, for the shot fired had spread the alarm.

Seeing this, Samson dodged into the wood that clothed the western side of the coombe, and by a little scheming crept out a couple of hundred yards from where the sentry was on the watch.

"Tricked him this time," said Samson, chuckling, and once more starting, for a bullet whistled by his ear, and directly after there was the report.

But he ran on feeling that he had passed two of the chains of sentries, and that now all he had to do was to clear the mounted patrols.

This he set himself to do with the more confidence that there was no horseman in sight; and, with his hopes rising, he kept on now at a steady trot, which he changed for a walk as he reached the irregular surface of the moor, scored into hundreds of little valleys running into one another, and the larger toward the sea.

"Nothing like a bow, after all," muttered Samson, as he ran. "Shoot four or five arrows while you're loading one of those clumsy great guns. Got away from you this time, my lad. Ay, you may shout," he muttered as he heard a hail. "Likely! You'd have to holloa louder to bring me back, and— Well, now, look at that!" he grumbled, as he got about five hundred yards away, and suddenly found that he was the quarry of two of the mounted men, who had caught sight of him, and were coming from opposite directions, bent on cutting him off. "Well, I think I know this bit o' the country better than you do, and if I aren't mounted on a horse, I'm mounted on as good a pair o' legs as most men, and deal better than my brother Nat's."

He said all this in an angry tone, as he made straight for a patch of woodland at the edge of the moor, when, seeing this, and that the man on foot was steadily running in Samson's track, the two horsemen immediately bore away so as to intercept the fugitive on the further side, and soon disappeared from view.

"I thought you'd do that," said Samson to himself; and he turned sharply round, ran a few yards towards his pursuer, and then turned along one of the courses of a stream, and in a minute was out of sight, but only to double again in quite a different direction along the dry course of another rivulet, which wound here and there to the south.

"Get round 'em somehow," said Samson; and, settling himself into a slow trot, he ran on and on for quite a quarter of an hour, to where the hollow in which he had been running opened out on to open moor all covered with whortleberry and bracken, offering good hiding should an enemy be in sight, and with the further advantage of being only about a mile from the Manor.

"I shall trick 'em now," he said. "Once I've told 'em at the old house, they may catch me if they like; but they won't care to when they see me going back to camp."

"Halt!"

A sword flashed in poor Samson's eyes, and he found that the opening of the dry course was guarded by another mounted man, who spurred up to him and caught him by the collar before he had dashed away a dozen yards.

"Don't choke a fellow. I give in," grumbled Samson, as the man held him, and presented his sword-point at his breast. "There, I won't try to run. It's of no good," he added; and he made no opposition to a strap being thrown round his neck, drawn tight, and as soon as the man had buckled the end to his saddle-bow, he walked his horse slowly back toward the camp.

Before they had gone far, the other two mounted men trotted up, and seemed ready to administer a little correction with the flat of their swords.

"Yes, you do," said Samson, showing his teeth; "and as soon as this bit o' trouble's over, I'll pay you back, or my name aren't what it is."

"Let him alone," said his captor. "Come on, lad."

He spurred his horse to a trot, and Samson ran beside him, while the two others returned to their posts.

As it happened, Fred was riding along the outside of the camp with his father as the prisoner was brought in, and as soon as he saw who it was, the colour flushed to his face, and he felt that it was all over, and that he would have to confess.

"How now, sir!" cried the colonel. "You?"

"Yes, sir. I was only stretching my legs a bit, and this man tried to run me down."

"Are you the man reported by the sentry as trying to desert?"

"Me trying to desert, sir!" cried Samson, indignantly. "Do I look the sort o' man likely to desert, colonel, unless it was to get a good draught o' cider?"

"But you were out of bounds, sir."

"Father," began Fred, who was in agony, "let me—"

"Silence, sir! He is a soldier now, and must be treated as a soldier."

"Yes; don't you say nothing about me, Master Fred, sir. I can bear all I get."

"Go back to your quarters, sir. You are under arrest, mind, I will deal with you to-morrow."

Samson gave Fred a meaning look as he was marched off, and Fred's agony of spirit increased as he asked himself whether he ought not to confide in his father. A dozen times over he was about to speak, but only to hesitate, for he knew that the colonel would sacrifice his friend on the altar of duty, even if he had to sacrifice himself.

"I must save them," muttered Fred, as he went slowly back to his tent. "I am not firm and stern like my father;" and then, as soon as he was alone, he sat down to think of how he was to contrive the escape unaided and alone.

Night came, with his mind still vacillating, for he could see no way out of his difficulty, and, to render his position more difficult, the colonel came to his tent and sat till long after dark chatting about the likelihood of the war coming to an end, and their prospects of once more settling down at the home whose open doors were so near.

"And the Royalists, father? What of them?" said Fred at last.

"Exiles, I fear, my boy, for their cause is lost. They must suffer, as we must have suffered, had our side gone to the wall."

"Father," said Fred, "if you could help a suffering enemy now, would you do it?"

"If it was such help as my duty would allow—yes; if not, no. Recollect, we are not our own masters, but servants of the country. Good night, my boy. I think you may sleep in peace to-night;" and he strode out of the little tent, where his seat had been a horseman's cloak thrown over a box.

"Sleep!" said Fred to himself, "with those poor fellows starving in that hole. I must, I will help them, and ask his forgiveness later on. But how?"

"Pst! ciss!" came from the back of the tent.

Chapter Forty Nine
Samson is not to be Beaten

"What's that? Who's there?" said Fred, sharply.

"Pst! Master Fred. Don't make all that noise. You'll have the guard hear you."

The mischief was done, for there was the tramp of feet, and directly after a sergeant and his men stopped opposite Fred's tent.

"Must have been somewhere here," said the sergeant, in a deep voice.

"Yes," said Fred, stepping to the tent opening; "it was I, sergeant. I thought I heard some one call."

"No, sir; all's well. Good night, sir."

"Good night."

"You nearly did it that time, Master Fred," whispered Samson. "What made you holloa like that?"

"You, sir. How came you here?"

"Slit a hole in the guard tent, and crept out; that's all, sir. Tent walls are soft enough. Now, then, are you ready?"

"Ready? Yes—no—what can we do?"

"What you said, sir."

"But we cannot take them to the place to starve."

"Who's going to, sir?"

"What do you mean?"

"Only that I crept out o' the tent hour and a half ago, ran down to the Manor—easy enough in the dark—and told 'em what to do as soon as it was light in the morning, and then ran back."

"But the rope?"

"Here it is, sir; wound round me like a belt. Come along, and let's go."

"But the horse—how are we to get Sir Godfrey there?"

"I dunno, sir, only that we've got to try. Come on; we can only make a mess of it."

Fred hesitated no longer; but taking his sword and cloak, he stepped out into the dark night, joined his man, and then stole with him cautiously along the tents to where the horses were tethered. Samson untied the halters which kept them prisoners, and led them silently away over the soft glass.

The task proved more easy than they had expected, for there were no watchers near. Strict ward and watch were kept, but only by those on duty. Those who were off devoted the time to rest and sleep.

All round the camp there was every precaution taken against surprise; but in the interior of the tented space there seemed to be none to interrupt.

"Bridles, saddles?" whispered Fred.

"If we can't do what we want without them, sir, we shan't do it at all," said Samson. "Tie your halter to his head, and leave the horses alone. The two beasts 'll follow us like dogs, and it's all right so long as they don't whinny."

Samson was correct. The two horses followed them like dogs, their hoof tramp being almost inaudible, and they went on through the darkness at a pace which seemed terrible to Fred in its sluggishness, nearly down to the lake, and then round its western end, and in front of the ruined Hall.

"We shall never get them there."

"Oh yes, we shall, if we can get them through the lines, and it's so dark that I don't feel no fear of that. Now, sir, we'll tether them to these two trees, and then get to work."

Fred followed his companion's example, glancing round from time to time, and listening as every sigh of the wind seemed to be the breath of a watcher; and then, tethering his steed, which calmly began to crop the luxuriant grass, Fred started for the wilderness, his sword drawn to feel his way beneath the trees, and at last contrived to reach the spot where they had entered from time to time.

"Shall I go first, Master Fred?" whispered Samson.

"No, no."

"Better let me. I'm thicker-skinned, and it's going to be all feeling, sir."

But Fred would not give up, and, entering the tangled underwood at once, he went cautiously on, till about half-way, when a rush through the bushes brought his heart to his mouth.

"Only rabbit, sir. Keep on," grumbled Samson.

"Think we are going right?"

"Yes, sir, far as I can tell; but it's blind man's work."

Instinct or guess-work, one or the other, led them right to the fallen tree, when the hole was soon discovered, and Fred crept through and dropped into the passage, closely followed by Samson.

"Don't find fault, sir," whispered the latter, as he touched the bottom, "I should ha' done it, only I was took."

"What do you mean?"

"Brought a light."

"Never mind; I can find my way."

"Let me go first, sir."

"No; follow closely, and don't talk now."

"Only this one word, sir," whispered Samson, holding tightly by his master's arm. "When we get 'em safe off, and my brother Nat starts boasting, mind, sir, it was to help Sir Godfrey and Master Scar I came—not him."

"Silence!"

"How like his father he do grow!" muttered Samson; and he obeyed.

Fred wondered to himself that he felt no shrinking at the strange task, before creeping step by step into the utter darkness of this place; but he was strung up now, and determined to carry his task through, come what might.

Never before had the way seemed so long ere he struck his foot against the first short flight of steps; and then, as he reached the top unchallenged, a horrible sense of dread assailed him, for all was as silent as it was dark, and he asked himself what had happened to his friends.

He stood listening, but could hear nothing; and at last he gripped Samson by the shoulder, and whispered—

"What does it mean? Have they gone?"

"That's what I was asking myself, sir. Speak—or shall I? Anybody here?" he said aloud.

There was a whispering echo, nothing more, and Fred felt the cold perspiration ooze from his brow, as he tried to imagine what could have happened since they were there last.

Those moments seemed long-drawn minutes, and then relief came in a long, low sigh; and as that ended, the breathing of a sleeper and a restless movement were plainly heard from the corner of the vault.

"Hist!" whispered Samson; "hear that, sir?"

"Yes; they are asleep."

"No, sir; that behind us?"

"No."

"Listen."

Fred listened intently, and his hand went to the hilt of his sword, for, sure enough, there was the sound of steps coming slowly and cautiously, and as if he who made them listened, along the passage from the direction of the lake.

"Some one tracking us," said Fred, with his lips to his follower's ear. "Stand aside. Don't strike. Let him enter, and then we must seize and gag him when I say 'Now!'"

A pressure of Samson's ear against his lips told of his acquiescence, and they stood, one on each side of the arched opening, waiting as the steps came nearer, apparently more and more cautiously, till the stairway was reached, against which whoever it was stumbled slightly, and then ascended with many pauses, and stepped right inside the vault, breathing heavily, and seeming to listen.

"What shall I do?" thought Fred. "Seize him, or what?"

"Master Fred—Master Fred, do say 'Now', or our chance is gone," said Samson to himself; and as if this was communicated to the young officer by some peculiar sense, he was drawing in his breath previous to giving the word and dashing at their tracker, when a low, piteous voice said half aloud—

"Gone, or he has forgotten us. What shall—"

"Don't you talk like that o' Master Fred, sir," cried Samson, in indignant tones.

"Scar!" cried Fred; and he threw his arms round his boyhood's companion, who uttered a low sigh, and would have sunk to the stony floor but for Fred's support.

"Samson."

"Well, sir, what did he mean by scaring us and talking like that?"

"Have you been outside?"

"No," said Scarlett, in a low, hesitating voice. "I was ill and feverish. I went to the end to get some water, and I think I must have fallen down and slept. I have not slept much, and it has been so long and dark, and I thought you had forsaken us."

"Forsaken you!" cried Fred, reproachfully. "But your father—and Nat?"

"I hardly know; they seem to have done nothing but sleep."

"Don't talk now. Rouse them at once. You must escape."

"Escape? Where?"

"I have provided the refuge for you. Horses are waiting in front of the Hall. Now, let's try and get them out at once."

"In front of the Hall?" said Scarlett, whose weakness seemed to be chased away by his old friend's words.

"Yes."

"Fred, we can get down from the oak chamber into the ruins. A piece of the wall has fallen. Will not that be a better way?"

"Of course," cried Fred. "Then wake them at once."

This was done, and the news of the coming of help conveyed to Sir Godfrey and his man, who rose with pain to their feet; but it soon became evident that the former could not stir a step, though Nat declared he could walk anywhere, and nearly fell on trying to cross the vault.

"It is of no use," said Scarlett; "but I thank you, Fred Forrester, and I can never call you enemy again."

"No," said Sir Godfrey, piteously. "I am too weak to stir; but God bless you, my brave, true boy—never our enemy again."

"Look ye here," said a gruff voice, "I don't know nothing 'bout no other way, so you've got to show me or lead me. I'll hold a strap in my teeth, and some one can lead me by that. What you've got to do, Master Fred, is to set Sir Godfrey well on my back, and I can carry him anywhere. Never mind about that brother o' mine. Chuck him down in any corner, if he won't walk. I aren't going to carry him."

Nat uttered a low grunt, and muttered something out of the darkness about kicking, as, after a vain protest, Sir Godfrey was helped on to Samson's back, the sturdy fellow stooping down, and then rising up with a bit of a laugh.

"Dessay him I was named after was pretty strong; but he couldn't ha' carried you, sir, any better than that."

"My brave-hearted fellow!" said Sir Godfrey, faintly; and he set his teeth hard to keep back a moan of pain.

"Now, then," said Samson, "what sort of a way is it?"

"Just like that we came," said Fred, quickly as he drew Nat's arm over his shoulder.

"Then I don't want no leading," said Samson; "some one go first, and I can feel my way with my ears."

"Go first, Scar," whispered Fred. "Don't speak; only tell him when you reach the stairs. Now, forward!"

"Forward it is, gen'lemen. March! Never mind about that Nat. Got him all right, Master Fred?"

There was a low chuckle by Fred's ear that sounded like one of Samson's, as he answered — "Yes. Go on."

"Go on it is, gen'lemen; give the old donkey the spur, if he won't go."

The long passage was slowly traversed, and then began the toilsome ascent of the stairs leading to the oak chamber, poor Nat being very feeble, and Fred's task hard; but the top was reached at last, and the soft fresh night air blew freely upon the rescuers' heated brows, as, under Scarlett's guidance, they crossed the little room to the corner where the wall had fallen away.

Here greater difficulties began in the getting down to the level of the ground floor, stones giving way, and the darkness adding to the difficulty. Once there was quite a little avalanche of calcined material; but perseverance won, and all stood safely at last on the trampled lawn in front of the ruined Hall.

"Shall we let them rest here for a bit?" whispered Fred.

"No, Master Fred, sir; they must rest on the horses' backs. Come on; they're not fifty yards away."

A low whinny from one of the faithful beasts followed this speech, and the party listened in dread that the sound might have been heard.   .

"Come on, sir," whispered Samson; "heard or no, now's our time;" and he walked quickly to where the horses were tethered, with the others close behind. "Now, sir," he said in a whisper, "I've got to get you on that horse. If you can put a leg over, do. If you can't—"

Answer came in the shape of a brave effort on Sir Godfrey's part, and the next instant he was sitting erect on the horse's back.

"Hooroar!" whispered Samson. "Now t'other one. Foot in my hands like a lady. Nat, old chap. Ready? Up you go. That's brave. Yah! I forgot as we was enemies. Come along. You lead him, Master Fred, as you would bring him along."

"Can you walk all right, Scar?" whispered Fred.

"Yes. I'll take hold, though, of the horse's mane."

"Ready, Samson?"

"Yes, sir."

"Then, forward, and not a word; we must leave everything to chance. Our only hope is that we may pass between the sentinels, and that the darkness may screen us from their eyes."

A quarter of an hour's slow and careful progress over the soft grassy moor, and then they stopped short, for there was the chink of metal and the sharp stamp of a horse.

"If ours challenge him with a neigh, we are lost," thought Fred, as he stood trembling, and patting his horse's nose.

"Poor old lad, then!" whispered Samson; and, their attention taken by their masters' caressing hands, the brave beasts remained silent, and then moved on till there was a road to be crossed, and Samson halted.

"Can't help it, sir; there's no other way," he whispered; "and it's all stones."

"Forward!" whispered Fred; and they crossed the road, but not without making a sharp sound or two. Then they were once more on the soft turf, and bore away more and more to their right, till Scarlett whispered—

"Are you making for the shore?"

"No; for the Rill Head—the cavern," said Fred.

"Then it must be close here, for we are only a little way from the edge of the cliffs."

Endorsement of his words came in the low roar of a breaking wave from below; and just then the stars peeped out from behind a cloud, and they saw exactly where they stood.

Ten minutes later they were close by the narrow entrance, and as Fred searched for the exact place he uttered a cry of satisfaction, for there by the gaping rift lay two large bundles, whose contents he pretty well guessed.

Chapter Fifty
Back to Camp

"Now, Samson," whispered Fred, "we must trust to our horses standing fast."

"You let their halters lie on the ground, sir, and they'll not move," was the reply. "Wait a minute, till I've unrolled the rope from my waist, and then I'm ready."

"What can I do?" said Scarlett, in a low anxious voice.

"Nothing, sir. Now, Master Fred, let's get them two down first off the horses, and they can lie on the grass till we're ready for them. Then, if you think as I do, me being strongest, you'll go down first, while I hold the rope."

"Can you?"

"Can I?" exclaimed Samson, in a tone full of contempt. "Then when you're down, I'll lower down the stuff first, and you take it and cast the rope loose each time; and next, I'll let Sir Godfrey down and Master Scar, and then—"

He stopped short.

"Your brother," said Fred, sharply. "We cannot do better."

Everything was done according to Samson's plans, beginning with the helping down of the two wounded riders, after which Fred took the end of the rope, and was lowered into what, in spite of his determination, seemed to be an awful chasm.

But he had no time to think, for directly he touched the shaley floor, the rope was drawn up, and almost directly after, he was hastily taking from the rope the burdens which it bore, while, to his surprise, Scarlett came next.

"You?" said Fred in his wonder.

"Yes; I thought I could help most here; and it seemed so terrible a place for you to be alone."

"Scar!" whispered Fred, quickly, as a thought struck him, due to Samson's general forethought, "open those bundles, and see if there is anything to get a light."

Sir Godfrey was lowered down, and when Fred was helping Nat to sink gently on the flooring of the cave, the sharp clicking of flint and steel fell upon his ears, and soon after the gloomy place was illumined by a candle stuck in a niche of the rock.

"I wouldn't be longer than 'bout an hour, Master Fred, sir," came down the opening. "We may as well get back safe if we can."

Fred answered, and then set to work, to find that the forethought of those at the Manor had provided ample store for the prisoners; and if ever wine was welcome to man, it was to the sufferers lying exhausted there upon the shaley bed of the cave.

"As soon as I am up," said Fred at last, "I shall throw down the rope, and with the light you can explore the lower part of the cave, and see what means there are of getting to the mouth; for sooner or later a boat and men shall come to take you both where you will. Now, Scar Markham, God bless you, and good-bye!"

Fred had previously bidden Sir Godfrey farewell. Nat had sunk into the sleep of exhaustion long before, and now he stood grasping Scarlett's hands in his.

"Some day," said the latter, sadly, "this war must end, and then we may meet again."

"And not till then, Scar, for I can—I must do no more. Good-bye."

He snatched his hands from the grasp that held them, caught hold of the rope, and calling up to Samson, in another minute he was half-way up, but only to call down to Scarlett—

"Have no fear about supplies; there are those not far away who will see that you have all you want."

There was no reply, for in his weakness and misery Scarlett Markham had thrown himself upon his face, and lay for hours almost without moving, and till long after the light had burned out, and the faint bluish dawn rose from the chasm below.

Meanwhile Fred had reached the top, lowered down the rope till its weight made it glide swiftly from his hands, and then mounted his horse to ride back, through the darkness, trusting to chance to reach the camp unchallenged.

This time they were not so successful, for all at once a sharp voice bade them halt and give the word.

"Forward's the word, Master Fred," whispered Samson, "full speed, knee to knee."

Their horses answered to the touches of their heels, and bounded through the darkness, the man who challenged trying to fire in their direction; but the match merely made the priming flash, and before he could communicate with his fellows, Fred and Samson were far over the moor toward the park, dashing by an outpost, whose men fired and raised the alarm. It was too late to stop the adventurous pair, who were close up to the tents and off the horses, which they left to their fate, while the men whom they encountered now treated them as others who had been alarmed by the firing on the moor. Drums were beating, trumpets sounding, and men mustered quickly, waiting a night attack, till the sentinels were questioned and told their tale. An hour more, and it was broad daylight, and the men dismissed, after what was treated as a false alarm.

"And when I went to the tethering stakes, Master, Fred, sir," whispered Samson, "there were our horses standing alongside o' the others, with their halters hanging down just as if they'd never left their places."

"But weren't you missed? You were a prisoner."

"No, sir, s'pose not. I should ha' thought they'd ha' looked at me now and then; but I'd done nothing very wrong, and when a man did tramp into the tent, he found me lying down, and didn't see the slit through which I crept out and in."

"Then you are released, Samson?"

"Yes, sir; your father ordered me to be let out, and, oh, how sleepy I do feel! I say, though, sir, if the colonel know'd all we done last night, what would he say?"

"Don't talk about it, my good fellow. I hope he would be glad at heart; but as a soldier— Samson, we must keep our secret, perhaps for years."

Samson gave his mouth a slap with his horny palm, and walked away.

Chapter Fifty One
Greetings after Long Years

During the month which followed Sir Godfrey's escape, the forces of the Parliamentarians achieved success after success, Colonel Forrester and his son being despatched with a little column to the east two days later.

The dilemma to Fred before starting seemed terrible, but just as he felt that there was nothing left for him to do but confess all he had done to his father, he encountered Samson.

"Why, Master Fred!" he exclaimed, "you look as if you'd got the worries on you."

"Worry? Why, man, we have to march almost directly, and those poor people in the cave are—"

"What poor people? in what cave? Only wish I was one of 'em. Having it luscious, that's what they're a-having, Master Fred, sir. Chicken and eggs, and butter and new bread, and milk and honey, and nothing to do. Blankets to wrap 'em in, and cider and wine, and ladies to go and talk to 'em."

"Samson, are you sure of this?" cried Fred, joyfully.

"Wish I was as sure as all this human being cock-fighting was nearly over, Master Fred."

"Then you've been over?"

"'Course I have, sir. I aren't like the colonel, about here all these weeks, and never going home nor letting you go. I got leave this time, for I met the general, and told him how near I was to my garden, and how anxious I was about the weeds, and he laughed and give me a pass directly."

"And my mother?"

"Your mother, Master Fred? Why, I couldn't get to know about them in the cave for her asking me questions about the colonel and her boy! She would call you a boy, sir, though you think you're a man, and no more muscle in your arms than a carrot."

"But the people in the cave, Samson?"

"Don't I tell you they're all right, sir—right as right can be; and first chance there's going to be a boat round from Barnstaple to take Sir Godfrey and Miss Lil and my lady away across the sea to France, and Pshaw! I never heard the like of it; they're going to take that great rough ugly brother of mine with them. They're all right."

Many weeks of busy soldiering followed, by which time the king's power was crushed, and the Parliamentary forces had swept away all opposition. Regiments were gradually disbanded, and the Forresters at last returned to the Manor, from which Colonel Forrester's stern sense of duty had kept him away, as much as the calls of his military life.

"There, Samson," he said, smiling, as they rode home, "you may sheathe your sword, and sharpen your rusty scythe; while you, Fred—what are we to do with you? Send you back to school?"

"No, father, I must be what I am—a soldier still," said Fred, proudly; "but I hope in peace more than in war."

"Yes; we have had enough of war for years to come."

The colonel drew rein that sunny afternoon as they were passing the ruined Hall, and Fred heard him sigh, but he forgot that directly after in his eagerness to get home; and soon after father and son were locked in turn in sobbing Mistress Forrester's arras.

There was abundance to tell that night as they sat in the old, old room, where mother and son exchanged glances, each silently questioning the other with the eye as to whether the time had not come for telling all; but still they hesitated, till all at once Colonel Forrester exclaimed sadly—

"This is nearly perfect happiness—home and peace once more; but it is not complete. You say Lady Markham and her daughter left a month ago for France?"

"Yes, dearest," replied Mistress Forrester.

"Ah!" sighed the colonel, "I'd give all I have to know that mine enemy was saved from the horrors of that terrible evening."

"Will you give your forgiveness, father?" said Fred, rising.

"Forgiveness?"

"Yes: to one who was somewhat of a traitor to his cause."

"My boy! what do you mean?" cried the colonel; and Fred told all he knew, Mistress Forrester supplementing his narrative with a vivid description of how the fugitive Royalists had been helped into the cavern, and had then escaped by sea.

The colonel rose, and stood staring straight before him, and then he slowly went to the door, signed to them not to follow, and they heard him go upstairs, where, in dread at last, Mistress Forrester followed, to find him on his knees.

When, half an hour after, he returned to the dining-room, his face seemed charged, and there was a bright look in his eyes as if a weight had been lifted from his mind, while twice over his son heard him whisper softly—"Thank God! Thank God!"

It was after years had passed, and various political changes had taken place, that one bright May day, bright as such days are sometimes seen in the west, a heavy carriage drawn by four horses, and attended by two gentlemen and a sturdy servitor on horseback, passed slowly up and down the hills along the road leading to the Hall.

One gentleman was stern and grey-looking, the other tall and grave beyond his years, while, seated in the carriage were a careworn-looking lady and a beautiful, graceful-looking girl.

As they neared the old entrance to the park, the gentleman ordered the coachman to stop, and himself opened the carriage door, after dismounting, and handed the ladies out on to the soft turf.

"It is more humble for pilgrims to travel a-foot," he said, with a sad smile. "Do you think you feel strong enough to bear the visit?"

The lady could not answer for a few moments. Then, mastering her emotion, she said, "Yes;" and, taking the speaker's arm, they were moving off, followed by the younger pair, the whole party looking like courtly foreigners, when, after tethering the horses to so many trees, and leaving them in charge of the coachman, the stout serving-man strode up to the elderly gentleman.

"Would your honour let me have a look at my old garden once again?"

"Yes, Nat, yes. Take a farewell look. It is a fancy to see the old place in ruins, and have an hour's dream over the past. Then we will say good-bye for good."

The man touched his hat, and turned off through the plantation, while the party moved on slowly along the familiar old drive, the ladies, with their eyes veiled with tears, hardly daring to look up till they had nearly reached the great entrance to the fine old place, when they started at a cry from the younger man.

"Father!" he cried. "What does this mean? This is your work—a surprise?"

"Scar, my boy, no; I am astounded."

For there before them, almost precisely as it was of old, stood the Hall, rebuilt, refurnished, bright and welcoming, the lawn, terrace, and parterre gay with flowers, all as if the past had been a dream, while at that moment Colonel and Mrs Forrester appeared with Fred, hat in hand, in the porch.

Sir Godfrey Markham drew himself up, and his eyes flashed as he turned upon the colonel.

"I see," he cried. "Usurper! Well, I might have known!"

"That this was the act of an old friend to offer as a welcome when you should return," said Colonel Forrester, holding out his hand.

Sir Godfrey looked at the extended hand, then in Colonel Forrester's eyes, and again round him in utter astonishment.

"I—I—came," he faltered, "to—to see the ruins of my dear old home. How could I know that the man whom I once called friend—"

"Till all those dreadful changes came, and set us wide apart. Yes, I heard you were coming down."

"Godfrey! husband!" whispered Lady Markham; "can you not see?"

"I am confused. I do not understand," he faltered, as he caught his wife's hand in his.

"Lil, can't you shake hands with your old friend?" said Fred, as the tall graceful girl looked at him half pleased, half shrinkingly.

"And your father has done all this, Fred?" said Scarlett, in an eager whisper.

"Yes; I found him busy one day when I came home for a visit, and it has been his task ever since."

"But—for Heaven's sake, man, be frank with me—he meant it for your home?"

"Scarlett Markham, because my father differed from you in politics, and sided against the king, don't brand him as a cowardly miser. No; he said that some day Sir Godfrey would return, and that he would show him that he had not forgotten they once were friends."

"Father, do you hear this?" cried Scarlett. "Colonel Forrester, is the old time coming back?"

"Please God, my boy, now that the sword is to be beaten into a ploughshare. Godfrey Markham, I did this in all sincerity. Will you accept it from your enemy?"

"No," cried Sir Godfrey; "but I will from my true old friend." And as, trembling with emotion, he grasped the colonel's hands, he turned to see Lady Markham in Mistress Forrester's arms.

Meanwhile, a curious scene had been taking place at the back of the Hall, where Nat had directed his steps to lament over the weeds and ruin of the neglected place. He had walked on along familiar paths through the plantation to the back of the kitchen garden, passed through an old oaken gate in the high stone wall, and there stopped aghast.

"Here, who's been meddling now?" he cried. "Who's been doing this?"

For, in place of the ruin he had expected, he found everything in the trimmest order—young crops sprung, trees pruned, walks clean, everything as it should be; and, worse than all, a broad-shouldered man, looking like himself, busy at work with a hoe destroying the weeds which had sprung up since the last shower.

Nat did not hesitate, but walked down the path, and at right angles on to the bed, where he hit the intruder on the chest with his doubled fist.

"So it's you, is it, Samson?"

"Yes, it's me, Nat," was the reply; and the blow was returned.

"How are you, Samson?" said Nat; and he hit his brother again on the other side.

"Tidy, Nat. How are you?" replied Samson, returning the blow.

"You've got a bit stouter."

"So have you."

"Long time since we met."

"Ay, 'tis."

"Like this here garden?"

"Middling."

Each of these little questions and answers was accompanied by a blow dealt right out from the shoulder, sharp and short, till the men's chests must have been a mass of bruises. Then they drew back, and stared at each other.

"Who told you to come and work in my garden?" said Nat at last.

"Nobody; I did it out of my own head."

"And pray why?"

"Because I thought, if ever you came back, it would make you mad."

"So it has. How would you like me to come and rout about in your garden?"

"Dunno. Come and try."

"Well, I would ha' put in that row o' beans straight if I did."

"Straight enough, Natty; it's your eyes are crooked. Come back to stop?"

"No; going back to furren abroad."

"Then what's the good of my master building up the house again?"

"What? Did he?"

"Ay; came and see me doing up your garden as it had never been done up before, and went away and ordered in the workpeople."

"Hum!" said Nat.

"Ha!" said Samson.

"Well, aren't you going to shake hands?"

"Ay, might as well. How are you, Nat?"

"Quite well, thank you, Samson. How are you?"

"Feel as if I should be all the better for a mug o' cider. What says you?"

"Same as you."

"Then come on."

And Nat came on.

For peace was made, and though rumours of the next war at the Restoration came down to the west, those who had been enemies stirred not from the ingle-side again till Fred Forrester was called away; but Scarlett had become a student and a scholar, and the young friends met no more in strife. When they did encounter, and ran over the troubles of the past, it was with a calm feeling of satisfaction in the present, and the old war time as years slipped by seemed to them both as a dream.

"Yes," cried Sir Godfrey, eagerly, as he laid his hand on Colonel Forrester's shoulder; "some day, with all my heart."

"I am very glad," said the stern colonel, smiling at a group by the house where the ladies were seated, and Fred and Lil, so intent on each other's converse, that they did not perceive that they were watched.

But other eyes had noted everything during the past year, and it was evident that the time would come when Fred Forrester and Scarlett Markham would be something more than friends.